(d)EVOLUTION

Joseph Bertalmio

PublishAmerica
Baltimore

ISBN: 1-4241-7554-2
PUBLISHED BY PUBLISHAMERICA, LLLP
www.publishamerica.com
Baltimore

Printed in the United States of America

My parents, my brothers, my love…
For better or for worse, you've made me who I am today.

"I don't think anybody anticipated the breach of the levees."
President Bush

"Didn't quite…fell apart, where the fuck were you?"
Trent Reznor

PROLOGUE

"Taylor?" the nurse asked while holding open the waiting room door with her hip. She was staring directly at her clipboard, not even looking up to see if anyone responded. Taylor didn't mind, though. He positively hated waiting rooms, since leaving one meant you had to wait in another for the doctor. But at least there you had some solitude. There wasn't an entire room full of strangers periodically glancing at you, wondering what would bring you to the University's Student Health Services. This office was, to be fair, where you went when one of campus' many frequent STDs found another host.

Taylor arose and raised his right hand, making a quasi-scout's honor shape to confirm that he was, indeed, the Taylor she was looking for. The nurse must have had amazing peripherals, because she didn't even look up to see if anybody was following before turning to lead the way to the new waiting room; the "examination room." Taylor quickened his pace to catch up with the nurse, certainly not minding that it also got him away from his fellow infected.

On his path through the hallway there was a moment when Taylor looked down at the carpet and noted that it was commercial. A very low-pile carpeting like that must hold up well even with a lot of patients coming through on a daily basis. The dark green and grey pattern also did a pretty good job of hiding the dirt. These were the types of things that Taylor noticed. Not to mention the cheap, fluorescent lighting.

Taylor's time spent examining the interior design was brought to an abrupt end when he and the nurse came upon a scale in the middle of the corridor. He was instructed to step on. As he did so the Student nervously ran his hand through his medium length, jet-black hair. One thing that he did not want to know was how much weight he had lost since he'd last checked. The nurse jotted down his information and asked him to follow her.

Taylor proceeded, turned a corner and was shown into a room. At least this time the nurse looked up at him and flashed a fake smile. There was no blaming her for being so callous, though. She must have seen at least 3 cases of genital warts every day. And she sure as hell wasn't about to let any potential carrier get too close.

The examination room had an examination table that was waiting for Taylor to grace its presence. Those things always made him uncomfortable. It wasn't really the fact that he was being examined on that table, as it was the realization the eventually he would have to get off of this table to take off his shirt, and possibly even his pants. Taylor nervously glanced around and was relieved to see a sink and some Hand-E-Sanitizer on the wall.

"Any allergies?" she probed.

"None."

"Smoke?"

"No."

"Drink?"

Taylor paused, grinning like an idiot. "Religiously."

The nurse grabbed his right arm and proceeded to wrap a device around it that took his blood pressure. Taylor didn't particularly like having this procedure done, as he would get anxious about his breathing and worry it would ruin the results. In fact, he was so caught up in emotion that she had finished taking his vitals before he'd had enough time to adjust his exhaling. Before making her way out the door the nurse handed him a clipboard and a pen, announcing that the doctor would be in "shortly." Once Taylor was alone he set to his task.

Last Name: Donner
First Name: Taylor
Middle Initial: R.

Date of Birth (mm/dd/yyyy): 08/28/1988
Insurance #: (blacked out for anonymity)
Student ID: (blacked out for anonymity)
Allergies: None
Smoke: No
Drink: Yes
Symptoms: sore throat, fever, headache, fatigue, night sweats, weight loss

For some time now Taylor had felt ill. He'd originally thought it was just 24-hour flu or perhaps a bad cold. But four days earlier he'd woken up drenched in his own sweat. He'd been having a fever induced nightmare that had something to do with a hand or a claw, maybe both. The next morning Taylor had stepped on the scale to see that he was about two pounds below normal. He still hadn't been bothered until this morning when he'd checked his weight again and seen that he was about twelve pounds below normal. The Patient was forced to change his self-diagnosis, and had now become fairly certain he was suffering from either strep throat or mono.

Setting the clipboard down on the examination table, Taylor realized that the nurse may have used the same pen with a previous patient. He pushed himself off the table and walked over to the sink. He also didn't like the idea that the Hand-E-Sanitizer dispenser may have been touched by other patients. But Taylor knew that the end justified the means. He proceeded to wash his hands, and while doing so was interrupted by the sound of the doorknob turning. Taylor panicked, afraid because he'd been caught doing something other than waiting on the examination table. He just hoped the water he'd used wouldn't go on his bill. Taylor was fairly certain that his student insurance didn't cover utilities.

By now it was too late, and Taylor didn't have time to do anything other than look up with a dumb, surprised look on his face as the doctor entered the room.

"Whoa, didn't mean to startle you there," the man in the striped shirt apologized. He was younger than Taylor had anticipated. This was generally the case, however, as Taylor operated on the assumption that all doctors were at least 52 years of age. This provided a pleasant surprise for him every time he was forced to seek medical help. The doctor extended his hand and introduced himself. "I'm Dr. Haskins. What brings you in today, Mr....Donner?"

Mr. Donner hated being referred to by his last name. He didn't dislike his last name. In fact, he rather enjoyed it. But it seemed so formal. However, he assumed that Dr. Haskins was just following protocol, and Taylor didn't want to be a nuisance. After quickly drying his hands on his pants he shot his right hand out and grasped the doctor's. It was a good handshake, but that didn't keep Taylor from wondering if the moisture that accumulated from washing his hands might make his seem like less of a man.

"Well, I've got a sore throat, a fever, and I've been losing some weight."

"It says here you've also been experiencing fatigue and night sweats. How long have these symptoms been going on?" the Good Doctor questioned while picking up the clipboard.

"It's been less than a week, although the fever is off and on. The fatigue is pretty constant."

"Alright, Mr. Donner. I'm going to need you to take off your shirt and get on the table. I'll listen to your breathing first, and if there's nothing wrong there I'll need to take a strep colony."

Taylor shuddered mentally at the thought of the strep colony. When he was about fourteen years old he'd had the same thing done, and had ended up vomiting onto that office's eerily similar commercial carpeting. Taylor pulled his t-shirt over his head and set it on the table. Then he turned his back to the table, braced his hands on its edge and hopped backwards onto the crinkling paper.

Dr. Haskins leaned in towards Taylor with his stethoscope poised and ready to be cold. The moment it touched Taylor's chest he felt chills run through his torso, but by then the Good Doctor had already demanded a "deep breath." With every deep breath Taylor was asked to take Dr. Haskins quickened his pace, deftly landing his stethoscope over more and more of Taylor's lungs. After about eight deep breaths the ordeal was over, and Taylor was hopeful that he would be allowed to put his shirt on.

"Breathing seems fine. I'm going to take a look at your throat."

Tongue depressor.

"Say ah."

"Agh…"

Dr. Haskins stepped back, looking a little unsure of himself.

"Alright, I'll have the nurse come in shortly to take that strep colony. In the meantime I'm going to start you on penicillin. If it's strep throat, that should clear it up in about ten days," he said, at the same time pulling out a pen and his prescription pad. He paused for a moment, and continued, "I'd also like to take a blood sample. There's a chance that you might have mono. If that's the case the antibiotic won't be very helpful."

Taylor considered being proud of himself for making such an accurate self-diagnosis, but decided instead to focus on the fact that he was going to have to give blood. Taylor didn't much care for blood, and he utterly feared needles. Hypodermics had never been kind to him.

Dr. Haskins handed Taylor the prescription, said his goodbyes and left. Taylor was forced, once again, to wait. Only this time he was waiting to be stuck by a needle. Taylor began to reminisce on a time when a younger Mr. Donner had sat in a similar office and nearly blacked out while giving a small blood sample. The nurses panicked and ran to get him some smelling salt. Taylor was trying to recall the best way to describe the nauseating smell of the salt when he remembered that he was topless.

He hopped off of the table and grabbed his black t-shirt. When he had been getting dressed that morning Taylor made the conscious decision to wear something easy to remove and put back on. The plain black tee had seemed the most obvious choice. He had also chosen to leave his coat in the car, although this was beginning to seem like a bad idea. Taylor worried that he might be too weak from the blood loss to battle the February chill on the way back to his car. The idea of dying in a parking lot in the midst of a twenty three foot journey just didn't seem flattering.

Right on cue, the nurse opened the door as Taylor was pulling his shirt over his head. Hurrying it over his neck, Taylor peered towards the doorway and saw that it was the same nurse who had shown him to the room. Holding fast for hope, Taylor continued to pull his shirt on. If there was any chance that he could get away with just rolling up his sleeve, Taylor was going to take it.

"Oh, I'm sorry. We're going to need you to take off your shirt. And if you could just have a seat on the table I'll start with the strep colony."

"Do you think I could just roll up my sleeve?" The Patient asked, becoming increasingly pessimistic with every word.

"Unfortunately, no. We're gonna need to tie you off for the blood sample," the nurse responded, becoming decreasingly patient with every word.

Taylor was confused as to how rolling his sleeve up would impede that in any way. He was also curious as to why the nurse referred to herself as "we." But he knew better than to piss off somebody who is about to find your vein with a needle. Hypodermics had never been kind to him.

PHASE 1
The Quickening

The steady rain that beat down upon the windshield blurred the red light that beamed from the traffic signal. The 1986 Le Baron idled roughly, waiting for permission to resume its trek. The streets of downtown Normal, Illinois, were running with rain water. This had been a typical Midwest winter, completely fucking unpredictable. The temperature had shot up to the mid-fifties for a few days, but also brought with it a non-stop downpour. The previous eight months bore witness to massive drought that brought the rivers down to record lows. Water's constantly rising price had badly hurt the farmers in the area. The USDA was doing its best to help, but the funding simply wasn't there. This had put the locals in a very volatile mood.

The "locals" of the twin cities of Bloomington-Normal were the ones who didn't attend the University. The economy had been steeped in agricultural history long before Illinois State University began with its own humble roots. This certainly wasn't lost on the University either, as it had catered its agricultural department to the locals. The reality of the matter, however, is that the students of the University and the locals didn't mesh extremely well. Their values and lifestyles were often at completely opposite ends of the spectrum.

As the rain continued to pound against the pavement, the light turned green. It was an evening during which you were only out if you had to be. The Le Baron lurched ahead while its wipers worked at the maximum pace to maintain visibility. Even with no other cars on the street, you always had to keep your eyes open. Normal was set up like maze of one-way streets and unnecessary stop lights. Add to the equation 25,000 students ranging from alcoholics to joggers to night-classers, and travel during the clearest of days was painstaking.

The car was making its way around the University's quad, which was located almost directly in the center of Normal. Everything on campus was located on the quad, or directly off of it. The University set up was very centralized, including the dormitories. Illinois State University was the proud home of the world's largest dormitory, although they were apparently supposed to be called residence halls. The word dormitory had reminded some people of the horrific living conditions of China, and now residence hall was the more politically correct way of saying it. The idea was that changing the term might somehow make Americans less guilty with their own standard of living.

The Chrysler turned onto Beaufort Rd. and headed east towards the University's pride and joy. Watterson Towers stood against the blackness of the torrential evening, looming like a dark sentinel over the town. It stood 28 stories in height, but seemed even taller next to the miniscule buildings surrounding it. The massive structure housed over 2,000 students, making it a very volatile place to be at times. Recent years had seen countless thefts, a few incidents of arson, and even rumors of deaths within the confining walls of Watterson. The car slid past Watterson unassumingly. Its agenda lie beyond the juggernaut, and it only slowed slightly to look out for pedestrians in the rain. From there the Le Baron proceeded further east.

As the headlights passed by the quaint downtown area they revealed plenty of bored employees standing under dim lights. The patrons for beer, antiques and thrift blue jeans always seemed to die down as the wind picked up. Every now and then a poor soul huddled underneath a hooded sweatshirt would run into or out of the movie store, but for the most part downtown Normal was dead.

In an effort to diversify the area and appease the student population there had been some corporate infiltration as of late. The downtown and Main Street played host to approximately a dozen fast food restaurants. Closer to the highway Wal-Mart was offering low, low prices to the entire student base, and Starbucks had finally opened up to sell $5 coffee to poor students. Somehow a cappuccino always puts a collegiate's poverty in perspective.

Another red light flashed up, and the Le Baron answered with its brake lights. The whole city seemed to watch the Chrysler, waiting for it to make a move. There wasn't even a dog barking in the distance or some random car alarm announcing that its owner wasn't at home. On nights like these only the steady thud of raindrops acted as a reminder that time did not stand still. Sensing that there was no cross traffic to be found, the stop light flipped green.

The car declared its intentions of turning left and did so with caution. The puddles by the curbs were turning into miniature ponds, and a twenty year old car can't be trusted to stay in complete control. Veering well wide of any hazards the Le Baron continued on its way. Its headlights cut through the rain in front of it as the vehicle searched for a decent spot to park on the street. The Le Baron didn't need a large spot to fit into. It was a pretty small car. The only problem came when it was thrown into reverse, which would sometimes result in the engine quitting.

A spot revealed itself between a Honda Civic with too much custom work to be merited by a Honda Civic and an oversized pickup truck that undoubtedly had been double parked intentionally. After pulling into the spot, the Le Baron's headlights switched off and the driver side door swung open. A young lady stepped out and threw the door shut while beginning to run towards the apartment building across the street.

*

Taylor had been lying on the sofa for the majority of the night. After some syndicated Seinfeld he had switched to an inconsequential college basketball game. He was feeling 100% doped up, as he'd been on a steady diet of penicillin, Tylenol, water and Dayquil since his trip to the doctor's office the day before. Taylor planned to take half a bottle of Nyquil before he went to sleep, as he'd been kept up by fever-induced dreams for the past week.

He was down sixteen pounds. The futon that Taylor slept on when he'd first gotten ill became so soaked with sweat that it had to be thrown out. His fever and nightmares would make everything that happened between 11 p.m. and 8 a.m. a blur between reality and absolute horror. The worst part of it was that Taylor had yet to hear from the Health Services about his test results. Fortunately, he was too drugged up to care at the time.

Lifting his head off of the pillow and adjusting his tired eyes to see the clock, Taylor realized that it was just past four in the evening. The rain outside must have made it seem later. The drugs probably played a small role, too. The slow tick of the clock had been his only real company for the past few weeks. Ever since he'd begun to feel ill Taylor had hardly left his apartment. It was beginning to give him some cabin fever.

The single-bedroom setup wasn't too crowded, by any stretch. It had a relatively spacious living room, complete with coffee tables, a sofa and an easy chair. The glow of the television both warmed the room and acted as a cold reminder to Taylor that it was his new best friend. The apartment was also equipped with a small kitchen that hadn't been cleaned since move-in day, an equally filthy bathroom with shower, and a small bedroom that Taylor almost never bothered walking down the hall to get to. Sometimes he would venture into the bedroom when he needed a new pair of shorts, but even that was becoming less frequent.

What truly made the situation difficult was Taylor's slight germ phobia. If he'd had the energy to clean his apartment from the outset, there wouldn't have been any trouble. Now, however, his disease-induced sloth had turned the apartment into a cesspool of grimy dishes and dirty laundry. He was completely mortified to touch anything that wasn't a remote control.

It dawned upon him that company would be arriving any minute. Taylor's real best friend was on her way over. He assumed that she had soup. She was the type of person that always wanted to take care of people when they were sick, and worked on the basic principle that soup was a panacea. Whether somebody was suffering from a broken arm or a case of leprosy, there was nothing a can of Campbell's couldn't fix.

Taylor had met Marcy Milliken when he was in sixth grade. Even then she wore pink and white tennis shoes nearly everywhere. Even then she had been way shorter than everybody. Marcy stopped growing in the ninth grade, topping out at five feet and three inches. Taylor had met her when she was a good foot shorter.

He and his friend Andrew had been at one of the local creeks lighting Black Cats and skipping stones. Marcy and her friend Paula were there to smoke. Paula had gotten her sister to start buying her a pack a week in exchange for doing her math homework. Cigarettes are nearly as valuable in middle school as they are in prison. When Paula's lighter wouldn't work they walked the shoreline until they found Andrew standing knee-deep in the stream with a lit firecracker in his hand. They'd found their light.

Andrew Johnson was a real gangly kid, his red hair only adding to the goofy appearance. He, unlike Marcy, had shot up like a weed at an early age, but had never filled out. He was a walking toothpick, as frail as he was insecure about it. Andrew never much cared for his appearance.

They had heard a rumor about girls who smoked, and Andrew was more than willing to find out if it was true. He asked Paula out that day, not wanting to waste any time. This was still the sixth grade, though, so he asked Taylor to come along and double date with him. That was the only date Taylor and Marcy ever went on, but Andrew and Paula stayed together for three years. Over the course of the relationship they would often turn to Taylor and Marcy to act as mediators. It didn't take long for the two of them to turn to each other when they wanted to get away from all the bullshit that comes with doomed relationships.

A frantic knock on the door snapped Taylor out of his deep thought. He muttered something about bestiality as he groggily got off the sofa to answer the door. Suddenly it occurred to him that there was a torrent outside, and Taylor sped up slightly. He reached the door and drew the deadbolt.

As he opened the door he welcomed his friend, "You woke me up, Marcy."

"Screw you, I'm getting fucking drenched out here," she snapped back as she pushed him aside and forced her way into the apartment. Seeing that she had brought chicken noodle, Taylor immediately forgave the rude entrance. If vegetable soup was a get-well soon card, chicken noodle was a shot of morphine. If he was still sick by morning then it was probably terminal.

Taylor remained in the doorway for a moment, looking outside to admire the rain. Something about a storm reminded him that he was alive, even if he felt like death. It teemed from the skies, running rampant through the streets and threatening a flash flood. It wasn't completely out of the question; Taylor hadn't seen the weather act this way in his entire life.

Across the street he spied the local nursing home. He had never questioned why his rent had been so low, but the second day into his lease it dawned on him. The first ambulance of the day woke him up, turning slowly, knowingly into the parking lot. It's flashing lights weren't screaming emergency. Rather, the red light acted as the bearer of bad news. Since then he'd seen at least a dozen people pass away, twice as many try to escape, and three times as many college students throwing things at the windows at night. He turned from the door and looked at Marcy. Her shoulder-length red hair had been absolutely manhandled by the rain. Maybe he should have gotten to the door faster.

"I'm gonna lay down, can you get me a glass of water," Taylor said, more telling her what to do rather than asking.

"Rough day?" Marcy asked. She struggled to find a clean glass. Eventually she came up with one, and poured the glass of water reluctantly. Any other time he told her what to do generally ended up with something being thrown at his head, but this was different. She'd never seen him look so sick. To be honest, she was surprised he had been able to answer the door. He told her that he had only lost seven pounds, but she could see that he was wasting away.

Taylor made a move towards the sofa, "I feel like utter shit."

He didn't even look up at her. Marcy remembered a time when his eyes would light up when she entered a room. She considered blaming the fact that he was sick, but dismissed the notion immediately. The thing that worried Marcy was that even before he got sick Taylor had started to act this way. He was getting distant and callous. Something had been tearing him apart for a long time, and she had an idea of what it was.

When they had first met he was the nicest person she had ever known. He was outgoing, energetic, and just plain fun to be around. Every year on her birthday he would show up at her house and make her eggs. Sure they were shitty, but he'd made the effort. Outside of Andrew, who was too busy being fucked up most of the time, she was his best friend. He treated her like royalty, and she loved him for it.

The real clincher was that he'd stopped hugging her when he saw her. He'd always been able to lift her spirits or make her day just with his embrace. It had been something they shared as a special way of showing how much each one of them meant to the other. Taylor didn't even hug his own mother, but then he didn't tell her any of the things he admitted to Marcy. They had been open books to one another, with only their true feelings about each other remaining a secret.

"I rented a movie," Marcy said optimistically. "It's supposed to be pretty good. I heard it might be nominated for some Golden Globes, and maybe even an Oscar."

"Go ahead and put it in, just don't get pissed if I fall asleep," Taylor instructed, sprawling out on the sofa again. He laid there for a moment, staring at the ceiling. He was reaching that point when the medicines start to affect reality. If only for an instant, Taylor was certain that the ceiling was collapsing in on him, like the lid closing on a coffin.

"Well, there's just one thing…" Marcy trailed off.

"What is it?" Taylor asked, more concerned with whether or not the ceiling was going to move again.

Marcy hesitated. She knew that the next words out of her mouth had to be chosen very carefully. "I heard there's, umm…a body in it. And it's kind of…mutilated."

Taylor didn't say anything, only opened his eyes and looked over at her. It wasn't a mean glare, more of a thoughtful look. He was clearly mulling it over. Something about the way Marcy was looking back at him made Taylor second-guess himself. She looked worried, and he never remembered seeing her that way. A momentary urge to comfort her passed, and the fear of seeing a corpse made his response sound angrier than he wanted it to.

"Just don't get pissed if I fall asleep."

*

Taylor was seventeen years old when he saw his first dead body. He had busted into Andrew Johnson's room to discover him lying in a pool of blood, his lifeless wrists slashed at least a dozen times. Andrew probably had to work up the courage, or the desperation, to cut himself deep enough to do any real damage. It hadn't seemed odd to Taylor at the time, but he wasn't disgusted by the sight. If anything, he was morbidly intrigued by it. He had even lingered in the doorway for a few moments, transfixed on Andrew's facial expression. It was a look of pure fear and regret. The mortician must have had one hell of a time getting him to look serene for the wake.

"Dr. Killjoy, we have a loved one for you."

His death had come at a time when both his and Taylor's lives were at extreme lows. Paula and Andrew had broken up almost three years earlier, but she still called on him to whenever she needed to waste her life away. Andrew was more than happy to oblige, never passing on the opportunity to partake in whatever chemical-induced haze he could find. Anything that could get him high would do. If pot was in supply, that was the weapon of choice. But for the most part he was forced to work with whatever household cleaners were available.

Never once, though, did Taylor blame his friend for his problems. Andrew had his share of shit to deal with. For starters, he was gay. Only Taylor knew. Even his own family had been left out of the loop. It was a catharsis that Andrew had realized two years into his relationship with Paula. He'd faked it for the final year.

The day Andrew told Taylor, also the night he and Paula had broken up, there was only one thing running through Taylor's mind. He remembered when he was younger that he'd overhead his parents talking about the Village People.

"They're sick," his mother had said.

"And they're only spreading that filth," his father had agreed.

Taylor had burst into the room, "Who's sick? What do they have?"

"They're gay, son," her mother had said. "And they're sick."

What really bothered Taylor wasn't the concept of being gay. He liked women, and he knew it. The scary part was having to go through high school in a conservative town that operated as a full-time rumor mill. There is a reason that brave people who are actually homosexual wait until later in their lives to tell people about it. It takes balls to come out of the closet.

And even if you're as straight as a congressman there are going to be times when you question yourself. Anybody who says they haven't even once, for a flash, had a minutia of a thought about it is lying. But that also breeds fear, and that fear leads to hate. Taylor didn't like men, but that wasn't what he was afraid of. He was afraid of being accused of it.

That was what he was tying to grasp, to overcome now, because he had rained that hatred down on his best friend. In a moment of extreme anger, Taylor had unleashed his Andrew's secret on the populace. Andrew had been run out of school. Some kids from the football team gathered 2x4's, pipes and chains from their garages and formed an impromptu "fag squad." They vowed to strike down any and all that were different. They never got to Andrew, though. He did the deed himself.

Suicide is far too common of a theme for adolescents. In life you sometimes don't realize how much you can do with your existence until you hit bottom. The reason that youth have such a difficult time turning their lives around is that they can't always cope. Life is a series of tragedies and miracles, but at that time Andrew's tragedy far outweighed anything positive in his life. With every fiber of his being, he was struggling to cope.

Taylor had fucked up. He could hardly remember what they'd been fighting about. Andrew had been with Paula the night before. Taylor knew they weren't having sex, so he got pissed at A.J. He knew that those two only get together when they were looking to party. The next thing he knew he was yelling at Andrew in the middle of the hall, shouting about how tired he was of covering for his friend. Then he called him a faggot.

Andrew sprinted, flew through the halls and crashed out the front doors. Taylor didn't follow. Worse, Taylor stayed at school the rest of the day. Guilt and anger mixed within him, but he was too proud to admit his wrong. He didn't rush immediately to Andrew's aid. As the day grew longer, and the classes left dwindled, Taylor's worry started to grow.

He knew Andrew's father wouldn't be home. And if his mother was, she wouldn't go into his room unless she smelled a rotting corpse. One time Andrew had shut himself in for seven days and she'd never even knocked or checked on him. She was finding solace in a bottle. Andrew found solace in a straight razor.

Andrew Johnson. Even his name sounded like a statistic. It was almost fitting that in death he had become one, just another teenager whose death the Senators would blame on music or video games. The truth of the matter was that Andrew had been just another statistic. His death hadn't come as a surprise to anybody, and it even amused some of his classmates. Every school has that kid who is goth just for the novelty of it, who likes to scare the hell out of the little kids and make a quick buck by selling them some pot. Andrew Johnson had been that kid, and everybody treated him like a joke.

That was one of the reasons Taylor never told anybody what he had found on the corpse that day. Hanging from Andrew's neck by a length of mint-flavored floss had been a piece of lined notebook paper. Typical of Andrew, he had written some cryptic, nonsensical message that was only meant to confuse people. It was the exact type of thing that all the other farm town hicks in Hudson gave him shit for.

Taylor didn't want his friend to be remembered for something as trivial as that. So he had carefully lifted the quasi-suicide letter off of Andrew's neck, neatly folded it up, stuck it in his pocket, and burned it later that night. He was scared out of his mind that when he reached down to grab the note Andrew's eyes would open up in typical 90's horror movie fashion. But his corpse had been so stiff that Taylor knew he was really gone. Even his bold, fiery red hair had lost some of its color, looking ashen and devoid of any life. Taylor shook off his fear and tore the note from Andrew's body, revealing a cross hanging from his friend's neck that Taylor hadn't seen in years. Though they made no sense whatsoever, the words on that paper stuck with Taylor the rest of his life.

"Martyr me you dumb fuck."

*

The term "God-fearing" had always seemed odd to Taylor. In the social sense that it's used, it implied a belief in God. Folks who regularly attended church and followed the guidelines laid down by the Bible were called "God-fearing Christians." However, so far back as Taylor could remember, he hadn't fit into that category.

Undoubtedly, Taylor feared God. The idea of an all powerful being that could wipe out anybody at anytime for any reason was enough to keep him up nights. That didn't mean, though, that he was a Christian. In fact, Taylor had stopped considering himself devout almost a half-decade earlier. But he was still scared shitless of God. He was even more frightened of God after he chose to stop being a Christian. That must have really pissed off the Almighty One.

The first time he had ever truly been afraid of God had nothing to do with a preacher's warnings or a threat of condemnation from a self-righteous prick. Instead, it had come near the playground of his elementary school when Taylor was just about seven years old. Andrew Johnson was the only other person in the world that had known about it.

The incident had started one spring afternoon when the two of them were playing hide and seek with a group of kids during recess. Andrew, being the adventurous one, had always found some of the most obscure hiding places. Sometimes he wouldn't be found for the entire duration of recess, showing up just seconds before it ended. It always amazed and impressed all of his classmates.

That day, however, Andrew didn't return from hide and seek. Taylor had sat in his desk all afternoon, constantly looking up at the door in expectation of Andrew's triumphant return. The hours ticked away, and slowly Taylor stopped being bothered by it. His friend had probably just skipped out. He played hooky about twice a week. Whenever the school phoned his house Mrs. Johnson wouldn't even flinch.

The school day had ended, and Taylor ran home. He wanted to phone Andrew's house immediately and find out what had happened. He was sure that there would be some fantastical story waiting for him as soon as he talked to his friend. When he'd walked in the house, however, his mother was sitting on the stairs just inside the front door.

"Taylor, honey. We need to have a talk."

She proceeded to tell him that Andrew had gone missing that afternoon, and had been found just a half-hour earlier. From what she had gathered from the local gossip, Andrew had wandered off of school property. Nobody was certain exactly what had happened, but Taylor's friend had been found unconscious outside of an abandoned barn just a short distance from the school playground. He was covered in cuts and bruises.

Inevitably, that scarring experience had been turned into a lecture by Taylor's mother. She warned him not to wander off of school grounds, no matter what. Later in life Taylor would come to realize the validity of her cautioning, but at the time all he wanted to know was why she was lecturing him instead of comforting him. He wanted to know what had happened to his best friend.

The next day Andrew showed up at school wearing long sleeves to cover his cuts, but he was quieter than he'd usually been. The whole morning Taylor had tried to get him to tell him what happened, but the teacher had shushed him at every attempt. He would have to hold his questioning until lunch, and the wait was excruciating. Taylor was almost squirming in his seat.

When the lunch bell finally tolled, Andrew had sped out of the classroom. Taylor finally caught up to him in the lunchroom. He spied his friend sitting alone at a table in the corner. Andrew had always sat in large groups, usually acting as the center of attention and entertaining everyone. Logically, Taylor understood that something was wrong. That was, however, only in a practical sense. He couldn't truly imagine what his friend was going through, and he couldn't really show any sympathy for something he didn't comprehend. Andrew hardly looked up as Taylor took his seat across from him at the table.

"So…?" he started, expecting that the mere act of asking what had happened would return Andrew to his former self, bragging and bullshitting. But Andrew had only bowed his head, suddenly overcome with an interest in the juice box he was brandishing. Taylor was about to follow that up with an overzealous "where were ya yesterday," but he stopped himself. There were tears streaming down Andrew's face.

The young Taylor was dumbstruck, even more so than his muted friend across the table. For the first time in his life, so far as he could remember, there was no one-liner or excuse that he could make to change the unfolding sorrow before him. There was no telling how long they sat there, one of them bawling while the other gaped, before Andrew finally broke the silence.

"Do you promise not to tell? Not anyone?"

"…yeah."

"So, you know how we were playin' hide-'n'-seek yesterday?" Andrew posed, waiting for Taylor's confirmation before he continued.

"Yeah," Taylor obliged.

"Well, I knew you guys would find me if I was on the playground," he began. His focus was mostly on the facts of the story, any attempt at conveying emotion would only cause him to cry even more. His face reddened as he leaned forward in his seat. He was speaking hushed, and Taylor wasn't even sure if he was supposed to hear what was being said. "So,

I crossed under the fence and headed into the field. I thought if I lay down out there for a while nobody would be able to find me."

Taylor took a moment to process what he'd just been told. The field that Andrew was talking about was massive, used for growing corn. At that time in the year, though, nothing had been planted. Even if Andrew was lying down he would be pretty visible to anybody scanning the horizon.

"But when I got out there I realized you guys could still see me, so I kept going," immediately Taylor's question had been answered. For a moment he wondered why he was so worried about the hide-and-seek logistics of the story, thinking that he should be more concerned with why Andrew ended up unconscious for three hours. Andrew continued. "That was when I thought about hiding in the red barn. It seemed perfect, since nobody would be able to see me and most kids are afraid to go anywhere near it. So I walked up to it."

Taylor knew immediately the barn he was referring to. He wouldn't admit it at the time, or ever for that matter, but he had been absolutely petrified of that barn. It had been abandoned for as long as he'd been alive, and the windows were all shattered. He couldn't imagine anything that would force him to go anywhere near that barn, but Andrew could.

"I wasn't too far from the door when I heard laughing come from inside. I thought maybe there were some older kids inside, and I didn't want them to know I knew they were there. So I turned to leave, but then I heard a voice. It was calling my name, Taylor. I sweat to you, it was as plain as day. It was like there was somebody inside the barn that knew I was out there, so I looked back up."

Here he stopped, and got choked up again. Andrew's eyes diverted to the juice box once more, the tears welling up in his eyes while Taylor could only look on in anticipation. The fact that his friend was clearly shaken by the ordeal didn't really register with him, and he pressed for more information. For Taylor, the promise of a good story, some juicy gossip, was too much to pass up. "Then what happened?"

But Andrew wouldn't talk. He only wept in embarrassment, and made a weak vow to Taylor through the tears and the sobs. "I'll show you at recess."

*

Taylor opened his eyes just in time to see the end credits rolling. His soup and water were untouched on the table in front of him. Marcy must have been in the bathroom, she always held it in until the movie ended. Letting out a groan, Taylor forced himself to sit up. The moment he was upright he let out a fit of coughing that brought with it a decent sized ball of phlegm.

Once the coughing subsided, Taylor was left with the unenviable task of finding a place to spit. His instincts told him to use the glass of water, but he eventually decided on the sink. Grabbing the bowl of soup as he pushed himself to his feet, Taylor walked into the kitchen. Still holding the phlegm in the side of his mouth, he popped open the microwave door and started the soup.

Taylor turned and looked at the sink behind him. It was overflowing with dishes, and smelled a little bit of mold. It was then that he realized he hadn't done anything other than wait in doctors' offices and test the frame of the sofa for the past week. He hadn't even made it down the hallway to sleep in his own bed. And Taylor couldn't remember the last time he'd showered. The mess of black hair that fell over his eyes felt like a mop that has just been used to clean up a grease spill. He must have smelled like a combination of cough medicine and broth.

"Charming."

He righted himself and started towards the sink. His legs simply did not want to cooperate, and the diamond pattern of the linoleum floor was making him a little dizzy. He wasn't going to give up that easily. He only had a few steps to go, and Taylor was not about to admit that he didn't have the strength to walk eight feet. It took him nine steps to reach his destination.

Placing his hands on the edge of the countertop, Taylor leaned forward and pursed his lips to let the spit slide through. He was aiming for it to drop into a bowl of Ramen noodles that had been left to coagulate for the past five days. Craning his neck to improve his accuracy, Taylor looked down at the stream of spit and noticed it was darker than phlegm should be. No longer caring about where it ended up, he let the spit drop. He looked down to see that his "phlegm" was actually blood, far too much blood to be comfortable with.

Before Taylor had any time to investigate further, he heard Marcy opening the bathroom door. Without hesitation Taylor started the faucet and washed the blood out of the bowl as best he could. Feigning as if he'd been washing his hands, he turned to acknowledge Marcy as she entered the kitchen.

"How was the movie?" Taylor posed, though his true intention was to keep her from asking why he'd be washing his hands in a sink that had probably spawned eight new species in the last week.

"More boring than it should have been, the characters were too self-centered," Marcy stated with a degree of deduction. Marcy could have been a movie critic if she'd ever taken the time to learn how to write. A puzzled look overtook her face, as if she was trying to smile but was also a bit troubled. "How do you feel?"

"Pretty fucked up, to be honest. But a steaming bowl of soup should change that," Taylor responded. He turned off the water just before the microwave beeped to indicate its task had been completed. "Do you mind getting that? I seriously can barely stand right now."

Marcy obliged, and Taylor now had to figure out his best way to get to the sofa. He stumbled forward a few feet and planted against the wall, which he would use as his crutch until he was close enough to the couch to collapse onto it. Meanwhile, Marcy glanced back at Taylor before testing the temperature of his soup with her index finger. She didn't even notice that he was putting at least half of his body weight on the living room wall. She just wanted to make sure he didn't see her finger in his soup, especially since she'd just gotten out of the bathroom. Marcy had washed her hands, but that wouldn't stop Taylor from freaking out.

"This'll need a minute or two to cool," Marcy said quickly, seeing an opportunity for conversation. "What did the doctor say?"

Taylor hesitated, clearly not wanting to discuss the subject. "He hasn't said anything yet. The office hasn't called."

"That's good then, right? If they don't call then it means they haven't found anything," Marcy was trying to be hopeful, but it was obvious that it wasn't working out. ISU's Health Services had a policy of only calling their patients if test results came back positive. The patients whose tests came back negative were left to wait, wondering what horrific disease could cause the results to take so long. It was an incredibly comforting system.

"They better find something. I'll be pissed if I don't get a doctor's note saying that I'm actually sick," Taylor lamented. Many of the University's professors had regulations stating that if you missed class, you needed a doctor's note as proof. Even then you weren't guaranteed the chance to make up any missed assignments.

Marcy made her way over to the living room and placed the soup in front of Taylor. "It needs another minute, yet," she said while sitting in the armchair adjacent to the sofa. She was in perfect psychiatrist position, and she saw her opening to find out what had really been bothering Taylor. She just didn't know if she wanted to take that risk. An uncomfortable silence passed, during which Taylor closed his eyes. Marcy spent the duration of ten minutes working up her courage, finally just deciding to blurt it out. She called it the "Band Aid Approach."

"Taylor?"

"...yeah?"

"What happened to you that day?"

Silence.

"I mean...you just wandered off after Andrew's memorial. And the next day you looked like you'd been to hell and back."

Taylor sighed, swallowed and opened his eyes. Marcy couldn't tell if he'd been expecting her to ask, and Taylor himself didn't even know. He didn't really want to discuss it, but he'd always known it was something he'd have to talk about eventually. He paused, rethinking for a moment whether or not he actually wanted to go through with it.

"What I'm about to tell you doesn't leave this room."

*

A procession of friends, family, and guilt-ridden classmates waited in line to say their last goodbyes to Andrew Johnson's corpse. They had put him in a suit, which Taylor knew he would have hated. Andrew probably would have wanted to be buried in his Radiohead shirt with the psychedelic teddy bear on the front. He also would have wanted to be naked from the waste down.

Taylor sat near the back row of chairs, looking towards the casket but not really looking at anything in particular. He'd been wracked with guilt since the moment he'd run into Andrew's bedroom only to discover he was too late. He'd tried calling Andrew as he'd driven out of the school parking lot, but his cell had been turned off. Sitting at the funeral home, Taylor couldn't help but think that Andrew would've wanted to have his phone on then, even in death. He would have found some eerie comfort in having his cell phone belting out his Tubular Bells ring tone as his corpse stiffened.

This thought made Taylor well up in the eyes, and he looked down at his shoes to keep from being seen. The whole process of looking towards the casket only to end up crying and look at his shoes had actually taken place nineteen times that morning, but Taylor never realized it. He numbly jumped from one thought to the next, sometimes reminiscent, sometimes depressed, but always guilty.

That was how it was for all kids who grew up in suicide surroundings. At some point in time they're going to feel a level of guilt for not stopping it. But the hardest realization there is to make is that it was completely out of their control. Some people just get pushed beyond coping, and from there it is a spiral. Not one of those kids in Hudson didn't cry at least a little bit for Andrew's death.

Taylor only knew the half of it with some of them. He was fortunate enough to have grown up with a supportive family. A lot of the townsfolk tried to claim that suicidal tendencies were just a way to get attention. Their naivety was unknown to them, even if they were right in a few select instances. Taylor just operated under the basic assumption that people who crave attention also want to be alive for it. Dismissal is just easier, though, especially in such trying times.

Eventually the crowd dwindled and only those closest to Andrew were left. Marcy was in the back room bawling into a pillow. Andrew's parents were in the front row, trying to maintain enough strength just to thank those remaining for all their help and support. It was around this time that Taylor slipped out the side entrance and began his walk.

He had been storing some heroin and a needle for Andrew. He hated to do it, but if Andrew's parents caught him with it he would have been in the military the next day. Taylor also viewed it as a way to keep Andrew from doing anything too stupid. The hypocrisy of his actions that night had seemed minimal to Taylor following on the heels of his friend's death. Pure sorrow always seems to justify self-mutilation until the next morning arrives.

Taylor walked for miles, leaving the city limits of Hudson, Illinois and entering the vast expanse that is Unincorporated, America. Eventually even the corn fields came to an end, and Taylor was left to wander through the forest, not even knowing how he'd gotten there. After he'd walked for about six hours, Taylor stopped. He didn't even hesitate as he pulled his shoelace out of his K-Swiss.

He had tried to avoid wearing anything made in a sweatshop, which meant he'd stopped wearing his Nikes in junior high. Next he grabbed the box out of his inside pocket and sat on the ground, resting his tired back against the trunk of an oak. He sat staring at the tiny wooden box, examining its design. On the top a carving of a floral arrangement had been painted in black. This was one of Andrew's modifications.

Once he had flipped the lid Taylor immediately chastised himself, "*No alcohol swabs.*"

He had what he needed, though. The set included some bottled water, a balloon of heroin, a syringe, a spoon and some cotton swabs. Taylor set to work tying off with the shoelace, just above the elbow. He'd seen it done a dozen times before on television, and had even read up on it on the internet once. The only problem was that he had no idea how much to use.

He used too much.

Taylor blacked out almost instantaneously. He succumbed to that which scared him most of all, his nightmares. Taylor's nights were what truly tortured him. Without fail, every night Taylor suffered in a never-ending battle with his nightmares. His most utter and hidden fears came to surface while he slept defenseless. Everything he'd ever been afraid of was out to get him, and Taylor spent the entirety of his slumber running from the demons of his mind. They were relentless, always at his heels ready to peel off any skin they could get a hold of. He awoke every morning feeling that despite the fact he'd won the war, he'd lost every battle.

Taylor still found the most frightening nightmare to be the one he'd had when he was just three years old. Mickey Mouse and the fat, purple thing from the McDonald's commercials had been singing and dancing with him.

Then, just for the sick pleasure of it, Mickey had grabbed a chef's knife from his pocket and cornered Taylor under his bed. Taylor had tried to slide out and run, but Mickey grabbed him by the ankle. The mouse's grip was like a crushing weight that rendered Taylor paralyzed. Taylor looked back over his shoulder to see the purple fatass singing and jumping, all the while Mickey was grinning, with teeth that looked like wood screws. Mickey didn't hesitate much longer. He bent down, opened wide, and bit down. A pain that seemed too lifelike to be from a dream shot through Taylor's ankle as Mickey tore his face back, a chunk of his young victim's Achilles tendon hanging from his jaws.

The demon's eyes were pitch black.

Taylor had woken up instantly, bound to his bed by panic. His ankle was throbbing, but there were no marks or blood. He didn't run to his parents' room, he just lay under his covers, soaked through with sweat, unable to sleep for fear of a once innocent figure in his life trying to exploit his vulnerability. Ever since that dream none of the figures in Taylor's dreams had ever caught him again. But he knew if they did, they would be relentless in their torture. That was the nature of Taylor's nights.

The night in the forest was different, though. Lying on a bed of twigs and ants, Taylor's eyes were open but rolled into the back of his head. His breathing became labored, and his heart rate dropped to a level just above perceptibility. Somewhere in the depths of his mind, Taylor became aware. Things were about to change forever. The nightmare had begun.

He was in the forest, but now it was the forest of his dreams. The grey that had overtaken the area over the winter was transformed into green, but not a normal green. It was much more brilliant, like the moss of decay. The veins in the leaves and the clouds in the sky were all pitch black, as if being fed by some dark force. There was a feeling of bitterness in the air. He could almost smell it. But worst of all, he couldn't move.

Taylor had always been paralyzed by fear to an extent. He felt it was something that everybody experienced at some point. Taylor's fear was the unknown. It was the claw waiting to reach out from under his bed. It was the feet standing outside of his doorway at night. It was the hand crashing through the stairs to pull him down, dragging him into obscurity. Whenever it happened, he was utterly unable to move. He could feel his arms, his legs, his susceptible neck, but he just couldn't get them to respond.

Taylor strained his peripheral vision to get a sense of what was going on around him, but the trees seemed to have closed in. He felt entombed, complete claustrophobia overtook him. There were rocks and twigs jabbing into his back, and then Taylor felt something moving. It was just below his thigh, like maybe a snake or some miscellaneous form of rodentia. At the time he was certain that it was a rat. He struggled to turn over or stand and run, but his body wouldn't respond. He was completely vulnerable.

*

Taylor was in full story-telling mode now. He wasn't really even cognizant that he was talking to Marcy anymore. Now it was just a monologue of his memories. His eyes drifted towards the walls, becoming unfocused on their off-white surface. Scratching at the stubble that had accumulated on his face Taylor decided on the best way to segue into the unfathomable account he had to convince himself had actually happened.

"Then I saw them. My pants had obscured 'em at first, but they were climbing...*crawling* from the ground. At first it was just a swarming blur that I saw. Then they started using my pants as leverage, pinching. They were clutching my skin hard enough to bruise, and pulled themselves out of the ground. By the time I realized that it was hundreds of them, they were tugging at my hair. They were behind my head so I couldn't see 'em. The army climbed from the dirt, covering over my knee and crotch."

Marcy had to stop him. She had no idea what he was talking about. "Hundreds of what, Taylor? What army are you talking about?"

He snapped out of his diatribe. Looking up at her he proclaimed, as if it should have been obvious from the outset, "Earwigs. Fuckin' pincher-bugs."

Marcy had lived near a nest when she was very young. She hated earwigs. They pinched like hell, and they were fast. Next to the cockroach they were the most disgusting bug she'd ever seen. Taylor went on.

"By this time I was panicked. I just kept telling my body to move, but it wouldn't. I could feel every part, every limb, but I couldn't get them to respond. Then the ones by my head came completely out of the dirt and started to slowly…creep…across my head towards my nose. They stopped just at my eyebrows, and then the ones at my legs came too. They were coming straight at my face."

"Then they attacked. They began pinching, biting, crawling everywhere. They twisted themselves into my hair. They snatched at my eyelids. They picked at my balls. They crawled into my ears, my nose. They burrowed into my bleeding vein, and swam through my blood. They burned my insides until I couldn't feel anything but searing and scratching. My skin screamed and tried to tear itself from my body."

Taylor trailed off, his breathing suddenly labored. Marcy couldn't tell if he didn't want to go on, or if he just couldn't explain it. He was staring through the wall now, as if fixated on a projection of what was in his mind.

"What? What happened then?" she was done being polite and concerned, she was just frightened. Nothing that he said after that could have been comforting.

"Pain shot through me, every limb and every nerve was seizing. The blood pooled up in my eyes, and the green that surrounded me turned to a red haze…and then it was over."

"So you mean you woke up?" Marcy asked.

"Sort of. I mean, there was some time in between when I blacked out in the dream and when I actually came to. But, the thing is, Marcy…when I woke up…I was bruised, cut and bleeding."

Marcy didn't have to be told that. She remembered how he'd looked when he came to her house that day. It looked like he'd just been jumped by eight men, mugged and left for dead. She didn't know what to say. She had no idea how somebody could get cut up as badly as he was. She hated to say it, but for all she knew someone or something actually did attack him while he was passed out. Taylor had closed his eyes and laid down again, which meant he was done talking. Marcy didn't mind, she was amazed she had gotten so much out of him.

Twelve minutes later, Taylor's cell phone rang.

*

Something seemed out of place from the moment Taylor gave his name to the receptionist. The Health Services office had about six or seven other students in there at the time, which was not uncommon this late in the evening. However, Taylor was not asked to wait this time. Immediately he was shown to an examination room. When the nurse had refused to give him the test results over the phone, Taylor had understood. But now he didn't know whether to be nervous or confused. Either he was going into that room to get a quick prescription or he was going in for something more serious. He hoped desperately for the former.

He was angry with himself for telling Marcy so much. He hated telling people his problems, because he felt that sympathy didn't make sorrow disappear. He also had a secret grudge that he was grappling with. It had taken Marcy this long to finally show some concern for his problems. Where had she been when he was in his darkest places? Why didn't she reach out to him when he'd needed her most? Sure, she had no problem asking for his sympathy and compassion, but this was the first time she'd outwardly given his situation any interest. He was still bitter about that, even though deep down inside he knew he was just as much to blame for not having reached out to her for help.

Marcy had insisted on coming with him after he'd gotten the phone call, but he had refused. Despite the fact that he could barely walk, he was far too stubborn to admit to needing that much help in a two-hour span. He had sent her back to her apartment, telling her that he'd call as soon as he got home. Walking down the Health Services hallway, Taylor was so caught up in his own thoughts that he didn't even have time to contemplate the carpeting.

Something inside told him that this was going to be a very ugly diagnosis. His inner-doctor had run out of possible diseases that his symptoms would indicate. Unless it was just a freak thing, spitting up blood didn't seem consistent with anything he'd heard of except the plague. This time the nurse didn't even come into the examination room with him. Instead she just averted her glance and told him that the doctor would be with him "shortly." Again.

As if Taylor wasn't nervous enough with the preferential treatment he'd gotten already, Dr. Haskins came into the room less than a minute after the nurse left. Something was wrong, and it wasn't a minor something. From the moment the doctor entered the room Taylor could read his face perfectly. It looked like the face of a man who had a heart-wrenching secret to tell. He asked Taylor to take a seat. Then he took his own seat, too close to Taylor for comfort.

Dr. Haskins took the awkward approach of listing chronological events. Taylor couldn't begrudge him for it. He had a feeling that the Good Doctor had gotten enough experience at breaking news to people to know what worked.

"Thank you for coming on such short notice, Mr. Donner. We…*I* want to thank you for coming in. You'll excuse me, but we had a few people bring in opinions on this. As you know, you came in on…Tuesday, I believe it was. You were complaining of fatigue and flu-like symptoms, which we had attributed to a bad case of strep or a common case of mononucleosis. For the mono we took a blood sample, which we tested for the Epstein-Barr virus. As we expected, the results came back positive. But they were much more…advanced than we had assumed. The EBV analysis was much higher than a normal case of mono. Sometimes this virus can be linked to other, more…terminal conditions."

This last line hit Taylor like a runaway train. He knew there was only a short list of diseases that could follow that line. He wasn't overly concerned about what he feared very highly in Alzheimer's simply because he was still fortunate enough to have his youth. He was scared shitless of the different forms of cancer it could be. Colon cancer would be atrocious to him. Testicular cancer would be unbearable, and brain cancer would be downright tormenting. Leukemia always seemed to creep around the corner, because he did have a small penchant for smoking, despite what he'd told the nurse. He knew pulmonary fibrosis was one of them, but he didn't really know a lot about it.

"*Is the Black Death still around?*" Taylor nervously thought to himself.

And then there was the one virus that trumped all of them. It not only encompassed nearly all of the symptoms of the different terminal illnesses, it also brought with it a lifetime of social exile. Taylor had always viewed it as the greatest danger facing society. To him, it was the mother of illnesses. It was the New Age Leprosy. He had never even considered it a possibility, though.

Taylor didn't even have time to brace himself for whatever was about to come.

"Mr. Donner…Taylor…you have AIDS."

*

Somewhere deep beneath Bloomington-Normal, the soil began to stir.

PHASE 2
Cocktails and Flesh Wounds

The thin layer of moonlight shone through the window of the barracks. It lingered on the cold cement floor. It lingered on the bars of the beds. It lingered along the white sheets, pale and without emotion under those lights. It lingered over the solitary recruit's shoulder. It lingered nearly as much as the man's mind that brutal night.

His mind was into deeper thoughts. One thing he'd grappled with his entire life was the tolerance society had for him. He could feel it when he walked in the door to class as a kid. He could feel it on the street. He could feel it at the DMV. He could feel it at every level of his military career. He could feel it every minute of every day when he wasn't by himself.

It was in their eyes. When he walked into a room he could read what every single person was thinking. He could practically feel them projecting every black stereotype onto him. He could feel when somebody hated him. He could feel when somebody was afraid of him. He could feel when somebody was simply uncomfortable with him in the room.

Second Lieutenant Leon Gibbs of the United States Air Force was contemplating the mistake that had led him here. He'd walked into a recruiting office, with hopes of somebody paying for his schooling. He'd been out of high school, and out of work, for five years. His only chance at making something of himself was to go to college, but he had nowhere to go for the money.

They'd told him everything he wanted to hear. They'd promised him a cushy job in some computer room, entering data or making phone calls.

Nothing he couldn't handle, and nothing that involved rifles, hand grenades, trip wires, laser sighting, depleted uranium or killing. He would be done in two years. He would receive funding for any university that would accept him. And in no way would he be in any danger.

Three years later, he was still in the military. None of the promises had come true. With a sigh he remembered everything he could have been. Then with remorse he remembered everything he'd been through in the past three years. Life in the military was difficult. Life in the military for a black man was hell.

All those commercials they play on television make the military seem like some great fraternity. They even let women join their club. All you had to do to be part of the group was sign your life into the hands of self-interested men with no regard for human life. Somehow that last part was omitted from the advertisements.

Gibbs sat, alone in the barracks. He wondered when somebody would walk up to him, hand him a sheet of paper, and tell him that he had to reenlist once again. He pondered how much of his life would be thrown away, serving the needs of a stratum of men who would ensure he was never as powerful as them. He sat alone, and he asked himself if there was anything in the world that was worth fighting for any more. His mind was into deeper thoughts.

*

Marcy was a mess. In the past couple of hours she'd gone through pretty much every emotion possible. She was crushed to see her friend so ill, devastated to hear his tale of self-destruction, frightened by the Health Services' refusal to give the diagnosis, furious that Taylor wouldn't allow her to drive him, and even angrier that he'd forced her to go home. She had stayed at Taylor's apartment to clean up before leaving, knowing that living in squalor didn't do much good for your health. Now she was making the same depressing drive through Normal that she had earlier that night, trying to convince herself that she'd made some headway by getting Taylor to finally finish his bowl of soup before leaving. It didn't provide much comfort.

Despite all of that, however, what was really bothering her was what had happened in the days after Taylor returned from near death after Andrew's memorial. She had helped him to clean his wounds and told him he could stay as long as he needed to. The truth of the matter, though, was that she needed him to stay. The loss of Andrew had been just as tough on her, even if she didn't feel as guilty about it as Taylor did. That was part of the reason she'd accepted Taylor's explanation of his physical condition, saying he'd "fallen." She was so frightened then that she never asked any more questions, but she had always secretly wondered if he'd had his own run-in with a razor.

Marcy never knew for sure, but she always suspected that he'd stayed for the same reason she'd asked him to. He could have gone home, but his parents didn't understand what he was going through like Marcy did. He'd stayed for three days, and on the third night they'd fucked. It wasn't making love, and it wasn't casual sex. It was purely a way to escape, for both of them. Just to feel something other than sadness for a fleeting moment was justification enough. She didn't even care that it was unprotected, or that some of his cuts had opened up again during. Looking back, she could barely remember anything about it other than the blood and semen. People often underestimate the human libido.

The next morning she had woken up and Taylor was gone. Graduation came and went, and the summer passed into the start of college. With every passing day Taylor had seemed to disappear, becoming emptier each time she managed to get him to spend time with her. She wasn't surprised when he told her that he'd be living in an apartment instead of the residence halls. She knew him well enough to realize how much he needed his solitude. In fact, the only reason they had been seeing each other so often lately was the fact that he was so ill. They may have grown apart, but she could never abandon him.

*

Taylor was in his car, and the engine was idling. He had to concentrate just to remember how to shift it into drive. His mind, his life, was completely blank. He weakly rested his hand on the gearshift, barely able to grip it tight enough to pull it back into the "D" slot. It refused to budge, and he numbly remembered that he had to engage the brake first. The brake lights flashed as he dropped his foot onto the pedal. The reflection of the light against the rain and the windows of the building behind him filled the rearview and side mirrors with red.

"Everything's red in this world."

Taylor would get momentary flashes in his head. He couldn't clearly remember anything after Dr. Haskins had announced his doom. He wasn't even sure how he'd gotten to his car. There was a vague recollection of being told something about shared needles, but his coherence was fading in and out so badly that he couldn't make the inevitable connection. He dropped the Pontiac Grand Am into drive, and it began to roll forward.

The drive back to his apartment was a long blur. Taylor didn't know how long it took or how many red lights and stop signs he failed to recognize. Suddenly he just found himself on the street outside of his apartment. There was no parking, not that Taylor cared. He was completely unaware as he put the car in park and left it to sit in the middle of the road. He toppled helplessly out of the car and fell to the street, landing on his side. The rainwater running along the pavement was nearly two inches deep, and it crept up his pant legs and swam along his left cheek.

He could have lain there for thirty minutes or thirty seconds. His perceptions of time and his surroundings were completely nonexistent at this point. Suddenly his insides began to heave, and he vomited a mess of stomach acid and half-digested soup into the gutter. The sweeping torrent of water lapped up the pile of vomit, tossing it back against Taylor's cheek. His senses were jolted by this a bit, and he became conscious of the fact that he was soaked through and in the middle of the road. Using his forearm for leverage, he reached towards the side of his car.

The rain simply did not want him to get up, and it pulled down upon his outstretched arm like a wet rug. It was then that Taylor began to consider whether or not he even wanted to get up. He knew for sure he wanted to die tonight, but the image of his corpse lying in a pool of rainwater and vomit in the freezing February night was too dismal. He wanted to go out in a blaze of glory.

With a proper suicide as the only incentive he had for living any longer, Taylor grabbed the side mirror of his Pontiac and clutched it. Straining every muscle in his body, he pulled himself up and rested against the side of the car.

Now that he was on his feet the distance to his front door seemed less impossible.

Staggering and dragging his green and white Pumas through the mud, Taylor pushed off of the hood of the car. The rain that had drenched his hair fell down into his eyes. Half-blind he made his way to the door. The mud wasn't as avoidable as the walking dead man would have liked, and his legs almost gave out on him halfway through. By that time Taylor was too caught up in his suicide plan to stop, and he pushed onward.

*

As she passed in front of Watterson's entrance Marcy leaned down to grab a new cassette tape. She didn't live in Watterson, but had the misfortune of living in the Tri-Towers. They were located a solid twenty minutes' walk from the quad. To counteract the weather, Marcy opted for some Neil Young. Something about his chant of "NO RAIN" on the Live Rust album always made her smile, even on the nights when there wasn't a cloud to be seen.

Marcy bent lower to find the tape she was looking for, taking her eyes off the road for only an instant. It was an instant too long, as Marcy was barely able to make out the shape of a man in the road when she lifted her head back up. She swerved just in time to avoid hitting him, but the Le Baron lost control immediately. Hydroplaning across the road the car hopped the curb and smashed into a parking meter, halting its momentum and sending Marcy's head directly against the steering wheel.

Something in the dashboard chimed three times, fading slightly with each repetition. Then the engine died.

A dull pain swam in Marcy's head, and grogginess overtook her thoughts. Slowly she raised her gashed forehead from the steering wheel. Once she saw the blood dripping from where her head had rested, anger and panic replaced lethargy. Almost out of instinct, Marcy pushed open the driver's side door and raised herself out of the seat. The fact that it was raining didn't occur to her.

Through the cacophonous rainfall Marcy placed a hand to her head, then brought it back down to examine it. Within seconds the deluge had wiped out all traces of blood, and Marcy lifted her hand to repeat the exercise. This time she saw the unmistakable blood that gathered at her fingertips before it was erased. She needed to find something to treat the wound, so she looked up to figure out where she was. Then she saw the dark shape that had caused the accident in the first place.

It was standing rigidly in the center of the street that Marcy had been traveling along. Behind the shape was Watterson, columns of yellow lights peering out over the scene. Lightning cracked, matching the fractured foundation of the concrete monolith. The light it afforded further outlined the dark shape that still stood motionless in the street.

"That bastard better be dying, or I'll kill him."

"HEY! Are you alright?" Marcy yelled against the drowning noise of the storm. Lighting flashed again, but Marcy was still too disoriented from the blow to her head to see clearly ahead of her.

No response.

"DO YOU NEED HELP?" she screamed, storming towards the shape, faltering in her tone as the cold made her start to shiver. Through the falling rain she could barely recognize that the form shifted towards her. She began to convince herself that this person was in need of assistance and took some of the aggressive edge out of her pace, while rubbing her eyes in an attempt to coax her senses back to full strength.

The falling rain was making it hard for her to make out the details of the offender, and she craned her neck out and squinted. It looked as though the figure was just as dark as the night itself, like it was covered in mud or emanating its own abysmal obscurity. Doubt overcame her.

The shape made a move towards her, almost cutting through the rain as it did so. Marcy halted and stepped back on her heels. She didn't need to see its face to feel the threatening nature of its body language. It shot in her direction faster than she had expected, coming at the pace of a power walk. Before she had any time to react it was upon her, knocking her to the ground and clutching at her chest and shoulders.

"Rape."

The unnerving thought shot through Marcy's mind and she froze. Being violated had always been Marcy's deepest, most base fear. Almost certain that she was about to be defiled, her system went into lock-down before she could clench her legs together. Just like Taylor in his heroin-induced nightmare, she was paralyzed and defenseless.

Wasting no time, the silhouette leaned in towards her face. Its features came into view, and Marcy's fear now changed into panic. Its face was decayed and ashen. Her assailant's eyes were completely absent. The sockets were simply devoid of anything, vacant and infinite. They fixed her eyes and drew her breath like a black hole. This abomination meant Marcy grievous bodily harm, but not in the way she originally feared.

Marcy began to struggle, sheer desperation willing her limbs to fight. It opened its sagging mouth and revealed a brood of decomposed teeth, shooting in every direction. Fully aware that death awaited her if she didn't escape this entity's dominating grip Marcy forced her forehead at its chin, smashing its mouth shut and cracking the teeth together. Emitting a cross between a grunt and a hiss the monster reeled backwards just enough for Marcy to pull her knees between their chests. Using the wet earth below her as leverage, Marcy thrust her legs outward in a powerful kick. The creature fell backwards off of her and smashed its head on the curb, spewing a stream of black and red liquid from its gaping skull. It twitched for a moment, and then fell motionless.

Marcy didn't wait to find out if it would get back up as she scrambled back to her feet and began to look around, not knowing where to go. The Le Baron was dead, she was sure of it. Making up her mind for her, another form materialized through the rain in the distance behind the fallen ghoul. Marcy didn't know if this was another demon or a random pedestrian, and she didn't give a damn. Spinning on the wet soil she turned in the opposite direction and fled.

*

Taylor looked at the concoction in front of him. Surrounding a plastic red cup were at least a dozen bottles of household cleaners, medicine and liquor. Something about the knowledge of his impending death, the end of his agony, had inspired Taylor. He'd somehow found the energy to empty his cabinets and create his very own red-eye mixture. Staring at it now, he felt excited.

He was about to start a new chapter in his life. This would be his epilogue, his eulogy.

Grabbing for the final ingredients, Taylor was forced to make a decision. The Dran-O would undoubtedly kill him, but he wanted to go out numb. He'd suffered enough. He decided instead to go with the vodka. He felt that would do a great job of complementing the crushed penicillin, Tylenol, Dayquil, Nyquil, Windex, and Jim Beam (Black Label, he wanted to go out in style, after all).

"I'd rather die drinking Absolut than live drinking Skol," he grimly muttered as he poured the remainder of the bottle into the red cup. His mixture was complete.

Cocktail.

Taylor remembered that the doctor had mentioned cocktails to him while he was handing him some pamphlets. The reading material must have still been in the car, or perhaps he'd dropped it sometime before he'd gotten into the car. Depression, nightmares, paralysis and a host of other unthinkable horrors are the known side effects of antiretroviral treatments; suicide is the unspoken side effect of AIDS cocktails. Taylor couldn't imagine a lifetime of force-feeding himself horse pills, especially if they only exacerbated the symptoms.

"I call this little cocktail the 'Midnight Hearse to Georgia'," Taylor declared, quite proud of himself for his famous last words. With that he grabbed the plastic cup and consumed everything in it, not even stopping to taste the chemicals. His stomach immediately rejected it, sending most of it back into Taylor's mouth. He clamped his hands over his lips and only a small amount escaped, with some making its way out of his nose. It burned like glass cleaner and hard alcohol should, which indicated to Taylor that it was working. He swallowed again, and this time it stayed down.

The regret that he had expected to follow didn't come. Instead, he flashed back to the doctor's office one more time, remembering that Dr. Haskins had mentioned some sort of dementia caused by cat feces. Taylor didn't want that torment. He was certain of his choice. Death swam through his veins now, and it was only a matter of time before it conquered his vitals. Knowing that he would never wake up again, Taylor closed his eyes and surrendered to the abyss.

*

Marcy's flight was taking her to the only safe place she could think of, and to the only person who she could think of. She raced across the flooded streets and mired lawns, never looking over her shoulder. The sound of sirens pealed off in the distance, but Marcy didn't want that kind of help. She needed comfort. Taylor's apartment came into view just down the block.

*

In the midst of his final moments, Taylor became aware. He opened his eyes to see that he was in a chapel near the altar. The pews were masked in darkness. There was no light coming in from outdoors. The only illumination came from a dim spotlight that revealed the Holy Table, and the area behind it. The altar stood in front of an inlet in the wall that served as a balcony. Below the balcony, where Jesus would usually be hanging from his cross, Marcy was suspended above the ground, floating.

She opened her eyes and recognized Taylor, who was just in front of the communion table. Marcy smiled and spread her arms out, welcoming Taylor. Then she raised her arms in the air and revealed her set of wings. They came out at her sides, ruffling a little as she stretched them out. Taylor knew that Marcy was, and had always been, his angel.

He knelt at the communion table and held his hands aloft, expecting some sort of salvation. Staring into Marcy's eyes he paused. He felt that she was pure love, yet he sensed something dark lurking in the chapel. If he was right, then Marcy didn't share his feeling. She just looked back at him, blissfully ignorant. That was when he noticed the movement on the balcony behind her. He tried to cry out, but no sound emerged from his dying lungs. Marcy stared back at him, puzzled.

A claw rose up behind Marcy, wielding a rusty utility knife. Taylor tried once more to cry, but his efforts were futile.

Wasting no time it slashed downward, slicing Marcy's right wing. She cried out in anguish, arching her back as if to keep the pain from spreading. The claw came down again, nearly severing the base of her wing. Taylor only sat on the ground, unable to help in any way. Hatred and misery came over him, and for the first time in his life he felt what true fear was.

Marcy was still suspended above the ground, and the blade came down again, splitting open a vein in the wing. Blood spewed out of the wound and Marcy screamed what was an unmistakable death cry. The hand stabbed again and again until it had finally hacked off the entire wing. With that Marcy plummeted to the ground, crashing onto the floor below in a heap. Taylor gaped at her, shocked at the sight of his best friend lying motionless in a pool of blood. Then he looked upward, horrified, and got his first look at the attacker.

It was more demonic than anything Taylor had encountered in his nightmares. It was an entity. His eyes were eclipses, his clothes tattered and torn, revealing his own ashen green skin. What was most remarkable, however, was the monster's face. It was like a mask of mud and burlap. Something underneath of it seemed to crawl, making the burlap waver in a sickly dance. Its grin shone through a slit in the mask. It was true evil, gleeful at its atrocious destruction of beauty and life. And its teeth were devolved from anything that could be called human, rusted over and primitive.

It turned its attention to Taylor, and for a moment it seemed that the sheer emptiness of the demon's being would swallow the huddled man. The dismay in Taylor at seeing Marcy ruthlessly murdered forced him to his feet. The entity on the balcony widened his grin, unleashing from its eyes a flood of green plasma that swept towards Taylor like water escaping a broken dam. It overtook him.

Taylor struggled to breath, but the fluid filled his lungs and rushed into his stomach. He was pounded into the pews, pinned against them by the unstoppable force of the inundating waves. Battered and broken he lay on the ground as the onslaught of gore swept past him, finally dying out. Taylor lay in a crumpled mess, the thick fluid still enveloping him. Hardly able to move he lulled his neck to look at Marcy. That was when he heard her call out for him, but it didn't sound like it was coming from the altar. It seemed more like an echo that resonated throughout the entire chapel. With that, the spotlight illuminating Marcy's fallen body faded out.

In the pitch black, something grabbed at Taylor's shoulder.

*

Taylor looked behind him and discovered that he was in his bathtub, with Marcy shoving her hand down his throat in a desperate attempt to make him vomit again. The water was running and it was shocking Taylor into waking up. She had come to save him.

"FUCK YOU!" she screamed. "YOU CAN'T DO THIS TO ME! I NEED YOU, YOU SELFISH ASSHOLE!"

Taylor spit out some of his cocktail and looked up toward her, not even able to focus or hold his head up. The brightness of the bathroom light contrasted her form, making her little more than a blur to him. "I'm sorry," he said, barely audible and muffled by Marcy's finger.

Marcy assumed he was apologizing for trying to kill himself, or maybe even for vomiting. "Just…just don't die on me…you can't."

She continued dumping water over his head and trying to make him vomit, working at a hurried and frantic pace. She could hardly keep her eyes open from the blood streaking down her face. The gash in her forehead was too deep for her system to combat alone. Still, she glanced at him for a moment with a look on her face Taylor had never seen before. He gagged and began to sob as the ceiling started spinning again. He was about to go under once more.

"I have AIDS…"

PHASE 3
The Noose Tightens

The twin cities were under siege, and mass panic had ensued. In one night the police had received reports of somewhere around sixty murders, hundreds of assaults, and a handful of disappearances. To make matters even worse, the rescue crews were helpless in the battle against the never-ending torrent. The military had been notified, and the police were preparing to declare marshal law. Local news reports had initially reported a terrorist attack, but switched their stories over the course of the next eight hours from a crazed army of methamphetamine addicts, to the apocalypse, to rioting students who had become depressed by the weather, and finally deciding to call it a local cult of cannibals before being taken off the air. The streets were lined with crashed cars, many of which were on fire despite the rain.

A state of emergency was declared, and the tornado siren was activated. Four dozen soldiers from the Scott Air Force Base had been dispatched, but had yet to arrive. The base was located less than two hundred miles from Normal, and managed an elite aeromedical evacuation team. At around seven that morning all radio and television stations had been switched over to the emergency broadcast system, advising all of McLean County to stay indoors and not to open the door for anybody other than emergency personnel. Those who did not have any place to take shelter were directed to the Redbird Arena, which was located just northwest of campus.

The arena was a massive structure with a cloth roof. Quite possibly, the stadium could have been the most unsafe place to put the citizens. If anything there was a greater chance of disaster because of its unstable structure. Still, the reports claimed that it would provide emergency shelter to between ten and fifteen thousand people. By noon it was almost at capacity with refugees, healthy and injured alike. Their claims of zombies were dismissed as a result of post-traumatic stress syndrome coupled with mass hysteria.

*

Fatigue tempted her to stop, but the current situation did not permit any break. Though her hands were raw and blistering, Marcy continued to fortify the single-bedroom apartment. She had been up for nearly thirty six hours and was having trouble staying awake. Only the intermittent sound of gunfire and her fading adrenaline kept her from falling asleep on her feet. She knew at any moment one of the creatures that had overtaken the town could come crashing through a window or even a door. Marcy grabbed another handful of nails and continued pounding.

The apartment was running low on lumber, and she started to eye the cabinets. By now she had already used a coffee table, the bedroom door, the bathroom door and had barricaded the front door with a dresser and a desk. The fact that she'd already covered up all three windows didn't comfort Marcy at all. She had felt the grip of the demon that attacked her, and a paper thin door wouldn't hold up for long, especially if more than one of those things showed up.

Taylor was still in the bathtub, but Marcy had stopped checking on him early in the morning. A few times he'd cried out to her, begging her not to take him to the hospital. She was more than happy to comply. He was going to pull through, although with his current status that didn't provide much comfort to Marcy either. Even if he did wake up soon he'd be of no use to her. She was alone in this apartment, left to fend for herself. She stopped momentarily to wipe the sweat from her brow, and it occurred to her that she probably smelled worse than Taylor. At least he'd been washed off.

The television behind her had been repeating the same message for the past few hours. She had it memorized, and the only reason she didn't switch the set off was in the event that some fresh news came on. Marcy glanced at the clock over her shoulder and saw that afternoon was becoming evening. She would have to stop soon, even if the task at hand wasn't as satisfactory as she'd like. She still had to find out what kind of food was in the apartment, develop an escape plan in case it came down to that, find something that could be used as a weapon, and sleep.

Marcy shook her head. Sleep would have to wait for the moment, and thinking about it wasn't going to help. She rubbed her right shoulder, stretched out her back, and went back to hammering.

*

The squeal of the brakes shot through the night, overpowering the crashing rainfall. The military caravan pulled onto the Interstate 55 exit and rallied along the roadside of the Business 51 ramp. The drivers were ordered to meet at the head of the caravan and receive their directives. The state troopers had blocked off I-55 and I-39 for nearly 15 miles. That would help keep the media out for some time. It would also attract the media. The Air Force was in charge of keeping any choppers from flying over the area. The last thing this operation needed was nationwide attention.

Second Lieutenant Leon Gibbs waited in the truck, holding to the warmth that radiated within it. Once his orders were issued he'd surely be out in the rain. He wasn't high ranking enough to be in charge of "supervision" or whatever bullshit term his officers used. He was the bottom rung, and he knew it.

He'd been told this was just a training exercise, but anybody with even the slightest clue knew that major highways weren't closed during rush hour unless there was something huge going on. No details had been given about this "exercise," but Leon took that to mean that there was something catastrophic happening. He peered out the windshield and saw his driver running back to the truck. The windshield wipers were throwing buckets of precipitation off the glass with every pass. The driver hurried back, hunching his shoulders as he did so to keep the rain from running down his neck and under his shirt. He grabbed the slick door handle, opening the door and jumping into the driver's seat in one motion.

"What's up?" Gibbs asked, ready to get the job over with before it even began.

"Barricade. We're gonna head to an overpass on College Avenue and set up a perimeter. We're not to let anybody out," the driver replied. He didn't seem overly eager to talk about it, but Leon needed more information.

"And if somebody tries to get through?" Leon pressed. He liked to know what he was getting into ahead of time, especially when he knew he was being lied to about the mission.

"Any hostility is to be treated with whatever force necessary."

*

At 5:17 p.m. all telephone service in McLean County, cellular and land lines, was shut down.

*

That night, none of the major news networks reported any incident in Bloomington-Normal.

*

With visibility low, the conductor had slowed his forty car freight train to about five miles per hour. He absolutely hated coming through McLean County. Every time, without fail, he'd have some drunken college student playing games on the rails. Sometimes they would lie down in front of the train, waiting until the engine was about fifty yards away and then scampering off. Other times they would simply run beside his train, shouting idiotic catch phrases and expletives.

As if that wasn't reason enough to slow down, the constant rain kept him from seeing more than ten feet ahead of him. He leaned forward and strained his vision, but it didn't help any. Obscurity lay before him. Knowing full well that rain wouldn't completely halt campus idiocy, he began to blow his horn.

The blare of the train's whistle bounced off of the raindrops, entrapping itself within them. Unless somebody was standing within a block of the engine, its warnings would fall on deaf ears. Still, it was a smart precaution to abide by. The last thing that the conductor wanted was an accident. That would mean he'd have to get out in the rain.

He'd seen the videos they show conductors when they're in training. He'd heard all the stories about death on the tracks. Yet he'd never seen any of it in person. And nothing, no video or story, could have prepared him for his very first experience. As the engine slowly rolled along the tracks, he saw somebody running almost directly into the flashing headlights that pulsed from the train.

It all happened far too quickly for him to react to. Before he'd taken in what he saw, the engine had rolled right over whoever had been in its path. His face turned pale white as he realized what had happened. He had killed somebody. It wasn't his fault, but he was surely to get the blame.

"Fuck…"

He'd lose his job. He'd lose his retirement. He'd probably even lose his wife.

"God damn drunk ass college fuckers."

He brought the train to a halt as quickly as he could, but it rolled another forty yards before it came to a complete stop. The conductor reached into his pocket and grabbed his cell phone, hitting the speed dial for emergency. He waited for it to dial, and pulled on his rain slicker. Still with the phone to his ear, the conductor clicked on his flash light and waited for the police to answer before leaving the train.

Instead, he got silence. The phone clicked a few times, and each time the conductor thought it was being answered. Then his cell beeped, and a message came across the screen reading simply "No Service."

"Balls."

He popped open the door alongside the engine and peeked his head out. The rain beat down on his slicker, slapping against the rubber. The conductor pointed his flashlight off to the side of the train. Seeing nothing, he pointed it behind him. As far as he could see, there was nothing out of the ordinary. Still, he couldn't see very far.

Lowering himself to the ground, the conductor began his slow walk. He would first check the front of the engine. There was a small chance that instead of being steamrolled by the engine, its victim was clinging to the front like a bug on a fender. The conductor would prefer that case, since it would mean less walking and less cleanup.

By the time he reached the front of the engine he'd begun to hear a hissing. At first he'd dismissed it as a trick being played by the weather. Then he'd heard it again, only louder. It seemed to be coming from all around him. Attributing it to the weather, he ignored the precursor to murder and pressed on.

The flashlight wasn't necessary as he approached the scene of the crime. It was grisly, of that there was no doubt. The poor bastard had apparently run directly into the engine, as if attracted to the light. He hadn't stood a chance. His face was indistinguishable, and the conductor couldn't really be sure that it was a man at all. The mess of blood, along with the mangling of flesh that the engine had performed, left any identifiable characteristic to be washed away by the rain.

The conductor bowed his head, partly to avoid the rain, but mostly to avert his eyes from the morbid sight. Inside the hood of his slicker he could only hear muffled pounding, and he was oblivious to anything else. That was the moment the demons, who had been hissing in the near distance alongside the train, chose to attack. The conductor hardly even heard their advance, only looking up at the very last instant to see dozens of darkened shadows rushing towards him. He threw his hands over his face just before being overtaken.

They flattened him to the ground, pinning him under the crushing weight of their small army. There was a slight pause before their steely fangs were shown, crude instruments of slicing and gnawing that were sunk into the conductor's shoulders and chest. Piercing flesh without mercy, they bit down. The crunching of ribs was only outmatched by the snapping of sinew.

The conductor screamed, kicking his legs hysterically and begging for mercy. His salvation arrived, and it came in the form of the devil. Blackness took over the sky, and the zombies relinquished the flesh they had torn from the man's body. Silence followed, only the train operator's pitiful whimpers could be heard as the night swallowed them.

A monster walked towards the train engine, slowly and deliberately. It stopped a few paces from the shivering victim and bent low. There it retrieved a rusty railroad spike that was lying amongst the rubble. Without a word it commanded its minions, and they lifted the conductor off of the tracks. He was smashed against the side of the engine.

The dying man looked downward, seeing a demon shrouded by a burlap sack walking towards him. It lifted a similar mask onto the man's head, just before driving the railroad spike through the conductor's trachea. Minor spasms shook the body before it went still, hanging from the spike like a fish from a stringer, acting as a warning for all who would see it.

*

Taylor's eyes scanned the note that Marcy had left for him. He had woken up, covered in his own puke, to find all of his windows boarded up, most of his furniture destroyed, and the television blaring a message about not leaving your house. Marcy was sleeping on the sofa, a bloody makeshift bandage around her head, and clutching Taylor's baseball bat that she had modified by pounding eight nails through its barrel. Apparently he'd missed one hell of a show.

"Taylor, don't wake me. Don't leave the apartment. Eat your soup."

"Oh…well that explains everything," Taylor bitched dryly. He was feeling surprisingly strong and well-rested. Something about his ordeal with death left him with a fresh perspective. It was almost as if he didn't completely want to die.

The depression that had dominated his life for the past year was no longer foremost in his mind. That mentality, the darker side of Taylor, had seemingly been washed down the drain of the shower, along with about a paycheck's worth of booze and painkillers. At this moment, unaware of the horrible dangers that surrounded him, he was just happy to have Marcy there.

The vision he'd had after his suicide attempt scared him enough to admit to himself that he'd been treating her like shit for far too long. He couldn't keep using his own problems as a crutch. After all, if he'd gotten his disease from a shared needle, then there was a strong chance that he wasn't the only one in the apartment who was infected. He owed it to Marcy to help her through this, just as she had tried to help him through his struggles.

The apartment was lit only by the television, which Taylor muted to keep it from disturbing Marcy's slumber. He had no idea why she'd worked so hard to quarantine them, but he did recognize that it must have been an incredible amount of work. He stepped into the kitchen, smelling the soup but unable to see it. The moment he caught the scent of food it dawned upon him that he was starving. The thought of flipping on the lights crossed Taylor's mind, but he chose not to. He owed it to Marcy to let her sleep as long as she needed.

It had been twenty four hours since he'd eaten, and that meal had only stayed in his system for a short while. He strained his eyes through the darkness and spied a pot on the stove. Moving towards it he held his hand over the top of the soup. It was still warm.

Lacking both the patience and the visibility to find a bowl, Taylor started greedily slurping straight from the ladle. He finished the bowl in less than ten minutes, hardly taking the time to taste it. There had been some okra in it. There was not doubt of that. This was the most he'd eaten since he first started feeling his symptoms, and the meal warmed him. He felt healthy, even though he knew that he was anything but. The only thing keeping him from feeling completely normal was the fact that his clothes were still damp, and he could no longer avoid that he wreaked.

Taylor grabbed the note that was left for him and located the pen it had been written with. Stepping near the television he angled the paper so that he could use the light to read it more easily. He thought for a moment, then uncapped the pen and began to write.

"Marcy, I'm in the shower. I have no idea what the hell is going on right now, but we'll discuss EVERYTHING when you wake up. I'm really sorry for what I put you through last night…"

Taylor stopped writing for a moment and stared at the last sentence. It occurred to him for the first time that maybe the ordeal of seeing her best friend try to kill himself, and finding out she most likely had AIDS in the same night might have been too much for Marcy to handle. Perhaps she'd freaked out and this was her way of coping. That wouldn't explain the television, but that could have just been an advisory about the weather. And the boarded up windows might have been a way keep the windows from shattering under the pressing wind. No matter the reasoning, Taylor knew that he had no room to judge. He would make his amends. Not even thinking, he signed the note, *"I love you…Taylor."*

He placed the letter on the coffee table and turned to the bathroom, stripping off his shirt as he did so. By the time he'd reached the tub he was down to his boxers, the idea of being clean giving him every reason to hurry. He started the water and walked to his room to grab a towel, scratching his ass as he did so. Reaching his arm out to push open the door he stumbled a bit, remembering too late that he no longer had a bedroom door.

It was now a decoration on the bedroom window, which allowed for only a small opening to see outside. The blackness inside the apartment was matched by the lightless gloom outside. Taylor flipped on the lights and began his search, not even wanting to know what it looked like on that dismal evening. The constant sound of rain gave him a good enough indication.

When he found a towel Taylor's back was to the window, causing him to miss the barely perceptible shadow that passed beyond it. Grabbing the towel he headed straight to the bathroom and was happy to know that he still had hot water, despite the fact that Marcy had been alternating between hot and cold every time she felt it necessary to douse him. He stepped into the tub, not even bothering to close the shower curtain as he flipped on the shower head. The night had brought him a newfound energy and mentality, but he wasn't ambitious enough to reach all the way to the curtain and pull.

Leaving the curtain open turned out to be a good idea, as it kept the odor from being trapped inside. Taylor hadn't thought ahead enough to know that once the water hit the drain it would bring forth the wonderful stench that had been fermenting in the pipes all day. Turning his head to the side he gagged a bit and struggled to gather himself. The very last thing he wanted was for the fate of the previous night's meal to repeat itself.

After a moment he felt confident that he would be alright, and closed his eyes as he thrust his head under the flowing water. He gasped as the water hit him, suddenly remembering vividly his vision from the night before. At the time he'd been so frightened of being drowned, suffocated under the crushing weight of the flood. Now he was just glad to be alive, and he opted instead to relish the feeling of the water as it cleansed him.

He stood under the stream for a long time, not wanting to move to grab the shampoo. This was the first time he'd actually reflected on what he'd done the night before. It was not an easy thing for him to do. He came close to tears for a moment, but was able to hold back. He was going to have to admit to a lot of things, and make a lot of apologies. Maybe that was what had held him back from salvation during his nightmare in the chapel.

Taylor finished showering after a thorough shampoo and some intense scrubbing, refusing to open his eyes even once. The thought of having some dried vomit, or worse yet dried *shit*, on his body wasn't very flattering. He'd made sure to get every spot, even struggling quite a bit to get between his shoulder blades. He stuck his head under the water, pausing to enjoy the warmth one more time, before shutting off the valve. He grabbed the towel and stepped out of the tub.

After quickly drying himself Taylor wrapped the towel around his waist. He looked into the mirror and stopped. He didn't recognize the figure staring back at him. He waited, hoping that steam would dissipate to reveal a more hopeful reflection. But the thing in the mirror remained, unwavering.

It had been a long while since he'd actually taken the time to consider his physical well-being, and the knowledge alone of his weight loss hadn't prepared him for this. The figure in the mirror was emaciated, ribs stretching the skin that protected them. Sores and scabs adorned his torso, making it look like he'd been stabbed repeatedly. Taylor shuddered and quickly looked away, going to his bedroom as fast as possible to get a shirt so that he could hide himself.

Taylor grabbed the first shirt he saw, the classic plain white tee. He hastily pulled it on and began to search for the rest of his outfit. He was about to pull open his underwear drawer when a bang in the distance stole his attention. Taylor jumped and looked towards the window. It had sounded like a gunshot, something he'd become far too familiar with growing up in such a rural area. Seconds later, two more shots went off in quick succession. Then silence followed.

Still staring towards the window Taylor blindly reached his hand backwards and groped for the light switch. He caught it with his middle finger and darkness entered the room. The shots had stopped, but Taylor got the feeling the threat wasn't gone. Just like he'd felt in the chapel, his instincts told him that there was something lurking. He suddenly remembered that Marcy was asleep on the sofa, and sprinted down the hallway in his t-shirt and towel to the living room. Seeing that she was still sleeping and unharmed, he breathed a sigh of relief.

The situation forced him to make a tough decision. There was only one spot in the apartment with a view of the street, and that was through the opening in the bedroom window. Taylor had to find out what was going on, but he didn't want to leave Marcy. For some reason, possibly because of his sudden rebirth as a decent guy, Taylor didn't even consider waking her. Eying the bat of nails that sat in Marcy's loose grip, he made up his mind to investigate.

Sliding cautiously between the sofa and the squared, wooden coffee table Taylor stood over his friend. The glare from the television hit his back, his body shading Marcy from its glow. He kneeled slightly as he reached downward and gripped the black bat. His hand inadvertently made contact with hers as he pulled the weapon away from her. She didn't even notice any of it; the day's work had collapsed her. He strafed slowly along the table and into the open room. Looking back at Marcy one more time to ensure that she was alright, he returned to the bedroom.

As he entered the room, Taylor worked a tight grip around the handle of the bat. The makeshift club was the only thing Marcy had found in the apartment that would work as an acceptable defense system. The hammer was too short. Raising it to shoulder height, Taylor examined the nails themselves. Each one of them stuck out of the barrel about two inches, and they weren't going to budge for anything less than a skull. Whatever had scared Marcy had done an effective job. Taylor had never imagined something so crudely violent, and he was fascinated with violence. Seeing it first-hand, though, made a world of difference. All the decapitations and disembowelments on television couldn't prepare him for the real thing.

Cautiously he crept towards the window, trying to shut out everything but what could be seen and heard outside. The floorboards groaned softly as they rubbed together under his weight. Two blinding bolts of lightning separated by mere seconds cracked through the night sky. The brief moment of illumination revealed a shape outside of the window, standing dead still on the right side of the opening. Taylor stopped momentarily to consider what it could have been, and noticed a faint scratching sound coming from the glass. It was most likely that a downed tree branch was being knocked against the pane by the wind, but Taylor had the unsettling notion that it was something far less innocent.

Reaching the nail-bat towards the boarded up window, Taylor hooked one of the nails on the lip of the lower board, which looked like one of his kitchen cabinet doors. He wanted to stay as far away from the glass as possible, even if there was nothing out there it didn't mean the windows couldn't implode. Pulling back carefully, the nail bent the board inward just enough for Taylor to see an extra few feet of the street. The scratching ceased.

Taylor was determined, despite knowing that the figure outside the window could have been the same individual who had just fired off three rounds. He pulled back even further on the board, and it let out a cracking noise that was far too loud for this stealth mission. Taylor changed his mind about his approach, and pushed the bat forward to unhook it from the board. He pushed too far, and the bat tapped the glass. As if waiting for the signal an arm smashed through the window from the outside, shattering it with little effort.

"JESUS!" Taylor screamed, stumbling backwards and dropping the bat, which hadn't been fully loosed from the opening. The arm reared back and struck again, this time cracking the lower piece of wood and reaching slightly inside the bedroom. The opening had widened enough for the arm to reach through, but whoever it belonged to wanted to get all the way in.

Taylor gathered his balance and stepped forward, staying low to the ground as he reached for the bat. If he got too high up the hand would undoubtedly be able to grab him, and he would be pulled face-first into a splintered plank. Ducking just in time to avoid a swipe at his hair, Taylor stabbed his hand at the handle of the bat and was able to grab the knob between his forefinger and middle finger. Still ducking, he tried to pull the bat toward him using just the strength of his wrist, but the nails had dug deep enough into the carpeting to prevent it from sliding.

The arm withdrew from the opening and prepared another strong blow. Taylor saw his chance and leaned forward, giving himself just enough leverage to lift the bat and jump backwards before the arm smashed into the board again. It came down with brutal force, showing complete disregard for its own wellbeing. The wood gave way, sending it to the floor inside the bedroom. The rain seized the opportunity and surged through the broken window into the bedroom.

With enough room to crawl through, the attacker stepped back and leaned downwards. It gripped both sides of the window frame and prepared to launch itself into the room. As it did so Taylor stood and readied his swing. He'd played enough Little League to know that when the ball's set on a tee you'd better be going for the fences. He waited for just the right moment as the attacker leapt inwards. Just as Taylor had expected, its legs caught on the wall below, leaving its torso hanging inside the bedroom. Wasting no time, Taylor cocked his arms back to add more strength to his strike and unleashed the bat of nails into the intruder's skull. A sickeningly wet thud sounded as the nails cracked through the bone. A dark fluid that Taylor assumed to be blood gushed from the wound, thumping on to the carpet below.

Still rushing with adrenaline, Taylor stood mortified with the handle of the bat in his tight clutch. The blow had killed whoever it was, and for the first time Taylor considered the consequences of his actions. What if it was just somebody trying to find shelter from the storm? What if some idiot frat boy had gotten drunk and didn't realize what apartment he was at? Taylor began to shiver, suddenly overcome with emotion. He lifted the handle of the bat upwards, using it to angle his victim's face into a better view, but he couldn't make it out in the darkness.

He leaned forward, trying to adjust his eyes well enough to determine exactly what he had just done. His jaw slacked and quivering, Taylor put his face a foot away from the corpse, and that was when the lightning struck. Taylor cried out, convinced that he had just seen one of the creatures from his dreams, crimson liquid expelling from the massive crater the bat had caved in from its skull. Another bolt lit up the sky, and Taylor's fears were confirmed. His nightmares had become a reality.

Wanting to be as far as possible from the thing hanging through his window, Taylor placed his size 10 against its face and wrenched the bat from its head. The nails made a wet cracking sound, ripping tissue and bone as it tore a chunk of flesh from the swelling head. The bat freed from the body, Taylor kicked the creature repeatedly until it fell back outside. He'd seen enough zombie movies to know what to do next.

Taylor set to work boarding up the window again.

*

By the time Leon had set up roadblocks along a four mile stretch he was beginning to wonder if he would ever get a break. His unit had been working tirelessly at the same tedious task for nearly twelve hours. Grabbing another roadblock from the flatbed he stopped a moment to stretch his back. The state police had been bringing truckloads of barricades, but always managed to leave before they had a chance to help unload them. Leon dropped the saw-horse style blockade and started to make his way towards the transport truck they had come in.

The work was hard, reminding Leon of his two-a-days in high school. He'd played center, his size at the time nearly double the other linemen. Since then Leon had stopped lifting, but he was still noticeably large. Still, his frame was beginning to tire from carrying so much weight for such a distance. He prayed for some help, but expected none.

For the duration of the night they had yet to see a single Bloomington-Normal police officer. Even if they had, the orders were to keep them inside the blockade. The other units hadn't reported any incidents either. Leon wondered how long that would last. He also had to question whether or not any civilians who did make their way to the blockade would buy the bullshit story that had been lined up for them. The official line that was prepared for such an instance was to ensure the citizens that they would be released soon. They were supposed to accept the fact that they were simply being held for "questioning."

Leon knew the truth without ever having been told it. These people were being quarantined, both from the media and anybody else that they might spread their disease to. Leon wasn't exactly certain what condition they had, but they had received radio reports that a team from the Center for Disease Control and Prevention was being sent in to assess the situation. Whenever that happened, it didn't bode well for the poor souls inside the contained area.

The headlights of the transport truck were still on, helping to light the work area. Leon raised an arm to shade his eyes from them as he reached the truck, which was on the outside of the area being warded off. The only acceptable reason for any Air Force personnel to enter the area was to work on the blockade, which meant they weren't permitted to enter beyond three feet. He opened the door to the truck's cabin and began to search the seats.

Finding what he was looking for, Leon stuffed it in his pocket and jogged back to the supply truck to pick up the roadblock that he had left there.

There was the unmistakable dull pain of a strained muscle in his back as he carried his load to the end of the line, which had become quite a distance away from the truck. He would probably have to move the truck the next time he came back to it. It would be a nice break from all the lifting, if one of the three other members of his unit didn't decide to take that break first.

As he continued along Leon passed two of his team on their way back to the truck. They hardly even looked up, and Leon couldn't blame them. They'd been at it so long that the polite nod as they passed had become unnecessary hours ago. Now they only wanted to finish their task and be relieved. Leon reached his destination and saw that the fourth member of his squad was taking a small breather.

"Any idea how much longer we're gonna be at this?" he posed, leaning against a saw horse.

"I'm about to find out," Leon replied, setting down his roadblock and pulling from his pocket the binoculars he had gotten out of the transport truck. He used one hand to shield the lenses from the rain while holding the binoculars up to his eyes with the other. The constant rainfall had long ago become more than a mere inconvenience. It must have cut at least three hours off of their work, slowing them in every way possible.

"I can't hardly see a thing through this rain, but you can't figure it'd be longer than another hour," Leon didn't allow any optimism to escape his lips, only an educated guess.

"Dammit. This shit's startin' to wear on me," the Second Lieutenant responded. Leon couldn't remember the man's name, and couldn't have seen it on his uniform through the darkness if he'd tried.

"There's just one problem," Leon replied, dropping the binoculars and turning his gaze toward the other officer. "There haven't been any reinforcements called in to take night watch, which means we're not relieved of duty until some help shows up."

"For real? What about state police?"

"They're only gonna help us in setting up the blockade. Outside of that, we're on our own until the powers that be decide how they want to handle this. Until then, it's up to us to make sure nobody gets in or out of this god forsaken town."

*

By the time morning arrived there had been enough of an uproar from commuters to get the media's attention. Two major interstates had been shut down for nearly twenty four hours, and no reasoning had been given other than that there had been an "accident." Television crews were sent away by state police, which wasn't completely out of the ordinary. But every local station had sent a chopper to get a shot of the carnage, and each one of them was scared off by the Air Force before they could get close enough to realize there was no accident, only a small group of bottom-rung Air Force officers setting up a bunch of roadblocks. It wasn't long before the news world realized that something strange was going on in McLean County, and news crews were dispatched shortly thereafter.

*

Marcy could tell from the minute she saw him that Taylor had changed. He still appeared emaciated and weak, but something in his eyes gave it away. His grey eyes that had been distant and cold were finally starting to show the shades of green that gave them life. He seemed vibrant and excited, at least as much so as one could be in their current situation. Most of all, he was being nice to her, really nice.

She had woken up sometime around noon to find him cooking with all of the lights out except for the television and a few scented candles. Taylor's apartment was stocked with Yankee Candles, he was absolutely obsessed with them. As much as she wished they were lit to set the mood, she knew that it was the only light they could use without attracting more zombies. She made her way to the bathroom and took a shower, leaving Taylor to cook and stand watch over the apartment. When she had come out lunch was almost ready, and she took her place at the coffee table after stealing some clothes from Taylor's room.

Zombies. She hated to use that word. It seemed so morbid, but in the end there was no other word for it. They certainly weren't living, and they certainly wanted to kill. Taylor had told her about the attack the night before, and she had told him about her own similar experience. Every few minutes he would look back at her, with an odd look on his face. Then he would go back to stirring the pot, acting as if there was something he'd wanted to say but didn't know how to start.

Marcy could sense his reluctance to talk about his suicide attempt, and she didn't press the issue. She had seen his note on the table and knew that eventually they would have to discuss it. For now, though, she was happy just to have him back, even if it was just in time to watch the world end. Taylor grabbed the pot that was on the stove and carried it to the sink, dumping it into a colander and turning to stir the sauce pan that still sat on the stovetop.

"*Pasta,*" Marcy thought to herself, not noticing that she was picking at her bandage. "*He's making my favorite, how sweet.*"

In reality, Taylor had chosen pasta for a multitude of reasons. For starters, it was one of the few things that he knew how to make. Also, he knew they might need their energy if escape became necessary. That Italian food was Marcy's favorite hadn't even occurred to him. He opened up one of the cupboards and pulled out two plates. He then heaped a healthy portion of spaghetti onto each one, and doused them in spaghetti sauce.

Pulling two Diet Cokes from the refrigerator he made his way to the coffee table, setting a plate in front of Marcy. Her eyes widened as she smelled the meal. She hadn't realized just how hungry she was until food was put right in front of her. She could hardly wait for Taylor to grab a couple of forks and dig in. When he came back, Taylor handed her a fork and stared at her in silence for a few moments while she ate.

"In case we don't survive this, I think there's a few things I should talk to you about," Taylor said in the straightforward manner of his that Marcy both loved and despised. He furrowed his brow and appeared ready to say something when Marcy cut him off.

"We can talk about whatever you want, but let's wait until after we eat," she said, a large portion of her lunch hanging from her mouth. She wanted to savor this moment. Even if the spaghetti wasn't made especially for her, and even if the candles weren't there for romance, Marcy knew that this might be the closest to romantic she would get Taylor to be for a long time. And if they did die in that apartment, at least they would have spent an intimate moment together.

*

"Well, I gotta say…it's about fucking time," the walkie-talkie blared from Leon's hip. He groggily grabbed the binoculars and looked off into the distance, spying the first group of people to emerge from Bloomington-Normal since the blockade had been completed.

Leon was in charge of a half-mile stretch of the blockade and had stationed himself below an I-55 overpass on College Avenue. The underpass acted as a natural barricade, and Leon could use all the help he could get, armed with nothing but a walkie-talkie, binoculars and an M16 rifle. The last thing he wanted was to hurt anybody, but he had his orders. Leon prayed that the threat of force would be enough to keep these people in line. If they assessed the situation properly, the survivors that reached the blockade would soon realize that overtaking it wouldn't be a very hard task.

Straining his tired eyes, Leon counted at least seven of them. It looked as if they were going to make their way to somebody else's stretch of the blockade, which didn't bother him one bit. He wanted neither to deal with them, nor to have his rest interrupted. He had been awake for one and a half days, and his superiors didn't seem eager to bring any more troops into the situation than they already had. Leaning against one of the underpass' pillars, Leon sighed tiredly and continued his waiting.

*

"Let me start by saying that I never meant to hurt you. The decision to…to drink that cocktail the other night…that was all about me. It may have been selfish, but I'd thought it through," Taylor started, choosing his words carefully. "At least at the time I'd thought it through…but looking back I forgot about a few important things."

Marcy wanted to say something. She didn't know if she should console him or yell at him. "*A few important things?*" she thought to herself. "*I don't know if that's an apology or an excuse.*" She could feel the bitter side of herself coming out, but she wasn't going to let it show as long as Taylor made more of an effort to take some blame. All she really wanted was an apology and to hear him admit some guilt, but she wanted him to do it right. For now she chose silence, giving him the chance to open up on his own.

"At the time all I could think about was myself, and I think I'm somewhat justified in that. But I didn't look at the larger picture. I couldn't consider anyone else at the time. I…I didn't even think about what it would have done to you," Taylor said, looking up at Marcy periodically to gauge her response. "So, I'm sorry. I'm sorry for a lot of things."

Marcy could tell that he was sincere, but she needed to hear more. Not so much for personal comfort, she'd gotten the apology she wanted. Now she needed to make sure of two things. First she wanted to know for certain that Taylor was honest about his sudden new outlook on life. Also, Marcy had to find out why he had abandoned her in the days following Andrew's funeral. Seeing that Taylor was struggling to continue, she decided to facilitate that matter.

"Like what? What are you sorry for?" she asked, coming off more bitter than she'd wanted to. She could see Taylor's reaction. He was a bit surprised to hear her anger but seemed prepared for it.

"For starters, I'm sorry for having been such a dick for the past year. I don't think I've been there for you once these last twelve months, and that was just plain shitty of me. At first I was bitter about what happened after…Andrew. I tried to blame anybody and everybody else for my depression. I figured that if I accused other people of not being there for me that I would have an excuse to be so withdrawn. But now I've come to realize that it was my fault. I can't expect people to constantly ask me how I'm doing, or to drop everything to make sure that I'm at peace. I was the one who didn't make an effort to seek help, and I'm the one who has to take the blame for that. My withdrawal had nothing to do with you, and I'm finally beginning to accept that. I care about you too much to abandon you, Marcy."

Abandonment. That was the admission Marcy wanted to hear most of all. She stared Taylor in the eye for a moment, her blue eyes averting from his grey pair to look at her pink and white tennis shoes. Taylor continued.

"After that night at your house, I just freaked out. I had just lost Andrew and I was scared shitless of losing you too. So, instead of getting closer to you I pushed you away. I think I was so fragile that I would have rather kept you at a distance than have been hurt by you in the long run."

"Taylor," Marcy interjected, "I wouldn't hurt you, not on purpose. But you have to understand that by leaving me hung out to dry you hurt me. You hurt me a lot, and I don't think it was fair to do that based on the assumption that sometime down the line I might leave you. Not only did I need you then, but I was vulnerable. I'm very insecure about my insecurities."

Taylor smiled grimly, trying to maintain the levity that Marcy clearly needed.

"But you also scared the living shit out me, Taylor. You showed up at my door covered in what could have easily been razor wounds. If the loss of Andrew hadn't hit me hard enough, you had to come and make me wonder if you were suicidal, too. That's not fair, even if its incidental. You held out on me then, and it's been keeping me up nights ever since. To see you actually try to go through with it…well that almost broke me."

"As if that wasn't enough, you've been wasting away in front of me. Every time I see you it seems like you're that much closer to death. I looked at you and I would see a ghost, nothing more than a shell of who you used to be. Maybe you've changed now, but as of last night you were ready to quit. You were ready to give up on everything, including me," with this she halted, gathering herself for the final revelation. "Honestly, Taylor, you've been dead to me for a very long time. Only my love for you, my foolish and inexplicable love for you, has kept me coming back."

She had come out and said it. It had taken her a year, but she had finally lifted that weight off of her shoulders. There had been countless nights when she had lain awake in bed, imagining Taylor's reaction to her accusation. She figured he would either become outraged or mentally break down even further. So, her surprise at his reaction was understandable.

Taylor sat across from her on the chair and a grin spread across his face. He hung his head and chuckled to himself.

"What?" Marcy demanded, "What the fuck is so funny? This isn't a laughing matter."

"No...no it's not. And I don't think it's funny. Actually, I think you hit the nail right on the head. I just, I just feel like such a bastard for what I've done, you know? I always felt guilty, like maybe I had taken advantage of your vulnerable state, even if I didn't mean to. I guess I'm laughing out of embarrassment more than anything. I know I can't change what I've done. I can only try to make up for it. And even if I have to spend the rest of my life doing so, I'm willing to try."

Given their current situation, Marcy didn't know if the rest of their lives was long enough to make up for what he'd done. There were hordes of undead roaming the city, maybe even the country. And it was almost certain that both of them had AIDS, but she appreciated his effort all the same. She was too in love with him to let that get in their way now that they'd made so much progress.

"I love you, Marcy. I always have. It just took me way too long to admit it to myself."

With that Taylor leaned off of his chair and knelt against the sofa, pulling Marcy in by the shoulder and kissing her. They made love under the flickering candles, not giving a damn about their diseases or the world around them. For that moment, they were the only two people that existed.

*

Maybe it was just because he'd been eating well over the past twenty four hours, or perhaps it had something to do with having faced one of his biggest demons by telling Marcy how he really felt, but Taylor was stronger now than he'd been since he first started feeling his symptoms. This was one of the very few things in his life that he had to be optimistic about, but he took some solace in it nonetheless. For the first time since he could ever remember Taylor's mind was at rest. It wasn't at peace by any means, but for right now nothing was eating away at him to the point where he couldn't function. He'd almost forgotten how that felt.

Realistically, though, he knew that his life had grown exponentially worse in the last few days. Despite having given his heart to Marcy and her accepting his love there were still a lot of factors he had to deal with. And he had to deal with them soon. The zombies outside weren't going to simply leave them alone. It was only a matter of time before his AIDS symptoms returned or worsened. And he had to figure out a way to survive in this apartment, despite running low on food and clean water. He was just thankful that the electricity, for some unknown reason, was still on even though the phones hadn't worked all day.

The big picture showed that electricity wasn't much of a help at this point, but having the television available in the event that some breaking news were to come on was one of the few things giving Marcy and Taylor any hope. And it was definitely a factor in holding onto their sanity. As it was, however, the television hadn't changed its tune since it initially switched over to emergency broadcast. Taylor would periodically turn the volume up to check for a new recording, but would inevitably mute it once more, disappointed at the lack of response to this emergency. His only rational explanation was that the rising of the dead wasn't centralized to Bloomington-Normal. He assumed that this was going on across the nation, and possibly around the entire world. That was the only practical reason that would explain why nobody had come to save them.

It was Friday night and they didn't have enough food in the apartment to last beyond the weekend. They decided to begin planning for escape. It would undoubtedly become necessary at some point, either because of diminishing supplies or increasing zombies. They had a lot of factors against them other than the obvious. The rain hadn't ceased for over a week, and they couldn't bank on it stopping anytime soon. The roads were almost certainly a mess of abandoned or crashed cars. And if the zombies multiplied by killing those around them, Marcy and Taylor would have to find a route that was less densely populated.

They sat at the living room table now, writing in the glow of the television all of their plans and ideas. For nearly four hours they had been at it, and their final strategy was almost completely formulated. Marcy decided now would be a good time to step back from the details and look at it as a whole. Taylor agreed, also a fan of the fact that this would give them a well-needed break. His eyes were tired and his brain had been devoid of useful thought for the past forty five minutes.

"So, this is what we've got," Marcy started, lifting up their official sheet of paper and skimming the important points. "Inside this apartment are four ways to escape. We have the front door, the living room window, the bedroom window, and the bathroom window." Marcy had always hated the bathroom window in Taylor's apartment. Being constantly afraid that somebody might be able to make out her form through the blinds, she couldn't comfortably do anything in there. Now, however, she viewed it as a possible blessing if she had to exit this deathtrap in a hurry.

"The front door is the easiest to get out of, because all we have to do is slide the furniture away," Marcy continued. She and Taylor had gone over all of this quite a few times, but they both agreed that it was a good idea to pound it home at least once more. "The other windows would be a bitch to get out of, but if the path to the front is blocked off then that's going to be our only alternative. We've got a hammer ready at all times in case we have to pry the boards off of the windows and jump out them."

With this last statement Taylor patted his pocket to show that the hammer was on his person, available and willing to smash anything in its way. He was carrying it with the hammer's head in his pocket, the handle sticking out. This had led to more than a few "is that a hammer in your pocket, or…" comments from Marcy over the course of the day. Normally Taylor wouldn't find that sort of humor funny, but ever since he and Marcy had their talk they'd been as giddy as junior high school kids. It sickened him.

Marcy momentarily shot a glance at the hammer, and Taylor could tell she was thinking about saying it again. She thought better of it, however, and kept reading their day's work. "The only weapons we have are the bat, the hammer and fire. Seeing as how those monsters are going to be drenched if they get in here, the flame will only act as a deterrent."

"*Damn, she sounds professional*," Taylor thought to himself. "*She sounds dangerous, too. It's kinda hot.*"

"The only flammable stuff in here is some household cleaner and a few cans of hairspray, because somebody drank all the liquor," Marcy teased. She knew that it was still pretty early to joke about Taylor's suicide attempt, but she would rather talk about it than ignore that it ever happened. Humor had always been one of her ways of coping. Taylor grinned dismissively, now just wanting her to get to the next part. That was what he actually wanted to hear, as it had taken them most of the day to settle on.

Taking a more grave tone to her voice Marcy proceeded with the escape plan. "If we are forced to leave the apartment we have a few options. First we can try to get to the car. Although the roads probably aren't going to allow us to get far, the car will get us away from whatever breaks into here faster than running would. It will also provide some safety, since we don't think those things could break a car window as easily as one of these apartment windows."

Taylor nodded. They had debated over that for quite some time, both of them knowing that there was no guarantee that they could get to the car, or that it would even start. After that it was a crapshoot. The whole city had to be a disaster area by now, and there was no way they could simply drive out of town without a hindrance. But they knew they'd rather take that chance than be left on foot to battle however many of those things there might be. A claw hammer and a nail-bat might be effective weapons when you've turned your apartment into a fortress, but they don't mean dick when you're outnumbered and in the open. For the first time in his entire life Taylor actually felt some regret that he shunned firearms.

"After we get out, whether we're on foot or in the car, we have to head west. To go south from here would put us into downtown Bloomington, which would be like asking for death. To the east is too commercial and too congested. Travel would be nearly impossible and there would probably be a ton of zombies roaming that area. The north is an even worse option than both of them. It's a maze of indirect streets, so travel is tough. But the worst part of it is that all the residence halls are there, especially Watterson. If those things have gotten into Watterson then there could hypothetically be over two thousand of them in that direction," With this Marcy trailed off a bit, a look of deep thought on her face. The notion that so many people could be dead finally hit her. To this point she had only seen this as a tragic ordeal for herself. Actually putting the reality of the situation into words had hit home with her. The lives of thousands of people had been ended and destroyed by this disaster. "Yeah…west is the only way to go."

The plan having been read, Taylor looked Marcy in the eye. She had initially wanted to go north, just because if they could get past the residence halls it would be a straight shot to the interstate. But he'd talked her out of it, convincing her that it was too risky to assume that the zombies couldn't multiply. If they were infected or cursed in any way, then they could spread that to their victims. Given the information that they had, Taylor couldn't rule out any possibility, and this was a major enough risk to calculate all the way. "I know you're still not one hundred percent on this, Marcy. But there are a bunch of roads running straight west, so we might actually be able to drive pretty far. And there's not a lot of people in that direction, at least not in comparison to the rest of the county. If we can just get to 55 we'll have a shot of getting out of here with our lives."

That wasn't the only argument that Taylor had presented over the course of the night. He'd also told Marcy that he was flat out mortified of Watterson, and that was before the possibility of tens of thousands of undead roaming around it. Before he had applied to live off-campus Taylor was originally placed in Watterson. He decided to tour it, just to see if it was even an option. The entire time he was inside of that place he'd felt like he was being suffocated. The air had the feeling of a catacomb, and for some unknown reason Taylor feared that Watterson would eventually become his tomb.

Ever since then he'd gone to great lengths to avoid it. He didn't just keep from entering Watterson; he took measures to assure that he didn't even go near it. His route to class in the morning took an extra ten minutes just to keep him from walking in its shadow, which had always sent chills running deep through him. Now the thought of going near it seemed absolutely damning to him, and he'd made Marcy fully aware of his feelings on the matter. Taylor didn't care if it was just his own neuroses or the sheer logic of his argument. He didn't want to go anywhere near that cursed place.

As it was, Taylor lived too close to Watterson for comfort. If he hadn't had to go through so much bureaucracy to be granted off-campus living there might have been a better shot of getting a prime apartment. The process, however, had delayed his ability to commit anywhere, and he ended up settling for his single-bedroom that was just a few blocks from the lurking nightmare.

"And Marcy," Taylor spoke up, breaking the uncomfortable silence. "You have to keep your promise."

Marcy looked down, not comfortable even discussing the pact that they had made. Yes, she thought it was logical. But she didn't really think she could go through with it if her fears were actually made real. They had debated for a good thirty minutes before she finally accepted the reasoning behind Taylor's morbid proposal. Now she just wanted to forget about it, to file it away in her mind as something that would never happen. She had agreed to make the promise, but now whenever she considered it she doubted herself. And it scared the hell out of her.

"I won't make you say it again," Taylor went on, "but I can't stress enough how important it is that you don't go back on your word. You can't waste any time out there, or you'll end up dead yourself. You can save the mourning for when you're safe, but the greatest thing you can do for me in that situation is to get yourself out of here safely. If I die, Marcy, you have to leave me behind."

*

All day and night survivors had been arriving at the blockade, most of them in worse shape than Leon, who hadn't been relieved of duty since he arrived. The only thing keeping him awake was a steady supply of energy drinks that were also threatening to send him into convulsions. His entire being was in a state of animated fatigue, and he had long ago begun to question why the military would leave four dozen men with no sleep to quarantine two cities of angry refugees. The citizens of Bloomington-Normal, battered and frightened, were less than receptive of the excuses that Leon had no choice but to present to them.

By this time there were about three thousand people who had reported to the entire blockade, and Leon guessed that somewhere around two hundred of them were in the zone he was assigned to. He sat atop the overpass now, with a bullhorn that had been brought to him by the state troopers. The last time they had come Leon simply stared vacantly back at them, begging for help without ever saying a word. They could only sheepishly retreat back to their cruisers and take off, leaving him alone once again.

Leon scanned the crowd, hardly able to bear their intermittent cries of fear and desperation. Twice he had been forced to fire into the air to maintain order, but he didn't know how long that approach would work. These people were far more frightened of what was inside the blockade than what would happen if they tried to break out. Sooner or later they would calculate the odds and make a move. Leon knew deep within himself that he wouldn't fire upon them.

He wasn't an overly motivated person. That was why he had chosen a military career in the first place. Leon liked the idea of somebody providing him with direction until he was able to figure out on his own what he wanted to do with his life. But he was smart enough, filled with enough common sense, to know that everything about this assignment was one lie after another. These people weren't a threat to anybody. They were like caged dogs, their animosity motivated only by fear.

The most telling realization that Leon had come to was that if the citizens of Bloomington-Normal were sick it certainly didn't merit a blockade. Whatever it was that they were running from wasn't airborne, otherwise Leon would have caught it long ago. As it was the only thing he'd caught these past few days was a shitty attitude caused by his lack of sleep. He still didn't know what was going on inside this blockade, but he was of the opinion that the first priority of the military should be to get these innocents out of the danger zone.

As a matter of fact, Leon was beginning to wonder if the claims of the refugees didn't hold some truth. There had been varying testimonials, but all of them were based off of the same concept. Something inside of Bloomington-Normal was on a murderous rampage, and it was eating people alive. While Leon was hesitant to believe all of the details he'd heard, there was definitely enough of a consensus to give some credence to the basis of their stories.

The situation itself made Leon feel somewhat fortunate to be where he was. For starters, he was much happier to be outside of the blockade than inside of it. Furthermore, he was provided some protection from an attack because he was atop a berm. Footing would be hard enough in normal weather, but these citizens would be hard pressed to battle the mud and still be able to reach him. If they were to rush his blockade, they wouldn't try to take the overpass. They'd shoot through the underpass, which was guarded by a few roadblocks and a supply truck that had been positioned to slow any foot traffic.

This made him pity these poor souls more than anything else. They were physically and emotionally decimated by their journey to the blockade. When they saw military personnel they must have been overjoyed, assuming they would be saved. Now they were being told that they would have to wait here indefinitely. All the while the rain was washing their hope further and further away. Eventually they would either choose to revolt, or they would simply wither away with the precipitation. There wasn't going to be an in between for them, there never was.

Unexpectedly, the crowd of refugees arose and looked towards Leon.

"Damn it, they've already had enough of this bullshit," Leon thought to himself. He readied his rifle, prepared to fire it into the air once more. If that didn't work then he would probably just give up. At this point he no longer cared. This wasn't his fight, and it wasn't his decision to make as to who should live or die. The truth was that he might run with them, especially if some of the things they'd been describing were true.

He was just about to pull the trigger when Leon realized that the survivors weren't looking at him. They were looking past him. In his weary state Leon hadn't even noticed that headlights were radiating over the area, illuminating the highway behind him. He stood and turned, just as interested in what was about to happen as those he was watching over.

There must have been at least twenty transport trucks coming towards him along the interstate. By his estimate, each would probably hold about ten men.

"So good of them to show," Leon muttered, too fatigued to even care what they were there to do. He hoped that they would relieve him, but at this point he had very little optimism about anything this assignment entailed. He shouldered his rifle and waited, knowing full well that if he left his post to investigate the trucks he could be given an even worse duty. After fifteen of the trucks had passed by him the remaining transport vehicles came to a stop. Their back doors swung open and dozens of Green Berets spilled out, making a beeline straight towards Leon.

Second Lieutenant Gibbs fell back on his heels for a moment. He'd always had a fear of authority, which was completely justified by the fact that he was a black man who grew up in a white suburban neighborhood. Now he was about to stand toe-to-toe with at least forty men who all out-ranked him, and he would have to do whatever they asked of him. His gut feeling told him that they didn't give a damn about him or his orders, but that didn't stop him from worrying. Leon regained his footing and flashed a salute as the men approached him.

"You Gibbs?" one of the men questioned, shouting much louder than he had to in order to compensate for the sound of the storm. He stood about six feet tall and was as broad as a barn door. He dwarfed the other Green Berets, even making Leon seem small in comparison. His wide chin and grizzled appearance were all business. He furrowed his thick eyebrows at the question.

"Yes sir, Second Lieutenant Gibbs," Leon responded, pulling his hand back down to his side. The other man stopped about two feet from him and gave a brief salute in return. He kept his hand at his brow to protect his eyes from the rain, and Leon wondered immediately if the man had actually meant to salute him or if it was just a coincidental move.

"Captain Wes Talbott, United States Special Forces. I understand you've been keeping watch here for a couple of days now?" the military man was strictly business, which was the way Leon preferred it. The last thing he wanted was to pussyfoot around the reason they were here, even if it meant bad news for him. At this point, all he wanted was for this ordeal to be over.

Talbott turned his back for a moment, signaling to his men that they should get to work. Immediately they broke towards the trucks and began to strap on various equipment and survey maps. When he looked back Leon responded with a simple, "Yes, sir."

"Well I want to let you know that we appreciate it. This has been one helluva situation for everybody involved. We're going to need you to keep watch over your post, but while we set up our incursion you'll be allowed to rest. We can put somebody else in charge of your post until we're ready to go in. Sound fair enough?" Captain Talbott finished, making the last question more of a statement. All the while that he was talking he failed to make eye contact with Leon for more than two seconds. He was watching the prisoners on the other side of the blockade, gauging them.

"Yes, sir," Leon answered quickly, the prospect of sleep momentarily overtaking his desire to know why twenty truckloads of Special Forces would be called in to handle the situation instead of a MedEvac unit. Even if Leon had thought of something to ask Captain Talbott, he had already turned and left to proceed with his operation. Forgetting his worries, Leon found his way down the berm and to the cab of the supply truck. He succumbed to slumber immediately.

*

Marcy was asleep, and Taylor had been left to security duty. He sat rigid on his barstool in the middle of the hallway, listening intently for any sign of intrusion. It had only been three hours since Marcy went to sleep in his bedroom, and he wasn't a bit tired. The majority of the day's work had been done with his mind, and his body was more than ready to take the first watch shift. Besides which, Taylor believed he needed the time to sort out everything before he fell asleep and ended up forgetting some important detail.

Marcy wasn't about to complain about second shift, either. She'd had a long day of taking care of everything and letting Taylor sit on his ass to think. That meant that she'd had to do everything from sex to cooking to writing a master plan in a ten hour span. She didn't think twice about giving him the job of staying awake at two in the morning with nothing but the TV glare to keep you company. She had fallen asleep with no sleeping pills, which was not easy for her to do given the flesh-eating populous that was just outside the window.

The knob of the nail-bat was leaning against Taylor's thigh, ready to be used with excessive force if anything should threaten to compromise the apartment's security. It was the kind of creepy night when you could only sit and try to keep the darkness from worrying you. Eventually your mind is going to wander just enough for the shish kabob skewers across the kitchen to begin to closely resemble a set of pikes preparing for impalement. To the benefit of Taylor, he was too engrossed in his own thoughts to worry about such unrealistic horrors.

The agreement he'd made with Marcy had clearly shaken her. In fact, Taylor was probably more frightened of it than she was. But he'd put on a strong face for her, knowing that if those fuckers outside did kill him he would definitely want Marcy to leave his corpse behind. If he became one of them, so be it. He'd rather turn into a mindless cannibal two miles away from her than two feet away. In his heart he knew that he would have a hard time doing the same for Marcy.

The night was starting to wear on him, and after leaning the bat against the wall Taylor stood up to stretch out. He checked the clock on the wall and saw that he only had two more hours to go before he woke Marcy. He decided to kill as much time as possible watching the television's streaming text. There was always the off-chance that something new had been reported, although Taylor held as much hope for that as he did for their survival. At this point it seemed like only a matter of time before something broke in and slaughtered them or they ran out of food. After all, Taylor was living by himself and was too poor to buy more than a few days' worth of groceries. Scratching the back of his neck, he made his way into the living room.

Taylor caught the television with his peripherals and stopped. He quickly snapped his head toward the screen, not exactly sure that he'd actually seen what he believed. The Emergency Broadcast message was flashing in and out of static. Taylor studied the screen intently, watching to see if another image flashed on the screen. There was nothing now, but Taylor was certain he'd seen something for a very brief instant.

He moved to the sofa, his eyes still fixed on the television. As he lifted up the remote and searched blindly for the volume button the screen flickered quickly. Pressing his thumb down and bringing the volume to half-power Taylor listened intently. He couldn't decipher whether or not what he was hearing was static or a low, laboring breath. He brought the volume up higher and strained one ear toward the television.

For no logical reason the speaker system kicked on, the receiver blasting the surround sound. Taylor jumped backwards against the sofa, startled by the sound coming from all around him. He could tell now that it was, in fact, the sound of struggling breath. The respirations were deep and rough, sending an abrasive vibe through the room. At first Taylor's thoughts went to Marcy, assuming she was in danger. But before he could react the screen flashed up an image. Taylor looked back at it again, but the picture reverted once more before he could clearly make it out.

Now he was torn. Part of him wanted to run to Marcy, to hold her in his arms. In his heart he knew that if anything happened to her the entire one-eighty he'd made with his life would be null and void. But another side of him wanted to wait. There was more to this than just an electrical disturbance. He was starting to get the same feeling he'd gotten just before the zombie had punched through the bedroom window. Something unholy was at work, and it was too powerful for him to ignore.

As if in response to his thoughts, the television made up Taylor's mind for him. The screen switched once again, and this time Taylor could see what was undoubtedly Watterson Towers. The mere sight of it lurking across the distance was enough to unnerve Taylor, but it looked alive on the screen. Slowly the windows of the twenty-eight stories began to fade on and off randomly. At first they seemed to have no discernible pattern, but Taylor began to notice that two of the windows lit up more often than the others. All too quickly he understood what they were. The medieval monstrosity had eyes, piercing almost as white as the Sun.

Taylor had to shield his face as the screen pulsed brighter. It tore through his fingers and eyelids, and he was beginning to see dots when the television flashed to a negative image. The same eyes that had just been pyres of light flipped to complete darkness. Taylor knew that they were the exact same eyes that had belonged to the entity from his vision. The empty swirls on the screen began to draw his attention like a vacuum. He was powerless to fight back.

Taylor's jaw dropped open slightly as the darkness clouded his thoughts, acting as blinders to the world around him. The entity was in control now, and it switched the shot on the television to display a demonic figment of Taylor standing in a dorm room. The wraith Taylor turned its head and grinned at the real Taylor, wickedly flashing the same teeth that belonged to the monster who had slashed Marcy's wings. As it did so its head tilted to the side, cocked in an overzealous grandstand. The impostor's eyes were also empty and lightless. It turned its attention to the window behind it and flipped the latch open.

Wasting no time, the zombie Taylor opened the window and climbed up to the ledge. Now the entity switched the picture of the television to show the viewpoint of the Taylor standing twenty-stories in the air. The distance to the ground was clouded by screaming, swirling winds that could have almost pulled him out of the window. As if willingly, the fake Taylor jumped, the air cutting past its grotesque face as it plummeted to the asphalt below. The ground rushed towards the television screen and the real Taylor screamed, shocking himself out of the entity's hold and coving his eyes with both hands.

He sat in the same petrified position for ten minutes, his hands trembling over his smashed shut eyes before he decided to look. Carefully he split his fingers and started to open one eye. He didn't want to pull his hands away for fear of seeing something he'd have rather missed. As Taylor's eye opened it became apparent that there was no light in the entire room. The television had gone out completely. Taylor switched his plan and went with the Band-Aid approach, ripping his hands away and forcing his eyelids open.

There was nothing. The power must have gone out completely. The television wasn't broadcasting anything, and even the VCR wasn't flashing the incorrect time. Taylor had known that it would only be a matter of time before this happened, and Marcy had planned for it. There were three scented candles placed throughout the apartment. One was in the bedroom, one in the living room, and the third rested in the hallway. Taylor had originally put the final candle on the barstool, but switched it down to the carpet so he could use the stool for guard duty.

Temporarily too worried about the pitch black of the apartment to dwell on the television incident, Taylor reached forward and groped in the dark, finding the candle in front of him. It was a Yankee Candle, but he didn't know which scent. A good aroma therapy was exactly what he needed to get over his vision. He pulled the candle towards him and fumbled in his pocket with his free hand. Finding his lighter he flicked it to a flame and reached it towards the wick. It blackened as it lit, emitting a faint odor from the moment it caught flame.

"*Honeydew*," Taylor thought to himself. "*Nice.*"

The room glowed, not even illuminated half as well as it had been by the TV. Sensing the need for another candle, Taylor made his way towards the hallway. Secretly Taylor was glad to have an opportunity to light the candles. The apartment had acquired a rather distinct odor, which was highly unpleasant to handle, since this ordeal began. It also helped him to relax, which he believed he'd earned after being mind-fucked by a television.

The glow from the Honeydew helped to accent the outline of the candle in the hallway. Taylor spotted it and bent to pick it up, lifting it to his nose first. His inhalation gave way to confusion. He was having a more difficult time figuring this one out. He stood straight up and lit the wick, lifting the candle above his head afterwards. He was going to try reading the sticker on the bottom.

"I know I have two that smell pretty much the same," he thought to himself. *"I just don't know if this is the Cherry or the Black Cherry. I can usually only tell by the color, but it's too damn dark for that."*

There wasn't enough light to read the stickers, so he placed the candle on the stool and waved his hands over it, trying to waft the scent to his nostrils. He didn't want to go into the bedroom and wake Marcy, but he had found a mission. There was no choice but to find out what scent the candle was. It struck him then that he could just take it over to the flame from the Honeydew and straighten out the whole olfactory debate in a matter of seconds. He had taken two steps towards the living room when he heard a window smash and Marcy scream.

Taylor switched out the candle for the bat, placing the former on the stool and scrambling into the bedroom.

*

Leon looked up. He had suddenly been roused from his sleep at the blockade. A cricket killed its croaking. Overhead a hawk flew freely over the blockade, weaving from one side to the next. It would be the first of many to reach the blockade. Leon guessed it would also be the last to be given such liberties.

Something about the deathly silence seemed to worry the Second Lieutenant. He wrapped himself tighter in his fatigue jacket. He braved the cold, hidden in the cab of the supply truck. From his vantage point, he could see everything that was about to unfold.

*

Two sets of arms had managed to punch through the boards covering the bedroom window. Taylor was frantically swinging the nail bat at them, but they didn't even seem to feel the pain. The ashen arms just pushed forward, grasping for anything that might fall into their clutches. Marcy had been on the bed, which had been pushed against the wall opposite the window the day earlier. She was unscathed, but too frightened to think clearly. Her mind began to race as she panicked. Was she supposed to help Taylor fight them, or should she try to open an escape path? What was their escape plan? Where in the hell was the piece of paper they'd wasted all day on?

"Marcy!" Taylor shouted, swinging the bat down and sinking the nails into one of the four wrists grabbing for him. The blow didn't even phase it. "Marcy!"

Marcy shook herself out of her stupor, suddenly remembering the plan. "Taylor! Holy shit, we gotta go!"

Retreating back a step, Taylor turned towards her, assessing the situation as he did. She was right, and he knew it. He would have to let the zombies in, or else Marcy and Taylor would have to contend with them outside. "Get to the living room!" he shouted, pulling her up by the arm. He had a plan, but it wasn't part of the one they'd written up.

The arms tore away at the wood, almost clearing enough room for the monsters to get in. Marcy exited the room and Taylor followed. She stumbled down the hallway and almost knocked over the burning candle, collapsing on the floor next to the arm chair. Taylor didn't follow her, instead rushing into the bathroom and grabbing a handful of bottles off the countertop.

"What are you doing!? Where are you!?" Marcy cried, grabbing the side of the chair and pulling herself to a stand. She clutched at her pocket and felt the shape of the car keys inside.

Taylor emerged from the bathroom and calmly strode towards her. In one hand he had the bat, in the other he was carrying hairspray and bug repellent. Marcy understood what he had in mind even before he said it.

"Marcy, you're gonna have to start the car. Get that furniture away from the front door and wait until I tell you to go," Taylor said as he handed her the bat. "I'm gonna hold 'em off for as long as I can."

Marcy took the bat and nodded, but she didn't turn. "Taylor…"

"I know…" Taylor stated as he swept her into his arms and hugged her firmly. He quickly released, though. He was all business, if not for Marcy's sake then for his own. "But we gotta get moving."

Marcy set to work removing the furniture barricade, struggling to disassemble it. She had packed it so tightly originally that it didn't want to budge this time. Taylor knelt next to the barstool, eyeing up the flame of the candle like a crosshair. He sat patiently, waiting to hear the zombies enter the apartment. Behind him Marcy was beginning to panic, still having a hard time clearing a path.

A crash from the bedroom told Taylor that they had broken down the big board, and were just moments away from entering the hallway.

"NOW MARCY!" he screamed, looking over his should briefly to see that she had only moved the desk. The dresser still stood by the door, preventing her from opening it all the way. Taylor looked up and saw the first zombie entering the hallway. It was clad in soaking wet blue jeans and a red collared shirt. The buttons of the shirt had been torn off, and a gap in the material revealed a massive crater in the beast's chest where its heart should have been. Dried blood caked the outer rim of the crater.

"JUST SQUEEZE THROUGH, THERE'S NO TIME!"

The second zombie was in the hall now, and they had spotted Taylor. Letting out a guttural hiss the lead zombie strode quickly towards him. Taylor lifted the can of hairspray and depressed the canister. The stream of flammable liquid caught the flame, sending it forth like a small flamethrower. The zombies halted instinctively and stepped backwards.

Taylor kept shooting the flame and looked back at Marcy again. She was trying to slide through the small opening of the front door. The doorknob was crushing the small of her back as she forced herself through. Throwing all of her weight outside she freed herself and escaped the apartment, but the nail bat caught the molding of the door and slipped from her grip. She ignored it and pulled the keys from her pocket. Spinning towards the street she saw the Pontiac, only a row of parked cars between her and the passenger side.

*

Taylor picked up the candle and continued spraying. The can of insect repellent was in his back pocket, and he might need it to buy time for himself to get out the front. The raging fire licked at the oncoming demons, forcing them to remain in the hallway. Taylor walked backwards and stopped spraying, wanting to conserve any part of the can that he could. Once the flame subsided the zombies made their way towards him again. Taylor let loose another quick stream of fire and continued to the front door.

*

Marcy looked around and saw that there were two more zombies outside. One of them was about twenty yards to her left, the other even closer than that. They were both dressed in plain white nightgowns that had been splattered with blood. Their hair was gone, replaced by a congealed mass of burgundy. Each moved slowly and stiffly, as if held back by the same physical constraints of their former living selves.

Assessing the situation quickly, Marcy realized she would have to run across the hood of one of the parked cars if she stood any chance of getting to the Grand Am on time. She didn't waste any more precious seconds, setting off across the front lawn and preparing her jump.

*

Taylor reached the front door, still eyeing the zombies as they closed the gap. They clambered within five feet and he sprayed again, sending them back once more. With his right hand Taylor grabbed the door and realized that there was no way he could escape through such a small opening. Bracing his foot against the frame he drove it backwards, cracking the wood of the dresser. The zombies took the opportunity to make another rush at him, but Taylor loosed a violent burst of fire.

*

Marcy landed on the hood of the parked car and took another step before noticing the zombie that had been lurking behind it. She was in mid-stride as

82

it reached for her, seizing her ankle as she was about to jump from the hood. Her flight turned into a tumble as the creature tightened its grip. Marcy pitched headlong to the street, smashing her cheek against the pavement. She fell unconscious immediately, feeling no pain while blood and teeth spewed from her mouth.

The zombie descended upon her.

*

Taylor had cleared enough room to escape the front door when he felt something tug at this leg. It was the nail bat, Marcy must have dropped it.

"*MARCY!*" the realization struck him.

Fending off the zombies, Taylor had completely forgotten to check on her. He mustered up all the force in his body and shot himself through the door, reaching back to grab the nail bat just before the zombies could snatch his wrist. Spinning on his heels Taylor looked towards the car, but didn't see Marcy anywhere. Then he spied two zombies outside the apartment closing in on him from either side. Marcy must have seen them and fled on foot.

Raising the bat to a traditional batting stance, Taylor didn't hesitate as he swung the nails directly at the head of the slow-moving zombie to his right. He connected with enough force to sink the nails completely into the soft, decayed cranium of the zombie. It fell to the dirt immediately, dragging bat and Taylor down with it. The zombie that had been on his left seized the opportunity to attack.

Taylor caught his footing as he fell and gripped the bat, jerking it back towards him with all his strength. It hardly budged. Knowing that there was another ghoul just seconds away from being upon him, Taylor turned and kicked outwards, catching it in the chest. The zombie reeled back, giving Taylor enough time to step on the fallen creature's skull and retrieve his club. He yanked it out, bringing with it a large chunk of gelatinous flesh that was dripping with a dark substance.

Wasting no time, he lifted it over his head and shifted his body weight towards the zombie behind him. This one, too, folded to the ground the moment Taylor planted the nails into its brain. It bellowed a defiling shriek as it fell, causing Taylor to turn his head. He then looked back to the two monsters that were still inside the apartment. They were almost out, and snarling straight towards him.

Thinking fast Taylor dropped his bat and whipped the can of bug spray from his back pocket. Then he grabbed his lighter. He rushed towards them, preferring to go on the offensive rather than wait for them to get outside. Taylor let out a cry of rage as he unleashed a flare of chemical flame upon them. He didn't relent until the zombies were completely engulfed, and he was certain they would burn in that apartment. Their dual cries nearly bled Taylor of his sanity, and he almost fell to the earth as he tried to block them out. He replaced the tools of fire in his pockets and covered his ears. After a few moments the shrieks of the demons died out, and the flames spat out of the slim opening of Taylor's apartment.

With the immediate threats taken care of, Taylor turned his attention to Marcy. She was nowhere to be seen, and he assumed she had to have run off. He didn't want to call out her name, as his scream moments ago had probably attracted more than enough negative attention. He decided to quickly check the car, in case she had gotten in and was hiding from sight.

Grabbing his bat Taylor made his way towards the street. He had to slide in between two parked cars to get to his Pontiac, and he proceeded cautiously. Taylor turned his body sideways and strafed along the bumpers, his bat ready just in case. As he placed his foot down in the middle of the street, the petrified Taylor dropped the bat.

Marcy lay in the street, blood seething from her face. A zombie was on top of her, biting at her neck and unleashing another wave of thick, red plasma. Taylor's eyes filled with rage as he rushed the ghoul and tackled it to the ground. He gripped the fiend's trachea like a vice, raising its head up and quickly thrusting it down against the wet pavement. Its skull cracked as it widened its mouth, trying to hiss and bite at the same time. Taylor pulled it up again and this time grabbed at its empty eye sockets as he savagely belted the back of its head once again. This time it went limp, but Taylor didn't stop. He didn't even notice that his hand had grown deathly cold from touching the zombie's eyes. Revenge and bloodlust were all that he knew at that moment, and he continued pounding the monster's head against the street until it was little more than a pulp of cerebral tissue and mucus.

After Taylor's rage subsided, he stopped. The rain beat down upon his shoulders, reminding him of the dread weight that had just been placed upon him. He was going to have to turn around and look at Marcy, but nothing save his own willpower could make him. All he could think about was Andrew Johnson's corpse, and the last thing he ever wanted was to go through that again. He wasn't even morbidly curious this time. Rather, he was filled with dread. He knew that she was dead. There was no need to take a pulse.

He had let his guard down for less than three minutes and it had gotten her killed. The rain pounded against him, urging him to act. But Taylor only knelt there, over the corpse of the zombie that had killed his best friend and lover. He didn't want to say goodbye. He didn't want to go on alone.

The time passed without notice. Rainwater soaked into Taylor's clothes and hugged them to his skin. His hair was matted down, and it fell down over his eyes, further blinding him in the obscurity of the night. The weight pulled him downwards, like a dumbwaiter to hell. All he had to do was sit in indifference and he would soon be dead as well. In his line of thinking, that had suddenly become a viable option.

Then he remembered the promise. He had made it in haste, not taking the time to look at the consequences realistically. She was in the exact condition the he had purposely avoided considering. But, in the same vein, how could he betray her in death? At the same time, though, how could he abandon her? Taylor got to his feet, ready to justify whatever move he was about to make.

The options circled around his head, dizzying him. To take her with would be nearly as dangerous as walking back into his burning apartment. For all he knew she would reanimate in the back seat while he was driving, putting him at risk of sharing her fate. But to leave her here unprotected for these abominations to defile would be the very last thing Marcy would want in death. Without turning around, Taylor thought.

"She would have to be buried in Hudson...she wouldn't have it any other way."

It was true, and he knew it before he'd really even thought it. Marcy would want a funeral. She would want her friends to be able to grieve for her just as they'd grieved for Andrew. She had understood the importance of closure. His mind was unofficially made up as he turned towards her.

The sight before him changed his decision. *"...unless it would have to be closed-casket."*

Marcy's once angelic face was grated into an indecipherable mess of exposed bones and still-gushing blood. There was hardly a distinguishable characteristic on the entire left side of her skull. Below that carnage, her neck was nothing more than a vat of violence. Her entire jugular had been savagely torn out, and it made a sordid slopping sound as the rainwater ran alongside the wound.

Taylor's feet dragged him towards her corpse and he dropped to his knees. Bending down he cradled her in his arms, the rain washing her blood down her face and onto his jeans. The left side of her face was one massive, gaping wound. At least eight of her teeth had been shattered. Her eye was shut, a mess of swelling and thick plasma.

Forsaking every concept of survival, Taylor let out a howl of misery. The tears streamed down his face more heavily than the storm surrounding him. He sat in the street, on his knees, clutching the body of Marcy to his chest and shivering. Her warmth was slowly fading, and he tried to avoid the knowledge that he would soon have to say his final goodbye.

Taylor brushed her hair back and kissed her on the forehead, the only part of her face that was relatively unscathed. He was about to grab the car keys from her lifeless hands when a chill ran through him. He could feel Watterson Towers behind him, staring at him. It was rising up and reveling in his pain. Taylor struggled to block it out, thinking only of Marcy. He hated the idea of leaving her behind for the undead army to have their way with. One of those zombies could come by and feast on her the instant he left. But he knew he had to keep his promise to her. He had to be honest with her now, if only to make up for the fact that he'd done so little of that when she was alive.

Taylor hugged Marcy tightly one more time, whispering "I love you" into her ear as he lifted her off the ground and carried her to the stoop of his apartment. He didn't even notice the flames fanning his face as he laid her on the ground. He grabbed the car keys, ran to road, retrieved his baseball bat, got in the Pontiac, and started the engine. He didn't look back as he drove away, the inferno from his apartment growing. He didn't want to know if her body burned before the zombies made it their carcass. As the flames grew in the rearview mirror Taylor's body temperature shot up four degrees. The fever, the symptoms, were returning.

*

A noticeable rift had emerged amongst the refugees. At first, when they were all little more than desperate escapees trying to survive the nightmare behind them, there had been an unspoken unity between them. Slowly, as more of them began to gather and settle in, the separate groups could be made out without much trouble. There were circles, each one of them gradually becoming its own camp. Some of them were made up of people with the same interests, others based upon gender or race.

The majority of them, however, were relying solely on age as their determining factor. The locals were distancing themselves from the college students. Their ideological differences were the driving forces behind the evolution of these cliques. For the most part the locals of Bloomington-Normal had very conservative viewpoints. This had been a source of conflict in McLean County for many years.

"*It just doesn't make any sense,*" Leon pondered. He was sitting at his post, high atop the overpass of Interstate 55, trying to grasp how the sociological climate of the blockade could have changed so rapidly. The instant that the survivors began to arrive at the blockade there had been an immediate feeling of compassion. At first, if only for a short while, it had seemed as if everybody inside the blockade was part of a single community. They didn't care one bit about each other's beliefs or backgrounds. All they cared about was that each one of them had suffered a tragedy, and the outpouring of support had been breathtaking.

Now all Leon could see was a regression, a step back in the social evolution of these victims. Instead of love and support, there was fear and distrust. It was as if the atrocities hadn't even happened. After thinking about all of that for quite some time Leon came to a dreary conclusion. The already precarious situation presented by hungry, tired and frightened refugees was becoming even more dangerous. It may have only been on a small scale at that time, but the climate was shifting to the point of a highly volatile storm.

That was how Captain Wes Talbott had come up with his plan for handling the civilians. All night he'd been implementing his invasion, a mission that had been dubbed "Operation: Damage Control." Now that the final plans were made, however, he was left with the task of ensuring that none of the prisoners try to organize an escape. There had already been a few attempts to rush the blockade, which had only been stopped by a hail of bullets. If there was any chance at holding them off until the mission was complete, he would have to organize a strategy much more complex than simply pointing a gun at them. After all, eventually some of them might begin to point their own guns back.

"Gibbs, I've got two men who'll stay behind and protect the blockade with you," the Captain dictated. He was staring at the crowd as he did so, almost as if disgusted by their desire to disobey a military initiative. "We're going to divide them further…pit them against each other."

"Sir?" Gibbs could only ask, not sure if the Captain was actually suggesting that they create a civil war amongst the civilians.

"You see, Gibbs, back when slavery was legal there was a far greater number of slaves working the plantations than there were whites to run them. So, slave-owners had to come up with a way to keep them from rebelling. What they came up with was the idea to pit the light skinned slaves against the darker skinned slaves, causing civil wars within the slave population that kept them from organizing. It was quite a brilliant strategy, really."

Leon's eyes narrowed as he wondered whether or not Talbott even cared about the massive implications of what he'd just suggested. Leaving alone the fact that he'd just lauded the work of fascist, racist hicks from centuries past, that still didn't excuse what such a volatile idea could create if implemented in the current situation. The people on the other side of the blockade weren't slaves, enemies or prisoners of war. They were American citizens, and to use fear-mongering as a tool to divide them would ultimately lead to killing.

"I'll leave two men with you, to help keep things under control," and with that Talbott went back to his squad. Leon was left to helplessly fume at the recent turn of events. With two Green Berets left behind to follow Talbott's orders, and keep watch over the Second Lieutenant, there was no way he could simply ignore the strategy that was being employed for crowd control.

*

Three hours had passed since Taylor fled from the scene of Marcy's graphic demise. Yet, he'd hardly covered any distance at all. A combination of shock, awe and sporadic car pileups had slowed his progress considerably. The Grand Am ran idle at an intersection little more than five blocks from the firestorm that had lit up Taylor's apartment. He waited for the light to turn green before he could proceed, but the power had been out for the entire morning.

He lay sprawled across the driver's seat, which he had reclined the full amount. The Pontiac's automatic headlights prevented him from going into complete stealth mode, but he was able to dim the car down to the parking lights level. The streets are terrifying in the pitch black, even in a familiar area. Marcy had never been able to walk downtown alone, and that was with all the lights. She would have absolutely despised this.

The thought of Marcy's death had struck him, and Taylor was mourning by crying uncontrollably. He clutched his hand to his heart and sobbed, the fever was inducing horrifically vivid visions of the zombie sinking its teeth into her. The impact of Marcy's death, however, had not yet hit him.

He'd tried to sound so fucking bold, telling Marcy that they would have to leave each other behind. Every fiber in his being wanted to be right back with her, whether that meant being eaten alive or engulfed and burned into a charred corpse. He wandered in his thoughts for many dark hours that night. Without realizing it, he shifted the car into drive and proceeded onward.

That morning the rain stopped.

*

The blockade had been opened, but only temporarily. Talbott was the first to make his way through, leading a group of three dozen men to the other side. Armed heavily enough to take on a small army, they made their way through the curious and desperate refugees. Any hostile movement by the civilians was met with the business end of a rifle, which had unbelievable power. Even the most pitiful of men could be made into a God with a loaded chamber.

Before setting off on his unholy crusade to kill anything in sight, Captain Wes Talbott had passed his strategy onto Leon and the two lucky men who had been left behind to ensure that Second Lieutenant Gibbs didn't give in to compassion. "These imbeciles are operating under the assumption that the bullshit we've been feeding them might actually be true. For some ludicrous reason they still cling to hope. Use that to your advantage, because eventually they're going to get angry enough to start to question it. That's when you have to use fear to rule them. The threat of a bullet in the head is so much more effective than actually wasting the bullet."

*

The Pontiac rolled slowly north on Cottage. Taylor had been driving for hours. He deciphered that he'd originally gone south, because that was where the tornado siren that had shaken him from his thoughts was in relation to his apartment. Now he was trying to find passage west. He was nearing double-digits for the amount of times he'd been blocked off by an accident. The damn locals had been too worried about living that they'd forgotten to obey traffic laws. It was a shame.

His plan was to reach Beaufort and head west. That route would take him fairly close to the interstate. If that was blocked off he might be able to hit College, which would almost certainly be a mess. The other problem was Taylor hadn't even thought about supplies yet. Gas was going to be needed sooner rather than later, and he didn't think he could make a daring escape again without any food in him.

All of this was lost on Taylor, who had been able to develop some semblance of a plan in spite of his fever. Other than that, however, he was still lagging behind mentally. He couldn't go longer than five minutes without thinking of Marcy. All the while he could feel the onset of what could be the late stages of AIDS.

According to the brochure Taylor had found laying the back seat, he might begin to suffer from AIDS Dementia. He had been unable to think clearly all morning, and it was starting to frustrate him. He could feel the heat rise in his chest, indicating the he was about to panic. He knew he had to stick to the plan in order to calm himself, but he couldn't remember what street he was looking for anymore.

Taylor started breathing heavily, his control on the steering wheel wavering. The Pontiac started veering to the right, and Taylor had to force himself to brake. He peered out the windshield, seeing that he was at the corner of Cottage and College. Suddenly it occurred to him that he'd passed the street that he had wanted. But now he wasn't even going to consider turning back to get to Beaufort. He believed he had a much better chance of escaping that way. But he was slipping, fading out of consciousness. The virus was getting the better of him now, and he fell asleep at that intersection with the engine still running. Holy Cross Cemetery loomed across the road.

*

Moments after the Pontiac Grand Am that rested under the shadow of the trees ran out of gas a well-armed group of Green Berets passed by it. So far they had been sorely disappointed in their lack of anything to kill. The sun had finally peaked out from the overcast clouds, and the haze of the morning made it impossible for the Special Forces to see the shape of a man sprawled out on the reclining driver's seat. Taylor's potential rescuers continued onward toward their destination, Redbird Arena. They lost the maroon vehicle behind them to the fog that was dissipating as the early morning turned into day. A chill overtook the Pontiac, covering it with a thin frost.

Somewhere near the middle of Holy Cross Cemetery, the soil began to stir.

*

Taylor's car was still encompassed in an ever-thinning layer of frost. It was the only thing protecting him from the creatures that were slowly starting to congregate in and around Holy Cross Cemetery. A few of them had passed within a yard of Taylor's driver side window, only their threatening outlines visible from inside the car. He hadn't woken, however, as their shadows passed over his closed eyes. For the time being he was oblivious to everything but his dreams, which would be faint memories by the time he rose.

*

Noon was still a couple of hours away, but the sun was finally overtaking the clouds. Only the areas that were still hidden from its reach remained cold enough to maintain a frost. Within an hour, though, the day would be warm enough to melt away any sign of the morning's chill. Leon rested his chin in his cupped hands, occasionally rubbing his eyes and scratching at his stubble.

The sudden shift in the weather was a welcome change to him. The line of trees that separated Normal's citizens from the carnage within the town was clearly visible under the light of day. The large knoll that played host to the growing number of escapees was littered with their weary bodies, almost all of them sitting or laying on the ground. They weren't as edgy as they had been in the past couple of days, and Leon attributed this to the fact that there hadn't been any attacks from within the blockade. Aside from the occasional refugee taking a walk along the blockade's edge, the morning had been quiet.

All of that changed, though, when the first fight started. A woman wearing a sweater streaked in dried blood had to be held back from attacking a college student who had walked near a section of College Avenue that the frantic woman had claimed as her own. The territorial feud grew into shoving, which escalated into punches before it was broken up. Leon watched in shame, while the Green Berets looked to him for answers. Leon returned their questioning glares.

"Oughtn't we do something?" the Green Beret named August asked. His short blonde hair lay flat in the wind, the dark blue of his eyes searching for an answer. The other Green Beret was more of an asshole than the ignorant August. That one was Crawford.

"*James Crawford,*" Leon recalled. It seemed to fit him quite well.

"I don't honestly know," Leon answered. "You're the ones that Talbott talked to, not me. I don't even know why I'm here anymore."

"We stick to the orders," Crawford directed. He shouted it as if he had something to prove, most likely a result of his short stature compared to the other Green Berets. In fact, Leon mused, he didn't appear to have actually served a day in his life. Still, his leathery face and scrawny neck created a hardened exterior. Leon figured anybody in Special Forces deserved to be there. "And don't go giving us any more lip."

"Lip?" Leon got on the defensive. "I'm just stating the facts."

Crawford glared at him, August looked away at the crowd that was slowly breaking up. Once the action had ended everybody lost interest in the scene.

"We do love our drama," August said. His sudden interruption broke the tension. Still, Crawford wasn't about to let an inferior rank, especially a minority, get the last word.

"We stick to the orders."

*

The dirt road in front of Taylor stretched on for endless miles, lined on either side by flowing tall grass. Overhead the sun tried to beat down on him, but a thin veil of clouds only allowed a dim phosphorescence to come through. He wanted to shield the light with his hands, but something pulled at his shoulders that kept him from doing so. Looking behind him, Taylor finally noticed the load he was carrying. It was nearly unbearable.

Taylor had a length of chain wrapped around his hands that led to a red wheel wagon behind him. It was the same style as a wheel wagon made for young children, but much larger. The sides were surrounded by two-by-fours, encasing the burden that weighed it down. The wagon was probably large enough to house a pair of medium sized pigs, or maybe a horse. Livestock, however, was not what encumbered Taylor's wagon.

The decaying bodies of Andrew and Marcy lay lifeless against the baking metal floor of the wagon. It was permeating the horrid stench of their spoiling carcasses, causing Taylor's stomach to wretch. The nauseating feeling that had overtaken him for the hours prior to his suicidal struggles three nights before had crept back over him. Taylor never came to the realization that this was only a dream.

His task laid out before him, Taylor commenced to pull the chains. With a surge of energy he was able to get the wagon rolling. Its momentum would have been useful on a paved road, but the heavy dirt did nothing but hold it back. The chains creaked with strain as Taylor heaved them over his shoulder, using his entire back to keep the wagon moving. He began to make his way down the dirt road, his burden still dragging behind him.

Taylor's journey went on for eons, the ultimate destination still unclear to him. He was nearing his breaking point when the fleeting shade that was the only factor making his work sufferable began to dissipate. He was now exposed to the dawning solar assault, which had suddenly come out in full force. As the heat hit his forehead Taylor doubled over, spewing up a stream of stomach acid as he did so. He hacked and gagged for a few moments before preparing to resume.

Lifting the chains up once more, he dashed forward. This time, however, he didn't have the strength to start the wagon. All that he could muster was a weak whimper, which was inexplicably followed by the ground shaking quickly. Taylor stopped, widening his stance to keep his balance. The quake hadn't been major, and he was able to remain upright. But another wave of quivering soon followed.

This was stronger, noticeable throughout the surroundings. The tall grass that had trembled uniformly in the wind was now convulsing in every direction. The clay-like dirt that stretch for miles was heaving slightly, sending large cracks throughout its surface. The jolting turned to churning, and the earth in front of Taylor began to swirl in a whirlpool of dirt.

He stepped back and clutched the chains to his chest in fear. The once impenetrable road in front of him was collapsing, making way to a drain of emptiness. The dirt continued to swirl, revealing a vast dark hole that appeared bottomless as it became larger, forcing its gaping edge closer to Taylor with each passing second.

Taylor assessed the situation quickly and turned to flee the widening void. Forcing his legs into an ambling rush Taylor struggled to push off against the dirt that was quickly vanishing below him. In a last ditch effort to escape the impending abyss Taylor leapt towards the wagon, clutching at its sides as he fell against the wooden panels. Using his velocity and the last of his power Taylor pulled himself over the edge and fell hard onto the floor of the wagon. He landed between the corpses of his fallen friends and gave way to momentary paralysis. Either the hard fall or the syndrome within him had stripped him of the ability to move, and Taylor lay against the rusted bottom of the wagon with the smothering chains strewn over his body. His eyes looked towards the sky as a darkness overtook the air.

*

A shadow had fallen over Taylor's body, and the line between reality and dream began to blur. Was he in a wagon along a dirt road, or was he in his car next to a mausoleum? Was the shadow a creation of the chasm that had opened up below him, or was it in reality a zombie standing just outside his window? Where had the clouds gone that protected him, and what had happened to the frost that had hidden him from view?

*

The Taylor that lay in the massive Red Flyer wagon peered into the horror above him. A gigantic hand had emerged from the black hole that was waiting to suck him down into the abyss. It was severed, slash marks at the wrist revealing how it had come free of its host. It was the hand of death, and it was here to deal out doom. Just as the understanding of his condemnation was occurring to him the hand smashed downward, shattering the wagon into splinters. The axle snapped and Taylor rolled off the slanted tetanus-laden metal, plummeting into the gash in the earth and disappearing into its null existence.

*

The flesh-and-blood Taylor who was thrashing in fevered pain inside the Pontiac Grand Am didn't even see the horde that had besieged his metal fortress. When the first zombie pounded the front windshield with its hand Taylor opened his eyes, seeing only the sunroof above him. Still in a dream-like trance and uncertain if the opening was his damnation or his salvation, Taylor reached out and turned the key to the power position.

The red radio lights flashed on and the dome flickered. Taylor reached upwards and depressed the sunroof button, sending it sliding open slowly. His sight fixed only on the escape that was revealing itself, Taylor completely missed the clock and odometer as they flipped themselves to display the most telling revelation of the young day. The clocked flickered in and out while the odometer dialed itself in all directions, both of them inevitably and simultaneously coming to land on "666."

When the roof had finally completed its task Taylor threw himself upwards without even thinking ahead of time what might happen once he passed through the portal. His pandemic-ridden body propelled towards it nonetheless, careless of what may lie on the other side. Taylor's exit was halted despite his recklessness.

He paused to figure out what had impeded his flight and looked downwards. There were chains around his chest, or so Taylor thought. His mind was too fried to tell the difference, and he ripped at them without regard. Upon grasping the restraint Taylor recognized its texture. A moment passed and he understood that it was only his seat belt. He unfastened it.

The lapse in reality had caught Taylor off-guard, but his ability to grasp the gravity of the situation returned because of it. This time he stopped to consider all of the possibilities, and none of them sounded optimistic. He checked the gas gauge, and immediately his spirits sank. He must have let the engine run out when he fell asleep. He was going to be forced to flee on foot. The only problem was that Taylor didn't have any sense of how many were outside of his car. The shadows completely choked off any light from outside. For all he knew there could be anywhere from ten to a thousand of them. Could he really barrel through that kind of group?

The sunroof had been vulnerable for quite some time now, though. None of them had even come close to getting on the roof of the car. Maybe he could squeeze out quickly enough to make a run for it.

"*Prometheus*!" Taylor thought to himself. He had forgotten about his aerosol arsenal. He had a weapon. All he needed now was a distraction. He gathered his half-full/half-empty can of mosquito repellent and his lighter. Next he readied himself for the getaway, preparing to deploy his diversions.

"Shit yeah…this is gonna be fun," he exclaimed somewhat honestly. This plan just might work if the zombies were as primal as he'd thought. Grabbing the keys from the ignition Taylor activated the alarm and burst upwards through the sunroof. Not even taking time to assess the surroundings as he exited the vehicle Taylor unleashed a burst of flame in all directions, spinning and rising from the sedan as he did so. He stopped the flame just long enough to brace his trembling fists on the hood of the car, clutching his only defense while raising his legs out of the car and onto either side of the sunroof. He was able to make out that there were somewhere between two and three dozen of them, making their ranks about two or three deep.

Just as Taylor had hoped the wraiths were still cringing backwards in uncertainty about the sudden outburst from the car. Knowing that there was no time to admire his work, Taylor flicked the lighter and sprayed it towards the left side of the car, jumping to the pavement below at the same time. The zombies all recoiled at the flame, revealing a fleeting opening for Taylor to escape their noose-like attack.

Pressing forward he took the gamble, having decided before he even left the Pontiac that he would use the element of surprise just long enough to keep them confused. The moment they realized that he wasn't capable of harming them all at once they would descend upon him, the same way that they had done to Marcy. The gap was little more than two feet, but Taylor's stumbling landing kept him moving forward fast enough to burst through it. Lowering his shoulder he knocked the two enclosing demons backwards, breaking free into the clearing.

He had taken three quick paces away from the mob when he froze. Holy Cross Cemetery stood before him, and it was teeming with the undead.

*

Supply trucks had arrived that morning and Leon was relegated to unloading duty. Crawford and August were supervising the watch post, leaving Mr. Gibbs conveniently by himself to distribute the Red Cross supplies that had been sent. The Red Cross workers weren't allowed to hand them out, as Crawford had pointed out that would entail them crossing the blockade. Now Second Lieutenant Gibbs, who was outranked by his two partners, was left to struggle without any help.

He'd been toiling all morning with the job, and it was starting to shut down his body. His back would give out briefly almost every time he bent to lift a box. He'd stopped lifting with his knees hours ago, their edemas threatening to blow out his ability to walk at the drop of a hat. He'd taken off his jacket to relieve the pounding rays of the sun, but Crawford had found it unpatriotic to not wear the entire uniform.

Leon hated to let the two of them watch him work, but he didn't have much of a choice. He was bound to his duty. He was outranked and outnumbered. Outside of the rifle that he kept on him at all times, Leon was absolutely powerless. That's a dangerous situation to put anybody into.

*

Taylor was still running at a decent pace, but he was starting to feel as though he couldn't go on much more. He'd sprinted with all of his life across the cemetery, using his sheer human speed to bypass his coagulated pursuers. They were following, no doubt, but he had gotten so far ahead of them that he hadn't seen them for at least five blocks. He was in a residential area now, still running along College Avenue. He'd lost his vehicle, but he was going to stick to the plan. College Avenue would lead to the interstate, even if it meant getting past even more of those things. Taylor continued west, the sun directly above him.

The distance that awaited him was unknown. Taylor rarely traveled this way, and he'd never taken the time to pay attention to the area. It was too far from campus to matter. He knew that no matter how far he had to go, the need for his body to take a break was going to get the better of him before he reached his destination. His infectious sores were taking advantage of his body's vulnerable state. It was only a short matter of time before the other symptoms followed. The syndrome was relentless.

Taylor held out hope that he had outrun the entire undead army, with nothing but peaceful expanses ahead of him. The idea of rest overtook him, and he barely had time to reach an abandoned front porch before collapsing. Taylor dragged his unresponsive legs towards his chest and pulled himself across the wooden slats towards the front door. He reached up and closed his eyes as he tried the handle, expecting disappointment to follow. It opened.

With everything that he could still muster Taylor pushed the door open and forced himself into the house. It was deathly quiet as he collapsed just inside the entrance, the door still partially ajar. He could only hope that he was hidden from sight as he once again surrendered to unconsciousness.

*

A shriek of anguish pealed through the darkening sky, snapping Taylor out of his dreams like a shot. The cry that came from the distance was all too familiar to Taylor. He had heard it before, when he'd torched the apartment and the zombies inside. They had cried out in such pain that he had to cover his ears, almost sending him to the ground. Nothing of this earth could make such a sound. It was as if death had a theme song, and it was little more than the screams of these creatures and their victims.

His long break ended abruptly. He'd slept six hours, and now Taylor had a decision to make. He could continue to hide out in the house or he could make a run for it. There was no third option. If he'd been stronger Taylor's mind would already have been made up. When healthy he could outrun those things any day of the week. Now, though, he couldn't accurately say if he was even able to stand up.

But he had no clue if they would be able to smell him or not. Taylor still wasn't sure how they had discovered him in the car. There was an off-chance that these beasts could track their quarry. If that was the case then there would be dozens of them crashing through the windows and breaking down the doors in a matter of minutes. That was not a gamble Taylor wanted to take.

He extended his arms up and grasped the door handle, using it to pull himself to a standing position. He was going to have to make a run for it, or else he ran the risk of being engulfed by the masses once again. Taking once last check of his surroundings, Taylor bolted, jetting out the door and down the stairs in a flash. Letting out a grunt when he leapt down the stairs, Taylor's feet hit the sidewalk in stride as he turned to continue west.

With a look over his shoulder Taylor saw that he was not being followed. As far as he could see, there was nothing behind him at all. That knowledge did nothing to slow his pace, however. The night had come quicker than Taylor had expected, and now he was running with frantic desperation. There was little more than the moonlight to guide his way, and it almost felt worse to Taylor than the rain had. All he could see as he ran were dim shapes and blurs all around him. The haze of the evening seemed surreal enough to be a dream.

He made his way past the first block, pumping his arms at his sides and pushing forward. The only measure of distance that he could use was the feeling of sidewalk, grass and pavement below his feet. The power outage had slipped his mind when he was considering the escape. It was too dark to make out different shapes now. Later it would be so entombed with darkness that travel would be impossible.

His thinking had caused Taylor to briefly lose speed as he maneuvered onto another stretch of pavement. He had probably gone four blocks now, but he couldn't keep track easily. He shook off his thoughts and focused his energies yet again on forging ahead as quickly as possible. The newfound burst lasted for half of a block before the sprinter stumbled across a mass sprawled across the sidewalk. He toppled, nearly catching his balance before diving to the ground. His left shoulder crashed onto the cement, sending a shock of torment through it. Asphalt lacerated his flesh, tearing open one of his infected sores on his chest. Pus and blood poured out, soaking heavily through his white shirt. The rest of his body landed harmlessly on the grass, but that was a small consolation prize.

Doing everything he could not to cry out in pain Taylor rolled onto his good shoulder. The whole left side of his torso had gone numb, and he couldn't tell if he had a broken bone somewhere. He whimpered softly for a short while before realizing what he was doing.

"Men don't whimper. Get the fuck up before you've really got something to cry about."

He took his own advice, sitting up and pushing himself onto a knee. The throbbing burn in his shoulder hadn't even begun to subside yet. It was then that Taylor remembered that he'd tripped on something in the first place. His landing had been so traumatic that he'd momentarily forgotten how it happened. Determination set in as Taylor shook off the pain, and the investigation commenced.

The night stood still around him as he crawled gingerly through the dark. He could hardly discern the faint mass that lay motionless before him. Taylor's mind started to race, and he began convincing himself that this was a bad idea. No good could come from investigating this matter any further.

But his curious desire got the best of him, and he continued inching towards the unknown. When he was just a few feet from it the shape became recognizable. It was undoubtedly a body, but everything else about it was still a mystery. Taylor crawled another foot closer and called out softly while reaching his hand towards it.

"Hello?"

Silence. Taylor's hand remained suspended inches from the body.

In the distance a flock of birds shot out of a tree, the sound of their wings beating against the night sky drowned out everything else. Even the blaring of the tornado siren had disappeared. An unsettling feeling followed, and Taylor's fragile mind replayed the sound over and over again. Forsaking his curiosity Taylor made up his mind to flee.

He braced his outstretch hand against the ground to push himself up. If he'd placed it just a few inches to his right he would have stood up and started running, most likely escaping unscathed. But his hand landed in something wet and warm. It was something that was streaming from the body's chest. All too suddenly the revelation hit Taylor, his hand covered in crimson.

He cried out in horror.

Somewhere nearby his cry was answered. A horrific howl rang out against the moonlight, defying any living creature to deny its power. Taylor just had enough time to figure that it had come from the north when another shriek tore through the darkness. This one seemed to come from the west. He was surrounded, and the noose was tightening once again.

Suddenly the carrion next to him seemed like Taylor's last concern. He righted himself and got to a knee once again, but he tried to stand too quickly. The world spun around him, the dizzying gyrations sending his senses into a frenzy. His nausea returned as another shriek cut at his ears. The cries were so close that Taylor could no longer tell which direction they were coming from.

Taylor's stomach wretched, doubling him over. He was still on one knee, his fists the only thing from sending him face first to the ground. He dry heaved, sending up nothing but a mass of stomach acid. As he gathered himself something unseen sped past behind him, pounding against the pavement. By the time Taylor whipped his head around it was out of sight, but whatever it was had been running.

Pure adrenaline allowed him to push off of the grass and reach a kneeling position. Another figure deftly swept behind him, slicing past so closely that

Taylor could feel the wind rush with it. He knew they had closed in, and there was no telling how many of them there were. He propped one foot forward, steadying himself to rise up. His body's energy was almost completely depleted.

With nothing going his way now but a shot in the dark, Taylor straightened into a stand. That was when another figure raced by him, crashing against his wounded shoulder and sending him sailing backwards. Time almost stood still as he flew through the nothingness. So many things occurred at the same time that his mind was forced to race faster than his body.

First, while he was plummeting Taylor's perceptions shifted into the otherworldly. The world changed from reality to his visions. Instead of being a fraction of a second from pounding against the earth Taylor was back in the black hole that had sucked him out of the Red Flyer. But, that wasn't the only thing he sensed.

Taylor achieved a dual-reality, melding his dementia with his surroundings. Did a light appear within the darkness, or was that a flashlight that just flickered on over his face? And did he hear the endless tug of the vacuum that was swallowing him, or did a rifle shot just ring out? Taylor had decided that both must be true just before he hit the ground. The aerosol can in his back pocket loosed itself, rolling loudly down the sidewalk. The last breath in Taylor's lungs was knocked out as the darkness took him.

*

Russell Singleton was a nut. He owned seven rifles (four of them automatic), four shotguns and a baker's dozen of pistols. His attic had been converted into a survival shelter years before zombies ever came to Bloomington-Normal, and so had his basement. Sometimes he wore camouflage just for a trip to the grocery store. Tonight he'd chosen his Mossy Oak fleece. It was a bit chilly.

The fleece complemented his dark blue jeans and hunting boots. His unkempt appearance only added to his intimidation, with stray strands of shoulder length cobalt hair pasted across his face. The stubble that had accumulated since the crisis began was already a thick, peppered beard. He stood in the middle of the street, pumping his left arm once in celebration.

"Got 'im!"

He raised his rifle again, scanning the road with the flashlight that was taped to it as he took aim. One of them skittered away from the motionless body that lay in front of him, and Russell didn't hesitate as he pulled the trigger. The zombie's brain matter spewed out the front if its skull as it crumpled to the dirt.

"Fuck yeah!" he cheered. This made four confirmed kills on the day, and he was fixing to break his previous night's record of seven.

He walked ahead, whirling in a circle slowly as he checked his surroundings. There were more of those things, and they would wait until his back was turned before they made another move. He'd come to rescue the dipshit that had been running blindly down the street. Now that poor idiot was huddled on the sidewalk, and Russell could only hope that he hadn't been bitten.

He reached the fallen body, doing one last check of the area before turning to pick it up. Sure enough, they had waited for him to reach their original quarry. There were four of them surging at him, one on each side. He cursed himself for not bringing the automatic. Either way, he figured he had time.

"Shit, son!" he cried as the first one's head exploded. He whipped the rifle over his head and spun his body one hundred and eighty degrees. The gun landed expertly against his shoulder, the second victim being queued up in his sights. He squeezed the trigger. "Holy Christ!"

He snuck in one quick fist pump before spinning his torso to the left and opening fire on the third attacker, his tying kill. The first bullet ripped through its neck, the second finding home between its eyes. He wasted a bullet, which only fueled his desire to battle. He might get to use his buck-skinning knife if this got ugly enough. With a grin Russell turned to face the fourth assailant, and celebrated his second straight night of hitting lucky number 7, "Violence is a virtue, motherfucker."

He'd always wanted to use that one.

The final attacker sprinted towards Russell, snarling out and prepared to lunge. Russell had different plans, however, aiming low as he squeezed. The hollow-tip tore the zombie's knee out from under it, sending it to a kneeling position. The Hunter dropped the firearm, allowing it to rest on its shoulder strap. Still high off of his one-liner Russell pulled out his knife, the serrated edge reflecting the moonlight across the demon's neck as it slid through the decayed flesh. Russell sawed off the entire thing in only a few quick strokes, letting it tumble heavily to the dirt.

Gripping the rifle again he swept the light around him, seeing that it was once again clear. Only the aluminum siding and hedges were there to greet him. Russell then turned his attention to the body, kneeling down to grab it. He hesitated, however, as he began to lift it.

"Oh…shit," he shook his head, closing his eyes momentarily in grief. The body was drenched in blood.

*

Leon was on his sleep shift. Before he left for the night to retire in one of the trucks he stopped by the overpass. August was there by himself, and a quick scan of the area revealed Crawford checking the arms supply on their truck. He shuffled roughly towards his superior. Ruing the necessity to even ask permission, Leon wasted no time.

"I'm going to sleep shift now, sir." Leon reported, already turning to leave before he got his approval.

"Go ahead," August started, but thought better of it. "Wait…Gibbs!"

Leon was screwed. He was probably going to be put on watch duty for the rest of the night. Crawford had obviously shown August a taste of power, and he'd liked it. From here on out he was at their disposal.

Yes, sir?" he answered.

"Good work, you know…unloading the trucks today. Really helped the uh…morale."

He said 'morale' with pride, like it was a big fancy word to him.

Leon smiled, uncertain of August's intentions. "Thank you, sir."

He started to ponder the usefulness of Special Forces' Benjamin August.

*

Russell made it through the front door of his house relatively certain that he hadn't been followed. He dropped the body to the ground and turned to close the door behind him. He'd constructed a series of hooks on either side of the door that allowed him to quickly drop in 2x4s to barricade the door. He put up four of the possible eight, knowing that a quick exit might be necessary. He didn't want any extra boards impeding him.

Stepping over his parcel Russell cut his path down the hallway and into the kitchen. He kicked open the refrigerator and grabbed a beer. The power outage had kept the fridge from running, but it still did a good job of cooling his American Beer, which was brewed two hours away in DeKalb. Russell's cousin would always bring down ten or twelve cases whenever he visited. The stuff only cost $4.99 per case, and Russell was able to use the saved money for a subscription to Guns & Ammo.

"You want a beer, son?" he called out behind him, laughing as he heard the silence in reply. This was going to be one fun night. If this guy turned out to be bitten Russell was going to get to increase his total to nine, which would be a cause for even greater celebration. Sitting down in a folding chair he continued to talk with his guest. "One beer for each kill seems fair, doesn't it? We gotta show some discipline, after all."

He finished the can after a few swigs, and sighed in aggravation. He was going to have to carry that sad sack downstairs if he turned out not to be infected. He decided to get it over with, preferring to finish the day's work before he started the party. He would just have to start the celebration over again and redo the beer he already drank.

Russell stood up, his chair creaking below him as he did so. With a grimace of regret he strode over to the body. This poor kid was probably about twenty one years old now. The humane side of Russell didn't want to see such a young life stolen away so ruthlessly. The hunter in him felt no compassion for the beast that this kid would become if he'd been bitten. He knelt as he reached the victim, not wasting any time for second thoughts as he tore back the shirt.

He revealed a mess of blood and mucus. There were wounds everywhere on his torso. It looked as if he'd been bitten thirty or forty times. With a regretful grin he made his diagnosis, and raised the rifle that still hung from his shoulder strap. Then Russell reached out and pressed against one of the wounds, which woke his temporary prisoner immediately.

"Repent, son," Russell ordered, standing tall and turning the flashlight on. It bore into Taylor's eyes, showing that if he had been infected, he hadn't turned yet. Taylor shielded his eyes briefly until Russell switched the flashlight off.

"Did you call me 'son,' man?" Taylor lashed, all at once realizing that his shoulder injury earlier in the night had gotten worse now that the numbing had subsided. He had no idea what in the name of hell was going on, but he had woken up to find one of the grinning hicks from Deliverance touching his bare chest. The last thing he wanted to be called was "son."

Not wanting to lose the element of fear, Russell dropped the rifle and pulled the knife from its sheath. He brandished it in front of Taylor's face. "Did one of those fuckers bite you, son?"

At least he and Taylor had the same pet name for the hell spawn that had overrun the town. The young college student quickly understood the reasons that the man with the knife had for asking. Still the sight of a steel blade approaching his throat made his response frantic. "Bite me? I don't know. I blacked out, man. I swear I don't know."

"If you don't know, then what are all these marks doing on your chest?" Russell was getting edgy, and he started to care less and less about this kid's survival. Even if he wasn't bitten there was something that Russell wasn't being told. There was no reason to take in a punk kid he couldn't trust. His temper was flaring quickly, so much that he didn't care if those things got inside. He was gonna open the door to throw this little bastard out.

"Put down the knife." Taylor instructed, trying to take some authority.

"I have a death wish." Russell countered, playing a wild card to throw his counterpart.

"I have a death sentence. Put down the knife."

"What are those marks doing on your chest?" Russell asked shakily. He wasn't backing down until he was certain that this kid wasn't lying. "And don't you fuckin' lie to me, son."

"Those are sores, man. I'm sick. I've got AIDS," Taylor revealed hesitantly. Russell's reaction made Taylor's revelation seem even worse than if he had been bitten.

"Oh shit…you ain't a *fag* are you, son?" Russell recoiled. Taylor couldn't tell if he moved back because he'd touched his blood or if he was afraid Taylor might be a homosexual. The way he'd emphasized the word "fag" with overwhelming disdain seemed to indicate that it was the latter. Taylor was about to respond when he realized he'd never actually been asked before. He wasn't gay, but he'd always figured that wasn't the point.

"Should it matter?"

Russell sheathed his knife. "Get up, son."

"My name is Taylor, and I can't get up. I can't even feel my legs right now."

Russell scooped down and lifted Taylor off the ground like he was a rag doll. His must have dropped at least four pounds since he fled the apartment. The hulking Russell had no trouble hoisting him over his shoulder, and he carried Taylor down the hallway, stopping at a door to his left. Wrapping one arm around Taylor's waist the he opened the door, unveiling a stairway leading to the basement. As Russell descended with one hand on the rail, Taylor looked up and saw a greeting painted hastily on the doorway above him.

"Welcome to the Seven Bridges Road."

*

The tornado siren trumpeted its unnecessary warning against the increasing wind. Anybody who was close enough to hear it was either dead or already well aware of McLean County's state of affairs. Wes Talbott wasn't deceased, but most of his squad was. He definitely didn't need a siren to tell him how dire the situation had become. He was holed up in an empty alley somewhere along Main Street. He was out of breath, and he didn't know for certain where he was, only how he'd gotten there.

The incursion had started with Talbott heading one of the four squads that entered Bloomington-Normal from the west, with ten soldiers under each captain's squad. The same amount of men had been sent in from every direction. Less than two hundred men were charged with the task of battling the hordes of thousands. On the bright side, though, the zombie's didn't have the same weaponry as the United States Army.

Initially, everything had been quiet. They had only encountered a handful of hostiles, and the number of dead they passed along the way was nowhere near as high as they had expected. Talbott and his men were just beginning to think that they might get out with their lives when the Redbird Arena came into view. Pillars of smoke billowed from the roof of the arena, and a sea of death surrounded it. The zombies writhed as one, almost in celebration of their conquest of the Arena. Nothing could have been left alive inside.

Waves of zombies swarmed from the makeshift shelter, over one thousand of them already standing outside of it. It was only a matter of minutes before they noticed the soldiers approaching. Talbott had started screaming into the walkie-talkie, pleading that the other troops come to aid them as quickly as possible. The response had been minimal, with almost every other squad involved in a massive firefight of their own.

The choices were obvious. Talbott could retreat and wait until he had the necessary forces to take on such a brutal army, or he could go to war. He was outnumbered and lacked the ammunition to finish the job. Captain Talbott knew that fighting would be suicide, but he also knew that he had his orders. If he didn't complete the mission there were dozens of other captains just waiting to take his place. He was not to exit Bloomington-Normal until every threat had been eradicated.

Sometimes blind pride can force a man's hand, and this was one of those instances. Unfortunately, this man had scores of young men under his charge. What had ensued was a massacre. Two other squads answered his cry for help, but they still hadn't arrived by the time they zombies realized there was fresh meat to be had. That left a handful of Special Forces to follow Captain Wes Talbott into his own personal war.

The horde came at them faster than they expected, splitting them and forcing them to the defensive. Talbott and his men hardly had time to fire off any rounds, and those that they managed did little to stop the snarling abominations. The auxiliary forces arrived just in time to catch the front lines of the undead bearing down on Talbott and his men. The demons had been screaming in anguish like a frenzied mob. The M16's had opened fire a heartbeat before the first bites would have been made.

Catching the attention of the wraiths, the squads had drawn a secondary wave upon them. Droves of zombies charged at them, some running in a frenzy, others walking stiffly and stalking the ranks. The special forces were soon being encircled by the monsters, their bullets too few to hold them back. The separated troops of Talbott, who had been momentarily forgotten by the creatures, could hear little more than the decreasing gunfire and the cries of destruction coming from their doomed reinforcements.

Talbott recognized the opportunity to escape and didn't hesitate. His orders were momentarily reprioritized as the chance to live another day became of relatively high importance. He had ordered the retreat, roaring it at the top of his lungs and turning his back to his fellow soldiers while charging away from the masses. A small group of zombies ran out to cut him off, but he had altered his course and was able to barely pass by them. He had continued to flee, not sneaking the time to look behind him.

That was how he had ended up in his current position, poised behind a dumpster on the north-south running Main Street. He hadn't heard anyone or anything approaching in quite some time, but he knew his impromptu hideout wouldn't last extremely long. Checking around the side of the dumpster, Talbott battled the dark to make out whether or not there was any danger nearby. When he was relatively certain that it was safe to make a move, the Captain sprinted out onto the road.

*

Andrew promised Taylor that he would tell him what had happened that day outside of the barn. So Taylor bolted for the doors when they opened for recess. He was literally pulling Andrew. It just didn't even occur to him that Andrew wasn't in any rush to relive the tale. Taylor had to hear it for himself. He thirsted for it.

When they were both outside, Andrew reluctantly told Taylor to follow him. Andrew then turned and faced the barn. His eyes lost their life when he gazed upon it. The blood in his veins turned cold. Then he walked at it, almost against his will. It was like something was drawing him to it.

Taylor followed behind impatiently, he was expecting something cool. He couldn't wait to find out and tell everybody else. He'd probably be the coolest kid for at least a day. That had to count for something in the long run.

The breeze was picking up as they closed in on the barn. Taylor didn't even hesitate to cross beyond where they were permitted. Andrew didn't even notice. He walked up to the barn door, sat down and crossed his legs. Then he cupped his hands over his face and began to sob.

That was the first time Taylor realized something was really wrong.

"What's the matter?" he had asked.

Andrew couldn't answer. His mind had shut down. He simply grabbed at the chain around his neck. "He took it."

That was when Taylor finally noticed that his friend's crucifix was gone. He wore that thing every day. Now it was just the chain.

"What happened?" Taylor questioned. Andrew was lost, though. He was no longer playing.

Taylor looked at the barn, and something made him want to go in. There was something unknown on the other side of the door. He had to find out. He had to be the only one to be able to say he went inside the haunted barn. He pulled open the doors, and slid through the small crack.

His eyes took some time to adjust to the change in lighting, there was only a small crack of sunlight coming in from the few windows and the slit shooting through the freshly opened doors. They revealed a room of dirt. The walls were caked in years' worth of it. The floors were simply a foundation of compacted soil. The pillars that held the structure together were aged and cracked, resembling the crumpled earth that they sprung from.

There was only one thing that didn't resemble dirt in the entire, empty barn. There was a red wagon. It was a Red Flyer. Taylor had always wanted one of those.

He forgot his fears for an instant, striding towards the wagon. It wasn't until he'd gotten close to it that he stopped. There was something placed directly in the middle of the wagon. It was a burlap sack.

The low-lighting died against the sickly surface of the burlap. It was wrinkled and damp. The mere sight of it made young Taylor's skin itch. He could already feel it scratch against his hands as he picked at it in a vain attempt to open it. He was becoming increasingly skeptical. Then he turned around and saw Andrew. He could only make out a portion of his face through the doors, but Taylor could plainly see the agony that Andrew was going through.

Taylor owed it to his friend to open the sack, regardless of what he might or might not find. He reached down and grabbed the burlap. It seemed to crawl within his hands, lying dead against every nerve ending. Then he pulled open the opposing ends.

Taylor should have just opened the sack in a flash. Make it as painless as possible, and don't let anything stop you. Unfortunately, at that young age, he hadn't yet heard of the patented "Band-Aid Approach." So he opened it slowly.

The instant there was an exposure to its contents, an army of earwigs poured from the opening. They emptied out in waves, covering first Taylor's fingers. He shook his hand wildly, to get them off, but they pinched down and refused to let go. So Taylor thrust his hands into the sack, feeling soil within.

The dirt swallowed his hands. It was cold and smothering. At the same time the number of earwigs climbing up Taylor's arms was increasing. They crawled over one another, searching for flesh to puncture. They made their way up his arm, and under his sleeve. They latched onto his armpit, sending a burning, crippling sensation through his torso. Still his hands searched.

A pincher bug found its way onto his neck. That was when he lost it. He shrieked, falling backwards over himself, his hands freeing from the swallowing burlap sack. He pulled them to his chest, clutching together. Taylor rolled on the ground in agony, writhing at the prickling sensation from all the earwigs. He heard them crunch under his body, their plasmatic innards bursting and smearing his skin.

He looked up, to see the red wagon. But it was gone. There was no wagon, no burlap sack, no dirt. Only the earwigs remained, and they suddenly released Taylor from their menacing attack and fled out the door. They crossed directly underneath Andrew's legs as he bawled outside, but the poor son of a bitch didn't even notice.

Taylor shivered on the dirt floor of the empty barn, his hands still clutched at his chest. He opened them, and saw in his right hand a crucifix. He didn't remember anything but screams and hospital beds after that.

For a long time that memory reran itself in Taylor's mind. His subconscious-self remained huddled in the suffocating darkness of the doomful, poorly lit barn. He felt like the walls were crumbling inwards on him. Any light that did make its way into the room was killed against the cold, musty planks acting as Taylor's crypt.

As the blurs faded, Taylor came to realize that he was in his rescuer's house. The dank wood of the barn melted away, unveiling a concrete fortress. Each wall of the shelter was covered from top to bottom in shelving.

The wall to the right of the staircase, which Taylor had seen first while hanging over Russell's shoulder, was stocked with nothing but Gatorade, gallons upon gallons of it. Russell had then laid Taylor into a sitting position on the sofa affixed directly in the center of the concrete basement. The pea-green, red and black plaid sofa had a small navy blue braided rug in front of it. All of this was illuminated by battery-powered floodlights placed in each corner. It was quite accommodating for a post-apocalyptic getaway.

Next, Taylor had looked to his right, noticing that the wall across from all the Gatorade you could ask for was lined with a lifetime's worth of Goldfish crackers. Apparently Russell planned on going gourmet with his meals if an H-Bomb fell. There was also a small, 1950's style television set on one of the middle shelves. Now this place was just starting to look retro.

Taylor sat on the sofa. In front of him, above the staircase, a wall clock ticked away the seconds. The exhausted Taylor was too tired to look behind him, and could only dream what might be on the back wall. From what he'd gathered about Russell, it probably had something to do with pornography, toilet paper, a confederate flag, or all three. There was also the possibility that it was another vice altogether.

"It's probably an entire steer on dry ice, with five jugs of moonshine to go with it."

As the infected Taylor pondered how often that much dry ice would need to be replenished, Russell was shuffling around behind him. The whole room had a chill to it, as if the reasons behind the room also set its atmosphere. All Taylor could hear over the cluttering behind him was the sporadic mumbling of the man that had rescued him.

"Oh dear...I think he just mumbled something about bestiality," Taylor scrutinized.

While Taylor's fever tried to rule his fears, Russell completed his task and fell silent in anticipation. A few short seconds later music began, and Taylor recognized it immediately. He hated that feeling, knowing what song he was listening to but not being able to actually remember the name. He spent the better half of the introduction trying to figure it out.

"That's Duran Duran." he muttered, shocked that someone like this stranger would listen to the writers of "Hungry Like the Wolf." In fact, if that had been the song that was playing Taylor might not have been so surprised.

But this was "Drive By," one of Taylor's all-time favorites. He tried to stand and turn to look at the man behind him, but his legs gave out on him as he rose, and he collapsed to the area rug in front of the sofa.

"Sure is! You ain't a *fan*, are ya, son?" Russell shot back, not even noticing that Taylor had fallen from the sofa. "Hold that thought. I'm gonna run 'n' grab some beers from upstairs."

He stood and ran up the stairs, jumping over Taylor as he went. Halfway up the steps Russell turned and stared at the stereo. "Oh, son? The name's Russell."

Russell then turned and climbed the remaining stairs. The fibers from the braided rug below him were starting to make Taylor uncomfortable. His dementia was trying to convince him that they were small shards of metal tearing into his flesh. In fact, Taylor didn't realize how much sway his fever had over his thoughts until he peered at the ceiling above him and saw a procession of earwigs crawling along its smooth surface, clinging upside down to the ceiling as they snapped their pinchers together. Taylor's eyes started to slip as Simon Le Bon proclaimed that this was, indeed, the story of his dream.

In a flash the earwigs dropped from their perches, falling at the half-conscious Taylor with rabid animosity. They landed in unison, framing the body on the floor but not actually touching it. Too confused and intrigued to be frightened, Taylor watched them as their black figures crept along the floor towards the corner where the staircase met the Goldfish. Their pinchers clacked in unison, anticipating a meal.

The music in the background no longer registered in his mind, and all he could hear was the snipping sound of the claw-like pincers as they made their way across the concrete. He struggled to stretch his neck to the side enough to see where they were going. Out of the corner of his eye he caught the image of the earwigs piling up in the corner, like they were crawling over a huddled mass. Taylor craned his neck even further, and saw fully what they were after. While his eyes widened in horror, Taylor spied his deceased lover, Marcy, lying lifeless in the corner. The insects began to crawl into the open wounds on Marcy's face and neck. The only way she was recognizable was by her trademark pink and white tennis shoes. Taylor stared, shocked, for a brief moment before pressing his eyes shut and crying out in dismay.

When he opened his eyes the earwigs, along with Marcy, were gone. All that Taylor could hear was Russell in the room above as he lay on the rug below. It had been yet another vision, one of a growing list problems that was beginning to haunt Taylor as much as his disease. Still looking towards the corner, Taylor pondered that maybe his nightmares and his infection were related. Perhaps the entire ordeal he was in, all of the zombies and death, were really just a creation of the AIDS Dementia. Maybe he was still in his apartment living room, waiting for Marcy to bring him more soup.

With a sigh he laid his head back down on the padded rug. Maybe Russell had put it there in the event that he actually did pass out. From what Taylor could gather, the man who had brought him here had quite a penchant for drinking beer. Landing on an inch-thick braided rug was probably less risky than smacking against three feet of concrete. He sat up, wanting to know what other surprises Russell had down here.

Taylor used the couch in front of him for leverage. He grit his teeth to keep from crying out from pain, his shoulder begging for mercy. Once he reached a kneeling position, Taylor glanced up and was bemused at what was before him. In the middle of the wall, firmly secured into the ground below, was a sparkling white porcelain toilet. It even had a fuzzy cover for the lid. Above it was a silver cross, standing watch as a sentinel over the fallout shelter. At the toilet's side sat a table, with only an ashtray and a Bible on it. Framing the throne were a collection of guns that could defeat some third-world countries.

Next to the table sat a stereo and a CD tower that probably housed between one and two hundred discs. Above that was a Kurt Cobain poster, portraying the tortured songwriter beating against his guitar strings with a closed fist. On the other side of the toilet, next to the handguns, was more shelving. The top shelf carried a large stock of toilet paper. The shelf below that was filled by three dozen bottles of Grey Goose vodka and a supply of D batteries. The bottom two racks were both filled with the same thing, ammunition.

"So cozy…" Taylor gaped. The sound of feet coming down the stairs stole him away from the peacemakers on the wall. "Nice place you got here, Russell."

"Thanks! Thanks a lot. I like to think it's pretty cozy. Don't you agree, son?" he had grabbed fifteen beers. Either he planned on persuading Taylor to drink a few or he had decided on an even larger celebration. Taylor didn't know if Russell had heard his quip a few seconds earlier, and he wasn't sure how to answer the question.

"Sure is."

"Hey, you want a beer? I don't want to have to drink all these myself."

Something about that statement didn't seem completely truthful.

"No thanks, Russell. I think it could kill me," the reply was made. Taylor was expecting him to ask why, or to show some compassion towards his guest.

"To each his own, son. All the more for me, right?" he snapped open a can.

Taylor began to notice that Russell was a big fan of asking questions he probably didn't even need answered. If he'd accepted the offer and finished three beers, Russell would have run upstairs and grabbed three more. There's nothing like a stockpile of alcohol and firearms. All they needed now was a recruiting officer to greet people as they walked in.

The song was coming to a conclusion, and Russell made his way to the stereo. After taking a hefty swig he set the beer on the ground and knelt next to the CD tower. Taylor took the opportunity to fall into the sofa. He was exhausted and miserable. His muscles ached, his shoulder screamed, his head was swimming, and he was having a hard time breathing without a searing pain in his chest. He needed a drink.

"Hey. Any chance I can get one of those Gatorades?" he piped up. He desperately wanted an Orange, but he was already begging. "It looks like you haven't even opened 'em up yet, so I don't want to waste 'em if you're saving up."

"Oh, those?" Russell glanced back. "You can open those. I was only savin' 'em for when it started, anyways."

"I'm sorry?" Taylor thought his new acquaintance might have made a slip of the tongue.

"Hell, I suppose it's already been started for a while. But nobody really knew for sure if it would be fire and brimstone all at once, or if the damn thing would just creep up on you. You know what I'm saying, son?" he peered upwards and saw the liquor on the shelves. "Hey, you want some vodka in that Gatorade?"

"What are you talking about, Russell?" Taylor snapped. He was far from being in the mindset to be fucked with.

Russell laughed. Taylor didn't seem to think it was quite as comical.

"Armageddon," he replied matter-of-factly. It must have boggled his mind that Taylor hadn't already jumped to the same conclusion. "The Apocalypse is upon us."

Taylor could only look at him quizzically.

"Well shit, son. Didn't you know? I mean, the signs are all around us," he leaned forward and grabbed his Bible, shaking it at Taylor. "You've read the Bible, ain't ya, son?"

Taylor squirmed, which sent a numb, chilling pain through his shoulder. Of course he hadn't read the Bible. One look at the size of that monstrosity had scared him off of reading in the second grade. The last time he'd even touched a Bible was when a local parishioner had handed them out on the quad. Taylor had politely taken one, then unceremoniously thrown it in the dumpster as soon as he'd reached the apartment. Still, he didn't want to seem out of the loop. "Most of it."

"Listen here, son. Judgment is upon us. Why in the hell do you think I went out there to rescue you? *My* motherfuckin' conscience is clean, but there are a lot more souls out there that need saving. Don't fuckin' tell me you haven't repented?"

"Are you saying the only reason you saved my life was to try to convert me?" Taylor was caught off guard. It wasn't that he didn't appreciate being given yet another chance at life, but he was still going to live under his own beliefs. Russell showed only the slightest hint of shame as he nodded his head, telling Taylor that he'd better choose his actions very carefully from here on out. The last thing he wanted to do was scorn the God of an armed man.

He'd always rejected the concept of Apocalypse. But here it was, unfolding in front of him as plain as day, and he hadn't seen it. The dead were rising from their graves and slaughtering humanity. Maybe Russell had a point. The rain was going to come pouring down again any day. It would sweep away all the sins of this earth, and nothing would remain. What if all his skepticism about religion had been false, and this really was endgame? In the end, though, Taylor told himself what he'd always felt. He wasn't going to simply give up and accept the fate presented to him. This ordeal was about more than just delaying the inevitable, and to give up on his hope of freedom outside the city now would negate all the maturing Taylor had done in the past few days.

"A cleansing rain can wash away all sins. Now, that much I truly believe," Taylor said. Russell began to nod his head and open the Bible in his hands. Taylor stopped him by raising his hand. "But if it rained all the time, nobody's convictions would ever be tested. I guess what I'm trying to say is…everybody needs a good drought at some point."

Russell stopped and thought on it. Then he closed the Bible.

"Well…alright. To each his own." Russell set down the Bible and walked over to the Gatorade. Now all Taylor needed was a little sustenance, even though his appetite hadn't been healthy for quite some time. His stomach churned at the mere thought of food, but if he didn't put something down soon he was going to be dead in the water. Once that was out of the way, Taylor was confident that he would be safe enough until they found a way to escape. If there was one thing he was certain of, Russell wasn't about to let anything get to them. He still had so many more lost souls to save. "So…no vodka, then?"

"Honestly?" Taylor asked, not expecting an answer. "No, I really think it would just end up on your beautiful area rug, here."

"Hell, son! Can't fault a fella for askin', can you?" the outdoorsman turned messiah pumped his fist, for reasons Taylor couldn't even begin to guess. His mood swings were starting to wear on Taylor, who felt that the wrong answer at any point in time might result in a hunting knife being pointed at his throat again. Religious fanatics were unpredictable at best.

"I gotta ask, Russell, how old are you? You can't be any older than forty." Taylor was only one man's son, and it sure as hell wasn't Russell Singleton's.

"Twenty eight," he stated, not grasping why Taylor would ask. He handed Taylor his beverage and walked over to the stereo once more. He thumbed through a few choices while Taylor sipped at his grape Gatorade. If it had been orange he probably would have finished it in a few swigs. Russell had purposely given his least favorite flavor to Taylor, who coincidentally hated grape just as much.

"*That cheap son of a bitch,*" Taylor griped mentally. And why was a twenty-eight year old going around calling other people "son?" Most importantly, how was he going to escape Bloomington-Normal. "If only I could make it to my car. We could get out of this town."

"Well shit, son. You can just take my truck if you want. It's in the garage."

Taylor turned and stared back at Russell, dumbfounded as he watched the man open a Bjork CD.

"*Is this guy being serious? Does he really have a car or is that some form of asshole humor? And how does somebody with such a massive gun collection own a Bjork CD?*" He was just going to have to find out. "Russell, do you actually have a car here?"

"Car?" with that the Hunter scowled, his eyes brimming with rage. "CAR!? It's a *truck*, motherfucker…and of course I do. You can take it if you want, son. I ain't gonna need it once the rapture hits full tilt."

He opened up the disc tray on his stereo and placed in the CD, hitting play before continuing. Apparently his anger had already subsided, but Taylor wasn't going to make the same misnomer again. "Bjork ok?

"Well then what in the hell are you waiting for? Let's take it and get the hell out of Dodge, Russell," he had his hands placed against the edge of the sofa now, just waiting for confirmation to go upstairs and hit the road.

"You can take it all you want, I ain't leaving. There's too much work for me to do here. Besides, son, ain't you always wanted to go out in a blaze of glory?" he both asked and stated with conviction. Taylor knew that Russell was just crazy enough to be serious. There was no point in arguing with him, and young Taylor wasn't going to let his golden opportunity for survival go to waste.

"I did once…but it didn't work out so well."

Russell only sighed, clearly disheartened at his new friend's refusal to go along with his ideals.

"Well, then I'm outta here. I might need some help getting to the garage, but I'm gonna make a break," Taylor declared. This was his only real chance at survival right now. He felt protected in that shelter, but he didn't know if he'd be able to battle his illness without some anti-retroviral cocktails to combat his worsening infection. He already had beads of sweat forming on his face, and he doubted strongly that an extended stay in a bomb shelter would help his condition. "There's gas in it, right?"

"Sure is, topped 'er off yesterday morning," Russell claimed, rising up to the sound of "Army of Me" blaring from the stereo. "You'll probably want to come up with a plan before you head out, though. Can't very well battle the undead on a wing and a prayer, right son?"

Taylor pondered for a moment. He had no plans other than to drive west. A full tank of gas would be a huge plus. But he wondered what would happen if he got swamped by zombies. Would the truck be strong enough to pull through? What if he had to get out and go on foot again?

"What kind of truck do you drive?"

Russell glared at Taylor. He actually looked violent for a moment, before returning to his normal, serene self.

"Motherfucker, what the fuck do you think I drive? Ford F-350, son!" he retorted. Russell finished the sentence as if he had a line in a commercial. Apparently he was built Ford tough. Once again, though, his anger faded just as quickly as it had arrived. "You wanna know what I think you should do?"

Taylor wasn't given time to respond.

"You gotta go west. Those things probably hit Redbird Arena already. The television didn't know what the fuck it was talking about. Ain't that right, son? That stadium was just a deathtrap. Think about it, why would they tell them all to go to the arena? It's the End of Days, they're just lining 'em up for the Horsemen. Makin' it easier on 'em, son. There's no escaping the Second Coming."

Taylor didn't necessarily agree with Russell's reasoning, but he did agree that Redbird Arena was a lost cause. When a disaster hits you don't tell everybody to hide out in some oversized bomb shelter and wait for the shit to hit the fan. You get them out of harm's way, and worry about the financial matters once every possible life has been saved.

"So far as your plan goes, you'd best take a few rations from down here with you. And I'd even be willing to part with one of my revolvers to help you out of a jam. Then you gotta distract those damn ghouls out there, cause once they hear me opening the garage door they're gonna come in a flash."

Taylor didn't deal in guns, even during the Apocalypse. He found his ideals puzzling now, since he'd used a baseball bat filled with galvanized nails to kill those things. What was the difference between that and shooting the fuckers? Regardless of the justification, he just didn't know how to use a gun. Unless the zombies were vulnerable to pistol whippings, he had no use for one. "No thanks on the gun, Russell. What kind of distraction have you got in mind?"

*

The moonlit shadows were almost as long as Captain Talbott's stride as he sprinted through the empty streets of Normal. He didn't know how far he'd gone, only that he was tiring quickly and needed a place to hole up. The zombies were gaining on him, he could tell from the quickly closing distance between himself and the bloodthirsty cries of the horde behind him. They had heard him fleeing along the street, the moonlight affording just enough visibility for them to make out his meaty figure.

Talbott didn't dare to glance back, it would only slow him down. At this point he needed all the time he could find. He was only human, incapable of carrying on at this pace forever. The monsters behind him were utterly inhuman, and they would not stop until they had feasted on flesh.

The Captain was frantic. He couldn't trust any of the buildings to hide in, something the thirty men he was in charge of learned the hard way. Their bodies were being torn limb from limb along the streets in front of Redbird Arena while Talbott's boots slapped against the pavement. Now the Captain's squad was just another meal for the cannibalistic undead, and if he didn't act quickly he would be little more than a palette cleanser.

As if answering his silent, crazed pleas for asylum, the Illinois State University tennis courts suddenly became visible in the near distance. The fencing that surrounded them was at least fifteen feet high. If he could make it to them, and find a way to lock out the zombies, Talbott believed he'd be able to wait inside of the enclosure until reinforcements arrived.

"*If reinforcements arrive,*" he leveled with himself, pumping his arms at his sides. Talbott's breathing was getting labored, and the sound of the zombies was growing perilously close. He was still about forty yards from the tennis courts, and there was no guarantee that they would be open even if he did make it in time. Talbott knew one thing for certain, though. If he couldn't get inside the fencing his time on earth would come to a bloody and violent end.

"*Zip ties,*" he mused. He had some zip ties inside his left cargo pocket. They were usually used to detain any unruly resistance he would run across during his missions. Now, however, they seemed to be the ideal lock.

Thirty yards away, and his left calf was starting to scream. Every ounce of strength that he had was being forced into a full-out sprint, but his muscles were used to being a captain, not a soldier. It had been a long time since basic training, and he wasn't as young as his ego told him he was.

"*Cowboy the fuck up soldier,*" he berated himself, "*Quit yer bitchin' and hike up your skirt. This is a god damned war.*"

Much to his surprise, and a little to his mental disappointment, this juvenile method of encouragement actually worked. For just long enough, the adrenaline rush returned and his aching muscles quieted. Now he was within ten yards, and his hand slipped down to his pocket, grabbing for the zip ties as he continued his sprint.

Talbott slammed on the brakes, slowing his pace and using the chain-link door in front of him as a crash pad. He ripped the zip ties from his pocket with one hand and flipped up the unlocked gate latch simultaneously. With nothing more to do but slide inside the enclosure and lock the door behind him, Talbott heard a guttural howl no more than twenty feet behind him. Panic doubled up with his existing knowledge that he had to hurry, and he pulled the gate out slightly, leaving only enough room for him to slide through.

Spinning his body one hundred and eighty degrees, the Captain strafed through the opening. He reached out and clutched the gate, pulling it in towards him hurriedly. The lead zombie, clearly the best sprinter in the pack, was only a few yards ahead of the rest. Nearly losing his concentration, Talbott gasped at the number of ghouls before him. Hundreds, maybe even a thousand of them surged towards the tennis courts.

With only a fraction of an instant to spare, Wes Talbott pulled out his pistol and fired a single round directly into the right eye of the zombie rushing the door. It flailed as it tumbled, so close to the fencing that it smashed into it, the creature's dead face wedging itself against the chain-link. Blood shot from its gaping eye socket, sprinkling across Talbott's chin and neck as he applied the first zip tie to the top of the gate. He tightened it and knelt to place the second one. The remaining zombies poured against the chain-link, bouncing off of it in a wave.

*

While some would have trouble calling crackers and Gatorade a meal, it was more than enough to satisfy Taylor's surprising appetite. When the offer of food had been made he almost declined, assuming that he wouldn't be able to keep it down. Now that the non-perishable feast was placed in front of his guest, however, Russell was afraid to put his hand anywhere near the box of Goldfish. This was Taylor's last chance to eat and restore his energy before making his final attempt at escaping McLean County.

Russell had switched off two of the floodlights. The imminent threat of attack was gone, and there was no sense in wasting battery power. The low-light made the room feel even smaller, almost like a mausoleum. The basement was already becoming a bit small for the two of them, and now Russell was contemplating using the facilities.

"Hey, there. You don't mind if I use the toilet, do you son?" Russell asked.

"It's your place, Russell. You can do whatever you want," Taylor consented, turning to face him and realizing too late that Russell might have already dropped his pants. Fortunately, he was still fully clothed. The discomfort on his face showed that he was obviously going to drop something that would make Taylor lose his appetite just as quickly as it had come back. "But do you think you could wait until I'm done eating?"

The toilet had already gotten quite a workout in the past couple of hours. The empty cans of American Beer that adorned the shelving next to the toilet had run their course through Russell's system. His erratic behavior was also affected heavily by the alcohol, and he'd become much more mellow and subdued, sometimes even forgetting to call Taylor by his worn out nickname.

As he shoveled handfuls of Goldfish into his mouth, Taylor's fatigue slowly faded. He now had some time to rest for a while and think. He'd been reflecting on the events leading up to his rescue for quite some time and something about it didn't quite add up. He hoped Russell, the resident expert on apocalyptic matters, could clear things up.

"Russell, there's something I don't quite get about these zombies," Taylor began. Russell gave a grunt to signify that he should continue. "Well, when I was being attacked outside of my apartment, the damned things must've been lumbering along at about half a mile an hour. And when I was escaping from my car they could hardly keep up with me, even though I was going slow as shit."

Something about the way he described his speed seemed inappropriate once he'd said it. In retrospect, Russell was probably experiencing some shit that wasn't exactly slow. Fifteen beers tend to exacerbate any gastrointestinal functions. He continued discussing his dilemma nonetheless.

"But when they were after me on the street, I could have sworn they were running. It was like they were fuckin' track stars. Now how can that be?"

All Taylor could hear in response was a slow, labored breathing. Just when he was convinced that Russell had fallen asleep on the toilet, waiting for permission to drop his load, the man behind him chuckled. Taylor could only imagine what was so comical, but he knew that he was probably going to get an answer.

"Son…those things out there are dead human beings. Some of 'em have been dead for years, some for a few days. I'm just spitballin' here, but I'd venture to guess that if you were to rise from your grave after lying in it for a decade, you wouldn't be moving too fast, either."

Taylor was starting to see what he was getting at, and it made sense.

"And hell…" Russell trailed off here, and once again Taylor was concerned that he'd slipped into unconsciousness seated on his porcelain throne. At least when Taylor fell asleep it was for good reason, and not while sitting in an indoor outhouse. He was just about to give up and resume eating when Russell came to again. "And hell…not everybody is as fast as the next person, you know? Now where is your apartment at?"

"Broadway, just north of Vernon," Taylor answered, not exactly sure what Russell might be getting at.

"Just across from the old folks home? Well that's why they were moving so slow. You were probably battling some zombies fresh out of geriatrics."

That seemed a little unsettling to Taylor, who didn't like the idea of killing a senior citizen…even one that was already dead. In fact, the retirement community across the street had spooked him enough before its residents began trying to consume his flesh. Nevertheless, he'd gotten his answer and he was satisfied with it. Though this logic had never occurred to him it did seem practical. He figured that Russell was done answering and grabbed the bottle of Gatorade.

"Also, the thing you gotta remember is that these things are hunters," he started up once again. Taylor was beginning to regret having gotten him started, since it seemed that he might go on about it all night. "They're gonna send out the fast one's first, the scouts. Then they're gonna find out where the most people are and push the hordes in that direction. You probably just got unlucky and ran into some scouts out there."

"*Scouts and hunters?*" Taylor thought to himself. "*Does this guy think that the zombies are organizing?*"

"I gotta tell you, I'm a bit lost. What do you mean 'scouts'?" Taylor questioned.

"What the hell you think I mean, son? They're hunting down any and every living thing. But they're not just going to scatter in all directions and hope to find food. They're finding out where the food is first, then overpowering it. Why do you think Redbird Arena fell so quickly? They knew…they saw all those ignorant fools piling into it. And the powers that be, those fuckers in hell, orchestrated the whole goddamn thing."

Taylor suddenly didn't have an appetite. If Russell was right that meant the situation was a lot more dire than he'd originally figured. He was going to have get going sooner rather than later, because those things knew he was out here now.

"When you're ready, I'm gonna get going." Taylor said, assuming that Russell would need a couple of hours to sober up before he started operating his heavy artillery. He assumed incorrectly.

"Grab anything you need from down here, I'll meet you upstairs," the man on the toilet replied as Taylor heard him unbuckling his belt. Just in case he needed another reason to leave quickly, Russell made one final comment as Taylor weakly pulled a case of Gatorade from the shelves. "Oh, shit…this one's gonna be rancid."

*

His intertwined fingers lined up like a congregation, and that thought alone added to the disagreeable nature of what he was doing. Looking back, the last time he had prayed was a distant memory. It had to have been at least five years. Not even the suicide of his best friend had forced him to talk to God, although that could have been because the tragic incident left him isolated and withdrawn. Now, for the first time since he'd stopped believing in the church, Taylor Donner sat down and prayed.

An unsettling silence had taken hold of the garage where Taylor waited in the driver seat of Russell's tank of a truck. His lips moved, but the muted words that ran through his mind were wholly inaudible. To talk to God was one of the most difficult things he could ever do. He had long since given up on the idea of a greater power in the universe, but in such a dire hour he was willing to believe in anything that might provide some strength. The Goldfish and Gatorade weren't going to be able to carry him all the way.

"Dear Lord," Taylor started, uncertain of what to say next before he'd really even begun. The fact that he'd started off as if he was writing a letter was already lingering in the back of his head. He doubted now that he even had the conviction to open up, to be honest. He closed his eyes, shutting out his surroundings and forcing himself to continue. "I'm not a churchgoer. I'm not even a believer, really. But if you're out there, I think you'll understand why there's so much doubt in my heart. I've had nothing to believe in all my life. I've seen no signs of your love, especially in those around me. This world is filled with...pain."

He was on a roll now. Surprisingly he had allowed himself to open up very quickly. It was what Marcy would have referred to as the "Band-Aid Approach." He wasted no time, "I think that's part of the reason I have so much doubt. In my life I have seen tragedies. I've lost family, and friends. And none of them deserved the deaths they endured. None of them. That's not testing their faith, lord. That's sadism. So I hope you can understand why I don't even know what I believe."

"The sad thing is that I'm not even sure why I'm praying now. I know your track record, and I know that no good can actually come of it. It's just a placebo to ease my mind. But I need it, 'cause right now I'm scared and I have nobody else to depend on. You've taken all of my friends, so I guess that means I have no choice but to come to you for help. Funny little coincidence, no?"

Taylor had acquired bitterness from Marcy. His honesty was losing its finesse. For an instant he considered slowing down, not wanting to anger any God that might be listening. But this was his confession, and if he was going to die tonight he wanted to make sure to get everything off his chest.

"How could you abandon me? How could you abandon this world? Brutality and crimes against humanity are done every day in your name. You have become justification for murder...why? If you're really out there how can that happen? For all the stories I've heard about your great power and love, when was the last time this world saw it? Maybe the reason spirituality is suffering is because there are so few reasons to believe in any good in this world. Poverty, hunger, homelessness, war, murder, hate, discrimination...these are devastating, each one of them. So for all of them to exist across the globe while the rich get richer, that's radical. That's hell."

Taylor opened his eyes, suddenly not only frightened of the zombies outside. When you bitch out God you get a sudden spiritual hangover, like maybe you've just condemned yourself for more than a lifetime. He looked at his hands to see that his fists were now clenched together, a ghostly white. All circulation had been cut off. From here he wasn't really sure what else he could say, so he opted for the only logical approach. He gave God an ultimatum.

"I don't care if I live or die tonight. My fate no longer concerns me, not in the least bit. But I'll be damned...I'll be damned if the rest of the world has to continue to suffer. Find a way to rid this world of evil, to restore hope to the hearts of the good. Otherwise, you just might find yourself losing all your followers quicker than you think. In the name of the father, the son, and the holy bullshit...amen."

He was trembling now. His entire being was rattled, both frightened deeply and totally liberated. He fully expected to be struck down where he sat, taken by the hand of God before he ever had a chance at salvation. Taylor laid his head down on the steering wheel and let out a long, disturbed sigh. As of that moment he had no mind for things as trivial as AIDS, zombies, Marcy or the throbbing pain in his shoulder. The only emotion, the only thought that he could conceive of right then in the cab of Russell's shiny, white pickup truck was that of utter doom. It had consumed him.

A knock on the window made him jump frantically. Taylor whipped his head to the left, spying a chuckling Russell standing outside the truck in the nearly pitch black garage.

"You ready, son?" Russell asked, still laughing hard at the expense of Taylor's shock. While Taylor looked bewildered in front of him, Russell opened the door of the Ford and handed over the item that Taylor requested during the brainstorming session they'd had earlier that dark morning. It was a propane torch, with two gallons of gas inside. The effectiveness of a lighter and some hairspray hadn't been lost on Taylor in his initial escape attempt.

Taylor came to his senses, shedding the feeling of damnation that had overcome him. "Ready as I'll ever be, Russell."

"Alright! Don't forget, take a right out of the drive and take the first right you come to. There'll be a stop sign," Russell reminded Taylor. They'd gone over the plan only once, as it was basically a crapshoot once Taylor made it to College Avenue. He didn't expect to be able to make it more than two blocks without hitting an intersection that was blocked by an accident. The only thing really going in his favor was that Russell had backed the Ford into his garage, leaving the nose pointed towards the exit. It was going to be a straight shot out for Taylor. "Oh, and son? Be sure to obey that stop sign, we wouldn't want you gettin' a ticket, would we?"

Russell laughed as he walked out of the garage and through the door leading to the kitchen. In just a moment the escape would commence, and Taylor's life would be in Russell's hands.

*

Earlier that morning, working under the generator-powered floodlights, Russell Singleton and Taylor Donner had sat down and worked out the plan of escape for Taylor. The strategy was so asinine, and they both knew it, that for it to work would take multiple miracles. The unfortunate truth of the matter, however, was that with their very limited resources the plan at hand just happened to be the best possible. Only at one point in the evening, during the height of their pessimism, did Russell question Taylor's conviction to go through with their plan.

"Son, I gotta ask," he had started. His eyes seemed calm for the first time since Taylor had met him. There was something in them that he didn't expect to see from the grizzled, gun-toting, beer-guzzler. Just beneath his bushy eyebrows, unmistakable in his bright grey eyes, was a look of concern. It was something that Taylor had seen very recently in the eyes of Marcy, when she had come to his apartment to care for him before the AIDS diagnosis. "Are you sure you wanna go through with this? I mean…it seems like suicide."

It took some restraint not to laugh, because Taylor figured that the man who had rescued him from certain death had no idea how well acquainted he was with suicide. It wasn't as though Taylor now considered suicide something to be laughed at, but he certainly didn't fear it as much as he had in the past. Actually, since his recent run-ins with death he was beginning to shed all of his fears of dying. Somewhere between losing his lover, the city being overrun by zombies, and learning that he had an incurable terminal illness Taylor had come to terms with his mortality. At this point in time he was just happy to have another opportunity to live.

"You know Russell," he returned the gaze, hoping to placate the man sitting on the sofa next to him. He searched for the right words to sum up how he felt. "I'd rather die trying than live dying. You follow?"

Russell had simply nodded and gone back to working on the map that they'd created. The sheet of lined notebook paper was laid on the table, a small square drawn in the center. It wasn't labeled, but they both knew that the square represented Russell's house. Off of one side of the square was a rectangle that was Russell's back porch, and inside of it stood a stick figure holding a pistol. The barrel of the gun had a stream of dashed lines shooting out of it. Above this portion of the map was the number "1" scrawled next to the stick figure's head.

The portion of the map that was labeled as number "2" featured another stick figure on the opposite side of the house, with the words "open door" written above it. The level of professionalism that went into the diagram really shined through. The third and final step of the map, which was aptly titled with a number "3," had a large vehicle running along a street that was drawn on the front side of the house. Noting the abnormally large size of the truck that

Russell had drawn, Taylor took it upon himself to scribe "not to scale" on the lower corner of the map.

With their masterpiece finished, and clearly a plan simple enough to remember without having a hand-drawn diagram, the two masterminds rose from the sofa. Russell had to aid Taylor up the stairs and into the truck. Once in driver's seat Russell handed over the keys to his prized Ford. A simple warning was all Taylor needed to know that Mr. Singleton's truck was to be handled with care.

"Scratch it, and I'll fucking kill you."

That was when Russell had left the garage, and Taylor had undertaken his prayer. Now Taylor was in the cab of the truck, their poorly laid plan about to begin. He pulled the lighter out of his pocket and placed it next to the torch that Russell had graciously given him. Next to those items were the food and drink rations that he'd taken. The keys were in the ignition. Now all he could do was wait.

*

The biting chill of the early morning hours greeted Russell as he opened the door to his back porch. As he strode out onto the 2x4's below him the memories of building the deck rushed back. He hadn't thought about that summer for quite some time, but something about the gravity of the current situation made him want to remember something that would make him smile. He was pretty well assured he wouldn't live to see the sun rise.

It had taken three days of hard labor to build that porch, with a handful of his best friends lending a hand whenever they could find time. When Russell decided to construct it, completely on a whim, he hadn't even taken the time to draw up plans. He simply bought the lumber and started hammering. Each morning he would wake up at seven and crack open a six pack. Then he'd walk out into the warm June morning and smile up at the sky.

The building process was now a blur to him. Part of that had to do with the beer, since he managed to drink about thirty each day. Part of it was because he didn't want to remember how hard it had been and how many mistakes he'd made. Those details weren't all that important to him. Now all he remembered was the sense of accomplishment he felt, and the ensuing drunken nights with his friends spent staring at the clear night sky.

Russell had lived in this house all his life, and when his parents passed it was left to him. If there was one thing that he was certain of as he stood on his porch, armed with a shotgun and two flare guns, it was that he wanted to die in this house. It was his home, and nothing on earth or from hell could make him abandon that. Russell raised his right arm and pointed the barrel of the flare gun over the top of the picket fence that surrounded his backyard.

"Lord, give me strength," he pleaded. With that Russell squeezed the trigger, and the flare rocketed through the darkness. In an instant the street behind his house was illuminated in a red light, revealing a small army of the undead. They were looking towards Russell's house when the flare went up, but their fear of the fiery streak it left behind forced them to the ground, if only for a moment.

Russell didn't waste any time, knowing full well that when the flare died out they would come to the source. He dropped the spent flare gun, backpedaled into his house and slammed the door shut, not bothering to put any of the 2x4's into place. The slam of the door coincided with the explosion of the flare, and Russell took that as an indication that his house would soon be under siege. He pumped the shotgun that hung over his shoulder and ran towards the front door.

*

The sound of the flare started Taylor's heart racing. Up until now the escape plan had only been spoken, but the reality of it came crashing down on him. In just an instant the garage door would open, and the protection offered by Russell's fortress would be forfeited. Suddenly it didn't seem fair to him that Russell was risking his own life just for Taylor's chance at survival, even if the man did have an obvious death wish. Taylor knew that Russell was just itchin' to get to the Pearly Gates.

He straightened in his seat, and double-checked the safety belt across his chest. With the number of zombies and abandoned cars on the road he wasn't going to risk launching through the front window because of a minor collision. He breathed a sigh of anxiety as he put his right hand on the keys that waited in the ignition.

*

Russell sprinted out the front door and down the steps. The faint red light from the flare could still be seen creeping around the corner of the garage to his left. In the dim light Russell could make out even more shapes moving towards his house. They knew where the flare had come from. They were coming right for him.

Russell reached into his pocket to retrieve the second flare gun. They were moving more quickly than he'd expected, and he would have to fire it off fast. He needed to halt their progress one more time if he was going to be able to open the garage door manually for Taylor. His hand grasped the handle and he jerked upwards.

There was a brief instant that Russell believed he had the flare gun in his hand. In fact, he was just about to squeeze the trigger when he came to the dread realization that the barrel of the gun must have gotten caught on the lip of his pocket as he was pulling it out. Unarmed and unable to raise his shotgun, he had just enough time to mutter a "shit, son" before a zombie crashed into him and drove him to the ground.

*

In the pitch black abyss of Russell's garage there was really no way of telling time. Taylor certainly didn't trust his mental clock, either. For all he knew he could have been sitting in that truck for an hour. The world outside simply didn't exist. But he knew one thing for sure, Russell should have started opening the door by now. Taylor should have started the engine by now. The headlights should have disoriented the zombies long enough for him to escape and Russell to retreat inside the house by now.

Something wasn't going according to plan.

*

The rotten stench of decay and must washed over Russell's face, the demon on top of him snapped at his neck. The only thing saving Russell Singleton from a bloody, painful death was the length of his arms. He had the zombie by the throat and was using every bit of strength that he could muster to hold it off. He knew that he would have to act fast, otherwise the other monsters would join the fray and he'd be a dead man.

As the zombie hissed and splattered a thick black spit over Russell's bearded face, the desperate man opted for a desperate measure. He removed one hand from the creature's throat and slid it back down to his side, searching blindly and frantically for the flare gun that he'd dropped. He didn't know whether it was still in his pocket or if it had fallen to the ground, but he had to find out fast. He didn't have enough free hands to get off a clean round from the shotgun.

Either sensing an opportunity for a kill or just acting through sheer frenzy, the zombie that had Russell pinned to the ground slashed it's jagged, clawed hand down on Russell's face. The man let out a wail of pain, a streak of blood rushing from his temple to his nose. His grip on the attacker's throat dissolved in the pain, and the zombie drove itself downward for the killing strike, its own bloodied hands grappling Russell's throat.

Rage pulsed through his veins now, and with a thrust of his free hand Russell was able to find the barrel of the flare gun just beside his pocket. A fraction of a second later, and Russell Singleton's soul would have been put to rest. He moved with pure desperation, though, and his instincts proved deadly. Crying out in despair, anger and agony Russell Singleton pressed the gun against the zombie's mouth and fired. The explosion of light was matched only by that of the demon's head, decayed flesh splattering in all directions like shrapnel.

*

His hand that had rested on the ignition now shifted to his safety belt. Taylor worked blindly to unfasten himself, his weakened condition and lack of firearms not even registering in his mind. He'd heard Russell's screams of terror, and there wasn't a thing in this world that was going to keep him from rushing to his friend's aid. All Taylor could think as he struggled to work in the darkness was that he was going to fail to help Russell the same way he failed to protect Marcy.

"The same way you couldn't get to Andrew in time, too."

Taylor found the button for his safety belt and depressed it, pushing the door to the truck open and preparing to leap out. Just as he swung his legs towards the opening beside him he remembered the propane torch that Russell had given him. He halted and shifted his gaze to the passenger seat. In the low light he was hardly able to make out the shape of the torch and the lighter. The moment he reached out to grab them the sound of the flare gun shot out, freezing Taylor.

"Did he shoot that off to distract the zombies or because he needs my help?"

Indecisiveness took hold of him, and panic dominated his mind. Taylor struggled to make a decision, but his nerves were muted. He felt utterly helpless, unable to even make himself get out of the truck and see if Russell's life needed saving. Not wasting an opportune moment to make matters worse, Taylor's stomach heaved and a stream of vomit came rushing.

The physical illness gave Taylor the unexpected ability to suddenly make one important choice. Knowing full well that Russell would castrate him for such an infraction, Taylor clenched his mouth shut and threw a hand over it to keep any puke from touching the inside of the loaned Ford. He surged forward and shot his head out of the door, letting loose what he had barely been able to hold back. His body convulsed slightly as he gagged, waiting for the second round to come. The tightening of his muscles caused his injured shoulder to go cold and numb, sending a shock down his arm and up his neck.

The garage door opened just as Taylor spewed out another load of vomit.

*

The weight of the door failed to register. The only thing that had a hold of Russell's mind was the red hot, searing pain that pulsed on the left side of his face. He'd lost all vision in that eye, and he was learning quickly that life without depth perception is difficult, especially in the dead of morning. The rapidly diminishing light provided by the flare was all that he had to see by as he worked feverishly to execute the plan. The garage half-opened, he heaved his arms upwards and fully exposed the getaway truck to the world. Simultaneously, Russell noticed that Taylor was physically and violently ill through the unmistakable smell of regurgitated cheddar cheese crackers.

"Motherfucker! I swear to Christ himself if there's any puke in my truck I'll fuckin' slit your throat, son," he cried out, blood streaming from the open wound across his face. Opting to focus on what he felt to be more important matters he had momentarily forgotten that there were a handful of demons behind him waiting to assault his jugular, too. There was no answer to his threat, and after squinting his one good eye Russell noticed that Taylor wasn't sitting in the driver's seat. "Son?"

The flare that had been shot up cut out, leaving them once again to battle the pitch black. The sudden shift in vision was enough to make Russell forget about his prized Ford momentarily. He spun on his heels and raised his shotgun in a fluid motion. There were four of them, at least that was the number that he could see. Taking aim he picked off the zombie closest to him, catching its forehead with a spray of pellets. Its momentum carried it forward as it crashed onto his driveway, landing just a few feet from Russell as he pumped the shotgun once more.

The remaining three rushed him from all sides, leaving little time and an even smaller margin for error. On a good day Russell could have dealt with them easily, disposing of each threat as it got close enough to blast into oblivion. But tonight was different. He could hardly focus on them as they closed in on him, snarling and hissing at the sight of fresh meat. Russell fired off one more frantic shot, shredding the shoulder of one of them to bits, but failing to halt its progress.

He threw his elbows out in a last effort to defend himself, but in a split-second they would have him pinned down, clawing and biting him to shreds. He stepped backwards and bumped into the side of the garage, putting him between a bloodbath and a hard place. "Oh…shit."

Then the Ford fired its headlights, and the zombies shrank back. It was only for an instant, but it was just long enough for Russell, who had already pumped and lifted his shotgun, to fire off another shell. This one didn't miss, disintegrating the head of one zombie and taking out a chunk of a second one's skull. The two of them simultaneously crumpled to the ground, leaving the final zombie to fend for itself as Mr. Singleton pumped his shotgun once more.

The F-350's engine roared to life, and its headlights dimmed slightly. The monster in the driveway was confused, uncertain whether to attack the man with the 12-guage or to throw itself at the windshield of the mammoth truck.

"Russell!" Taylor shouted out the open door. "You mind clearing a path for me?"

"Taylor," he yelled in reply, using the God-given name of his partner in crime for the first time. "Have I got to do everything for you? Floor the fuckin' thing and do it yourself. I'm goin' inside to get a beer."

Not waiting to be told twice, Taylor closed the truck's door and smashed his size 10 Puma against the accelerator. Immediately he felt the fury of eight cylinders jerk the monstrous truck forward. All that stood between Taylor and freedom was a lone zombie, which realized its demise just in time to bellow one final death cry before the Ford bowled it over, leaving little more than a splatter on the driveway.

*

Russell reloaded his shotgun and prepared to cover his retreat. They'd be coming at him from all sides now. The ones that saw him shoot the flare from the porch would be crashing through the back door any minute, and any that might have seen him in the garage would be rushing at him that very moment. Retrieving the final shell from his pocket, Russell loaded it into the shotgun and walked backwards through the garage. Once he reached the door he opened it and rushed inside, flying through his hallway towards the basement.

He hardly noticed the sound of pounding fists and shattering glass coming from the door at the back porch as he passed by. He fled down the stairs and leapt over the sofa, ready to use it as a shield from the impending horde. The columns of firearms hanging on the wall behind him were his only chance at survival. Russell stood and grabbed a revolver from the hooks holding it up. He would save that one for himself, just in case.

Next he grabbed a semi-automatic rifle and a bottle of vodka. He was quite a sight to behold there, preparing for his final battle with a gash over one eye, a bottle of liquor in hand, an arsenal and a cross behind him. Russell

Singleton knelt behind the sofa of his fallout shelter, and waited for his judgment.

*

The last thing that Taylor saw in the rearview as he turned right at the stop sign was a score of shapes emerging in the darkness. They were headed towards Russell's tomb of a house. The red of the brake lights shot out through the night as he slowed to make his turn. He deftly spun the wheel, pulling out onto the two-block stretch that would take him to College Avenue.

The headlights stretched out over the blacktop ahead of him, revealing more demons standing in the road. Taylor punched the accelerator and ran them down, swerving whenever necessary to mow through them. The truck wasn't even phased as it passed over their undead corpses, chewing them up under its front tires and spitting them out from the rear.

Taylor signaled a left hand turn, a force of habit, and pulled out onto College Avenue. He silently and unconsciously thanked God for Russell's sacrifice. Then he hit the gas once more, uncertain of what lie ahead of him. All he knew for sure was that his time on earth was rapidly running out. Even if he did manage to escape the undead army behind him, there was still much work to be done. He had to get to a hospital. He had to get medicine. Hell, he probably even had to get proof of insurance.

PHASE 4
Devices of Bodily Harm

A gust of wind battered against Leon's statuesque head, trying fruitlessly to deter him from his watch. The signs of sunrise were beginning to show, with a dark purple settling over the horizon to the east. His breath shot out in front of his face intermittently while he struggled to battle the winter's morning freeze. There was no comfort in the cold, only a numb reminder that the coming day would bring more of the same.

At this point Leon was just hoping that when the refugees awoke they would come to terms with their divisive cliques. As the situation currently stood there were battle lines being drawn at his sector of the blockade. College Avenue split the young from the old.

The north side of the line was made up of anxious looking college students, to the south a pack of angry locals. He couldn't help but wonder if every stretch of the barricade was experiencing the same social civil war. If so, it was only a matter of time before somebody pissed off the wrong person carrying a gun or a hunting knife. The last thing that they needed was bloodshed amongst the survivors.

There had been a flare shot up in the sky about ten minutes earlier, but Leon stopped caring about them long ago. When the darkness permitted the ability to see them he would spy about ten flares per day. By this time he simply didn't pay those unanswerable pleas for help any mind, since he'd learned quite quickly that there was nothing that he could do about them. For now he just sat atop the I-55 overpass, waiting and worrying about what the coming day would bring.

*

College Avenue, the main route out of Normal and to the interstate, was a graveyard of abandoned vehicles. While the headlights pushed forward through the early morning hours Taylor scanned the wreckage around him. Most of the cars seemed relatively unscathed. The only thing out of the ordinary about them was the fact that they were abandoned, scattered across the street and in the surrounding lawns. Some of them, however, told tales of death.

Taylor had maneuvered his way through one block of obstacles when he came upon a minivan running straight across the road. Initially, he slid his hand across the wheel in preparation to swerve around the car. As he neared closer, however, his hand froze and he slammed on the brakes. The Ford halted, its beaming headlights revealing a grisly scene within the van.

There was a bloody handprint on the inside of the driver's window, which the headlights enlarged across the passenger window like a projector. Taylor peered forward, barely able to make out the shape of a woman slumped in the driver's seat. Through the glare and the blood it was difficult to be certain of anything, but it seemed that her chest was heaving slightly.

"*Shit*," Taylor panicked. Before he'd even had time to think the situation through his conscience was tearing at him. His survivor's instinct told him to leave her behind for dead, that she was a lost cause and would only expose him to further risk. His good side, the part of him that had recently reemerged in his life after his suicide attempt, wasn't about to go away that easily. "*I've got to try and save her.*"

It was, after all, the least he could do to make up for the all the help he'd gotten along the way. If Marcy hadn't risked her own life to board up all his windows he wouldn't have made it this far. If Russell hadn't been a maniac that roamed the streets with shotguns to hunt zombies, Taylor would have been eaten alive. Now he was in another man's vehicle, with the possibility of freedom just beyond a few more blocks of abandoned cars. He owed it to them to risk his own neck for once to save a life.

With a sigh of reluctance he grabbed his torch and lighter. Immediately he grimaced as a shot of pain in his shoulder scolded him for the motion. Knowing that any time wasted rethinking or pitying himself would only allow his headlights to draw more negative attention, Taylor unfastened his safety belt and swung open the door. He slid out quietly, leaving the door open to allow for a fast getaway.

Secretly, part of him wished that when he arrived at the window he would find that the woman was already dead, and he would be able to scurry back to the truck and continue on his way. The absence of zombies was more frightening to Taylor than the alternative. At least if he could see them he didn't have to constantly wonder where they were. Now he was alone in an empty street, and the presence of a bloody handprint before him was a grave reminder of how dead the world truly was.

He stepped forward, the van only a few yards ahead of him. The muffled plop of his rubber soles against the pavement was greeted only with a low whistling through the trees. The wind was announcing the coming of morning, but the sun wasn't yet high enough to provide any light that Taylor could use. His eyes adjusting to the strong beams from the headlights, he slowed his cautious pace to a near stop as he came within two feet of the window.

His mind suddenly raced as the new evidence before him unfolded. The woman was no longer moving the same way she had been when Taylor first drove up. She was now completely motionless, just as Taylor expected her to be after getting a good look at her face. The side of her head that was visible from where Taylor stood was ghostly white, with streaks of blood running across it. Her neck was a mess of torn flesh as well, her throat ripped out just like Marcy's had been. Most gruesome, however, was her skull. It was gaping wide open, and brain matter adorned the raven black hair that ran down to her back.

She was D.O.A., but that wasn't what had made Taylor's mind go from cautious to paranoid. She was killed by a zombie, of that he was certain. All of the doors to the van were closed, all the windows up. The blood that decorated the window was on the inside. And, most telling, Taylor was certain that her body had been moving when he first saw her.

"Oh…" Taylor muttered, not having time to come up with an obscenity fitting enough for the situation.

Almost as if sensing that Taylor was no longer coming to the van on a rescue mission, the zombie inside that had been feasting on the woman's flesh crashed against the window, smearing the bloody handprint with its grotesque face as it landed across the corpse at the wheel. The window was unshaken by the blow, but that didn't stop Taylor from jumping back and falling to the road. The demon immediately withdrew to try again. As it backed up the headlights unveiled the creature's features. It was, much to Taylor's dismay, a child.

A small wave of relief came over Taylor, the initial fear being assuaged by the fact that this zombie had no chance of breaking the glass. The child couldn't have weighed more than sixty pounds. Even if it hadn't been trapped in a minivan, there was no way it could get enough momentum to escape. Taylor gave silent thanks to the creator of child safety locks. Then he stood back up and mourned the child and its mother.

He had to jump to the conclusion that the zombie was the dead woman's child. Most likely what had happened was that the child was infected, but the loving mother had loaded it into the van anyway. At some point during their escape attempt the young child had turned, coming back from death as an undead demon. Then it had eaten her alive. Taylor bowed his head, paying his respects to the two dead inside the car. As he did so, the living dead occupant of the vehicular coffin bellowed a youthful, yet effective, ear-splitting death cry.

It was enough to catch the attention of any zombies out for a stroll in the area, and that was enough to get Taylor moving again. He turned back to the Ford and trotted to the door. He'd tried to do his good deed for the day, now all he wanted was to get back on the road and put this harrowing experience behind him. He climbed into the driver's seat and slammed the door shut. Then he flipped on his turn signal, a force of habit, and swerved around the minivan before him.

Twenty eight minutes, thirty seven avoided cars, and two blocks later, he was forced to stop once more. This time there was no amount of maneuvering or swerving that could help him. There was a massive pileup of cars, dominated by an abandoned semi-truck, in front of Parkside Elementary School that was absolutely impassable. Feeling the fatigue from the previous twenty-four hours creeping up on him, Taylor swigged down half of a Gatorade.

Then he killed the engine and grabbed his pyrotechnic devices. Killing the engine, he left the keys in the ignition, a gift to anybody who might come along and need a truck that couldn't leave McLean County. With nothing more than the shirt on his back Taylor forged ahead on foot. All that lay between him and the interstate was a mountain of crashed cars, some of which had obviously gotten stuck trying to jump the pile.

The previous half-hour, in which Taylor had done nothing but drive in and out of cars for a whopping stretch of two blocks, had given the sun time to show its face. It was just enough light for Taylor to spot all of the glass shards that were scattered throughout the cars and trucks. Immediately he placed a shoe on the bumper of an SUV and stepped up onto its hood. He then walked across the hood, which dipped under his weight, and climbed onto the roof.

The morning's cold wasted no time in taking hold of his body, chasing away the toasty warmth that had resulted in leaving the Ford's heater at full power. The sudden shift in temperature disoriented Taylor, and as he placed his hands upon the top of a Toyota the world around him suddenly started to swirl. Then, before he'd even tried to pull himself onto the top of the car, his shoulder went numb. Taylor fell backwards, crashing onto the hood of the car and landing on his injured shoulder. He struggled, barely able to hold in a roar of pain.

The AIDS symptoms had returned in a fury, and it couldn't have come at a worse time. If he tried to climb back down, he risked falling off the SUV and injuring himself even more. If he passed out on the roof of this car, he would be left defenseless. There was no choice but to continue on, but he really only had one good arm to do it with. He knew, deep down inside, that there was no way he could make it over this pile of cars. There was no chance of him making it to the interstate.

"And if I make it there, then what?" he posed, finally asking himself the question he'd been avoiding during his entire escape attempt. *"There's no guarantee that making it to I-55 will be any more productive than sitting on top of this car. If this is the Apocalypse, then the dead aren't*

going to be rising in McLean County alone. Face it, boy…you're a dead man."

All at once, the futility of his efforts came crashing down on Taylor. He'd spent the past few days being deliberately ignorant of the fact that he was going to die. He didn't know if it would be from disease, suicide or being eaten alive, but there was no doubt now that it was going to happen.

The floodgates of reality had opened, and Taylor lost the one thing that had kept him alive this long. He no longer held any hope. He simply didn't care. Forsaking any chance of life, Taylor chose not to stand back up and continue onward. Instead, he rolled off of his shoulder and onto his back. He was going to lay there until death took him, regardless of what manner it came in.

*

The first of the refugees were starting to stir, the new day having been announced as the sun rose over the tree line. Leon could already see it on their faces before they even had a chance to express their sentiments. They didn't even expect the situation to have changed, and that broke Second Lieutenant Gibbs' heart. In just a few days they had become acclimated to their detention, so much so that they didn't even bother to ask Gibbs or August if they'd received any news. Leon couldn't fully blame them, either, since he knew he'd just have to repeat the same old company line.

"We cannot divulge any information at this time. Please be patient and await the quarantine unit."

It was becoming apparent, though, that the line had worn thin long ago. First they had bought it, believing that their government couldn't possibly leave them stranded in a disaster area. Then they had questioned it, only to have their concerns perpetuated by a lack of new information. Next, there had been rebellion. That was still ongoing, to an extent. It was no longer anywhere near as bad as it had been a couple days earlier, though. Firing a few bullets past the detainees' heads changed their stance pretty effectively.

Now, after all that they'd been through, came the stage of acceptance. They'd come to realize their futility. There were no more attempts to cross the barricade, no leader of the group rallying them together. If anything, the ordeal had torn them apart, the citizens of Normal and the students of Illinois State University congregating on their respective sides of a paved division line.

"What's the difference between a peacekeeper and a peacemaker?" Leon wondered. Talbott's plan to pit the civilians against one another had worked to perfection. The unfortunate part was that Leon hadn't done a thing to implement it. The entire rift had occurred on its own, unless one of the Green Berets had done something that Leon didn't know about. Regardless, it didn't change the sad truth that human nature seemed aimed at distrust and prejudice.

The confusion and hopeless anger that had plagued Leon since he was first assigned to this blockade was swelling up again. Rolling his shoulders to stretch them out, he tried to clear his head. The night had been long, but that almost didn't even register. To Leon, time was starting to meld together. Night and day were the same to him, each day a continuation of the deception that preceded it.

"Gibbs, we s'posed to be gettin' any more 'mergency supplies today?" It was August. He'd been silent all night and morning, so the mere fact that he was speaking startled Leon. He was glad to have the interruption, though. He was starting to dwell on things that he would be better off forgetting. Also, he'd been wondering if August would ever talk to him again. Leon knew it would be in his best interest to get on the good side of at least one of the special forces. He got the feeling he might need an ally before all was said and done.

"I believe so, sir." Leon couldn't help but sound weary and dejected, and he immediately wondered if August would catch on. He must have looked the part, to be sure. Since arriving he hadn't had a single change of clothes, and the deluge he'd sat through earlier probably didn't help his appearance. Most importantly, though, he needed a good shave.

"Come on now, Leon. You got an itchy beard and the people on the other side of this god damned road block have to shit in the woods. Don't martyr yourself just yet."

"What time?" August followed up.

"I think before noon, sir. But I'm not sure."

A silence followed. It was heavier than it should have been, and Leon could sense it. After a few awkward seconds, Leon turned and looked at August, who'd been seated to his left out of view. August was fidgeting, tugging slightly at his dog tags and staring at the dirt off to the side. His mouth was twisting open and shut. Leon couldn't tell if he had something he wanted to say, or if he was already talking to himself. His right knee started to bounce nervously.

"You know, Gibbs…I ain't…I ain't really a racist." August's eyes never shifted from the dirt.

Leon didn't know what to say. His lower lip dropped open, but he couldn't find the words to push past it. Another brief silence followed. Once again, August broke it.

"It's just that…well, James has got a way of…takin' charge, you know?" as he asked the question August lifted his eyebrows and shifted his gaze from the ground to Leon. There was sincerity in his brown eyes, and Leon wasn't one to turn down a possible peace offering, especially one from an armed man.

"I believe you, sir," Gibbs said, giving a quasi-smile and bowing his head. He was both embarrassed and uncomfortable, but he was grateful. "Thank you, sir."

"Gibbs, you can call me Ben."

Leon was on the verge of accepting the proposal when a scream interrupted him. It was coming from the near distance, near the pileup of cars a few blocks down College Avenue.

*

The screams coming from Parkside Elementary School were too laden with fear to not be human. They weren't like the horrific cries of the zombies that he'd heard many times over the course of the past few days. Taylor feared the worst for the victims inside the school. He looked towards the place of learning and realized who the most likely victims really were.

"Children…innocence…now that's something worth fighting for."

Taylor climbed to his feet, a purpose-driven man. Almost effortlessly he slid from the roof of the car to the ground below. The fatigue was gone, the doubt forgotten. Taylor power-walked to the Ford, opened the door and jumped in. He checked the passenger seat to make sure that his pyrotechnic tools were ready. They were.

Taylor grabbed the key, started the engine and threw the truck into drive.

*

The line of piled-up cars that ran along the left hand side of the Ford led towards Parkside Elementary and ended at a baseball field. The field was surrounded by six foot high fencing that had been crashed into and closed off on the other side by five or six different cars. The end result was that the diamond was completely closed off save for a small opening next to the school's doors. They were the same doors that currently played host to about fifty blood-thirsty zombies. It took Taylor less than five seconds to recognize all of this and formulate his rage-inspired plan.

The Ford had already reached fifty miles per hour, and Taylor was head straight towards the doors and the zombies. Most of the creatures had failed to hear the engine start over the sound of the screaming children inside. A few of them had turned around and seen their oncoming death. Mindlessly, they ran towards it.

The pickup truck swung wide to the right, skidding across the lawn as it did so and spitting chunks of mud out its rear tires. Taylor's eyes squinted and widened all at once, a mixture of concentration and fury. There was no denying his will to save the children within the school, and there was nothing that could stand in the way of his burning desire to exterminate every fucking creature that may have been responsible for Marcy's death. Survival and fear were thrown out the window. Taylor was operating purely on hatred.

He straightened the wheel as the skidding Ford was aimed towards the opening of the enclosed baseball diamond. There were a score of zombies between him and right field, but a simple slamming of the accelerator would be all that was necessary to change that. Disregarding the repercussions for vehicular undead-manslaughter, Taylor punched the gas and gripped the wheel, turning his knuckles white.

The Ford had accelerated all the way up to fifty-five by the time it reached the crowd of zombies. Taylor's entire plan operated on the basic assumption that when a two-ton killing machine takes on a mass of decaying flesh, the former wins every time. His calculations had been correct, save for one unforeseen factor. Immediately after impacting with the front lines of the undead, the explosions of flesh and blood soaked across the windshield, blinding Taylor. Expertly he flipped on the wipers, the hemoglobin that had caked across the front window smearing as the blades ran back and forth.

Fortunately for the speeding truck, the temporary absence of vision hadn't altered its course. The Ford shot through the opening to the baseball field, the windshield cleaned well enough to reveal yet another error in judgment. Somewhere amongst the crowd of zombies the truck had separated the torso of one of the demons from its legs. Now the upper body of the monster, wearing flannel and a Budweiser hat, was sprawled across the hood of the Ford, clutching to the side with one hand and scratching at the windshield with the other.

"How much do you want to wager his lower half had some Wolverines on?" Taylor's mind spat. For the time being, however, he would have to ignore that issue and continue with the original plan.

He drove forward another fifty feet and slammed on the brakes, the red lights on the back of the truck only further frenzying the zombies that chased it. Taylor had hoped that the quick stop would jar the torso of the monster on his hood loose. It remained, however, its free hand clawing at the windshield despite the interference from the wiper blades. Paying no heed to the hissing beast, Taylor spun the wheel all the way the right and slammed on the accelerator once more.

A shot of chalk was sent into the air as the wheels hit the third base line. The rear end of the truck circled around one hundred and eighty degrees, the oncoming zombies framed by either side of the windshield. Using the zombie torso as a hood ornament, Taylor paused the truck for a moment and took aim at the pack of grotesque mob rushing towards him. He had to hold steady until the last one had entered the baseball field, otherwise his plan could easily backfire on him.

The brief downtime allowed the army of zombies to renew their war cries, another outlier that Taylor hadn't considered in his short window of time to formulate a plan. Fortunately, he was able to counter their howls. Scanning the sound system of the Ford, Taylor found the power button and punched it. Immediately the CD that Russell had last been listening to started up, and a rousing chorus of "Suffragette City" filled the cab of the truck.

Just as the Thin White Duke proclaimed that he couldn't afford the ticket, the final remaining zombie entered the killing arena. Taylor saw his window of opportunity closing and hit the gas, speeding around the closing horde of zombies and racing towards the only exit that existed. Instead of using it to escape the massive threat that pursued him, however, Taylor swerved the truck and skidded it across the turf. Its bed crashed hard against the side of the elementary school, the nose coming to rest against the fencing. The truck pinched off the only way in or out of the baseball field. A shudder rocked Taylor's shoulder from the impact, but he ignored it. The zombie that still clutched to the hood hissed in defiance as Taylor threw the truck into park.

"Shit yeah…this'll be fuckin' fun," the furious hero muttered, gathering his propane torch. The zombies were closing in on the passenger window, and they'd be upon him within ten seconds. Taylor knew he had to work quickly. His hand shot underneath his seat and searched blindly for the tire iron. Instantly his fingers felt the irrefutable steel shape and grasped it. With that, Taylor opened his door and jumped out. In his rush he forgot to turn off the CD player.

"Nothing like torching a mob to some jams."

With the force of a churning waterfall the zombies reached the Ford, crashing into the passenger side. Their front ranks were immediately crushed by the mob that followed, pinning them against the side of the F-350 and temporarily immobilizing them. They would regain their footing soon enough, though, and it was only a matter of time before they were able to climb into the bed and onto the hood.

Using the open door frame as a step, Taylor stabilized himself with one hand. He climbed up and onto the roof of the rocking truck, struggling to hold his footing as he raised the pry end of the tire iron. Without hesitation, he leapt down onto the hood and struck down at the Budweiser cap of the halved zombie.

Perhaps it was the vulnerable open netting of the trucker style hat, or maybe it was the fact that the corpse had clearly been dead for a few days, but the unforgiving steel dug into the brain of the demon like a hot samurai sword through butter. In a flash the beast halted its struggling, entering the realm of non-existence. The corpse's usefulness, however, had yet to pass.

In the background the cries of the children continued. The idling engine grumbled, angry that the zombie crushing had ceased. The guitars built up then slowed, giving the perfect segue for Mr. Bowie's trademark "Wham! Bam! Thank you, ma'am." None of this mattered to Taylor, though. He was too caught up in the moment, too desperate to complete the most important part of his mission before it was too late.

He released his grip from the tire iron, leaving it to protrude stiffly from the gushing skull like a flag atop a conquered mountain. Next in line was to crank up the propane, which he did excessively. It didn't take long for the pungent stench of gas to invade Taylor's nostrils, momentarily tickling his gag reflex. He quickly gathered himself, though, and dug his left hand into his back pocket. He pulled the lighter from it and flicked at the striker. The flame shot up, thirsty for the gas around it.

Hurriedly, perhaps too much so, Taylor raised the flame to the tip of the propane torch. With a "whoosh" it was lit, the blue pyre licking close to Taylor's stubble-riddled cheek. Despite the slight singeing, Taylor wasn't slowed at all. His own blood-lust was surging, surpassing even that of the horde that frenzied just a few feet to his right. The whistling flame reflected in the whites of Taylor's eyes as he lowered it to the torso beneath him. The air surrounding it became distorted. The flannel of the zombie began to blacken.

There's always room for error when making zombie-based calculations. This is mostly because of the lack of research in the field, but also because of the shortage of supplies for people in zombie survival situations. Taylor had jumped to the conclusion that the zombies, dried up and decayed, would burn fairly well. It was, to be fair, the entire basis for his current strategy. Should his calculations falter, there was nothing that would keep the horde from splattering his infected blood at the doorstep of Parkside Elementary. If he was right, however, the flames would spread feverishly, engulfing the mob in a matter of minutes.

In a way, Taylor's calculations were wrong. Much to his benefit, though, they were wrong in the right way. Instead of burning "fairly well" as he'd hoped, the corpse went up like kindling the instant the propane flame touched its skin. The result was a miniature bonfire on the hood of the Ford that was out of control before Taylor even had time to get out of its way.

As the explosion of flame shot upwards it knocked Taylor backwards, sending him smashing against the blood-stained windshield. Something cracked below him, but he didn't have time to figure whether it was his spine or the glass. Instead he rolled to his left, off the hood and away from the clawing, grab-hands on the other side of the truck. He landed shakily on his feet, leaning against the hood to keep from falling forward. Still clutching the propane torch, Taylor improvised the coup de grace of his plan. Flashing a grin of victory, he slowly lifted the torch with his outstretched arm.

The gas-fueled flame billowed from the end of the torch violently. It seemed to cry out like an excited dog that is about to get a steak bone. The anticipation was nearly worth more than the actual final act. Taylor wanted badly to savor his moment to torture the same fucking abominations that had stolen Marcy from him. Fortunately, he still had the presence of mind to know that time was a major factor. Lingering would only put him at further risk.

"Suffer, you sadistic fucks," he flipped the torch in the air. It spun end-over-end in the sky, seemingly moving in slow motion as it counted down the final seconds that the zombies had on earth. When it hit the first zombie in the chest their escape became impossible. The inferno spread in a heartbeat, overtaking every single one of them.

Wails, utter shrieks of misery, rose from the congregation of conflagration. Apparently their nerve endings were still intact. That didn't stop Taylor from wishing that somehow he could have made them suffer more before dying. Unfortunately, the tools at his disposal were quite limited. The next time he planned to take on a squadron of zombies he should think ahead.

The new dawn rose behind Taylor as he watched them all burn. With it rose green smoke that spewed from the still-flaming zombies. One by one they fell to the dirt, spinning and raging against the scalding flames. It took nearly half an hour for the flames to die out, a few corpses still twitching amongst the smoldering debris. Taylor didn't seem to care, though. They weren't a threat anymore.

As he stood back admiring his handiwork it suddenly became all too clear that Russell's Ford had taken quite a beating from the assault. There was blood splattered across the cracked windshield. A zombie corpse adorned the hood with a tire iron, which almost certainly scratched the paint, protruding from its skull. To make matters worse, the burn marks from the mass demise probably weren't going to buff out. If Russell were alive to see it, Taylor would have a lot more to be afraid of than a few walking dead. Russell would separate his head from his neck in record time, probably stopping to pump his fist in celebration afterwards.

"But that's not possible," was the logical reassurance, *"Russell's dead. There must have been at least one hundred zombies getting ready to siege his fortress. No...Russell's dead...he has to be."*

It was then that Taylor remembered Russell's sacrifice wasn't all a waste. After all, Taylor had chosen to battle these zombies for a reason. Until that moment he hadn't even noticed that the screaming from within the school had ceased. There was only silence now, save for the intermittent crackling that came from the ashen bodies trapped within the baseball diamond. Taylor tore himself away from the morbid scene and turned towards the school's doors.

He approached them with caution, despite his earlier certainty that the noises he'd heard were the screams of the innocent. Given the gravity of the situation, being wrong once could be fatal. Peering inside he saw an empty hallway that split off in either direction. There was a bulletin board immediately inside, littered with flyers about intramural softball, Black history month and tips on staying warm in the winter. Standing in the frigid cold wearing nothing but a bloodied white t-shirt, Taylor couldn't help but wish he was able to read some of those tips.

The glare from the sun cut down on his ability to see down the hallway. As he used his hands to shield the rays, a slowly moving shadow became visible in the hallway to Taylor's right. He didn't know whether it was man, woman, child or cannibal. Taylor simply wanted into the school.

Balling his hands into fists, Taylor used what little strength he had left to pound on the glass in a desperate attempt to catch somebody or something's attention. As the pounding commenced so, too, did the screams from within start up again. Whatever was inside was afraid of what was at the door, and that information led Taylor to believe that he'd found more humans. He stopped pounding on the glass and opted for a more civilized approach; shouting.

"Please! I'm here to help! Please, let me in!"

The cries quieted, but did not quit altogether.

"My name is Taylor Donner! I've killed the creatures that were trying to break in here! Please, I need to get inside!"

Silence ensued.

Taylor shielded the sun from his eyes once more, looking down the hallway to see that the shadow was no longer there. It had retreated at the sound of his voice.

"Shit...I scared it away. It's probably just a bunch of kids in there. I can't blame 'em for not wanting to open the doors," he thought, dismayed. *"I'm fucked."*

The episode had left him drained, and his forehead was on fire again. The fevers were getting more frequent, and it seemed to him that their severity was also increasing. He pressed his head against the glass pane of the door and closed his eyes. He would need to sleep soon. He hadn't gotten a good night's sleep under his belt for longer than he could remember.

With fading strength he turned to brace his back against the doors, and slid down to the concrete. With that he slid his knees up and rested his arms on them. Just as he was positioning his head there was a sound above him. It was tumblers clicking, the deadbolt was being drawn.

"Get in," a voice commanded, urgency ruling each word. "Hurry."

Taylor didn't waste time arguing, or looking up for that matter. He struggled to his feet, turning to see who had come to let him in. The door was held open by a woman in her mid-thirties. She had short, brown hair and thin, stylish spectacles. She wore a look of determination, and it masked the obvious fear that must have ruled her. Her thin frame was trembling to hold open the door with one arm, while the other arm clutched a bright red fire axe that dragged across the floor.

A group of children stood behind the woman, all of them lingering in the hallway with looks of curiosity and suspicion on their faces. As Taylor scurried through the doorway he tried to take a quick head count, but it was pointless. There must have been at least thirty children there, maybe even forty.

Taylor made it into the school, and the woman closed the door behind him.

"Move, we've got to get back to safety before more of them come," she instructed, locking the door before hastening ahead to lead the group. "Follow me."

*

Just thirty minutes prior, the blockade had been asleep. A few insomniacs and stragglers were up and about, but for the most part the camp was as deathly quiet as its guardians. The sunlight had just begun to peak over the trees, spreading its warmth over the quarantined survivors. The panic had begun as the widening rays of the sun revealed a mysterious scene in the distance.

As the sleeping mass began to wake, an increasing number of them also began to point towards the rising plumes of green smoke. Their ranks were divided still, the counter-productive tactics of James Crawford creating a greater rift with every passing moment. Intermittently the locals would sneak suspicious glances at the gathering of students, which would be met by glares laden with matching amounts of distrust. The friction had built into a conflict, and reluctant tolerance was nearing action.

Leon watched all of this with a restrained anger, and a strong desire to leap over the blockade to unravel the thick mesh of deception that Crawford had spent the past few days intricately weaving. Leon wanted to do this, but something still held him back.

It wasn't fear of consequences. At this point in time Leon no longer gave a damn about being reprimanded. It wasn't the fear of the two Green Berets around him, not even the powder keg Crawford. Leon was only holding himself back for one simple reason; it was the last trick up his sleeve.

If he gave himself up now and crossed the barrier prematurely, it would blow his one and only chance to diffuse the situation for good. And if he didn't do this right, if he didn't use the diminishing clout he had to make things right, then he'd be court marshaled the instant he crossed the line.

For the moment, Leon bode his time and waited, hoping that this storm would pass without a downfall.

*

Captain Talbott had huddled against one of the interior walls of the fenced-in tennis courts. In the past hour the size of the mob that hunted him had doubled. He didn't know much about these abominations, but it seemed to be only a matter of time before they learned to climb the fence. Talbott picked up his pearl-handled pistol, which had been lying on the concrete court next to him. His thorough examination of the gun revealed one telling, morbid truth.

There was only one bullet left. And the shaking of the fence was incessant, maddening.

*

Taylor couldn't remember the last time he'd seen something so beautiful. Maybe it was the trials he'd had to overcome to get to this point. Perhaps it was his fear that there was no future in a world overrun by violence. Or there was the other option, the possibility that children are innocent and remarkable. Whatever the reasoning, Taylor couldn't remember the last time he'd seen something so beautiful.

There were thirty six of them, each with a look on his or her face that was completely devoid of fear or hate. Some of them displayed sheer curiosity at the man that had saved them from the monsters outside. Others didn't seem to care at all, simply forgetting the horrors that had been at their doorstep just an hour ago. They played with each other, there in that fallout shelter of a classroom. They didn't care about each other's differences. They didn't discriminate. They simply enjoyed life, even if they were too young to fully appreciate it.

"They're completely innocent," Taylor whispered to himself, a tear running down his face. The struggle to escape McLean County may not have ended yet, but for him this moment was its culmination. For the first time in Taylor's life he felt as if he'd actually accomplished something. He had truly made a difference in the world. Even as the acquired immunodeficiency syndrome stole his life away, leaving him weakened and immobilized, Taylor Donner felt invincible.

"Oh my goodness, you're covered in blood," the woman who had carried the axe spoke softly. She still hadn't identified herself since leading him and the mass of children to the classroom, but she had abandoned the axe for the moment. "We need to get you some new clothes."

Taylor remembered a fleeting instant when he was on the hood of SUV, ready to die, when he'd chastised himself for not having dressed better. The thought of his body being found in such an unimaginative outfit was utterly embarrassing. If only he'd had more time to prepare before the zombies flushed him out of his apartment. It was just plain inconvenient.

"I think there are some clothes in the teacher's lounge. Can you watch the children while I go look?" she asked, truly concerned. She wasn't on her way out the door until he answered. She was worried about both Taylor and the children. She wouldn't leave either of them if it meant they'd be in danger.

Taylor tore his gaze away from the playing children, who wrestled on a thick-piled area rug. The frail woman was squinting at him, her brow furrowed in a troubled manner. Her look made Taylor feel helpless, and initially he was upset by it. Then he remembered how he must have looked. His t-shirt was torn at the shoulder, exposing a gash from his tumble on the sidewalk two nights earlier. His face was unshaven and must have been ghostly pale. The blood from the windshield he had crashed against was caked heavily on his back. He was glad that the sores on his back and chest weren't visible.

"*Man, my hair must look like hell. I wonder if there's any mousse here,*" he wondered silently. His mind was wandering easily now, and he'd completely forgotten what the woman had asked him just seconds ago. Before he'd had any time to answer, a young blonde girl ran up to him.

"What's yer name?" she sang. She wore a yellow sweatshirt. Her ears were too big for her head, and her freckled cheek blushed. She smiled a goofy grin, standing on tiptoes and leaning in as she waited for the answer.

He smiled back at her, "My name is Taylor. What's your name?"

"I'm Claire!" she exclaimed giddily. "You wanna play patty-cakes with me?"

Taylor cleared his throat and smiled. "I'd love to play with you."

Claire led him to the play rug and showed him where to sit. He plopped down hard, barely able to muster the strength to lower himself to the ground without breaking his tailbone. As he sat cross-legged on the floor, the still unidentified woman smiled back at the pair as Claire expertly baffled the novice Taylor. Once Taylor was fully immersed in the game she slipped out the door, knowing that the children were in good hands.

*

The dim hallways of the school were silent, but for the first time in days Julie Patterson wasn't afraid of the emptiness that greeted her. Rather, she found comfort in the absence of ravenous moans. It had been far too long since the last time she could slip from room to room without the fear of a fiend overtaking her. Now she felt safe, and it was all due to that brave young man she had left with her students. In his condition, though, she wasn't sure if he was taking care of the children, or if it was the other way around.

His feat had been truly spectacular, and awesomely reckless. In one courageous act he had purged Parkside Elementary of any threat. That was why she had been so shocked to see him crumpled against the doors. He looked to be in worse shape than the zombies he'd torched.

"He said his name was Taylor," she recalled. *"I almost didn't even let him in. One look at him and I was certain he was a zombie, too."*

She was trying to justify her apprehension at permitting the young man entrance. What she couldn't seem to convince herself of, however, was that in the same situation nine out of ten people would have left the barely living heap to rot on the doorstep. His outward appearance alone was enough to merit reluctance. The skin hung from his bones, and his unkempt features certainly didn't help his cause. There was blood all over him, and his shirt had been torn at the shoulder.

"For somebody who isn't a zombie, he sure looks like he's been to hell and back," Julie observed as she reached the teacher's lounge. She turned the knob and entered with less caution than she'd exercised in recent history. She knew that some of her fellow teachers left spare clothes at the school. It was a fairly common practice, especially considering that some of

the kindergarten teachers were forced to endure boogers, spit, and other unknown bodily fluids on a daily basis. *"Let's just hope I can find something that will fit him."*

While Miss Patterson, as she was called by her students, searched the lockers and cabinets of the lounge she started to reminisce on what had gotten her into this situation. The school had been planning a science fair for a few months, and she'd been put in charge. With only a week left until the big day Julie had invited all the participants to come to the school for a few hours and run through their projects with her. The reasoning given was that she could "assist in the proper execution of the projects." The truth, though, was that she just wanted to make sure some fifth-grader wasn't going to try something that would result in a small explosion or a massive chemical spill.

All the parents had gone, with Miss Patterson's assurance that their children would be in good hands until nine o'clock. Normally those types of extra-curricular activities saw parents lining up to take their children home fifteen minutes before they ended. So, when nine o'clock came and no parents had come to pick up their kids, Miss Patterson was surprised. By quarter after she was just plain worried.

Not wanting to upset the children, and definitely not in the mood to have them impatient, she decided to run a science experiment for them. Whenever one of the children asked where their parents were, she would just tell them that the storm had caused some traffic delays. For all she knew, that was the truth anyways. It had been pouring for days.

Just as the "lava" began to cascade out the top of the volcano, little Rob Lehman starting shrieking at the top of his lungs. Before Julie had any time to calm him down, assuming he'd been afraid of the billowing lava, all the other children started screaming as well. Miss Patterson looked up, and saw the source of their anguish.

A monstrosity was pressed against the window outside, its gaping jaw biting at the glass. The presence of anything trying to break in might have been enough to scare the children, but this putrid being was anything but human. Its face was wretched, the very skin on its skull seeming to stretch and wrinkle all over. Its teeth were little more than jagged, decayed, blades. The head was missing all of its hair, and instead was covered in dried, crimson blood that emptied from the pores where its hair used to be.

The absolute worst, though, was the demon's eyes. There was nothing there. They were like vacuities, swallowing anything that dared to venture near them. She had almost been drawn into them. It took the shrill yelps of the children to steal her attention.

Hurriedly she had locked the students in one of the interior classrooms, with no windows and only one way in. Then she sprinted down the hallways to the main entrance, the only one that was still unlocked at that hour. In a rush, she whipped through her key ring, selecting the right one just as the creature found its way to the doors. Julie had pressed all of her body weight against the door, inserting the key and turning it right before the zombie crashed into the glass.

"Then I ran..." Julie thought. She had run back to the classroom and not left for two full days. The children had cried and pleaded with her to let them out. They wanted their parents. They wanted their homes. They wanted food. They wanted to go to the bathroom. Finally, after two days of forcing them to use a bucket, Miss Patterson had led the children in a group to the restrooms. While they were inside, Julie searched the utility closet for a weapon, and found her shiny red axe.

She left the doors to the bathrooms open to let the light in, and also to keep a watch on anything inside the stalls. Once the children were finished, one of them had made a run for the doors. He reached the foyer before stopping in his tracks, skidding against the linoleum. He had awakened an army in waiting, and upon seeing him the zombies began to howl. They hadn't stopped until Taylor came and exterminated them.

Miss Patterson found a new outfit for Taylor, folded it neatly and left the room. When she arrived back in the classroom Taylor was reading to the children, all of them listening intently as he energetically narrated the picture-book to them. It was a story about a kitten that climbed a tree and couldn't get down, so it kept climbing. Miss Patterson was a third-grade science teacher, so the story was new to her, too. Despite her hesitance, and her desire to figure out what happened to Mr. Whiskers, she had to interrupt.

"Taylor? Could I talk to you for a minute?" she posed, the entire classroom looking up at her with eyebrows lifted high. Even Taylor had a look of surprise and curiosity on his face. Still, he set down the book and slowly rose out of his seat. The chair had been far too small for him, but he was glad just to have anything to rest on. Gingerly he walked across the classroom towards her, before she further instructed the class, "I'm going to talk to Taylor out in the hallway for a minute, class. When I get back we're going on a field trip, so get bundled up because it'll be cold outside."

*

The darkening green smoke that still filled the morning sky was starting to spread. The eerie harbinger of death refused to dissipate into the air, but instead began forming a cloud. It was sickly green, with black sewn into the creeping tendrils of smoke. The cloud slowly reached out, seemingly grabbing at the air around it to further stretch itself out. The mere sight of it was enough to fill one's soul with despair. It would only be a matter of minutes before it widened enough to block out the much welcomed sunlight, pushing its darkness onto the refugees.

Leon watched with growing impatience as the two rival mobs began to shuffle with panic. The dark cloud of fear hovered over them, willing them to do its evil bidding. The war had begun.

*

Taylor pulled on his new shirt, doing so quickly. The last thing he wanted was to see his own torso. He knew how bad it must look now. With no rest or sustenance the sores would be having a field day. In fact, he was surprised that they hadn't spread to his arms yet. He hoped it wasn't just a matter of time before they did.

He was in the men's room of Parkside Elementary School. The woman with the axe, who had finally identified herself as Julie, let him in and gave him the change of clothes. She'd also provided him with a First Aid kit, at which he could only scoff. He appreciated the gesture, but his condition was slightly more advanced than some ointment and butterfly bandages would handle. Taylor had long been a believer in not looking a gift horse in the mouth, but he was also wondering if Miss Patterson couldn't have done a slightly better job of finding him an outfit. Nevertheless, he had swapped out his plain white t-shirt for a grey knit shirt.

"*The blood's gonna leak through this thing in a hurry,*" he considered, thinking of his wounded shoulder. If his sores should open up, the new shirt would soon be a mess of coagulated cotton.

Then he looked suspiciously at the boxers Julie had somehow managed to find for him. Taylor may have been infected with an STD, covered in zombie blood and kept from a shower for days, but the prospect of wearing a stranger's underpants was pushing his limits. Not to mention the fact that they were novelty underpants, with the words "Slippery When Wet" printed across the crotch.

"*Just who in the hell do they let teach our children these days? And are these men's boxers or women's? Something doesn't add up here.*"

In the end, Taylor opted to pass on the anonymous promiscuous teacher's donation to his outfit. He did, however, accept the new jeans and socks that were provided for him. All that was left was the jacket, which Taylor was quite happy to receive. His fight against the undead had nearly been easier than his battle with the winter cold.

He stuck one arm through the navy blue winter coat, noting how well it complemented his jeans without looking too "denimy." Taylor had long ago begun to fear the prospect of wearing denim on his upper body. Something about it made him feel like the type of person who would be comfortable with handlebar mustaches and wearing cowboy boots in public. Pushing his other arm through the coat, Taylor pulled it up to his collar and checked himself out in the mirror.

"*I think I'll go with the unzipped look,*" he decided. It would give him the walking-against-the-wind effect that made him feel like a superhero. Since he was dying anyway, he had no trouble sacrificing the function for the form.

Next he started the faucet and ran some water through his hair. The grease that had accumulated since his last shower acted as a natural gel, and he pushed the mess of black hair to the side to keep it from falling over his eyes. Then he straightened and looked in the mirror once more. He lingered there for a while, gazing thoughtlessly at the reflection of himself that was almost impossible to see in the low glow. The only light he was afforded was the radiant sunlight that came in from the hallway.

"*You're stalling,*" he scolded himself.

Yet, he knew that he had every reason to stall. Julie had dragged him out into the hallway and told him that after he changed his clothes they were going to leave the confines of Parkside Elementary School. She said they were already low on food, and they wouldn't last more than a couple days longer if they didn't move soon. Now, with the enemy defeated for the moment, they had an opportunity to escape.

Taylor, though, didn't want to leave. He understood the logic behind Julie's urgency. He even agreed with it. But he was so tired, and he was so happy to be with those children. He wanted to stay just a little while longer, even if that meant they had to go on rations. In the end, though, he knew it wasn't his decision to make. He couldn't compromise the lives and safety of anybody else just because he wanted some rest.

He turned and left the bathroom, walking briskly down the hallway. The soft padding of his sneakers hardly made a sound against the linoleum. As he strolled between the rows of lockers, he couldn't help but wonder how many lives had been cut short so tragically by this disaster. There were thirty-six children alive inside. That didn't bode well for the amount that was undead outside.

Taylor reached the classroom and opened the door. As soon as he entered the students looked up at him. They were all dressed in their winter jackets and boots, sitting in a semi-circle around their teacher. Taylor turned to Julie and nodded.

"I'm ready."

*

There were a select few events that could have happened to make Second Lieutenant Leon Gibbs leave his post. Only one of them was foremost in his mind now, as he sprawled over the barricade, flying hurriedly from safety to the front lines of this civil war that had erupted before him. His focus laid several dozens of yards ahead of him. It was held within the hands of a young man, no older than twenty two years of age.

Its steely glint had first caught Leon's attention. It flashed devilishly beneath the student's coat, teasing with its power. Leon recognized that cold, crude instrument. He knew of its power, and he knew of its doom. His reservations were all abandoned. His sole purpose now to reach that revolver before it was fired.

Nothing could have prepared that crowd for what would happen if it was drawn. Any other guns in the crowds would inevitably be obligated to make an appearance as well. Before anybody knew what hit them it would turn into a bloodbath. As it stood they were mere seconds apart from catastrophe.

Neither August nor Crawford had seen him yet, as he continued on his full-tilt sprint to the scene of the crime. This was his pre-emptive strike. If the logs the locals had been gathering from the woods were solely for brandishing, Leon wouldn't have cared quite as much. But mobs don't brandish items unless they intend to ignite them, throw them, or bludgeon with them.

Leon swung his rifle into his hands as he tore down the side of the overpass, skidding onto the point of no return, College Avenue. He had hoped to reach the crowd before that fucking gun had been pulled, but he was a breath too late. The mob of locals had begun to advance, and the ignorant boy had clutched at the handle instantly. Leon had no choice but to be the first to fire. He had to seize power and opportunity. He had to pull the trigger.

The reverberating ring hit the sky. All attention suddenly shifted towards his desperate strides. Crawford, Ben, the locals and the scholars all waited on Leon to make his next move, to play his next card. The problem was that Leon hadn't planned that far ahead. He'd already taken to his wing, and his prayer was starting to look like a long shot.

"HALT!" was the best that he could come up with. He shouted it as he came within talking distance of the groups. They did wait long enough for him to get out, "I'm here to help" before they lost their patience.

A local whipped a massive rock from within the crowd. Leon figured the kid must've been a quarterback or a pitcher, 'cause that thing came with some zing on it. A spritz of blood hit the darkened sky as Leon's temple pushed his head backwards. He toppled without ceremony, punishing the ground with his impact.

Second Lieutenant Gibbs was clutching tight to that prayer when one of the locals rushed him, a peacemaker pointed directly at the young soldier's brain. He drew close enough to pistol-whip the shit out of Leon, but chose instead to press the barrel of his gun hard enough against the man's skull to leave bruising. It was deathly cold on his skin.

His finger tightened on the trigger, lingering long enough for Leon to fully understand its implications. Then he started to squeeze.

A blond-haired girl, about nine years of age, saved Leon's life.

"Daddy!" she screamed at the top of her lungs, more a shriek than an exclamation. She rushed through the crowds, who began to look around in confusion. The blonde continued on her path, weaving in and out of the startled people until she reached her father. She was so excited to see him she didn't even notice he was holding a bullet with a soldier's name on it.

He dropped the gun.

"Claire! I thought you…"

She jumped into his arms.

Behind all of this the stunted mob had come to rest its attention on a surge of children, coming upon them in pure joy at seeing new humans, all of them hoping instantly to find their parents there. Traveling with them were two older people. One of them was a thirty-something woman with a fire axe in here hands. The other was almost indeterminate of age, but it was a man who appeared to be on the very verge of death.

*

Taylor labored to keep up with the children. His senses hadn't yet gotten a chance to adjust to what was happening. He knew there was some shouting, and that the children were running. But he didn't know why. Before he could figure it out Miss Patterson started running, too. Taylor did his best to keep up, but once he reached a jog he doubled over, hacking for a moment before resigning himself to a power walk.

When he finally realized what the shouting was about, he had already come upon the large group of shapes. They were people, and as far as Taylor could decipher in the haze of his infected mind, they were living, loving, non-flesh-eating people. None of them had taken a swipe at his neck, and it didn't appear as though they really wanted to…so far as he could tell.

He slowed and looked around, trying to take in more of his surroundings. His head was swimming, and this sudden burst of action was only making it worse. He saw a group of people, and he noticed they were all circled around something. He craned his neck to see what they were looking at.

It looked like there was something on the ground, so Taylor inched closer, gliding past the curious people, who were all so struck with the presence of the children that they didn't even pay attention to Taylor. He moved closer to the scene in the middle of the crowd, and came upon the victim. It was a bloodied black man lying on the ground with a pistol at his side. The pistol was at the feet of a man with an empty holster, standing above the bloodied man while holding Claire.

"*I think Claire just averted a disaster,*" he echoed in his mind, not quite getting it yet. Still, he moved on towards the wounded man. He walked up the body, which lay still save for the frighteningly telling movements of breathing. He knelt down.

"My name is Taylor, I'm here to help," he grabbed the man's hand and leaned in to listen for a heartbeat.

*

Leon rolled his head around, taking check of his surroundings. He wasn't yet sure of how he'd gotten to where he was. He wasn't even sure of where he was. There were trees, he could see the leaves above him.

"*I think I'm dead,*" he thought, loosing the sentence into his mind. Then his hearing returned.

There were conversations going on. There was some laughter. And there was a voice right beside him. He lifted his head slightly, and saw a boy holding his hand. That was when the pain returned.

He winced, and settled his head back onto the ground. Then he went unconscious.

*

The rattling of the fences that had surrounded Talbott's life for the past hours had halted suddenly. The devils and demons, ghouls and goblins that surrounded the tennis courts were no longer clambering to get in. Now it appeared as though they were taking check of their surroundings. They were starting to figure out a way in.

*

"What the fuck happened here?" Taylor asked. The crowd around him had turned to see that he was tending to the victim. They had turned around, and remembered firsthand that a man had been stoned. They saw his body convulse suddenly. They saw the blood spew from his temple. They stepped back.

Julie ran up and examined the man. She peeled back his eyelids and saw that his eyes had rolled into the back of his head. "He's unconscious."

"What the *FUCK* happened here," Taylor demanded. He was beginning to pick up on it, all the evidence pointed at the same conclusion. But he still couldn't believe it. He'd finally found a large group of people, some of them armed, and they were executing each other. This was not civilization. This was not humanity.

He looked around. He raged. "*STOP FUCKING STARING!*"

Julie cried, "*SOMEBODY, PLEASE HELP ME!*"

The crowd stood in a unified insecurity. Nobody knew for sure what to do next. Finally a young man came forward, the rows of earrings and cocked hat belying what was about to say. "I'm second year pre-med, I'll take a look at him."

Then a woman stepped forward, "I'm a nurse at BroMenn."

They both went over to Leon to tend to him, telling Julie that they could handle it. Taylor wasn't finished.

He grabbed the man who was holding Claire. "Claire, sweetie. Tell your dad you want to know what happened here."

The man looked away, almost hurt. He seemed ashamed.

"Claire, tell your daddy how I saved you from that school."

The man looked up, a wave of uncertain gratification on his face. "You saved her from those zombies?"

Taylor nodded once, slowly. He held his hands out in front of him, spread apart to show he didn't have any tricks up his sleeve. "Tell me what happened here."

The man looked at Claire, who played innocently in his arms. "All right, I'll tell you."

Taylor hardly flinched.

"But I'll have to tell it from the beginning."

PHASE 5
The Bleak

Andrew had asked Taylor to meet at his house after school. It was a request that Taylor did not want to fulfill. The last thing he wanted was to watch A.J. get high while he sat back and watched. They'd probably end up watching some stupid ass horror movie or anything with Bruce Campbell in it.

So Taylor's surprise was justified when he got to Andrew's house and his friend handed him a freshly packed bowl. It wasn't like Andrew to share drugs, even with his best friend. Everything was nickel and dime shit with him. Even when he was with one of his connections there was no sharing.

Not being one to turn down a free hit, Taylor grabbed the green lighter on Andrew's desk and lit up. Something monumental was about to happen, and Taylor figured if he was going to have to sit through it he might as well be high, too. He looked across the cluttered bedroom at his friend.

Andrew was fidgety. He didn't even sit down before he started talking. There was a chance he'd taken an upper before leaving school, but Taylor thought it was just more likely that he was fried mentally from the years of hardcore drugs.

"Somebody's been trying to kill me," he stated bluntly. With that he plopped himself onto his bed, not really even looking up at Taylor to gauge his reaction. He didn't even betray a hint of emotion as he dropped the next bomb. "I think it's Satan."

Andrew's thumbs jittered, twitching randomly while Taylor tried to take in what he'd just been told. There was, to be certain, only one logical explanation. A.J. had been doing far too many drugs. It was a truth that had been revealing itself for years, and one that would have to be dealt with inevitably. The only problem was that Taylor wasn't ready to stage an intervention.

"You're just strung out, man," before Taylor even finished the sentence Andrew was shaking his head.

"No, this is different. This is real."

There was no arguing with Andrew when he got like this. All anybody could ever do was to try to reason with him. Even that was a cumbersome task, though. Nothing you could ever say would appease him. Taylor didn't have the patience for it today.

"Is he pink, fuzzy and only appears when you're tripping?"

Andrew stopped twitching and looked up. He stared intently at Taylor. His eyes were cold, his voice wavering. "Fuck you. The pink, fuzzy man would do something like that. This isn't a god damn joke."

"Calm down, man. I'm only dicking around," Taylor felt bad. He was beginning to have less and less time for his eternally-fucked-up friend. He was supposed to meet up with Marcy after school to work on algebra. "Why don't you just buy a gun and scare him off?"

"Guns, bro? Guns are for pussies. Guns are for people who can't handle matters with logic or reason. Fuck guns." Andrew jumped to his feet. He was riding a tangent now, and nothing was going to slow him down.

"Guns are the reason we have so much crime and homicide. You get rid of the guns and this nation suddenly looks a lot nicer to live in. But fuckin' interest groups like the NRA and the entire midwest scream their slogans to the heavens. 'Second Amendment! God Loves Guns!' And the god damn things have been grandfathered into our society."

"That's a pretty general statement…and don't say pussy," Taylor egged him on. He liked playing devil's advocate.

"Fuck you, pussy! The Second Amendment is as antiquated as people who support it. No, I'm not buying a fucking gun to shoot the devil."

"Really, Andrew? The devil? Are you sure you aren't seeing things again?" Taylor was suddenly high, too high to handle the situation at hand. He couldn't control his inner asshole. It was just too easy to mess with Andrew when he was acting this way.

"I DON'T SEE THINGS! IT'S THE DEVIL! IT'S THE DEVIL! IT'S THE FUCKING DEVIL, AND HE LOOKS THE EXACT SAME AS HE DID IN THE BARN!" the screaming caught Taylor off guard. Andrew fell backwards onto his bed, sitting up on the mattress and clutching at his face. "You weren't there, Taylor. You didn't see him. But he was there. He had a burlap sack on his face, and he was wearing a muddy tuxedo. He marked me for death that day and he marked you, too, when you went into that barn."

"Don't talk like that. You're not marked for death," the gravity of the conversation was beginning to dawn upon Taylor. "Andrew, it was a muddy burlap sack. You probably just got into the earwig's nest and panicked. There was nothing sinister or demonic behind any of it."

"Really? Then how did my crucifix get inside of it?"

Taylor remembered not having an answer then. It was the same feeling that he was grappling with now, as he sat listening to the end of Claire's father's story. He hadn't even heard the last few minutes, but he was able to fill in the blanks from what he'd seen. Instead, he kept replaying the scene of those earwigs crawling up to his neck on that crucial day in the abandoned barn. The stinging pain of the earwigs and the archaic splattering of red paint stood out. It was all he could think about, all he could envision, as the story of the irreverent stoning wrapped up.

He wished Marcy was there to help him. She'd have an answer, even if it wasn't the right one. Then Taylor wouldn't have so much pressure on himself to make a choice. Another part of him, though, was gratified that Marcy didn't make it to the blockade. Something told him that she would have gotten herself shot by a Green Beret when she found out that a quarantine had been set up. Marcy had never been one to put up with bullshit.

They'd had a chance to escape. They'd had a chance to organize. But they listened to some wily fuckin' Green Beret's sweet nothings. They turned on the only ally they had, each other. They devolved into earwigs, clambering in the soil.

Now he sat on the dirt, looking up at the underpass where the barricade had been erected. "*And I'm just a piss-ant scramblin' through the mud, too.*"

He had to get this soldier to the barricade. That much he knew for sure. Without medical help he could lose too much blood, or go into shock, or something else even more grave. The pre-med kid and the nurse were doing all they could, but without the proper tools it might not matter.

Then he had to get these dipshits to kill their fuckin' egos and band together. They had to be doing whatever it took to get across that barricade. But they'd be best to do it without bloodshed. This soldier that was bleeding to death behind him had risked his life to calm the crowd. He was a brave individual, and Taylor hoped that he could be their ticket out.

"We'll cross that bridge when we get to it."

He needed to take initiative, of that he was certain. Everybody else was standing around slack-jawed and motionless. Every moment that passed was precious, and he couldn't afford to leave the action up to anybody else. Taylor turned into a dictator, if only for a little while.

"I need some people to get this man to safety," he spoke softly to the crowd. "Right now survival is our number one priority."

Nobody moved, so Taylor provided an impetus. He pointed out two members of the crowed. One of them was an older man, most likely not a college student. The other was younger, and wearing a grey hooded sweatshirt with the letters "ISU" scribed at its front. Both of them had shoulders wide enough to block out the sun.

"You two look like you're built Ford tough. Carry him to the blockade, and if anybody up there gives you trouble, tell 'em to go fuck themselves."

They were startled at first, only looking at the other, then searching for anything but evasive glances in the crowd amongst them. When it became apparent that nobody else had a better idea, the two men acquiesced. They stepped forward, stopping at Leon's prostrate body and bending to lift it.

"Then tell them I'll be there soon," Taylor commanded, suddenly angrier than he'd felt in years. The sudden dismal change of plot in his life's story only reminded him of the shit he'd had to endure to get here. "And no matter what, tell them to go fuck themselves."

His breathing was heavy now, and he started to pace in front of the astonished crowd. He had to be careful not to overexert himself, but nothing could hold back his rage. He glared at the mob before him, running his hands through his unkempt hair. He paced a few moments longer, then stopped when he stood where the soldier had just been laying.

"This is sickening," he proclaimed, echoing the sentiments of all those within earshot. The crowd mindlessly nodded there heads, not expecting what Taylor would say next.

"Don't nod your heads at me. You've done nothing to stop this."

Suddenly their demeanor, as a whole, became much more alert.

"What have you all seen in these past few days? Sunshine, lollipops and motherfuckin' rainbows?" his voice rose, an anger distorting his words slightly. "Cause I've seen abyss. I've been through hell to get to where I am now, and what I discover once I get here is that society is pissing on itself. You should all be ashamed."

"Look around," he shouted. The masses hung on his words, but some still seemed ready to jump him. They'd rather be right than be wronged. "Go ahead, look at yourselves and what you've become. You're parked here, just inches from freedom, and you're at each other's throats. Why?"

A few more nods began to appear. Taylor was now rallying them just as much as lecturing.

"It's not because it works to your benefit, that much is for damn sure. No…" here he paused, scanning the crowd before him. He had their full attention, now was his opportunity to make something happen. He could probably get them all to break down the blockade right now if he wanted to. "It's because THEY want you to. It works to THEIR benefit. The less of you there are alive to talk about the incompetence shown by our government makes it that much easier to silence the truth."

Somebody in the crowd shouted, "Fuck yeah!"

Taylor was raging now, his fury belying the fact that his body could hardly hold together. "Well I say it's time we stopped fuckin' around and got something done. But the first thing we have to do is take a good, hard look at ourselves, because I see a lot of hate here. There is a common bond between each of us, and that is what matters. Not age, not skin color, not which side of this god damn war you're on. All that matters is life. And if those assholes up there try to take that away from us, then we fight back."

He stated the last two words carefully, with force. They crowd cried out at them, ready to go to war for Taylor. "Now wait here, I'm going to negotiate the terms of their surrender."

*

It was cold. That was the first thing that came to mind. It was dark out.
"*I'm in the barracks.*"
He looked down and saw the knife in his hands.
He wasn't even sure how he'd gotten there.
"*The last thing I remember ...,*" his thoughts trailed. What was the last thing he remembered? He didn't have a specific memory. It was only a feeling. "*Doom.*"
His grip suffocated the knife's handle. "*Futility.*"
That was all he knew. His final memory was simply the knowledge of a doomed futility. It was utterly lonely, there in his barracks.
He acquiesced to his blade, and placed it against the soft, padded section of his graven neck.
The moonlight suddenly burst through the window, dancing beautifully across the end of Leon's knife. It twinkled against his eyes. He looked up. He closed his eyes.

*

The soldier opened his eyes. He looked around, disoriented. It didn't surprise Taylor one bit.
"The last thing he remembers he was on our side of the fence," he turned to Julie. She was listening to him, but too engrossed in the drama of the wounded soldier to look at him. "And it was still light out."
Julie continued to stare at the soldier as he regained consciousness. She agreed with Taylor. If they had any chance of getting through this ordeal without a hail of bullets it was imperative that the wounded soldier live. He might have enough pull and compassion, but mostly pull, to get them out. That, plus the two mobs had elected her and Taylor to act as ambassadors. "Oh, I don't think he'll remember any light from this ordeal. I believe the last thing he saw was a whole lot of darkness."
The soldier lulled his head to the side. His glossy gaze fell upon Taylor and Miss Patterson. They were fixed on him. He didn't recognize them. At least, their faces didn't trigger a specific memory to match them with.

But he knew them somehow.

They marveled at the wounded soldier's will. They had both pegged him for dead. It had almost become easy to do. Over the past few days they had seen so much death that this one almost seemed a statistic. It was elementary. When one is exposed to nothing but darkness, it will consume them. Julie had even given him odds.

He was 12-to-1. This soldier was one hell of a fighter.

In the time it had taken to stop the bleeding, the life of the prisoners had been renewed. Taylor had coaxed the truth out of Claire's father. Julie had been a hero for reuniting four pairs of children and parents. Together they had taken control of the situation. Once the mob settled completely, it was decided that the fate of the detainees was in the hands of Julie and Taylor.

He had assumed, however, that the soldier would get proper medical treatment upon his return to the military side of the blockade. When he saw the bloodied man laid out on the ground and abandoned, without so much as a second glance, he reassessed those assumptions. Eventually one of the two Green Berets came back and wrapped some bandage around the victim's head. That had been nearly thirty minutes prior, and the ambassadors' patience was running thin.

Now, with the two Green Berets ignoring their demands for freedom, their only hope of a non-violent outcome appeared to rest in the hands of the mystery soldier. Only he had the clout to keep his compatriots from opening fire on the innocent masses.

The wind had picked up since the time that the soldier was brutalized. It ran across Julie's face and made her skin tighten. It made her face look tough. She was committed. There wasn't a thing in the world that would keep her from getting the rest of her students, the ones who hadn't found their families, from getting across the blockade if terror struck.

Since that time it had also darkened quite noticeably outside. The sickening cloud had grown from a fester to an omen. Taylor's condition had followed suit. Julie chose to lean against the roadblock to prove a point, that it was nothing more than a piece of wood to her. Taylor did it out of necessity.

His breathing had never quite caught up to him after he'd browbeat the mob. Also, there was an incessant and shrill ringing in his left ear. But mostly his head swam. His psyche was a setup waiting an eternity for its punch line.

There was no connection to reality in him, save for Julie's random comments. It had taken all of his strength not to sleep before the soldier woke up, but he was beginning to regret that move.

He pushed that nonsense out of his mind. For now he had to focus on the development unfolding in front of him. It was his highest priority to get to the soldier before anybody else did. But he wasn't sure if he wanted to risk jumping the blockade. That could spell suicide.

It wasn't as if the task of jumping the blockade actually worried him. Even in his pitiful condition, the roadblocks were quite porous for a blockade. If any of the detainees had actually tried to it would've been a cinch to lead a mad dash through the barricade. It would undoubtedly have ended in a lot of deaths, but it wouldn't have been too tough.

"The military would've seen that happening anyway. There's got to be a secondary perimeter out there," he calculated. There was no other reason for them allowing such an ineffective blockade. He wondered if the soldiers knew about it. The civilians sure hadn't said anything about it.

"I think they're trying to keep something from getting out," he blurted, taking a small gasp for air after he had finished. His was on the verge of coughing. Coughing usually led to hacking. Hacking usually led to gagging. Then he would puke.

This seemed to catch Julie off guard, but before she had time to react the soldier sat up quickly. She left Taylor to his struggle for breath and waved at the soldier, cautious not to alert either one of his guards. He looked at her and his eyes brightened. The look of familiarity was still in them. Gingerly his eased onto a knee, then rose to his feet.

The soldier did a quick check of his surroundings, giving Taylor time to suppress his dilemma to a mere scratchy breathing. After he seemed to have a decent idea of where he was, the soldier strode at Julie. The other soldiers still hadn't noticed that their patient was alive, and somewhat stable.

He walked up to them, slowly. He seemed more cautious than a man with a rifle should have been. He had a puzzled look on his face. He came as close to the roadblock between them as was allowed. Then he stopped, studying his counterparts on the opposing side of the blockade. Taking a last breath, he proclaimed, "You were there, just before it went black."

Taylor and Julie glanced quickly at one another. They'd already agreed to let Julie do most of the talking. She cleared her throat, and spoke lowly. The man across the blockade had to lean in to make out every word. "I'm Julie Patterson, this is Taylor Donner. You were struck in the head. We got you some medical attention"

"I'm Second Lieutenant Leon Gibbs," he responded. He gave a mini-salute, unsure of how to respond to these two that had kept the mob from killing him. "The last thing I remember is running at the mobs. What happened?"

"They came to their senses," Julie summed up. Leon looked back at her with uncertainty. She pointed at his bandaged forehead, "Just after they did that to you."

Leon remembered it. He'd been about to address the crowd when something had pelted him in the face. Leon touched his hand to the bloodied bandage at his temple, and winced slightly as he pressed it. Then he withdrew his fingers, and saw the trace amounts of blood at their tips. Then a man had put a gun to his head.

Now he was here, on his side of the blockade again. From the looks of things, the civil war had been successfully foiled. Seemingly, he had these two to thank for it. Which, he realized, he hadn't actually done yet. "Umm…thank you."

"I don't think I would have made it out of there alive if you hadn't stepped in, and that's God's honest truth. But how'd you manage to get 'em to work together? I mean, they were ready to start slaughterin' each other."

A second elapsed, Julie was trying to find the right way to put it when Taylor jumped in. He waved his arm to the open field behind him, filled with playing children. "We gave them something worth fighting for."

Leon looked upon it in stupor. This *was* what he had been fighting for. He nearly broke down at the sight. It was one of the most spectacularly beautiful scenes he had ever been fortunate enough to set eyes on. These children weren't biased. They didn't give a damn if they were on the east or the west. They couldn't care less whether it was sunlit or gloomy. To them it was celestial just to be alive.

"Then you've done a great service to this world," Leon marveled.

Julie took over, still holding tight to the agenda. "So what's this State of the Union Address you have to read to us?"

"Huh?" the Second Lieutenant queried. Then he remembered where he was, and why he'd been sent there. "Oh! This…this is a quarantine ma'am. The United States Military requests that you wait patiently for the Health Services officials to assess the situation. Thank you."

He took on a mocking tone, still maintaining a whisper to keep his countrymen from hearing what he told his cohorts. He said as if adding, "How can they expect anyone to buy this bullshit?" He knew it was bullshit. He knew they knew it was bullshit. He knew that everyone knew it was bullshit.

"Yeah, and what's the State of the Union Undressed?" Taylor probed. He didn't want to seem so cold, but he couldn't hold out much longer. Either the giant mob behind was going to break, or his grip on reality. Regardless of which won out, time was a major factor.

Leon got the picture. It was high time somebody around there actually saw eye-to-eye with him. This might be the closest he ever got to a chance to end this thing, and he wasn't about to throw it to the wayside. "We're basically fucked."

"Nobody's allowed out. Nobody's allowed in. Press have been here for a few days now, but nobody's done shit about it, which means nobody knows about it. It's total martial law, only we don't know what the fuck we're doing."

"Jesus…" Taylor gaped.

"How long has this been going on?" an astounded Julie chimed in.

"Too long."

A totalitarian shout from the north ended their conversation, Crawford was forging his way toward them. His raised rifle cut like a knife through the wind as he pointed it at Taylor's chest, loping towards them. "*Gibbs*!"

"Shit." Leon held back further cursing. "He's coming to tell me I've been court marshaled. I'll try to get back in contact with you later. Keep these people calm, but let them know what's at stake. Bloodshed is…"

That was all he got off before the Green Beret rung Leon's collar with his rifle. "Step away from the blockade. You need to retreat 10 feet from this roadblock."

The pair stood frozen. Julie didn't falter. She was driven to push the boundaries, to test the Green Beret's limits. Taylor didn't move simply because he couldn't.

"What are you doing? This man just saved dozens of lives," her steel glare was relentless. The man of war, however, was unphased.

"He disobeyed orders. Step away from the blockade," he responded, unbending. He was already pulling the zip ties from his belt to detain Gibbs. There was no mercy in him, only anger.

Julie was stunned, she tried to think of something to say, but her astonishment let out something a bit more primal. "Who the fuck do you claim to be?"

"Julie," Taylor cautioned. He didn't want this to escalate. Not yet, at least. He reached out to her shoulder.

The military man fully cuffed Leon and stared with animosity at the woman who was clearly getting on his nerves. It seemed like a matter of mere seconds before he aimed his rifle at them again, only a bit more convincingly this time.

"C'mon. Help me back," Taylor pleaded. They wouldn't stand a chance if he put a hole in Julie's chest. She was half the reason they had gotten this far, axe or not. Their odds at forming a non-violent revolution would be pretty grim if one of their ambassadors suddenly got murdered. "Let's wait this out."

She relented. Turning briskly she pulled one of Taylor's arms over her shoulder and walked him to the mandated ten foot line. As they passed out of earshot of everyone save themselves, she vented on Taylor. "Don't handle me. Side with me, don't side with me. That's fine. But don't handle me."

They reached their approximated destination, and she helped Taylor to a sitting position. He knew what she meant. You don't invalidate your ally's stance once the shit hits the fan. "I'm sorry, Julie. I shouldn't have done that."

She pursed her lips and nodded, closing her eyes as she did so. She needed some time to let her temper run, and Taylor needed to sleep more than ever. Everything was put on hold as Taylor fell backwards onto the ground, asleep before he even hit.

*

The tennis courts that had become his current sanctuary were divided into three sections. They were all equal in size, each containing three courts. There were only two doors on the interior that allowed somebody to pass from one section of the court to the next. The nets were all down at this time of year. Once it was warm enough in the mornings they would probably get them up, but it would only damage them if they were left on in this weather.

That meant there was nothing out there that would impede Captain Talbott if he had to flee from one court to the next, which was becoming an increasing possibility. He had placed zip ties on all of the exterior doors to the courts, but he only had two left. The bitch of it was, one of them on each door wouldn't be sufficient, but two of them on one door would ultimately lead to the second door being wide open.

If the zombies were to find out how to get the metal latch opened, it would just be a matter of them smashing down the doors through the feeble zip ties. If Talbott had thought about it at the time, he would have just placed the zip ties over the latches so they couldn't be opened. But he had been in a bit of a rush when he'd put up the initial, and final, defenses.

None of this would have mattered, however, so long as the zombies hadn't picked up on the notion of sliding the door latches around. It had taken them quite some time, and Talbott had even considered trying to secure the doors while they were in one of their thinking spells. They had literally gone dead for certain instances of time, staring off at nothing and unmoving. The Captain got close enough to the door to try it, but their growling at his approach gave him second thoughts.

So now he was stuck between a rock and a death warrant. He would have to retreat to the inner section of courts. Then he would have to simply wait for the zombies to come crashing in, and decide which of the two interior doors to block.

Talbott rechecked his chamber, and the lone bullet remained where it had always been, where it was meant to be.

*

Taylor wasn't sure if he was awake, asleep, alive or dead. Somehow reality had slipped, because minutes earlier he hadn't been standing atop the pile of cars just a short distance down College Avenue. And Watterson Towers hadn't been illuminated at all. Taylor tried to look around, but his body was frozen. There was nothing but fear in him now.

The windows that were lit in Watterson Towers numbered two. They were both on the twentieth floor, and they both looked like deadened eyes. The empty, cold, yellow glow shone out dimly through the windows. Taylor stared back.

This limbo played out for an immeasurable amount of time, ending only when flames began to drop from Watterson's eyes. They weren't flames shooting off in all directions. They looked more like burning bags being dropped from the windows. What seemed like an eternity passed, all the while these orange and crimson teardrops cascaded through the air, down the side of Watterson Towers.

Finally Taylor saw a torch in the near distance. It was growing closer, slowly. From what Taylor could tell it was moving at intervals. The blue to black backdrop of the darkened skies allowed the torch to cry out with its presence. It was like a beacon, and more of them were following.

Taylor waited. He was unable to move and didn't entirely want to. He didn't know yet if he should run away or towards the lights. On television they always told you to turn away from the light at the end of the tunnel. But this wasn't television, and he hadn't seen light in a really, really long time.

Slowly the torches grew closer. They marched together, each one growing incrementally closer with each movement. Taylor was able to make out the nearest one a little more each time. With this latest movement he could tell that there was a partner to the nearest torch. They were traveling in twos.

There was something warm and inviting about their glow. Taylor began to let his guard down slightly. The moved closer yet.

"...*taylor*..." they moaned. It echoed slowly, reverberating throughout the murky dark.

He tried to run towards them, but he was still frozen. They moved closer.

"...*taylor*..." It echoed faster, digging away at his mind. He grew cautious again.

They moved closer.

A bullet to the chest wouldn't have hit Taylor as hard as this did. His shattered mind raced to find the words, but he only managed a slight curse as the air collapsed from his body. "...oh....fucker."

He just wanted to raise a hand to his mouth to stop the sobbing. He just wanted to close his eyes. But his body simply wouldn't respond. There, side by side, marched two living effigies. Andrew Johnson's burning, boiling skull raged on the left side of the pair. Marcy's was being engulfed by flames as well, her features hardly distinguishable beneath the veil of charred flesh and licking flames. They cried out to Taylor in the same, lamenting moan.

"*...taylor...*"

He screamed, but no breath came. Their eyes were black. Their moans were death cries. Their faces living death masks. Taylor's body could only attempt to wretch.

They marched on, lining the middle of the street and moaning once each time they moved closer. Their moans ate away at Taylor. To him they weren't simply saying "Taylor." They were saying "Taylor, why didn't you rescue. Why weren't you there for us? Why did you let this happen to us?"

It destroyed him. He was broken by their slow, anguished moans.

Finally they reached Taylor. They sat next to each other for a moment, each different set of Andrew and Marcy's decapitated heads staring ahead at Taylor. Their gazes were empty. They couldn't even see him, only sense him.

One final moan set them in motion, carrying out their macabre dance in grotesque fashion. They split into two rows, one of each. Slowly they bounced along the pavement in unison, their burning flesh making a sickly slapping sound every time they landed. When both rows had reached the ends of the road, they stopped and turned their dead stares back at Taylor.

One last time they called his name, only this time it was shrill and painful. It was physical pain that rang out, not the pain of a damned eternity. That type of pain was already implied. The shriek flailed boundlessly in Taylor's cavernous mind.

"Taylor."

He woke up. Julie stood over him. It was still very dark out.

Blinking heavily to chase away his demons, Taylor slipped from the realm of dreams into the straightforward heaving of the real world. Almost immediately his dizziness took him once more. The world was all a big blur to him. It spun endlessly in an effort to find itself. So far it didn't realize it was chasing its own tail.

Still, he was able to recognize Julie. He even recollected that they were at the blockade. So far as having any semblance of time, he was on his own. It wasn't entirely surprising, though. The heavy cloud cover that had accumulated since the green smoke began to billow from Taylor's zombie barbecue was still very prevalent. In fact, it had decided to announce its arrival by smothering the entire eastern quadrant of McLean County in its opaque oblivion.

"Taylor," she repeated, sounding slightly more alarmed. "Get up."

He didn't even care how much time had passed, though. To him the ordeal was so near to the end that he was willing to expend whatever energy he had left to see it through. All he wanted to know was what revelation had merited waking him. He hoped against everything he loved that it was over.

"What's happened?" he put forward, itching for an optimistic answer. The founding of this blockade had been bittersweet at best. He was due for some good news.

"It's Second Lieutenant Gibbs," she ushered him. "He needs to see you immediately, while he's still free."

It defied every law of nature, but Taylor rose to his feet without flinching. The fever was back. The sores were throbbing. He was dizzy. He was nauseous. He was nearing the edges of sanity, if he hadn't already run past them. All he had was a fleeting hope.

"I can't wait," the civilian soldier beamed, standing as tall as his body would allow.

*

He was making his peace with Jesus. He was on his knees.

"Forgive me," he begged, not holding back to pride. "Forgive my atrocities."

He was seated inside the middle section of the tennis courts. The zombies hadn't moved more than three inches in the past hours, up until that very minute. The time had come. They were prepared to launch a strategic offensive. Captain Talbott's moments on Earth were dwindling quickly.

"I have sinned against humanity more times than I care to know."

He *was* a sinner. He *was* in need of the savior's forgiveness. Nothing else could bring him back from the brink of exile. He was leveling with himself now. There was no chance that anybody would come rescue him now, not even God.

"I have destroyed your beautiful creations many times over."

The murders piled up. He was running through the missions he'd been a part of. Chronologically, of course. At last count he'd single-handedly murdered twenty two people. Some of them had been enemy soldiers. Some of them were innocent civilians. So far he'd made it through 1986.

His days in South America were countless. His missions were nearly as numerous. Not a single one of them hadn't warranted a shoot-first approach in the rules of engagement. He hadn't even flinched on his first killing.

She had been some bitch from one of the tribes. She was saying something about respecting their holy land, or some bullshit. He wasn't always able to note everything the translator was able to tell him. After all, the bloodthirsty side of him always managed to win out. Just after she had fallen to her knees, begging for empathy and peace, he'd put a bullet in between her eyes. He didn't have a choice, really. The scene she'd been making was starting to draw too much support. There was no choice but to suppress it.

He had even developed his own serial killer one-liner;

"*I am death incarnate, and I will mow you down in my path of destruction.*"

A bloodbath had ensued. He'd ended up having to slaughter three other civilians that day. They'd been described to him as hostiles, though. According to the reports, these unarmed citizens were capable of destroying democracy with as little as eye contact. They were absolutely frightening.

Now Talbott knelt, his own version of an innocent peasant praying for reason. With death around every corner and knocking down his door it was only natural to plea for retribution. After all, he'd only been following orders.

"*Ah, but denial plagues us all until the bitter end,*" he reminisced.

The truth of the matter, he scolded himself, was that he had done all the awful things he'd been shocked by as a child. He'd carried out every foul deed he'd denounced as an adolescent. He'd broken every commandment that had been engraved on his soul all throughout his life. Nothing could truly save him from that.

Still, he prayed until the very moment that the zombies burst through the southernmost door, filing into the section of the tennis courts directly through the door to his left. Talbott was at his feet in a flash, hurtling towards the door to his right. He would set up in there, barricading the door behind him and waiting for the door to his destiny to be torn asunder.

*

As Taylor walked towards the blockade he had to put his hand to his face in order to stabilize his head long enough to make out Leon. The apprehended soldier was standing stoically on the opposing side of the token roadblocks. The meaning behind the barricade had taken on a meaning that was far more than physical. Even with their unadulterated honesty with each other, Taylor and Leon couldn't help but feel as if there was an unwavering wall between them. Physically it was a mere speed bump, but symbolically this line of painted saw horses was an insurmountable mountain.

"How did you manage to free yourself?" Taylor got right down to brass tacks.

"One of the Green Berets is sympathetic to my dilemma," the loaded reply came back.

Taylor was instantly intrigued. The opportunity to gain another ally on the rival side of the battle line was quite promising. He didn't have time to be coy. "Can he be trusted to fight for us?"

Leon paused. There was a definite uncertainty to his reply. He wanted to vouch for Ben, just based on the truth of his character. In the end, though, he just couldn't overlook the twisted loyalty that he held for Crawford. There was nothing but indecision to be taken from that. "Not definitely."

There was a brief silence while Taylor slouched himself onto one of the road blocks. He braced one hip against the blockade while holding his torso up with both arms. The weight of the world was on the small of his back. Sometimes it seemed like it was more on his stomach. The wind felt amazing against his burning forehead. His fever must have returned while he was dreaming of detonating brains.

And he could still feel the earwig guts and zombie blood on his back.

Julie had caught up with them. She'd been walking behind Taylor to ensure that he was safe, but wanted to check on the children before she joined the conversation. Judging by her somewhat eased demeanor, the children were quite secure. She wouldn't have walked away from them otherwise.

"So it's just the three of us, and our misinformed army of misfits?" she put bluntly. If she'd honestly wanted to she could have tried to sound more cheerful. Seeing as though she did enough of that during the school year, she figured this was the last time to bring out the Prozac bullshit.

Leon bowed his head. The decimated ranks of McLean County had produced more people willing to fight for what was true than the United States' military had. It was quite humbling for him to consider. It was also a very urgent revelation.

"What are our assets?" Taylor was forcing most of his diminished body weight against the road block. He knew that Leon had a rifle. He also knew that he had a hungry and frightened mob at his disposal. There had to be a little more than that to work with, though.

Leon gave them the wild card. "The press is here, but they haven't been allowed to broadcast anything yet. They haven't even been able to get to this blockade."

"So there is an outer blockade?" Taylor perked up slightly. He had to take some pride in his own deductions.

"At least one," Leon replied.

"So how do we get them on our side?" Julie threw out.

"A story," Leon stated. It wasn't a suggestion, it was the answer. If the poor bastards who had been waiting out here with cameras on their backs for the past few days were hungry for anything, it was a story that would help build their names up.

"But the fucker of it is that they won't broadcast it." Taylor was still a little confused. "What can we do to get them to put this story on the air?"

"Not a damn thing, my friend."

Taylor was taken aback. He'd become so distant from every aspect of humanity since Andrew's death that he hadn't gotten close to anybody. He hadn't even held idle chit-chat with anyone in a long time. To think that Leon considered him a "friend" was something he wasn't prepared to comprehend. Taylor didn't have too many friends.

The cold wind blew across the abandoned highway, dancing playfully off of the guardians at the overpass. Over the slight howl, the sound of children's yelling could be heard. Julie looked out to see that one of the boys was pulling the girls' hair. She excused herself to remedy the small social disruption.

Taylor looked across at Leon. The Second Lieutenant returned the stare. They were both quite stumped. Undermining a top-secret government cover-up was harder than they'd wished. Taylor was the first to break the unconstructive silence.

"Where you from, Leon?"

"Detroit...you?"

"A town about three miles north of here. It's called Hudson."

Another silence ensued. Leon took the initiative this time.

"Do you have anybody outside the blockade?"

"Yes."

Leon deferred and muttered a soft condolence.

"Do you have anybody back home, Leon?"

"Nobody who gives a damn.'

Leon studied his ally. His was still in disbelief at his counterpart's appearance. The pitiful body before him told a story of pain and suffering. He must have seen some atrocities over the past few days. "Have you anybody...on the inside?"

Another silence came over them. This one was palpably uncomfortable. Taylor's optimistic air emptied from him. He closed his eyes. It was a long time before he opened them again. Leon just looked on in uncertainty.

Finally Taylor looked up again, and Leon could see the tears welling in his eyes. Taylor gave an ample synopsis. "My angel...she died."

It was the way that Taylor said it. The mere words weren't poetry by any means. In fact, they were pretty chilling in retrospect. But his demeanor, his angst, said it all. Leon empathized. "Jesus...I'm so sorry."

Taylor bit his lip and shook his head, fighting off the onslaught of sobbing that had suddenly overcome him. He wasn't even worried about his feverish symptoms any longer. All that mattered to him was getting Marcy out of his mind, and fast.

"She was a godsend." With that he gathered himself and went back to his original state of ruin. "What if we staged something to get their attention?"

"Sorry?" Leon started to ask. He didn't realize that Taylor had shifted subjects so quickly. He was still reeling from the sincerity behind Taylor's sorrow for his lost "angel."

"We're on our own out here, Taylor. Nobody's coming in until people start coming out."

Taylor had already come to that conclusion, but he didn't realize the extent of the media deception. If there was something in place that was keeping anything from being broadcast, then it was very likely that the government planned to simply let the situation play itself out until they could send in some troops for a nice CNN montage. Until then, though, it was every man for himself.

"Do you realize how utterly shitty this feels from my side of the blockade?" Taylor blurted.

"In a deeper sense, yes, I think I do."

"There's no Health Services coming?" Taylor asked.

"None."

"There's no reinforcements on the way?" he continued.

"Not that I know of."

"There are no more than three rifles for every quarter mile of this blockade?"

"That's right."

"Does this blockade even mean a god damn thing?"

At that question Leon stopped to think. The obvious answer was that it was nothing more than a minor inconvenience. Any real escape attempt would prove that point with astounding ease. The truth, though, was a little more complex. There was definitely some reason that a row of road blocks encircled the entirety of these cities.

"I think it's come to represent a breaking point."

Taylor's mind wound itself into a tight ball of intolerance. The fever was rampant, and his insides were churning like the earwigs in the dirt. The breaking point had already hit for him long ago, this was more along the lines of a boiling point.

"Oh, for fuck's sake," he started. That was a relatively mild opening for his delusional rantings and ravings. "So we're left to he die? We're left here to fuckin' wallow in the wake of this shitstorm? God damn motherfuckin' Uncle Sam can't reach into his wallet to save his own countrymen but doesn't mind sending them off to die for his self-serving agendas? This is treason. This is an absolute betrayal of Americans."

He was struggling to spit out the final bits of his rant. His lung capacity had been steadily decreasing ever since he left Russell's catacombs. It was probably pneumonia. Somehow Taylor thought he remembered reading in one of his pamphlets that he might get pneumonia. That would explain a lot of how he'd been feeling lately. It didn't explain why he was seeing visions of his slain childhood friends eternally perishing.

Then again, he wasn't sure if anything would fully explain that. Some folks would be willing to accept a hefty amount of money to take a crack at it. "If you see some shit going down, you fix it. Leave the part about how the fuck you're gonna spin it for the aftermath."

He was furious now. His blood scratched at his veins as it coursed through them. He needed to calm down, or maybe even get some more sleep. He should probably eat, but he wasn't hungry.

During all of this Leon watched the encumbered ambassador with a nod growing perpetually empathetic as the bitchings progressed. He agreed completely. Of course, he couldn't say such things. Crawford might actually fire a round into his bowels for that infidelity to freedom. He was beginning to feel that they needed to look at the issue from a different perspective, and they should probably change the subject. Taylor was looking pretty wasted.

"In essence, society is devouring itself," Leon summarily agreed. "…in essence."

"How'd you get here? You look like the most…" here Leon caught himself. He respected Taylor, so he didn't end that sentence the way that he'd originally intended. He'd wanted to say, "*You look like the most pitiful person I've ever laid eyes on.*"

He stopped himself for one reason. Leon knew that it would dishearten Taylor, who must have been on the very verge of survival. The jacket might have fooled some people, but Taylor had left the zipper open. Every time the wind blew his shirt would cling to his ribs like white on rice.

"You look like you've been to hell and back."

Taylor jerked his head up, looking slightly over Leon's. The distance seemed to be talking to him, and Taylor lost himself in it for a moment. Then he remembered.

"Oh sweet shit, I can't believe I forgot to tell you," he shot at Leon. "There's a reason you haven't been attacked…yet."

Leon didn't like the sounds of that for an instant. Nothing could have torn him away from whatever Taylor was about to tell him. Not God, not death, not even Crawford. He was engaged.

"There's a school just down the road, past that pileup of cars," he started. He didn't want to waste much time. "The children were trapped inside by a swarm of zombies."

"Zombies?" Leon asked. He'd heard the rumors, but it was still pretty tough to believe there were actually zombies inside.

"Real life, undead, motherfuckin' zombies. They ate the man who saved my life," the veteran replied. He'd seen it all, he knew firsthand. Then he thought, "*But did I actually see Russell die? Either way, he's dead. He has to be.*"

There was no doubt in his voice. Leon also noticed that there was less fear than fact. Evidently Taylor knew how to handle these things.

"You've seen these things?" he drove at the point, knowing that Taylor wanted to stick to the fact that zombies were a threat to the blockade. Leon felt responsible for these people. The time could soon be approaching that he'd have to let them through the blockade. If zombies attacked, he'd have to let them through in a mad rush.

"The ones that swarmed the school, I killed them. The smoke you saw rising was from their burning remains. And the only reason they hadn't gotten to your blockade was because they were drawn to the school. They had no choice but to pass by it because of the pileup."

Leon got the point all too quickly, "Now they don't have any reason to stop at the school."

"They're gonna come straight through, and they're going to be drawn by the smoke," Taylor stated. This wasn't a guess. It was the same reason he hadn't gone to Redbird Arena, and the same reason he'd seen smoke towering out of it. "It's their defense mechanism. You can only kill them a handful of ways, and one of them is to burn 'em. But it's gonna bring the rest of 'em out of the woodwork."

"Jesus...even zombies are evolving."

Taylor chuckled. He actually chuckled. His sides hurt while he did it, and he had to stop to cough up a lung for ten minutes afterwards. Still, it felt amazing. All he wanted was a little laughter in his life right now. It seemed like forever since the last time he laughed.

Leon couldn't help but laugh a little as well, but when he was done he didn't rip his throat out for ten minutes coughing. Still, it reminded him of what he'd been missing out on all of this time as well. He couldn't remember the last time he'd had any reason to laugh. The entire experience in the military had just been one series of racial hate before another.

Taylor was dying. There was no reason for him to ignore the obvious dismay that still held Leon's face when Taylor stopped retching. "This is all you have to fight for, isn't it?"

Leon was stunned. Taylor was right.

"I'm guessing a military base in the Midwest is the last place you want to be a low ranking black man," Taylor fired. He could sense the hate in the Green Beret who had cuffed Leon. He could sense the detestation that Leon felt in return. "If it means anything, I don't think like they do."

"It does mean something."

That was all. The frigid breeze screeched in the ensuing silence.

"I feel like we should talk about football or something now," Taylor jibed.

It got them laughing again, but it also got them back on task again.

"Taylor, with what you know is there any way that we can defend these people?"

"With the number of men you have in here? Not a chance. Even with the guns in the mob you're only going to hold out for a short while. I mean, one of those things could be handled. But, one dozen would be a different story."

"Do they, like...spread? Can these people turn into them?"

It was weird. Taylor hadn't actually seen anybody change into one. It was obvious, though. He'd seen zombies wearing Skechers for fuck's sake. How could they not spread?

"I think so."

"How? Is it fast or slow?"

"I don't know about any of that."

"Fuck."

The whole thing seemed futile to Leon. There was no way to get the prisoners through the blockade. There was no way to handle an attack. It was looking more and more like the only way this drama would play out would end with the detainees being attacked.

Then he looked at Taylor, "How do you manage to be so cool about all this shit?"

A wrinkle of insight appeared at every corner of Taylor's face. "There's nothing quite so humbling as the knowledge of your own impending death."

He thought it was very clever. Leon found it more confusing.

"Yeah, but those people weren't anywhere near as cool as you are right now."

This threw Taylor. He'd been given a rare opening to divulge his secret to somebody else, somebody alive. He weighed out how he wanted to break the news. He opted for the Band-Aid Approach.

"Leon, I have AIDS."

*

There was a memory that had been running through the Captain's thoughts right up until the door had been smashed in. It was from his very first mission ever. He reminisced heavily on it. It had been his first taste of deceit. It coincided with the first time he could have been convicted as an accessory to murder.

That was the last thing he had pondered. It was the night he witnessed a higher ranking officer shoot a civilian in plain sight. There was something cold in the way he recalled it. The piercing rain probably had something to do with it. Regardless, he was the only other witness. Instead of making it two murders on the night, the officer had simply asked the man's name and promised him promotions.

"I didn't even flinch. I said 'Talbott' faster than he had shot the woman. I didn't give a shit if she was unarmed. That was her own goddamn fault. I'd just look the other way."

It's funny how life's little coincidences work out, but that should have been the last thing on Talbott's mind at that moment. Because right then and there he was knelt on the concrete court, a single bullet held within the chamber of the gun pressed against his chin. He was hoping to wait until one of them was actually upon him before he pulled the trigger. That way he could leave the world knowing his one last bullet might have also gained him some retribution.

As he had mused just fractions of seconds before the zombies surged through his final defense, *"I need all the retribution I can get."*

He was here to do God's work.

The slapping cadence of their feet on the cold, unforgiving surface was the call of the beast to Talbott. Its rising cadence signaled only one thing for him. This was his final mission.

He opened his mouth, lifting the gun from his chin. Then he placed it in between his teeth.

The pulsing mob grew louder. His death knell ran closer still.

He breathed his last breath, savoring the wisps of evening breeze that lingered. Then he closed his eyes and put the very notion of pressure on the trigger.

But the relentless death squad stopped short, and his kamikaze mission was ended. He listened for the final lurch of the nearest zombie, leaping just before it smashed into him at full speed and toppled him for the rest of the carnivores to fight over. But that never came.

Only silence ensued. The pounding of the zombies sprinting across the tennis courts toward had simply halted. Talbott was almost too afraid to open his eyes. Almost.

His left eye flashed open first. It was a sight to behold, in actuality. The entire scene reflected off of Talbott's grey eyes, as his jaw opened completely. He released his final breath very quietly.

The zombies had stopped completely. They were all staring off to the east, none of them moving an inch. Then, in unison they shifted their glance to the west. With that, they were off. Each and every last one sprinted for the exits, making their way down the streets to the west.

Talbott was left all alone, his one bullet unspent. The instant the zombies were out of sight he bolted out of the tennis courts and down the streets to the south. He'd seen what was happening to the north, and he didn't want any part of what was going on in either the east or the west.

*

The change in the wind that followed Taylor's announcement was eerie. Suddenly his affliction was something he longed to hold secret again. The look on Leon's face on its own was enough to make him regret his decision. His friend was shaken, unnerved.

"So what was that company line again?" Taylor offered.

"Huh?"

"The line you had to give everybody who came to the blockade? Didn't it have something to do with a quarantine?" he followed up. Leon was still feeling the effects of knowing how readily dead his greatest ally could be by morning. It was shocking.

"Uh…yeah. This is being called a quarantine."

Taylor shook his head in frustration. This wasn't a quarantine. If it was there would be a team of scientists at every station looking to figure out how to cure and treat the disease. No, this wasn't even close to something of that scale.

"This is completely a quarantine of information." Taylor theorized.

Leon was of the same mind. "If America knew what kind of shit was going on we'd have our people out of here by now. Can you imagine if somebody did find out? There'd be a shitstorm."

The break gave Julie time to come back and join the fray. She still toted her fire axe wherever she went. To her it was more of a security blanket than anything else. During some dark times it had been the only thing that made her feel even remotely safe.

She had just rejoined the trio when Taylor got a look of graven concern on his face. "Leon, what do you suppose the military is willing to do in order to keep this story from breaking?"

Leon had never considered it. To him the idea of failure had never seemed an option. Despite his hardships, Leon didn't allow thought for anything but evacuating the civilians. What if they did send down orders for him to slaughter all of the witnesses? What if he had to kill one of his Green Beret escorts to keep them from killing any witnesses?

"I believe the level of deception is limitless."

"God…I just want to rip my eyes out," Julie lamented. She had temporarily forgotten that getting a rambunctious child to tweak his interactive skills didn't quite compare to the feeling of a pallbearer that came with being a decision-maker with people's lives. She wondered, "*How in the hell did I end up in this position?*"

"Hush," Taylor teased. "You're far too pretty to be a masochist."

Julie looked at him with a perplexed grin. The experience had changed her as well. She felt like she couldn't fall asleep, or everything around her would simply disappear when she woke up. She feared that she could blink and the children would vanish. That was, without a doubt, her greatest fear.

A hawk flew overhead. Taylor spied it and laughed. "Quarantine my ass."

Julie caught on. Leon was too busy watching the vulnerable prisoners over Taylor's shoulder. They had no idea what they had coming to them. They were completely without defense, and they were being targeted. Worst, there was no cavalry on its way. There was nobody coming to rescue them.

"What'd we decide on? Any course of action yet?" Julie inquired. She was pretty well tapped for ideas, and she doubted they could have seen something she didn't. It was all pretty bluntly laid before them; there was no chance they'd all make it out alive.

"Nothing concrete," a sigh of desperation poured from Taylor's lips. The wind picked it up and carried it along. There was enough despair in the atmosphere to make it rain teardrops. That was when Taylor decided he should show his cards.

"I'll let all of you take care of that, though. I've got to get going."

Leon looked at him, his eyes the definition of concerned. "Do you need to sleep again? I can get a hold of somebody, maybe they can bring some medicine for you."

Julie just looked on, her attention suddenly focused on the conversation.

"It's pointless, Leon. I don't have much time."

"So it's true…" Julie cut herself off. Taylor looked to her, silenced. She had obviously thought there was something wrong with Taylor, but she wasn't sure what it was. "You have AIDS, right?"

Taylor didn't say a word.

"Oh my God…I'm so sorry," she held a hand to her breast, her mouth agape. She felt crushed. This man had saved her life. She began to cry slightly. She sobbed, "Oh my God."

"Don't cry for the dead, dear. What I want most is for my passing to go my way," he stopped to look them both in the eyes. "Part of my soul is still inside that war zone, and all I want before I die is to get it back."

"Think this through, Taylor. You could hold fast here for another couple of days. We could get you some medicine." Leon reasoned. He didn't know what in the hell Taylor would want to go running off to certain death for, AIDS or not.

"Sorry, I've already had this conversation with myself. My side won out."

"Why?" Julie asked.

"Because it's what I want," Taylor was suddenly more sharp with them than he'd ever been before. He detested their very efforts to keep him from going his own way. He wanted nothing more than for their farewell to be brief and painless. Still, he loved them for trying, for wanting him to fight.

"Why do you have to go now?" Leon grilled. He was far from willing to let this go much further.

Taylor looked overhead. "I should leave before sunset."

"Sunset? The whole sky's choked out in smoke, there's no light to guide you,'" Leon pressed.

"Taylor you can't even carry yourself. How do you propose to make it more than an hour out there?" Julie jumped in.

"There's no guarantee that I will. But I'd rather die alone, my way…with my dignity."

Julie and Leon quieted for a minute. Taylor knew that he was nearing the end. His body was ready to give. His mind was beginning to stray. "I don't want to die in some hospital room. I don't want tubes sticking out of me or people poking me with needles. I need to find peace somewhere, and I know I won't be getting any here."

He looked up at the cloud that thickly veiled them from the daylight.

"Aren't you afraid?" Leon questioned, his blunt manner belying the sincerity behind it.

"Bitch, please...I'm about to meet my maker," Taylor joked at him, cracking a grin.

Julie wasn't satisfied. "How do you plan to defend yourself?"

Taylor shook his head. "I haven't got much. Just my will."

"At least take my rifle, we can find a replacement in one of the supply trucks around here," Leon offered. Just like that he found himself accepting that Taylor was really going to feed himself to the wolves. Now all he wanted was to make it painless for him.

"I never much liked guns. They put the power of God into the hands of foolish men," he'd finally figured it out.

"But none of that matters now. You two are in charge, and I'm on my way out," he proclaimed, rising from his leaning position against the blockade. "Leon, I'll get you the trust of the townsfolk on my way out. Julie, I'm counting on you to get those kids through this safely."

Taylor glanced at her fire axe, held closely by whitened, paranoid knuckles. "Do whatever it takes."

He reached his hand out to Leon, who glanced at it. Reaching out and grabbing that hand could mean big trouble if anybody saw it. He would be voluntarily crossing the blockade again. But he didn't give a good god damn about that. He shot his hand out and pumped Taylor's firmly, a stoic look of respect on his face.

Then Taylor released Leon's hand and turned to Julie. He leaned over to her and gave her a hug. There wasn't much strength behind it, and Julie was amazed at how light Taylor felt as she held him. Then he released and turned to walk away, both Julie and Leon too mystified at the sudden turn of events to really know what to say. He took three steps away from them before stopping to glance back.

"I think if I could have anything, it would be one more chance. I think if I could go back, have one more shot at childhood…I'd do a lot of shit differently. Still, I can't help but feel like this is exactly where I'm meant to be right now."

Then he walked away, zipping up his jacket and walking with the wind at his back. It was about the only thing that had worked out for him in a long, long time. He stopped when he saw Claire. She was still standing next to her father. He spoke to her father for a moment, shook his hand, and disappeared into the darkness.

*

With the daylight fading, Captain Talbott had to find his target soon. He needed some way to communicate with his officers on this matter. There had to be a communications tower in the area somewhere. Ideally it would be one with a locking door and no "unexpected" occupants.

His boots clicked against the pavement as he whisked southward. He hadn't seen any zombies since they fled the tennis courts in terror of his pistol-whippings. He had, however, seen traces of zombies all around him. The entire city was a monument to the wave of death that had struck.

Bodies had been strewn across lawns. There were bloodied corpses pulled halfway through shattered windows. Every block hosted a massive bloodstain where someone must have bled to death before becoming one of the others. The macabre had been delivered to every doorstep of this poor town.

He continued through the still streets. The long shadows were stretching across the road ahead of him, seeming to throw themselves in his way. Regardless of whether he blamed it on old age, fatigue or bad luck, Talbott was moving rather slowly. His heaving got heavier.

"It can't be all that bad," Talbott told himself. *"At least I've still got that one bullet."*

*

"Where do you think he's going?" Leon wondered. He thought Julie might know something from spending the past day with him.

"I don't know…but I know him. He wouldn't just give up on this cause for the selfish reason of dying. He's definitely got something he needs to do," she reflected. She sensed there was something deeper to all of it.

"From the little I knew of him, he seemed troubled. I don't know, maybe it was because he was sick. Maybe he really did just want a little dignity," Leon considered. Still, he felt like there was a missing element to all of it. It was almost tangible.

"Well, it's certainly not over. We could very well get to him before all is said and done," Julie said.

Leon nodded, adding, "I should go."

Julie looked confused. She had just gotten here, hardly had time to talk things through, and then both of her partners were abandoning her. Nobility should take a back seat to common sense. With them both gone there was nothing for her to do but wait for the crowd to turn on her.

"Why? I haven't even had a chance to take part here? What's going on?"

"I've got to talk to August. He's a sympathetic ear, and I need to get some medicine for Taylor. I'll be back right after I tell him, alright?"

Julie was shocked, "Don't you think you could at least tell me what we're supposed to do if zombies come trying to kill us?"

Leon thought on it.

"That does make sense."

"Yeah."

"Alright, basically if zombies attack you're going to have to rush the blockade. Now, I won't be firing upon you guys. I'll be providing cover fire, at times. But I can't say what these two assholes might do. I think one means well, but he's so fucking by-the-book that he might start shooting civilians. The other I believe would relish the opportunity to play God."

"There are going to be some casualties, but if you don't rush it you'll be massacred. We just don't have the firepower to defend you. What happens after that is totally up in the air. So far as I know there isn't any help on the way, so this is all we've got."

"Three guys with guns standing behind roadblocks," Julie put it together.

"Exactly."

"Shit."

Leon straightened, stretched his neck and shoulders, then said his farewell, "Julie, that's all there is too it. I know it sounds like a no-win situation, and it really is. We're just going to have to accept that there might be some loss. I'll try to get back here after I see Ben, but I can't guarantee that I won't get sanctioned or some shit."

"Ok, good luck," Julie stepped back. Now that she was in the loop, via Leon's synopsis, she could keep a closer eye on the score of pre-teens running free. She and Leon nodded at each other, then both turned to set off on their respective tasks.

*

"At least it's all downhill from here," Taylor told himself. It was true, after all. Once he made his way through the dugout and back to Russell's abandoned truck it would be nothing but clear sailing through a stretch of road teeming with zombies. Once he got to the other side he had a secret plan.

"I'm gonna get me some Goldfish and some Gatorade," he whispered to himself, almost giddily. "Then I'm gonna see if that ol' Ford is still running."

The thought hadn't even occurred to him that nobody was listening to him, nor did it register that he was supposed to be on a stealth mission. He was becoming quite demented. The fact that he was able to remain on task was only due to the fact that he still saw the flames of the burning skulls licking at the pileup from the other side. To him the dark pathway to Watterson was lit and paved just for him. To him there were rows of decapitated heads lining the road. To him reality was about to cease to exist.

What Taylor didn't know, what he couldn't know, was that his mind had succumbed to dementia. With AIDS it can be temporary, or it can be very permanent. It was just now beginning to set in on a massive scale. By the time he reached the truck it could very well have set in completely. So far he had been able to battle against the physical ailments that came with his terminal lifestyle. This mental attack was completely indefensible.

What was about to happen to Taylor Donner, troubled youth, was the closest thing to hell he could imagine. He was about to enter a world of death while mired in the deranged nightmares of his warped psychosis. His world would end the moment he reached the cab of Russell Singleton's snow white Ford truck.

*

Leon worked his way along the blockade, periodically glancing behind himself to see if Crawford was watching him. So far he hadn't seen Crawford since he was handcuffed and left by the truck. His body was still sore, and his head was absolutely pounding, so it was understandable that he wasn't moving as quickly as normal. Ahead of him he saw August standing guard at the southern end of their section. With no Crawford in sight he picked up the pace.

When Ben saw the struggling Leon cutting a path to him, he decided to meet the Second Lieutenant halfway. They met far enough from prying eyes for Leon to be able to get straight to the point. He dropped any phoniness from his smile and looked the Green Beret square in the eyes.

"One of the civilians is very sick. I need you to get him some medicine."

"How sick?" Ben drilled. He wasn't so much concerned with Leon's motives as he was about whether or not he'd be breaking orders. He knew damn well the guys upstairs wouldn't break blockade for some fuckin' Sudafed.

"Dying."

Ben's eyes glossed over for a moment, as if the passing thoughts were visible on his face. He swallowed dryly and shut his eyes for a moment. Then he gave his answer, "So far as you know what 'n the hell we ought to be gettin' I can let 'em know."

"Antiretroviral treatments," Leon shot, adding, "Whatever they can get their hands on."

His superior seemed to be confused, so Leon tried to find a simpler way to put it. He was still thinking it over when the crushing calls of James Crawford disrupted him. He was tearing along the blockade, jetting straight for Second Lieutenant Gibbs.

"Gibbs! What in the fuck are you doing walking around like a god damn free man?" he cried. His hand reached to the zip ties at his side. "Don't you know you're under arrest, boy?"

"Damn, I'm not gonna be able to get Ben to cut loose those zip ties again. This is it."

"Ben, remember," he said lowly. "Antiretroviral treatments…COCKTAILS!"

The man only looked confused. He remained looking that way when Crawford grabbed Leon and roped him with the zip ties. Leon was taken back to the supply truck and fastened to the steering wheel. Then he watched as Crawford and August talked at length, sharing everything they knew.

*

"They're all dead, sir."

A silence, amplified by the darkness surrounding, ensued.

"Yes sir, all of them."

Another quiet.

"We were ambushed."

…

"No."

…

"No."

A sigh is heard.

"Yes, sir."

Nothingness.

"Only one bullet left, sir."

A set of red lights began to blink on the radio tower's switchboard.

"Disease of the blood?"

…

"No, I understand. I'll await your orders, sir. Thank you."

*

Julie sat on the ground, watching as her charges tired out and settled on the grass. They were almost all falling asleep. Julie wanted them to be rested, but she wanted them to be alert. She looked around nervously, waiting for it all to come crashing down.

PHASE 6
Tales From the Cryptococcal Meningitis

Taylor was looking upon Marcy. She was so vibrant. The way that her hair ran from her neck down her shoulders was always so gorgeous to him. She flowed, touching the very heavens when she smiled. They were snacking on Goldfish.

Taylor couldn't recollect how he'd gotten back to his apartment. It didn't even occur to him that he was with the same Marcy whose corpse he had identified just a few days earlier. His only care in the world was that the Goldfish were making him thirsty.

He took a swig of Gatorade.

"You know, Marcy. I never gave you a fair shake," he opened up. He cradled some cheddar cheese flavored crackers in his hand, waiting to finish his sentence before popping them in his mouth.

She just looked up at him and smiled.

"I never listened to you, either."

She twirled her finger on the rim of her Gatorade bottle.

"I sure do wish I'd done a lot differently," he said, looking up with one eye cocked.

Marcy was gone. He was left alone in his apartment, which slowly began to change around him. The walls turned from white to a grey, their texture shifting as well. What was once an eggshell enamel turned into cloth, and Taylor soon recognized that he was not in his apartment at all. He was in Russell's truck.

He took check of himself, and saw that he'd destroyed an entire bag of Goldfish without even knowing it. He must have nearly inhaled it. Looking to the south he saw a row of burning pyres lining College Avenue. Then he turned the key and went through a long process of backing up and going forward before he was able to right the vehicle. Taylor had driven it into an immovable wedge before he'd abandoned it. Loosing it from that grip required more concentration and patience than Taylor possessed at that time.

He scratched Russell's Ford.

He slammed on the brakes.

"Russell's dead…he has to be," Taylor assured himself.

Then he hit the gas and drove slowly towards the row of burning skulls on College Avenue. Taylor vaguely remembered being back in his apartment as he motored towards the path. Then he shook it off, chalking it up to confusion and moved it to the back of his mind.

He had his gunship, he had his snacks, and he had enough fuel. Gas prices had dropped significantly since the dead had started to rise. As he neared the candlelit artery that Marcy and Andrew had so kindly opened up for him he realized that the sun was still lying low in the sky. The smoke that had encompassed the area was gone.

"*I don't remember that.*"

He turned left. With the lane magically cleared of any traffic it was clear sailing for him. The route to Watterson should have been a facile sojourn of no more than five minutes by automobile. That was based on the basic assumption that Taylor didn't stop and traveled at a modest pace.

Taylor stopped. He jumped out of the truck. He was mortified.

"What is this?" he yelled. Only the crows fleeing their perches answered him. He was utterly frightened by what he was seeing.

The faces, the boiling and screaming faces, were crying out at Taylor when he came towards them. Then, as he passed them, they would remain facing to the west. They wouldn't turn to face him as he crossed beyond them.

He could proceed and face their tormenting lashes, each one intensifying the pain emanating from Taylor's sores. Or he could turn his back to them and shut them out. That would keep their stinging moans from tearing him apart so badly, but it wouldn't allow him to make any progress.

Not knowing what he was getting himself into, Taylor turned his back to the path before him. He nodded a goodbye to the Ford and began to walk backwards. He held his hands to his ears. The unbearable torment became somewhat bearable.

*

He wasn't certain how far he'd gotten. Walking backwards is disorienting to the mind and the body. What bothered him most were his arms. He had his hands glued to his ears from the moment he turned around. After the rigorous climb up the car pileup the constant strain of keeping his arms aloft was beginning to add up. He wasn't about to drop them, though. One earful of the tormenting cries around him would be reminder enough to never let his guard down again.

He wasn't sure how he felt about his deceased childhood friends facing the opposite direction. Part of him was glad just to have less acoustics to the hymn of his lament. The other side of Taylor was torn. Why wouldn't they look upon him? Had they turned their backs on him?

"Will I ever see them again?"

He hadn't had any time to take things in. All the running to and fro, killing zombies and drinking Gatorades, had kept his mind occupied. Taylor did notice that, unfortunately, one does tend to lose himself in thought when traipsing backwards through a darkened path, their soul filled with the wails of dying cohorts.

He seized this opportunity to finally actualize what had occurred. He started out with the basics.

"Marcy's dead," the words died as quickly as his lips after they had passed.

He'd meant to bring it up real quick-like, as if clicking through topics in a PowerPoint. But the moment he breathed those two words together, it knocked into him like a wave of sand. Marcy had died.

Suddenly he wasn't on the run anymore. He was just in mourning. At that very moment, Taylor Donner was indifferent to the outside world. He was apathetic to everything around him. Right then, though his body continued to live on, a major part of him died.

"There's no room for complacence in this world," he muttered. Once he stopped caring, he stopped living. The only problem was that he had nothing left to care about. After Andrew died he had only Marcy to care about, even if he'd acted like he never cared about her at all. Maybe that was why he had been so mean to her. He couldn't stand the thought of going through such a major loss ever again.

So he shut himself off. If he was never close to anybody again he could never lose them.

"And I started with Marcy," he wallowed. "She was dead to me long before she died. That's why I'm just shrugging it off like it's no big thing. But it's monumental. It's disastrous. The loss of one life kills so many more."

Taylor came to realize that he was no longer walking backwards. He had stopped completely. The wails had quieted, but there was still something shrieking through the sky. Taylor dropped his arms, feeling the weight of exhaustion as they toppled limply to his sides. Then he turned.

The demon in burlap had returned. It was in the pathway before him, hovering a few feet off of the asphalt on College Avenue. He was despicable. The badly tattered cloth that hung from his skin was a reflection of the very fall from grace he had become. He grinned widely at Taylor. Crude stalactites and stalagmites filled his carnivorous mouth.

Taylor only stared back. He didn't cower in fear. This wasn't one of his nightmares, where he could sprint until sunrise. He was wide awake, or at least he believed he was, and running would only delay the inevitable.

"What the fuck do you want?"

The monster only widened his grin, the pure black of his eyes pouring out against the only slightly darkened sky. Taylor thought he saw a remnant of his Achilles Tendon in there. Then he thought better of it and began to walk straight ahead.

If he was supposed to get to Watterson this fucker would step aside. If not, then he'd have to do battle eventually. What better time to start than now?

The entity of muddy burlap and rusty instruments only responded with a wave of his hand. With that one wave he brought a squall. Then he dissipated into the air, like a liquid dissolving.

The wind rose into a fury. Taylor planted one foot behind him for support. He wasn't about to give up any ground, and he would battle this tempest for all it was worth. Hunching his shoulders low he began to walk forward again. The sky crashed against him, buffeting his very progress into a standstill. His very strength was gridlocked by the storm. It was going to be a war of attrition. The first to stop pushing would win.

Without warning the air became rancid. It stank of decay. The fading day was noxious of spoiled meat, or some sort of carcass that had been out in the sun. Taylor's insides heaved. He bent low. Having doubled over, Taylor lowered his center of gravity. It made the battle against the wind much easier. But the onslaught of vomit that followed killed any celebration outright. All of Taylor's coveted Goldfish lay at the ground before him. That was the last of his food.

*

He still didn't know how far he'd gotten. Now he didn't know how long he'd waited, battling the constant wind that had been launched at him. The stench hadn't left. The nausea had. Finally, without a sign or reason, the storm ceased. Taylor had outlasted it.

He was slow to rise. His muscles had been blasted by the cold wind, locking them in position. They didn't want to stretch. Taylor's legs fought back, and he almost fell forward onto the pavement. Luckily he caught himself, avoiding the pile of half digested Goldfish beneath him.

With a great effort he finally made it to his feet. The screams had ceased. The flames were put out by the wind. Taylor glanced at the curbs at either side of him. There were no skulls. There was also no path.

The distance he'd traveled surprised him. He had walked all the way back to Holy Cross Cemetery. The open graves were all exposed before him, crying out against the sunlight. He'd come quite far on the path of despair.

The options were up in the air for Taylor. He could follow College Avenue all the way to Watterson. Then again, he could choose his own direction. There didn't appear to be any reason why he couldn't go check on Russell's house. Or maybe he could hit up the local bank.

A rustling of leaves didn't worry Taylor until he realized there was no breeze to cause it. He looked behind him to see a zombie clearing his way through a row of hedges. It disappeared behind one before soon reappearing between two others. He moved through them like a ghost.

Taylor wasted no time, shuffling off in the other direction. He was going to have to make himself unknown quickly. It wouldn't be long before the creature emerged from the tall bushes, and if Taylor was in sight he'd be an easy target. He would have to find sanctuary, but there was nothing but an open field before him.

The rustling continued, growing neither nearer nor farther, only remaining constantly ominous. Taylor raced forward, stopping only when he noticed an opening in the mud below. It soon became apparent that it would be his only viable option. He saw that it was going to be a tighter squeeze than he could have hoped. Apparently zombies don't leaving big gaping holes in the earth as they emerge. Taylor had been banking on that assumption.

Still, he had little other choice. Save for the infested row of hedges, he was in an open field now. If he went back the way of the street he'd run into houses and the chance of fenced-in yards. His options exhausted, he dropped to the ground. He slipped into the grave feet first.

The recent rain helped his entry into the earthen tomb. He hurriedly eased himself in, the slick mud expediting his journey. Unfortunately, Taylor realized too late that by sliding in he'd eventually have to climb out.

It was too late, though. Taylor's lower half was already immersed, and before he had a chance to rethink his strategy a shriek cracked through the sky. Taylor recognized it instantly. He looked backwards, knowing that if he was spotted then he'd be a sitting duck. He would have to pull himself out of the dirt.

What he saw was somewhat reassuring. The demon had emerged from the shrubs, but was not looking at him. Instead, it was sniffing at the air. The blood-soaked Taylor knew too well what the zombie had caught scent of. He continued, immersing himself completely into the grave.

The hole widened at its base. Taylor figured it must have been where the coffin door was smashed open. Regardless of its origin, the extra room gave Taylor a chance to spread himself, sinking his frame as far as possible into the earth. His shoes planted against the coffin door. A chill ran through him.

He was completely under now, his head cocked to the side to allow him to breathe. Only a small portion of his face was exposed. All of the blood on him was now under the ground. He prayed that was enough to keep him from being smelled.

"At least if they find me they'll have to earn their meal."

They weren't going to pull him from the mud easily.

"And I'm not gonna crawl out too easy, either."

Despite having his ears underground, and being nearly deaf, Taylor could feel the zombie approaching. Taylor looked up with one open eye and saw the beast just a few feet from him, standing still. It screamed again. The cry rang inside his head. It made him lose himself. His mind began to swim again. He closed his eyes, keeping one open only slightly. He didn't want the whites of his eyes to show, but he couldn't tear himself away from the scene developing before him. He was a voyeur to his own demise.

The scream had drawn more zombies. Two of them, if Taylor wasn't missing any. They congregated on the soil near him. He pursed his lips and exhaled lowly, slowly. His heart skipped as the air escaping his lips whistled slightly. The zombies didn't react.

Then he inhaled. Lowly. Slowly.

The zombies also inhaled. They sucked in the scent of his blood as it mingled with the air.

Taylor clenched his eyes closed, unwittingly. Then he reopened them, and the demons were gone. He craned his neck to look for them, and spied all three disappearing into the hedges. They were headed west, towards the blockade.

*

It was like a vacuum, and it sucked him further down with each passing second. The mud clung to him and tightened around him, like a body cast. The trauma of Taylor entering the hole must have compromised its support structure. It was ready to come down in a mudslide.

Taylor pressed his feet against the lid of the coffin. The weight of the mud between his legs was almost immovable. His best chance was to get up to his full height. If the grave was exactly six feet, he figured the coffin must have accounted for at least another foot and half. If he could push himself up his head would be fully exposed from the ground. He was able to slide his foot an inch before the space it had just occupied was completely filled with mud. One false move and he could further imprison himself.

Strain was slowly building on his chest. The weight of the mud combined with his pneumonia was threatening to cut off all of his air. It was altogether possible that getting just his head out of the mud wouldn't guarantee free breath. He might have to unearth his entire torso before breathing could commence again.

He continued to force his feet together. The task was arduous, with the mud compacting further between his shoes. Recognizing the futility of simply sliding his feet together, Taylor used the sliver of room that still barely existed near the lid of the coffin to lift his foot. It came up begrudgingly, trying desperately to snake its way back to the abyss. Taylor claimed his foot, the mud claimed his shoe.

"Shit...my good Pumas," he mourned. It had also cost him about half an inch of height. Still he slammed his foot straight down. The force behind the move pushed Taylor up a couple of inches. His ears were exposed. The struggle was arduous, and Taylor was realizing its futility before he'd even overcome a fraction of the task. His muscles ached. They didn't simply ache, they were nearly in atrophy. Every time he reached his arms over his head he had to will himself out of the near paralyzation that had taken him. He was on the verge of tightening up into a gnarled ball, his nerve endings nothing more than a spasm.

Next he lugged his other leg up, losing a little ground as he did so. His ears became half-submerged. He also lost the other shoe. None of that registered to Taylor, who was too frightened to do anything but panic. He smashed this foot down also, rising up to his neck. He continued the process, fighting the cumbersome weight that dragged him to the grave. His burden was wet and dense, and it was a heroic effort every time he garnered an inch.

After he'd climbed through enough mud to expose his shoulders, Taylor's skin began to itch. Shaking it off, he lifted a leg once more. But the itching only grew, bringing with it a slight burning. It stung at his back, and crawled along his legs.

Taylor could no longer ignore the pain, and he strained his neck downwards. The earth beneath him churned like quicksand, earwigs materializing from the soil. They clambered about the earth, searching blindly for anything to latch onto. Taylor could feel them rising from the grave as they climbed his struggling body. He watched in petrified horror as they came at his neck once more. This time, however, unlike when he was a child, Taylor didn't wait for them to reach his exposed flesh.

His legs began to work frantically, the near-realization of one of his worse fears waking them from their sloth. In a blur, Taylor toiled through the mud, freeing his arms and using them to lift himself upwards. The pincher bugs clung to him, burrowing into every crevice that presented itself. They broke through from the mud that was pasted on his body.

Taylor freed himself from the grave, falling onto his face and beginning to roll before his right ankle had fully left the earthen sepulcher. He spun his body along the ground, feeling the earwigs crush under his weight. This time their guts mixed with the mud, caking to his skin. After he'd thrashed for a few minutes, the last of the insects finally loosed its grip. Taylor stopped.

He lay out on his back, looking up at the still light sky. There he remained for some time, gasping for air. The mud hardened on his skin and in his hair. It swam inside of his pant legs and caked his jacket. He had been seconds from fading out.

His body was shot. The trial had spent him. With the remaining energy he had left he rolled onto his side, staring east. He spied a cloud of smoke over Redbird Arena.

"*I knew that place was nothing but catacombs.*"

Then he turned his gaze slightly further south, still gazing east. There was a line of trees blocking the distance, but he knew it was there. Watterson was getting closer still. If he could survive long enough, he'd make it there by nightfall. None of that mattered for now, though. He'd been fortunate to escape the grave, but he wasn't lucky enough to have any remaining strength. As his eyes closed he prayed that the cloud over the blockade had vanished early enough. Otherwise his friends would all die, and more zombies would be headed this way to end Taylor's slumber.

*

It was dark out when he awoke. His judgment put it around seven. But he wasn't worried about the time. Taylor's had just done something that hadn't happened to him for years. He had shut his eyes for what seemed like a couple of hours, and nothing had happened. There had been no nightmare. He wondered if pure exhaustion was the key to his dreamless night. Or perhaps it was because he was already in the nightmare.

Taylor wondered at the sky above him. It was filled with stars. It was breathtaking. The muddied Taylor pondered sitting there for even longer, savoring his last cloudless night. Even the dark, night sky seemed to be brimming with shades, bouncing with starlight. But his experience with the open tomb and the zombies had taught him one important thing.

"Don't stand around holding' your dick...ever."

He shook off the sleep, then he struggled to his feet and shook off the dirt. He decided that he'd be better off without a muddy jacket bearing down on him, and stripped it off. His grey shirt was relatively unscathed and surprisingly dry. Taylor rolled the sleeves up, despite the cold, and made his way to the street again.

It was silent save for the cold grass crushing under his bare feet. His toes were numb to even a stab wound. Despite the purpled sky, there was still good light for Taylor to move by. He couldn't make out every shape, but the walk did give him an opportunity to pick up on some of the scenery he'd missed out on before.

The whole route was an obituaries page in the newspaper. Taylor imagined it as he strolled.

"Doe, John. Born May 17th, 1979. Leaves behind one daughter. Predeceased by two sons, wife, mother and father. Chased down, cornered, slashed, hacked and torn to pieces by ravenous cannibal demons spawned from hell during the Great Zombie Plague of the Twenty First Century. Cremated."

Corpses were gathered at the gutters, swept there in the floods. Some were impaled on their own fences. Far too many of them were in their cars when it happened. Each other vehicle was a vacated mausoleum.

As he neared College Avenue once more, he spied his own car at the side of the road. The maroon Grand Am had been abandoned on the side of the road, gasless. Without fuel the damn thing was no more than an outlandishly large paper weight. Taylor wondered if the nail bat was in it.

"I don't even have the keys," he realized. He could hardly even remember leaving the car. That had seemed generations ago to him. It took him a moment just to recall why he'd even left the car.

"Oh shit! I went through the sunroof."

Then he shifted direction towards the Grand Am. If he could get into it he might be able to retrieve his weapon. He had turned down the offer of a rifle, but there was something different about the bat. It couldn't run out of ammunition. It didn't have to be reloaded. It was made by Marcy. She made it solely to defend Taylor.

He approached the vehicle. The open sunroof had let in the weather, and the weather had wreaked havoc. The insides and outside were glazed over, either by frost or another frozen liquid Taylor didn't even care to think about. The vehicle was a shell of its former glory.

Taylor dropped the jacket to the ground, reaching his still weary arms to the roof and jumped up as strongly as he could. His sleep had helped slightly, but he wasn't back in slam dunk form quite yet. His four inch vertical was, however, enough to get him enough leverage to pull himself up. He spun on his stomach to get his head to the opening, then gazed in.

The vehicle was flooded with soot, but there were no signs of a fire. It caked every feature of the interior, blacking out every definition. The entire scene looked like a dark canvas. Taylor reached in, forced to feel for the bat.

The length of his arm wasn't adequate enough to touch the seat, so Taylor leaned in slightly. The extra inches didn't allow him enough reach. The backseat, the spot Taylor assumed the bat to most likely be, was still about a foot further away. Taylor retrieved his arm and braced it at the edge of the sunroof, using it to pull his body even further into the car.

With a gasp of realization, Taylor slipped. He toppled helplessly into the vehicle below. Plunging, he held his hands before him, expecting to land against the back seat. What greeted him was a thick puddle, instead. Three feet of something, maybe rainwater, had accumulated inside of the vehicle

Taylor's new shirt was already dirty. He landed on his shoulders, they hit the water just above the back seat. Then his body followed, dropping all the way to the floor and further forcing Taylor's head down with it. Taylor splashed through it, blindly reaching for the surface.

Finally he found the headrest of the seat in front of him and lifted himself up, the mud at his fingers impeding his grip. As his mouth broke the surface he sucked at the air. It was becoming a common trend for him. Then the sickening water began to run down his neck, thickly clinging to it. He was sitting in muck up to his neck. His legs were stuck underneath of him. The landing hadn't gone quite as he'd planned. To his knowledge, and much to his benefit, he hadn't landed on the bat of nails. There were no noticeable punctures wounds on him.

As he gathered himself he began to slowly reach his hand through the water for the bat. All this water would make it nice and rusty, so he was sure to be careful. The last thing he wanted was to add tetanus to his growing rap sheet.

His knees cried out in pain, but he ignored them. The positioning of his body had forced his right shoulder to become stuck. He wouldn't be able to grip anything to pull himself out with unless he found the bat. And he was becoming increasingly certain that it was no longer even in the Grand Am.

The water cut a flowing "v" around his knuckles as they waded through the thick. Eventually he struck pay dirt. He felt the barrel of the bat with his thumb. It was wedged along the groove of the back seat. His outstretched fingers felt along it to find the handle. Then he gripped it.

Pulling at the handle, Taylor's grip slipped. The bat had refused to move at all. One of the nails must have gotten smashed into the center console. Taylor yanked at it again to no avail. It was somewhere around the time that he was repositioning his grip to push on the bat that he wondered how the bat got stuck on anything in the first place.

A third hand, one that did not belong to Taylor, and was even more decomposed, shot through the filth from the front seat, latching on to Taylor's wrist. It squeezed like a vice, crushing the bones on the backside of Taylor's hand. All blood flow was halted, and Taylor could feel his veins rushing into a log jam. It gathered there, pushing back against itself and out at the walls of Taylor's very circulation system.

Then the claw pulled its arm out, which was followed by its snarling, dripping mask. The demon in the car was wearing a burlap sack, snapping wildly despite the thick material. It hissed outwards, the sound's scratchiness only increased by the rough sack it wore, revealing nothing but the same, dread black eyes.

Taylor jerked his hand backwards, hoping that the substance coating his body would provide enough lubrication for him to escape the grip. Instead, he ended up pulling the demon further up from the pool of slime it had lain dormant in. The beast snapped again, only the outline of its jaw scratching the burlap evidence of the action. Taylor came, despite his fear, to understand the defenseless nature of his assailant.

He snatched at the zombie's mask, tearing at it for solid grip. With a surge he pulled his free hand downwards, straight into where Taylor hoped the spiked end of the bat was. The beast struggled, only increasing the tension on its death grip and ripping its head upwards.

The zombie dug its boned finger tips into Taylor's wrist as Taylor pressed its skull down once more against the nails at the end of the bat. This time he succeeded, lifting his body from the ground as he pulled at the mask. A gruesome squishing was heard for a brief instant when the mask first made contact with the rusty nails. Then there was only a sound similar to wood splitting. For every crack of bone that Taylor heard the zombies fingers dug deeper, until finally it lay exorcised on the rusty nails of Taylor's trusty baseball bat.

As he impaled the demon, Taylor began to sob, screaming, "YOU FUCKER! YOU FUCKER!"

A dark fluid escaped from it, Taylor didn't stick around to see what it was. He rose up, standing on the back seat. He wrenched the deadly bat free of the writhing body, and pulled himself through the sunroof. After sledding down the hood, Taylor hit the ground running. He wasn't going to stop until something stopped him, or his own body finally gave in.

*

A rushing, crashing cacophony announced itself in the near distance. In the dark, Taylor could only wager a guess as to what might be causing it. He slowed briefly, taking in his surroundings. The dusk sky greeted him, a palette of oblivion.

He must have been nearing the retention stream that ran alongside Redbird Arena. The mere thought of it turned Taylor's feet to stone. He had remembered all the warnings, all the signs that pointed to the stadium as a place of great death and suffering. What bothered Taylor the most was that he had far less fear of this place than he did of Watterson. It would consume him, of that he was certain.

The wearied Taylor continued onward. His silhouette stood against the deepening sky, a lone figure walking down his path. All that was good was behind him, all that he feared lay before him. It was also where he hoped to find his salvation. Not that he believed in any of that.

His forehead clung to his skull as he squinted to see the stream ahead. Slowly, dimly announcing its presence was a ghostly light. It emanated from the water, breathing death into the air. Taylor could only wander towards it, his mind no longer coordinating with his body. With each successive stride the truth unveiled itself.

The stream cut a straight line across the horizon, but failed to hide behind the bridge that Taylor knew to be there. Instead, the unforgiving fates had destroyed his bridge, and any hope of crossing with it. Still, Taylor walked onwards.

When he had reached the end of the boulevard, the fate of the bridge became apparent. Taylor hardly slowed as he passed the corpses of men in military uniforms. The road was exploded, chunks of road protruded like large shrapnel from the bodies of the victims framing the grisly sight. Taylor's path cut right through the unnervingly still bodies around him. Then he climbed to the lip of the precipice that framed the burning flow of the retention stream.

He stepped off the edge, and sank into the water below.

*

The first thing that Taylor remembered was the burning. It had torn at his skin like mustard gas. Then he had choked, swallowing the fiery water. His insides turned to fire, his eyeballs raged.

Then there was darkness.

He had wandered there for a long time.

When he awoke he was stretched out on the pavement in front of Redbird Arena. The flames still roared against the night sky. It was a tomb of thousands. None could have escaped alive. The demons would have collapsed on it, mercilessly slaughtering any and all who fled the flames.

And his head was on fire. The fever ravaged him, shooting his body temperature to 102. His clothes were soaked through, either from the rain or his own sweat. Most likely it was a combination of both. Beads gathered at his face.

A quick scan of his surroundings revealed an even more macabre scene. Charred corpses, half-corpses to be more specific, littered the sidewalk and street. Bloodied soldiers lay lifeless amongst them. Death had come to all.

Taylor slowly, slowly lifted himself off of the ground. Sitting up he saw a parcel next to him. It was a first aid kit. The kit was neon green, probably something carried by a hunter. Next to it, imprinted in the ash that had rained from above, was the outline of a Wolverine work boot.

"But…he has to be…"

Taylor flipped the kit open. Inside laid a bag of Goldfish, and a bottle of Gatorade.

"Jesus fuckin' Christ."

He lunged at the Gatorade. His throbbing throat insisted upon it. In an instant he was suckling at the bottle like a calf to its mother. After finishing it he turned his attention to the Goldfish, their salty goodness called to him to relieve the sweetness left in his mouth. Soon his snack was finished.

Only then did he fully ponder the implications. If Russell really was alive, he would have to be close. Taylor fought to his feet, and whirled towards Watterson. Taylor would just have to hope that whoever left him this gift had also been going that way. Then he took his first steps towards his own personal slice of hell.

PHASE 7
The Riveter

The division along College Avenue had all but disappeared. Julie had prepared the populace for the worst, and suddenly the quarrels that had fueled the mob's hatred seemed trivial. They stood nervously, anticipating that they might have to charge the blockade on a moment's notice. The children were scattered amongst the group, each entrusted to a group of volunteers. Julie had stressed the importance of future generations' survival.

Second Lieutenant Gibbs, on the other hand, was completely at the mercy of the situation. The zip ties that held him to the supply truck dug tightly into his skin. His hands were slightly numb from the cut-off in his circulation. There was no chance of survival so long as he was cuffed to the supply truck.

He sat in the driver's seat, with the door wide open. To his left lay College Avenue, the path that Taylor had chosen. Leon couldn't grasp the torture that haunted the soul's mind, but something about Taylor's departure seemed utterly appropriate. He peered off into the darkness that had swallowed his friend as he disappeared from this earth.

Any moment he knew that the hordes of hell could spew out of that very darkness. He was beginning to believe the reports. Demons, thousands of them. It seemed to be only a matter of time before they arrived, drawn, perhaps, by the putrid smoke that choked out the air above the blockade.

Benjamin passed by, glancing over his shoulder at the imprisoned patriot. Leon couldn't read his emotion. There was fear within it, to be sure. The attack was hanging in the air, like the heaviness that announces a storm. All that waited was the release, the downpour.

He stared, mostly, at the waiting mob. They held until Julie gave the order. The only thing holding them back was the rifle that Crawford pointed at them. It was aimed straight at Julie's heart, and Leon didn't doubt that he was a dead shot. The madman would shoot anything that tried to cross his horseshit blockade. Man, woman, child…all would be fair game.

*

Julie held steadfast at the front of her army. She stood, fastened to the middle of the avenue. Her axe was the only thing that lay between her life, and James Crawford's M-16. She crossed it over her heart, the blade facing the ground, and slightly outwards.

There were only a handful of options left, and time was quite a factor. A quiet discomfort pulled at the gathering like a sadistic marionette. Their hopes rested on Julie's decision to act. She could either wait for the monsters to come for them, or lead the charge into the Green Beret's poised bullet.

The night had just begun to slip upon them. Julie had long ago given up any hope of a bloodless resolution. Her fears, her world, came shrieking to reality as a cry shot from the back of the crowd. The living dead had descended upon them. Her mind was made for her.

Miss Patterson had hoped to shout something inspiring, something rallying as she led her charge. What emitted, however, from her grinding scowl was a guttural cry of rage. Its effect was just the same, as the mob roared to life, to anger.

Crawford fired instantly, spinning Julie like a puppet. She crumpled to the pavement.

*

Gibbs' life was drawing to an end before his very eyes. Soon the zombies would clear the fleeing mob, and then they would come upon Leon. He was a free meal.

Leon didn't have any time to take it all in. A gasp was all he could manage. Then he saw Miss Patterson go down. That was when Gibbs panicked. He thrust his shackled wrists up, wrenching them against the ungiving plastic. It dug deep into Leon's skin, slicing thinly into the side of his wrist. If he wasn't careful, he could sever something much more important.

Leon bared his teeth and bit down, trying desperately to cut through his ties. It was hopeless though. Leon could only look up, and watch as hell consumed him. With livid wrath he tore at his shackles, blood beginning to stream along his forearms.

The punishing crush of the zombies was merciless. They happened upon the blockade in scores, overtaking the crowd before most of them even had a chance to react to the first cries. They were a hideous army. Crimson dyed their skulls, revealing the bloodied pores beneath. Their jagged scowls snapped at any flesh within reach.

What haunted Leon the most, though, was the surreal way that the zombies moved. Their exposed joints told a horrid story of death. The hell beasts' movements looked like a scene from a strobe light. They proceeded upon the crowd like a series of snapshots.

A young man, carrying nothing more than a backpack and a log he'd hoped to use as a club, was overtaken by a demon. The sickly sound of flesh ripping could not be heard over the roar of the crowd, yet it echoed in Leon's mind as he watched. The ghoul's claw emerged high above it's head, the chipped and scraggly nails at its end pointed directly at the young man's face. It struck down without remorse or restraint.

Next an old woman was taken down. She landed on her wrist, and Leon could spy the unmistakable flash of white that could only mean a broken bone. Then the monster latched onto her neck, clamping its teeth down to her shoulder bone. She wailed into the night, the bright red blood pooling around her.

Leon watched helplessly as his fellow American's were mowed down, one by one. His gun was only a few feet away, and he could do nothing to help them. The only wild card he had, one which he had completely counted out, suddenly came through in a big way.

Benjamin August, the same man who had a few days earlier spit in the face of Leon at the request of an officer, snuck along the side of the truck. A knife was held tightly in his right hand. He walked up to Leon calmly, a twisted smile on his face.

"Time you be getting' along," he beamed. He was almost so proud of himself for having done the right thing that he was forgetting the urgency at hand. With that he gripped Leon's wrist and cut the zip tie, as close to the wrist as possible. He did the same for Leon's other hand.

The Green Beret said nothing, only grinned for a moment. Then August fled, leaving the freed soldier to fend for himself. Leon didn't plan to flee, though. He had something else in mind. He bolted to the rear of the truck, making certain to stick tightly to the side of the vehicle. Peeking around the corner, Leon saw that the nearest zombies were a dozen yards away, and none had taken notice of him. Once he reached his arms he snatched them up, holstering the pistol and raising his rifle.

The initial charge of civilians had passed Crawford, and they squeezed between the truck and the walls of the underpass. Some climbed the hood. Now that Gibbs was no longer blocking the way, some even crawled through the cab. With them came a spattering of zombies, the first barriers to Leon's plan.

With skill, Leon looked down the crosshairs of his rifle, and aimed squarely at one of the demons that straddled the corpse of a middle aged man. It was tearing away at the dead man's bowels. The inhuman imagery made it easier for Leon to pull the trigger. His bullet tore through the ghoul's spewing mouth, knocking it to the ground.

Next, Gibbs' attention was shifted to a wraith that was sprinting towards him. Hardly having time to think, Leon spun his barrel and fired. The round dug into the zombie's chest, only slightly slowing its progress. Leon raised his rifle higher and fired once more. The echo of the shot reverberated off the side of the truck, the monster's brain matter with it. It spun and smashed against the rear tire, just to Leon's side.

He had created enough space to clear a decent path for himself. Wasting no time, Leon shot through the opening, making his way towards an outnumbered James Crawford.

*

Julie clutched at her shoulder. The wound went straight through her, an inch over her left lung. Blood pooled around her hand, as she tried in vain to apply pressure. Nothing could clot the flow. She was laid out, amidst a primal battleground. The humans beat at the demons with their clubs, and the demons fought back with tooth and nail.

So far she hadn't been noticed by any of the undead predators. The only motion left in her was the shaky heaving of her breaths. It was at that moment, that brief glimpse of defeat, that allowed Julie to stop caring. It was then that she looked into the sky.

A dark veil shut out all of the light that would have been afforded by the night stars. The air was darker than black. It was soulless. Miss Patterson lay dying in the field, and only then did she question hope. It was her first time.

Just as it seemed nothing good could come, that no light was going to arrive, Julie Patterson heard a child's scream around her. Disoriented, she sat up. A crippling numbness shot out from her shoulder, more blood streaming from the wound as she moved. The demons hadn't taken notice of her yet, but now that she was on her feet they surely would. With a spinning in her head the teacher shot to her feet, lunging forward aimlessly.

Her feet struggled to keep up with her momentum, and the aching in her arm dragged her down. She plummeted to the street once more, her cheek bone scraping along the pavement. With a frantic shake she pushed herself off of the ground one more time.

Desperation had come to Miss Patterson in an instant. The only thing that slowed her was the presence of a shiny, red, fire axe that she spied three feet to her side. With a heave she reached towards it, grabbing at the handle with her good arm, then using it to prop herself and stand.

Doing her best not to cry out from the pain, the grade school teacher slung the axe over her should with one arm. Then she searched for the screaming. There was fighting everywhere. The living were fighting as boldly as they could, but the demons didn't even feel pain. A blow to the chest with a 2x4 couldn't even slow their ferocity.

The cry sprang across the dark sky once more. Julie staggered towards it, the loss of blood doing everything in its power to cut her down. Fighting through, she made her way towards the scream.

The violence swelled, trying to hold her back. The moshing battle threw a body against her, which she deflected off of and quickened her pace. The shriek came again, and Julie spotted the source. Laid across the body of her father, and clutching at his hand, was Claire. The blond-haired girl wept at her father's side. He was dead, his chest cavity torn open. All that remained was a splatter of heart matter and gushing blood that was still warm.

"Come with me, Claire."

The little girl only wailed. She would bring the fury of Satan himself on them if she didn't shut up.

"Claire!" Miss Patterson snapped, in the voice she used only if a student was getting sent to the principal's office. She'd perfected it during her first year of teaching when a group of students had taken to writing "bitch" across the blackboard whenever she left the room.

This grabbed Claire's attention, just long enough for Julie to run over and grab her. She used her bad arm for that. "You have to come with me, honey."

Surprisingly, Claire didn't argue. She was in some sort of shock. If she lived to see another day, this event would haunt her for the rest of her life. As they turned to cross the blockade together, Julie spotted one of Claire's father's legs twitch. It sort of jerked up quickly, then lay still.

"Claire, baby?" she spoke calmly. She let go of the little girl's hand. "I need you to cover your eyes and promise not to look."

Julie didn't even check to see if Claire was following her instructions. She gripped the axe half-way up the handle, and lifted it over her head. Then she thrust down, splitting the man's skull. As the last breathe left the zombie's lips, the hair began to sluice bloodily from his scalp.

Then Julie spun and reached out for Claire's hand once more. Claire, who had failed to cover her eyes, witnessed her father's execution. Still, she did not fight. Miss Patterson grasped the child's hand and pulled her towards the blockade.

*

Leon opened fire on the beasts that had his fellow soldier surrounded. The first shot, from afar, came from his rifle. It pierced the back side of a demon's head, showering bone in every direction. The victim fell in a heap. Crawford took care of one of the others, slinging it to the ground and stabbing it in the cranium with his short blade.

From there the Green Beret drew his handgun and fired a round under the neck of another beast. His move was too slow for the last of the group, though. It hurled itself at Crawford's knelt frame, knocking him flat to the ground. As it scrambled forward it snapped its jaws at the soldier's hand.

The struggle caused Crawford to drop his gun, and he was pinned by the snarling monster. Its teeth widened against the darkness of its mouth. The fangs cut through the air like a bullet as they slashed downwards at Crawford's neck. Leon pulled his handgun and fired, aiming by pure instinct.

It was a direct hit, felling the beast. Under the spewing liquid Crawford pulled himself to his feet. Thanks were in order, but all he managed was, "Gibbs! Give me cover fire. We can't have one of those fuckers taking me down."

"I'm going in, Crawford!" Leon pointed beyond the blockade, back into the heart of the city.

"Like shit you are, boy. Do as I say and one of us might make it through this alive."

"I'll take my chances," Leon started sprinting towards the fighting. But his superior had different plans. As the Second Lieutenant tore across the field the Green Beret leapt out at him. Crawford rung Leon's neck, dragging the combatant to the ground.

Then he straddled Gibbs, gaining leverage on his victim and tightening his choke hold. Leon kicked blindly against him, but it was futile. Spots began to speck the horizon of Leon's eyes. He started going under. Spastically, reflexively, he kicked out against the air once more.

Dull pain throbbed in the Second Lieutenant's head, the cut at his temple reopening. His bandage began to dampen, the red that had seconds earlier formed a large circle now spreading all the way across Gibbs' forehead. A wet cracking noise then followed. Gibbs feared that his neck had broken. He waited, hoping that death would take him before the pain that was sure to come. The only thing that met his waiting was a warm sensation along his neck.

Then Crawford's grip gave out. Gibbs swallowed air, sucking at it like a vacuum. He fell to his chest, landing abruptly on the asphalt. Frenzied, he rolled onto his side and kicked out at Crawford. His aim was off, though, and he came up with nothing but air.

The Green Beret failed to attack, though. As he fell to the ground, as dead as the night sky around them, the bright red axe in his back came with him. It told the story, and Leon looked up at Miss Patterson. She stood, bloodied, with Claire clutching to her leg.

"I'm gonna get out of here," she spoke. It was calmer than it should have been. She knew what Leon was up to. She wasn't going to begin to try to stop him, but it was a journey she couldn't make. Her responsibilities lay elsewhere now.

"I'm gonna go in there," Gibbs responded. He nodded towards the fighting. He nodded beyond the fighting, to where Taylor went. Something inside of him, something hidden and brave, moved him away from safety and into the heart of danger. It was, perhaps, the hope that he had seen in Taylor.

"I know," she forced. "Don't get yourself killed."

Then Julie straightened, and saluted Leon Gibbs, Second Lieutenant of the United States Air Force. He saluted back, and they parted ways.

PHASE 8
The Survival

The streets were ominously clear of any cars. Taylor had imagined the corner of College and University to be a parking lot, a pileup of steel coffins. Instead he was greeted with an open pathway. It took less effort to get so far than he had anticipated, and he supposed he had his snack to thank for that. It had been quite the little cocktail.

"I'll call that one the 'Booster Shot'."

This was, to be fair, overlooking the nauseating fever Taylor was fighting. Intense heat and crushing pressure from every joint nearly crippled him. All the while his head swam frantically while brief, flitting visions and swirling lights danced before him.

He dared not speak aloud. At this point in time it was assumed that if he made too much noise he would summon hell itself. Still, it was hard not to spit out at least one obscenity. "SHIT!"

From the second story of a building came a gunshot and a flash of light. It was quickly followed by a howl and another gunshot. Then silence fell. Taylor knew that was where he had to go next, but he certainly feared it. The gunfire was coming from the Health Services Building.

The site of Taylor's diagnosis, his death sentence, protruded from the concrete jungle around it. The windows glared ever so dimly with the reflection of the Arena's flames in the distance. It defended Watterson as a pawn would a king. Still, it was evidence of another living person.

The night swirled quietly around him as he ran towards his fate. The streets had been completely emptied. Taylor got the sudden feeling that he was walking into a trap. It wasn't the first time, though. He hurried along, not letting the dread feeling slow him.

It wasn't until he had reached the very doorstep of the Health Services that Taylor noticed the rising cadence of footsteps all around him. They had ambushed him. He surged forth, into the depths of the medical office. It was a blind dash, as darkness had completely overtaken the night. Not knowing where it would take him, Taylor battered through the doors.

There was hardly enough light around for him to find his way once he was inside. The claustrophobia that comes with darkness encased Taylor. He stopped, reaching out with one hand. He felt nothing as he stretched further and further out. He was on his tiptoes when pulled back.

Widening his blind stance for stability, Taylor once again reached out, this time with the other arm. He waved wildly at the air, but felt nothing. There were no walls in reach. There was no way of knowing which way to go.

It took the smashing of the glass door that Taylor had slid through to force him to make up his mind. In an errant guess Taylor rushed straight ahead, ramming his shoulder squarely into the wall. His wound ached once again, screaming out in anguish. It melded with the dissonant wails of his pursuers.

Bouncing through the setback, Taylor rushed forth again, this time plunging down a hallway. He sprinted forward without regard for his own body. Any bit of air that he could consume was that much further away from the grisly death that was about to be meted out to him. He crashed into another wall, his chin taking most of the impact.

Cutting a right, Taylor spied wisps of red light calling to him from the end of this hallway. They flickered and beckoned, drawing him in. Unquestioningly he followed, pounding his way down the hallway, listening as closely as he could for the sound of assailants behind him.

Once he reached the end of the corridor, Taylor rounded the corner and headed past the lit flare that was guiding his path. Once he was out of the light he could hide from the death brigade. He quickly jut around another corner and halted. Pressing himself up against the wall, Taylor waited.

He listened. The silence was interrupted only by the low crackle emitting from the flare. It spit out just loud enough for Taylor to wonder whether he was just hearing things. He strained an ear closer to the corner of wall he was hiding behind. There was only silence.

Taylor crept further towards the lip of the wall, moving one slow step at a time. He prayed that the flare would drown out any noise he might make. He peered around the wall, and saw the fading light struggling to reach down the hall. It revealed nothing to him.

He strained his sight further, and waited a hair too long. The light afforded to his vantage point had nearly died out. Then a zombie crashed into the wall, keeping its pace and footing as it turned the corner and closed in on Taylor.

The demon strode faster down the hall at Taylor, who did the only logical thing he could do. He ran forward, into the unknown darkness. He ran from all the pain and suffering that he'd put behind him. The pit of darkness ahead him held more promise than what he'd known in his lifetime, and its possibilities enticed the man.

The distance seemed like a mile to Taylor. However long it was, however long it took, Taylor's legs were drained at the end of it. Once the gunshot rang out, Taylor hit the deck. He couldn't have stood up if he'd wanted to.

One blast had sent him to the ground. The second had curled him up into the fetal position. By the time numbers three and four screamed out Taylor was paralyzed by fear. The pitch black smothered him. He just had time to suppress a coughing fit before the flare was lit above him, and dropped from the top of the stairwell he'd collapsed in.

"Well shit, son! You're still unscathed."

The voice loosened Taylor's nerves. He looked up, suddenly able to move without fear. There his savior sat at the top of the stairs, a pair of Night Vision Goggles strapped to his face. There were four corpses strewn across hallway. Russell hadn't lost his touch.

"Well, that's the beauty of stain protectant. It can add years to a carpet's life," Taylor wondered, his eyes never leaving the pools of blood that gathered. "On second thought, you might need to do some spot work on that."

"What the fuck're you talkin' about, son? This ain't no time to lose your cool."

Taylor stood, his legs hardly able to support him. All the while his muscles wasted away. Russell sprung from the stairs down to Taylor, scooping him up like a six-pack of Miller High Life.

"C'mon godammit!"

Russell took off, Taylor over his shoulder again. He scaled the stairs in a few lengthy bounds, going through the doorway that led to the second floor medical offices. The burst through the doors to the second floor. Taylor's diagnosis had come on the second floor. That was reserved for more private matters.

The Hunter moved masterfully through the darkness. He carried his parcel to an exterior office. There he gently set Taylor into an office chair, the diseased student only able to watch the events unfolding before him. He lulled his head into a raised position, suddenly fatigued and helpless.

The run into the building had spent all of the strength that was left in him. Now he was lucky to wiggle his fingers. Meanwhile, Russell pulled off his Night Vision Goggles. His breathing was heavy now, something Taylor hadn't seen him do even on his record-breaking night of zombie hunting. The Hunter then stripped off his jacket and set it onto a desk.

Taylor looked on as Russell moved swiftly to the shades of the window. He opened them, and the moonlight fed into the office. It brought with it an eerie gloom that lingered over Russell's shoulders, revealing that he had been shirtless under the jacket. Only the shoulder strap for his shotgun covered him. The moon exposed the man who had saved Taylor once more.

His torso was covered in open wounds. He had been eaten alive to the point of near-death. Gashes laced his arms and back, framing the man's completely skinless shoulders. Pus and blood mingled there as Russell stared at the moon for what seemed like eons. Then he looked to Taylor.

"I won't hold out much longer. They bit me too good, son," The Hunter was dropping to his knees as he spoke, pressing the business end of his shotgun against the grizzled patch of beard at his neck. He nestled it tightly, bracing the butt of the weapon between his legs. "I came here hoping to find some medical supplies, but they've been picked over like a carcass on the battlefield. There's no chance for me anymore, son. You weren't supposed to find me like this."

"Russell?" was all Taylor could ask, the bearded man savoring his last breaths before him.

"Son…you weren't supposed to find me. I left you out there so I wouldn't turn into one of them anywhere near you. Now I've only got one option."

226

"No!" Taylor cried, halting Russell just as he was placing his finger against the trigger. The wounded man stared at Taylor, a well of tears forming at his eyelids. There was resignation in his eyes, a serene sort of acceptance. It was apparent from the moment Taylor looked the man in the face that he wasn't going to be talked down.

"You'd go to hell, Russell. You can't do this," even as the hypocritical words passed Taylor's teeth he wondered at his own audacity.

"Hell?" Russell looked back. "Why on earth would I, a devout Christian from birth, go to hell? You think me pulling this trigger is going to make God forget my faith. This is just a flash in the pan."

"That's a pretty big leap of faith."

Russell's demeanor calmed. "That's what faith is, son. Haven't you realized that yet?"

"No," Taylor was being as honest as he'd ever been. "I don't have any idea what to believe anymore."

A solemn silence took the suddenly smaller room. Both men traded stares, looking dismally at each other. Russell swallowed. Taylor blinked.

"God won't give up on you, even if you've forgotten about him. Eventually, he reveals himself to all of us, and provides the answers to our prayers."

There was certainty in Russell's statement. He didn't doubt that for an instant. "For your sake, Russell…I hope you're right."

"I can't handle the pain, Taylor. It burns…" Russell pressed the barrel against his chin. Taylor screamed, yelling the only thing he knew of that would stop the man from taking his own life.

"I scratched your truck!"

The man with the sawed-off shotgun paused. The moon played against his retinas as he pondered his options. His failure to leap into an instant tantrum worried Taylor more than a violent outburst would have.

"It was just a possession, son. That's not what really matters in life," he sighed. Russell inhaled sharply, then he squeezed. The shot resonated, booming throughout the room and into the hallway, raising the alarm for the searching demons. The pool of blood that had collected before Russell's body even hit the floor widened at the base of the door.

Taylor wept. It was the crying that came with sobs and wails. It sounded like the shrieks of the zombies. He stayed seated and motionless, succumbing to the fever and no longer able feel his legs. There he sobbed, until a crashing against the door cut through the haze in his bewildered mind. Taylor looked up to see dark shadows frenzying in the moonlight at the base of the door. They smashed, one by one, against the wooden barrier.

Each successive blow brought the barrier ever closer to splintering inwards, granting passage to the fiends that assaulted Taylor. The constant beating sounded like a satanic war drum. It beat within Taylor's mind. Each blow seemed to grow louder until the crescendo. The door smashed inwards, a charcoal and crimson monster pushing its body through the opening. With a howl it decimated the splintering wood. The dark creatures entered the room.

*

Leon's path was almost unimpeded, at which he was surprised. From all accounts he'd heard there were supposed to be cars bumper to bumper all along this road. He'd been running for fifteen minutes, yet nothing had slowed him down except for his own ailments. He was deprived of sleep for the past week, and the cut on his head was opening up as he strained to continue on.

He knew that Taylor couldn't have made it very far. He was in such bad shape that Leon expected to find his body strewn out across the street. So far he'd only seen a handful of corpses, none of them moving. To his knowledge, none of them had been Taylor, but light was pretty low. He had to pray that the young man was still alive. Now that the blockade was broken there was still a chance at survival.

The only compass that Leon had was vision, which directed him towards the only thing he could really see at that hour. A tower of smoke and flame in the near distance stood out against the dark, barely illuminating the street that Leon shuffled along, trying his best to keep a decent pace. He was making too much noise, that much was certain. But he had some firepower on him, and he figured if Taylor could survive, then his chances were pretty solid.

What had been truly odd was the path of embers that lined the street. It was as if a fire had just burned out at either side of the avenue, only the emanating red embers remained. They created a path that went straight towards the flame, and Leon could only imagine what that could imply. He had no clue what he was up against, only that Taylor probably hadn't strayed from the beaten path.

Something slapped the pavement to Leon's right in a quick, heavy succession. Leon looked to his side just in time to see a dark shadow blocking out the embers, coming straight towards him. There wasn't even time to raise his firearm before he was on the ground, the heavy attacker grabbing at his mouth. Leon began thrashing in panic, reaching to his side to find his combat knife. He kicked his legs maniacally, trying desperate to shake his attacker. Only the sound of a human voice calmed him slightly.

"Fucking hell! What in the name of Christ are you doing leaving the blockade?" Captain Wes Talbott leaned forward, revealing his face against the glare of the embers. His grizzled expression drilled through Leon's bullshitting. Talbott withdrew his hand from Leon's mouth.

"The blockade has been overthrown, sir."

Talbott stopped at this for a time. He was still kneeling on top of Leon's shoulder and chest, pondering what plan of action would best help him to complete his orders. He'd gotten one objective that outweighed all of the others.

"Then we'll just have to call in reinforcements." He pulled the walkie-talkie from his breast pocket, clutching at the side to depress the "talk" button. A muted lull of static preceded Talbott's orders.

"Base, this is Talbott," he paused. "Open up the outer blockade, kill anything that moves."

Leon gaped in astonishment. "They've been here the whole time…"

Talbott continued into the Walkie-Talkie, "Give us one hour for the extermination, then send in the press for some photo ops."

*

Julie sprinted as fast as she could, but Claire was a heavy burden cradled in her arms. College Avenue was wide open before her, only fellow refugees running along it. The zombies hadn't yet cleared the supply truck. Once they began to slip through the empty barricade they would be on her heels. She had abandoned her fire axe, the idea of going on the offensive seemed impossible. Escape was the only thing on her mind.

The numbness in her shoulder was unbearable. Claire clung to Miss Patterson, gripping her torso. She was getting dizzier as she ran, the amount of blood she'd lost slowing her senses. The road gave way beneath her legs, and Julie crashed to the ground. She spun as she fell, landing on her gunshot shoulder. Claire was unscathed.

The pain shot from her shoulder, stinging her neck and ribs. She tried to move her arm but it wouldn't respond. A digging agony scratched at the bullet hole. Julie only grunted, not daring to scream. Then she released Claire.

The little girl stood up, still visibly devastated from what she'd witnessed. There was more serenity on her face than one would expect, though. Most likely she was in shock. Julie writhed on the pavement, rolling onto her good side to relieve the pain. The cold wind bit at her open wound. Leveling her head just long enough to focus on Claire, Julie came to understand just how much blood she had lost.

"Run," she muttered, hardly able to utter a word.

Claire stared back blankly for a moment, after which she spun and tore off down the avenue. Julie watched on, the world around her fading to grey, then black.

*

He was floating. Like a buoy in a thunderstorm his head bobbed uncontrollably. The zombies that carried him over their heads could hardly contain his withered frame. They proceeded with his body, walking slowly like pallbearers. Taylor could make out the treetops in the night. They were on the quad.

Up above he spotted the American flag that adorned the middle of the quad. Halfway up its pole, stranded and clutching for its lost life, was the stiff corpse of a student. A squirming in his stomach began, challenging Taylor to keep his food down. The food he'd gotten from Russell was his only source of strength. It was the only thing keeping him going. Taylor's chapped lips rustled together as the funeral procession continued. His eyelids, caked with filth, stuck every time he blinked. Then he vomited.

Facing the sky, Taylor's stomach acid only pooled in his mouth, choking him and burning his esophagus. The mess of Goldfish soaked in body fluid and Gatorade poured out over the marching zombies. It splattered against their slick, decaying hides.

Taylor gagged, swallowing his own puke. He writhed in an effort to turn himself, to spit out his choking burden. The zombies stopped, steadying their victim and dropping him to the ground. Taylor landed on his back, taking the wind from him as he was choking. He looked up, seeing only menacing zombie faces and crude treetops.

Retching and hacking, Taylor's gag reflex spun him to his side. There the remaining vomit spewed forth, splattering against the sidewalk of the massive quad. Taylor remained there, knelt against the concrete, with a stream of saliva falling from his slack lower lip. He was completely oblivious to the demons around him, only the act of surviving in his mind.

Another surge of vomit made him hack once more, this time only a small amount of burning acid coming forth. It slapped against the pool beneath Taylor, whose chest heaved as he breathed heavily. The sound of him sucking wind was countered by the growls of the demons. Taylor looked up.

The demon's home struck out against the night. Watterson Towers stood menacingly before Taylor, only a pile of puke and about fifty yards between them. Its twin windows at the twentieth floor glared down at him, their deathly pale as emotionless as the moon. At its peaks rose sets of antennas, piercing the heavens above. Taylor shrunk back in fear.

Sensing his fear, the demons began to hiss. They circled Taylor, swarming around him and drawing tighter. He cowered from them, throwing his arms in front of his face. He was sobbing, so afraid of death as it faced him squarely in the eyes. He wasn't ready to go, he hadn't truly come to terms with his place in the universe. The demons began to shift, forcing him in one direction.

Taylor could only crawl, the last of his energy being sapped away with the quickly fading grains of sand. He fought, until the very end, but now he was defeated. All he could manage as the zombies poked and prodded his body, hissing and growling, was a weakened crawl. He dug his fingernails against the unforgiving ground. They split, cracking off and leaving his fingertips exposed to the abrasive concrete.

Still, he pulled onward, using the strength in his fingers to gain leverage. The sweat perspired from his forehead; it glistened underneath the windows of Watterson. Their eerie emanation was now the only light available, the night having fully overtaken the dusk. A slither of chill ran along his neck, and into his shoulders. His forehead suddenly became a glacier, melting away and flooding his face.

He made it onto an elbow, the unpadded bone smashing pavement. He was going to have to be all elbows if he wanted to pull it off. His legs wouldn't respond at all, so he wouldn't be able to get to a knee. That meant a lot of pain, a minefield of hairline fractures and ruptured bursas. Taylor wasn't of the mind to make that decision, however. He was on auto-pilot, not even wanting to know what would happen if he disobeyed the monsters.

They raged alongside of him. Their cavernous eye sockets somehow stood out against the emptiness of the night. They were beyond dark, they were eternal damnation. Their bellows pulled at Taylor's soul, tearing pieces of it away as they pierced. It was their teeth, however, that truly got Taylor moving.

Rows of inward bending, flesh-shredding incisors greeted him. They menaced in the dark, glinting lowly with their grave threats. Taylor didn't want to know the extent of their capabilities. He pressed forward. His elbows pounded against the sidewalk, lifting him just enough to push onward.

*

"What the fuck are you talking about? Reinforcements? How far away are they?"

Talbott only looked up, disdain for the black man more than apparent on his face.

"*Of all the low ranking shits that had to find their way in here, why him?*" Talbott wondered.

Leon wasn't ready to accept silence.

"They'll be here in a few minutes, shut the fuck up."

"How many men could have been there at the blockade with us?"

"It wouldn't have made a difference," Talbott scowled. All he wanted was a battalion, instead he got Gibbs. The man didn't even want to point a gun at another person.

Leon wasn't ready to accept lies. "You could have ended this eons ago."

Talbott drew his gun. The pearl handle was muted by the night. He only held it aloft, saying, "It's only been a short while."

The Second Lieutenant knew the captain was not going to have second thoughts. Still, he wanted the last word. "It's been lifetimes to some of us."

Talbott holstered his pistol, looking in Leon's direction. "Shut the fuck up."

The flashlights of the reinforcements swept over the two men, coming in a sea of brightness. Talbott straightened, flagging them to his position. "The time has come to erase the infection."

*

He crossed the parking lot, coming face to face with the main entrance to Watterson Towers. There he fell flat, his elbows giving way. Taylor's face planted against the jagged pavilion of asphalt. Breaking his fourth and fifth fingernails, the embattled young man ignored the wet, tearing noise and raised himself up once more. His head rolled to one side as he cocked an eye. The mouth of the beast awaited him, the eyes having finally drawn him in.

Taylor was aghast, only able to stare vacantly back at his tormentor. He gazed at the windows, fully expecting to see Marcy and Andrew's head come hurtling down at him. Nothing could have surprised him anymore. He'd seen it all.

One particular sore, one that lay directly over Taylor's exposed sternum, was pulsing shockwaves through him. The wrenching sensation shot all the way through Taylor's limbs, rendering his legs completely numb. Taylor could no longer feel anything below his waist.

Propping himself against his elbows once more, Taylor continued onward into the emptiness. The zombies closed in behind him, swallowing him.

*

The entire quad was brimming with zombies, their ranks standing chest to back. The flashlights revealed the scene, the demons' front line infantry dressed in street clothes. The zombies only stared back, their eyes as empty as their souls. They stood steadfast, unflinching at the advances of Talbott's army.

The only soldier not holding an AK-47 was Leon, whose M16 was running low on ammunition. He was just like the zombies who gazed vacantly at him; front line infantry. He stood, paused, waiting for Talbott to give the orders. For the time being he was willing to follow orders, but only because it was his best chance at finding Taylor. He just had to pray that he could find the dying man before a soldier confused him for "anything that moves."

The quad was a blaze of flashlights, flooding from every direction as the reinforcements arrived in droves. They came from every direction, entrapping the entire zombie horde. They circled the quad and Watterson, the zombies canvassing an area of four city blocks.

A bullhorn blared, Talbott's raspy voice screeching out.

"Charge!"

*

The only obstacle between Taylor and his destiny was a revolving door. He entered it, having no other choice. Once inside its confines, the embattled boy threw his hands against the glass. He lacked the strength, the leverage, or the weight to push the door any further. He pressed, his feeble wrists shakily giving out.

He lay huddled, shivering in the cold that had finally caught up to him. Still, his clammy face was moist with fevered sweat. The unshaven stubble on his chin belied how tightly his skin clutched to his skull. The wind from outside entered the half-exposed opening of the revolving door. It ran through like a wind tunnel, stinging at Taylor.

One solitary demon stepped forward, clad in black. It shoved the door, sending Taylor toppling into a pile. The door swept him up, forcing him forward and spitting him out on the other side. He entered Watterson in a heap, too disoriented to even know that he was now inside of the dark sentinel that had plagued him, called to him, haunted him.

But he didn't need to see it to know. He could feel it. There was a cold that bit at the air. Low-lighting, the first sign of electricity Taylor had seen since Russell's battery powered flood lights, hung over the concrete interior, reflecting sickly back at itself. A whirring noise came from the distance.

Taylor struggled to right himself. He couldn't even feel his legs to know where they had collected as the door forced him out. Using only the palms of his hands, Taylor grunted as he tried to push himself off of the ground. The whirring noise screeched in the background. Whatever it was needed a new belt and some WD-40. The cold, mechanical sound haunted Taylor as he struggled to move.

Weakly, he continued lifting himself, the ache in his arms turning numb. He was on the verge of going into atrophy. He had to keep moving. Taylor screamed in misery and threw himself onto his elbows.

Taylor didn't weigh much anymore, but what little weight he did possess crashed down against his elbows, their already bloodied and bruised state leaving them defenseless. The brittle humerus that were exposed cracked the ground, shattering into splintered shards. The bone chips poked through his skin, drawing even more blood from them.

Propping himself on his mangled arms, Taylor finally looked upon the insides of Watterson. Everything was grey, save for a sofa and an arm chair. They were blood red. Concrete lined the walls, the floor, the ceiling and the stairs leading up to the elevators. Everything about this room, the atrium of Watterson Towers, was soulless.

Its rows, symmetry, grey tones and low lighting reminded Taylor of a cubicle, a prison, or a line of lockers. Everything was monotonous, emotionless. There was a sense of emptiness in the cold.

"This is the place were souls come to die."

In front of Taylor lie two sets of stairs on either side of the lounge. They ran up to a pair of steel elevators. In the lounge was the aforementioned red furniture. In each of the two chairs Taylor could make out the shape of a body. The first one, the one to Taylor's left, was unmistakable. A pair of pink and white tennis shoes adorned its feet. The burn marks along its body only proved the undeniable truth to Taylor. It was Marcy's corpse.

This time it didn't appear that the sight would simply disappear as it had in Taylor's previous visions. Under the dim, yellow lights Taylor could hardly make out any details. The roar of machinery continued its whir as Taylor strained see if she was still "living." He didn't know what to hope for.

Taylor couldn't yet identify the second body, the one in the chair to his right. He would have to crawl even closer in order to get a strong enough vantage point.

The light above the elevator, the one between up and down arrows, illuminated. Taylor spied it, his eyes widening. He was not alone in the residence hall. His host was about to reveal itself. It was the moment of truth, the revelation Taylor had fought for. He was about to come face to face with his tormentor.

"*It's got to be Andrew*," Taylor concluded. There was no other person, living or dead, who could hate him that greatly. Just like his assumption that Russell had been dead, however, Taylor was wrong once again. Resolve and fear battled within him. The desire for closure wanted to go on, but Taylor's utter dismay at the idea of further pain held him back.

The whirring of the elevator stopped, a slight bang resonating from the top of the staircase. The light dinged once more, and the doors began to slide open. Like a bad Dracula movie, a smog emitted from the elevator. From it emerged Taylor's tormentor, along with an instant increase in the temperature. In a flash it went from icy to sweltering. It made Taylor dizzy, making it difficult to focus on the dark figure making its way down the stairs.

It walked slowly, methodically. Each step was taken in a surreal stride. Its movements never seemed to be impeded by the steps. Instead, it simply floated along, cutting an unobstructed path downward. When it reached the lounge it stopped, pausing for Taylor to regain his focus.

The fever gripped Taylor, making the figure before him seem like a vision of a kaleidoscope. His head remained still, but his sight swayed from side to side, bouncing against his sore eyelids. Each ensuing swing brought a deeper headache. With no sweat left to expend, Taylor's pores began to ooze a sort of oily film on his face. Shakily, he clenched his eyelids closed. He reopened them slowly, making sure not to lose his sense of balance. The confusion, the darkness lifted, unveiling what stood above him.

The beast before him was most certainly from hell. Its flesh was a mixture of mud and rags. Earwigs swam in and out of it like the dorsal fins of a speeding shark. Their clacking grew increasingly louder as the demon waited, wanting Taylor to make the revelation for himself. Over its head lay a burlap sack, the eyes and mouth blackened out in a thick, dark paint. It appeared that they'd been branded by pokers from the depths of Hades.

Within the emptiness of the mouth were rows of teeth. They were all razor thin and razor sharp, bent inwards for hooking and shredding. A hungry saliva dripped from them, hardly able to restrain themselves from decimating the flesh before them, and consuming its soul. Underneath the layers of mud a dark cloth could be made out. It looked like the remnants of a suit.

Taylor's eyes widened.

"The suit I was buried in," the demon, Andrew, spoke.

He began to choke, the ghost before him grinning through its primal teeth.

"The suit I was in when I made my pact with Satan," he calmly proclaimed, stepping forward deliberately. Taylor could only sputter.

"But…"

"BUT WHAT!?!?" Andrew, the devil, raged. The flesh within its suit hulked, revealing itself to be nothing more than dirt, the blackest earth imaginable. "YOU KILLED ME!"

"But…"

"You stabbed me in the back. You BURIED ME!"

Taylor withdrew, shaking his head and closing his eyes. It simply wasn't possible. He couldn't believe what was happening. Not in his wildest nightmares could he have thought Andrew Johnson would come back from hell to personally claim Taylor's soul. "No…"

"I went to *HELL* because of you. Don't sputter bullshit justifications at me."

Taylor opened his eyes. His baffled doubts aside, something about the ordeal didn't seem right. The zombie canvassed in burlap that towered over him was hiding something. Propped on nothing but his elbows, he asked, "Who's in that chair?"

The beast only grinned. Its massive size hulked beside the chairs. The creeping insects that inhabited his earthy flesh fell intermittently to the ground. Slowly, they were finding their way towards Taylor. They scrambled noisily across the concrete, a small army of them headed to Taylor's corner.

"Who is it?"

"Guess."

Taylor didn't want to guess. He didn't want to waste any more time. He just wanted to...

"Die?" Andrew asked.

"What?"

"You were about to say that you wanted to die, no?"

Taylor cocked his head, baffled. Could the devil before him really...

"Read your thoughts?" he finished.

"No..." Taylor shook his head. He couldn't tell if it was the devil, dementia or the amount of drugs he'd done since Andrew's suicide, but something was giving him a major mind fuck. "You're just a cheap parlor trick."

His resolve was returning. "Tell me, Andrew...what am I thinking now?"

The demon's grin continued, though he no longer strode forward. Now he was stopped again, between the two chairs. He bent low, gripping at the sides of each chair with crude claws. The veins in his hands swam with bugs. His fingernails were decayed and mossy.

"You're thinking you'd really like to know who's in this other chair."

"Who are you?" he asked. Something about the devil's bluff didn't sit right with Taylor. "You're not Andrew."

"No?"

"No, you bag of shit," Taylor was mad again. "Andrew Johnson wouldn't wish this upon anybody. He was a victim, not a predator."

"Your victim...you killed him," the monster was less confident.

"No...I just failed to save him. And I have to live with that. I've had to live with that for the past year, and it haunts me every minute of every day." Taylor shot back. "That's more than any hell I can think of."

"You haven't thought hard enough," the demon answered, straightening. Just because Taylor had forced it to admit that it was not Andrew didn't change the fact that the devil had the upper hand. "I will show you suffering."

He clapped, and the demons in the chairs began to move. They rose up, revealing their full selves. The body wearing Marcy's shoes had a burlap sack over its head as well. It lifted to its feet slowly, giving Taylor time to realize how badly burned it was. She must have burned to a near crisp before she turned undead.

238

Marcy's corpse's movements were slow and stiff. She swayed under the burden of her own weight. It was a miracle that any muscle tissue was left at all under her torched flesh. She was little more than a swollen mass of blisters and blackened pus. Every inch she crept upwards, into a stand, forced her dried skin to crack even more.

"I bagged her myself," the demon spoke while Taylor's gaze turned to the second body, the mystery corpse. The dark lighting unveiled a zombie with no hands, they had been slashed off at the wrist. This one, too, wore a hood, along with a decayed suit.

"The suit he was buried in," the devil continued.

"You fucker…" Taylor couldn't even comprehend what was unfolding. If it was hard enough for him to believe that Andrew had come back from the dead to steal his soul, then it was impossible to imagine that the devil had managed to arrange for the zombies of both Marcy and Andrew to be here now, to haunt him. Even more slowly than Marcy, the corpse of Andrew rose to its decrepit feet. A year in the earth had left him crawling with maggots and earwigs, the latter seeming to be the trademark insect of hell.

"So eloquent in your hatred," the devil spat at him, with poison on its words. "

The zombies of Taylor's past clambered blindly, only searching out the sound of Taylor's voice.

"WHO ARE YOU?" Taylor's voice gave out, the final breath barely squeezing out of him. It was just enough to give the blinded demons a direction to flail towards. Their rotting bodies were both nearly pitch black, the damage to one of them done by the flame, the other by the ravages of decomposition.

"They'll reach you soon," the entity ignored him. He nodded towards the wall to Taylor's left. There lay a burlap sack, covered in earwigs. "You'd better find some way to defend yourself."

Desperation overtook Taylor, who's lungs could no longer produce any plea for mercy. He hurtled forward, smashing his broken elbows against the unyielding floor. His legs dragged helplessly behind, slowly making their way towards the sack. Once Taylor reached it, he plunged his hands into the sides.

It was wet and scratchy. It squirmed and stabbed at him all at once. The earwigs inside latched into his fingers, making their way to his hands. This time, however, he was using the Band-Aid Approach, if not by design, then through sheer fright. He ripped at the bag, tearing off chunks of the heavy material and mud until he clutched at the slippery contents.

Taylor's fingers felt something hard, and he snagged at its side. His slick fingers lost their grip, and he snatched wildly until his fingers looped something. Then he pulled backwards, spinning onto his back and clutching his hands to his chest.

His right hand loosely grasped a pistol, the mud making it difficult to hold onto. The earwigs shook from him, falling to the ground and crushing beneath his rolling weight. Taylor continued his roll and flattened himself on his chest. There he pulled the pistol from underneath him, pointing it instinctively at the zombie nearest him.

Taylor didn't even take time to weigh the consequences of his actions before he fired, unflinchingly. The gunshot was an act of pure instinct, but that didn't change the instantaneous remorse Taylor felt at killing his best friend, once again. The echo rocked throughout the atrium, shaking the revolving door. Andrew Johnson's corpse fell flat. Only at the sound of the crumpling body did Taylor realize what he had done. His breathing quickened, his heart raced. The sprawled out man tried to sputter an obscenity, to rage against the demon. Only a spattering of phlegm was produced.

"Now finish it. Every time you pull the trigger you sell a little more of your soul."

Survival was the only thing on Taylor's mind, and he aimed his shot once more. This time it was directed at Marcy's burlap-wrapped head. Once he had her in his sights, though, he hesitated. She was the only thing left on earth that had made his life matter. Once she was gone, his life would be gone with her. If he pulled the trigger, if he used the device of murder that he so flagrantly detested, his soul would truly be sold to the devil.

"In exchange for yours," the devil pressed, "I'll loose her soul from my inferno."

Taylor had no way of knowing whether or not to trust the demon. But Marcy's zombie was making it way towards him, the sound of the first gunshot acting as an impetus. He had no choice but to aim.

And fire.

PHASE 9
Black Americana

Two distinct gunshots caught Talbott's attention. They sounded like they came from within Watterson. It was difficult to tell against the other gunfire, but it was a risk Talbott would have to take. The press would be arriving soon, and he had orders to carry out. The line of zombies protecting the residence hall was dwindling, Talbott would have to make sure that he was the first one through.

*

Leon heard two gunshots coming from beyond the hordes of zombies he was decimating. The ghouls didn't even fight back, they just stood between the military onslaught and the dormitory they were protecting. Leon had run out of ammunition, but his knife was silencing the dead just as effectively. The ranks of zombies continued to thin.

He glanced beyond the demons, seeing that Talbott had already found his way past their defenses. He was approaching a revolving door, and his backwards glances alerted Leon. Talbott was hoping not to be seen. Something about that bothered the Second Lieutenant.

He pushed forward, forsaking his duty to slaughter the beasts. They didn't even resist, simply bouncing aside as he toppled through them. They stank of rot, like a fresh carcass on the highway that had gotten too much sun. Through the stench he shouted, "Captain! Talbott!"

*

"This isn't really happening." Taylor proclaimed, his voice little more than a rasp. He was staring at the still corpses of his childhood friends. Marcy had burned so badly that all the blood in her had already coagulated. Andrew's body was reduced to dust months before. There was almost no mess, no gore, from the shootings. Only a surreal sense of closure that was somehow unsettling.

"Isn't it?" the entity asked, its black eyes glowing with glee at the killings.

"No," Taylor continued. "This isn't even real. In real life I'm laid out on my couch, hallucinating from the horse pills they've prescribed me. And Marcy is taking care of me, and none of this has even happened."

Taylor began to cough, hacking on his words. The devil in burlap could only stare back, still holding all the cards in this equation. "Well if that's true, what happens to you here doesn't mean a thing. Why not play along?"

The dying body could only writhe, wanting to scream but unable to. The look on his face, helpless and frantic, said it all. He couldn't stand the mystery anymore. He needed to know who the masked figure was.

"*Who are you?*" he wondered, hoping this time that the demon truly could read his thoughts.

A silence ensued. The earwigs that had clambered at the stairs quieted. Only the devil and Taylor Donner remained. "I am the dark harbinger of hell."

"*Hell cares about me enough to send escorts?*" Taylor didn't know what else to ask.

"PETULANT FUCK!" the devil lashed, suddenly enraged. "You still greedily assume this is all about you? I am in this god forsaken cesspool on a mission of fear. Hell feeds on it, consumes it, along with the lost souls it breeds. You, Taylor Donner, infected piece of shit, were just a small, meddling inconvenience."

Its raspy voice rose into a fury with every statement. Taylor could only look back in utter confusion.

"*But…*" he started, only to be cut off by the burlap monstrosity before him.

"SILENCE! Succumb to fear…give in to oblivion," with that it pointed a single, bony finger at Taylor, piercing the young man's mind and crippling his thoughts. Then he lowered his hand and pointed towards the fallen bodies of Andrew Johnson and Marcy Milliken.

"I was there as the tainted blood rained from his slashed wrists. I watched while she choked on her own mangled jugular, waiting in futility for you to rescue her. And I reveled as you plunged a contaminated needle into your own arm, condemning yourself to my touch. You still want to know who I am?"

Taylor could only look back vacantly as the devil grinned.

"I am death incarnate, and I will mow you down in my path of destruction."

Then the devil disappeared.

*

Second Lieutenant Gibbs vaulted towards the Captain, who had turned to face him as he entered the revolving door. The momentum of the crash knocked both men into the turnstile, trapping them within its confines to do battle.

Immediately Leon had the upper hand, smashing Talbott across the bridge of the nose. He then clutched at the Green Beret's neck, hoping to choke him out while smashing his head against the glass pane. But Talbott was too wily, too battle-tested to go down so easily.

The Captain smacked Leon's hands away and thrust a punch into the Second Lieutenant's throat. Then he pulled the lower ranking officer by his jacket, pummeling him with a hail of head butts. Leon's nose split and three teeth smashed inwards. He choked on them as they were swallowed in the gushing of blood. Then Talbott cracked the young man's head against the windowed door. A thud resounded, and Leon went limp.

Talbott let him fall to the ground and turned to push through into Watterson's atrium.

*

The warmth and strength fading from his body, Taylor pushed himself off of the cold concrete floor, rising up to his knees. Donner closed his eyes and clutched his hands together, the hot barrel of the pistol sticking out. All he had time to get out was "Give me strength" before the demon reappeared behind him. Taylor spun, the grinning devil standing almost directly on top of him. The young man recoiled, raising his firearm and pointing at the demon's head.

He was on the verge of firing again, of killing the villain that plagued him, but then he saw…

*

…a military officer standing in front of him. Taylor blinked. When he reopened his eyes…

*

…the devil had returned. It bent low, pressing its head against the pistol. Then it whispered…

*

"Are you Taylor Donner?" the military man asked him. His hand went to his hip, clutching at the handle of a pistol. "Are you the one who has AIDS?"

Taylor struggled to breathe, to respond. If he couldn't speak this man would put a bullet in his head without question. But…

*

…the monster in burlap squeezed at his neck, choking the breath from him. Taylor's voice failed, only a faint squeak emitting. He gripped the trigger on the gun, its barrel aimed squarely at the head of…

*

Leon looked groggily through the glass of the revolving window, seeing Taylor knelt on the ground at the base of a staircase. The diseased young man pointed a gun directly at Captain Talbott, who shouted something and drew his own pearl-handled revolver. Gibbs watched the stalemate, not sure if he should act. Bursting through the door could lead to a gunshot.

So he waited, thinking through his options. The shards of glass that stuck in the back of his head gashed through his skin and scraped against his skull. The cut on his nose was pouring blood, disorienting the Second Lieutenant. He leaned against the revolving door, and heard a mass of shouting coming from outside.

Leon shifted, a shot of pain running through his face. Hundreds of red, blinking lights were tearing along the quad. They forged their way through the piled bodies, pushing forward at the line of armed forces that were dispatching of the final zombie threats. The red lights bounced, weaving through the darkness.

Soon the military men recognized them, too. They poised their flashlights on the oncoming lights, and revealed the men and women carrying the illuminations. The lights blinked from their beacons, the news cameras. The press had arrived, and Leon saw his golden opportunity.

Rising up, he pushed the revolving door back the way he had come, and went out into the cold night.

*

...a man in uniform holding a pearl handled revolver. Taylor still held the gun up, but nodded at the man's question as he repeated it a second time. "Are you Taylor Donner?"

Taylor's nod was slow, methodical. By the time he finished bobbing his head he had forgotten what he was answering. He only stared back at...

*

...the nightmare that held his life in its hands. His oxygen, his life, was dissipating quickly. If he could just break the monster's grip he could answer,

245

could scream. But the devil was unrelenting, his teeth flashing in bloodlust as Taylor's strength emptied. Then it spoke.

"I have orders to take your soul."

*

Talbott continued reading Mr. Donner his final rights, his finger begging to squeeze the trigger. "These orders come from high up, higher than you can know."

Then he paused, resting the tip of his gun squarely between the eyes of the AIDS-stricken young man before him. With ice water in his veins, the Captain proclaimed, "I am death incarnate, and I will mow you down…"

*

"…in my path of destruction," the devil spoke.

*

Leon walked gingerly towards the other militants, who stood in an arc around the entrance to Watterson. Streams of blood flowed from his bandaged head and his mouth. They held the media at bay, awaiting the official word to let them in. Operation: Damage Control called for the press to be allowed to film only after government permission was given. Until then, all transmitted footage was held from the air, seized on government orders. The Second Lieutenant made his way up to the front lines.

He looked over the crowd, seeing the eagerness on the part of all for the ordeal to be over with. The news crews were hungry for their stories, and the soldiers were simply tired of it all. It had been a trying experience for all of them. There must have been over twenty thousand dead bodies inside of the blockade, most of them lying at their feet right now.

The eyes gazed back at Leon, assumingly. They waited, ready for the words. Leon didn't disappoint. "Captain Talbott's inside waiting for his photo op. He says to let them in."

*

Realization set in slowly, like a shot of morphine spreading through his system. The man standing before him with the pearl-handled pistol was nothing more than an unwitting minion of death himself. Taylor slapped the devil's hands, Talbott's gun, aside. At the same time he held his gun aimed at Talbott, at the devil. He inhaled, savoring the oxygen as it hit his lungs. It gave him strength, just enough to stamp out his last will and testament.

"You would send me to hell for that?"

"This is a quarantine, and you have a disease of the blood," Talbott aimed his shot once more, measuring the distance to Donner's eye socket. Taylor flinched, wanting to shoot but not having the will. He was still had so much more to say.

"It was one mistake, one fleeting moment…you can't judge my entire existence on an accident."

"Make these words wise, boy," Talbott dictated. "They'll be your last."

He knew it was true. Whether it was the soul sucking entity or the soldier of ill-fortune before him, Taylor would die inside of Watterson. But he was no longer fearful, as he had been in his past. He'd faced his demons, and severed all of his earthly ties when he'd blasted the corpses of his childhood friends without a hint of remorse. There was no use fighting back, he had no place else to go. His words were deliberate, from the heart. Taylor eulogized his generation, his existence.

"I'll go to hell when you execute me, if hell exists. The Word looks down upon suicide, and a handful of other things I've dabbled in. But there's something that doesn't fit, to me. People look at suicide like some easy way out, like anybody who considers it is just weak. The thing is, though, if people knew how many teens have considered suicide nowadays, they would be baffled. But it doesn't surprise me, not one bit. If you were born into a world with so much conflict, so little hope, you'd choose death, too. We're born zombies."

Talbott waited patiently, looking pitifully down at the young man before him. "Is that all?"

"I haven't even gotten started yet."

The Captain regripped the gun in his hand, no longer as patient as he had been a moment ago. Breaking his resolve, a smashing behind him stole the soldier's attention. The revolving door swung, a cameraman and reporter squeezed into each quadrant of the door. They clambered inwards, the red lights on their cameras blinking, announcing their arrival. Within seconds the entire atrium of Watterson Towers was teeming with news crews, thirsty for a bloody story. All of their cameras were directed towards the drama taking place at the barrel of Talbott's pistol.

Taylor smiled, the Captain wavered. He was taken off guard, unsure of what to do next. Taylor Donner, weakened, lacerated, contused, sweaty, chilled, feverish, emaciated, fatigued, bruised, unshaven, varicose, sinewy, skeletal, deathly, sore, itchy, scratchy, scarred, bloodshot, but never ever broken saw his one and only opportunity to make his death worthwhile.

"We are a society, a world which possesses the capabilities to create utopia, a heaven on earth. Instead we choose to lend our efforts to greed and hate. War, poverty, pandemics, handguns…we're destroying ourselves instead. And all we can do is lean back and say that God will come one day and save us. But we can't just lay back and wait for a miracle to show us the way. This is a fight that has to go to the government, the people, and even the streets in order to succeed. You're not going to win it by suppressing the truth, you'll only multiply the lies until one of them finally makes us all snap. And then the toll, the blood, will be on *your* hands."

He stated it as a man possessed, no longer a dying body suffering at the whim of fate. Then he lowered his gun to his side, showing the news cameras, the entire world, that he was no longer any threat. He dropped the pistol to the ground, his palms pointed upwards as it tumbled off of his fingers. Then he whispered softly, only perceptible to Talbott.

"Here you stand, a gun to my head, and all the world as your audience. And I'm saying all the
things they can't hear. There's only one thing you *can* do…"

Wes Talbott looked back in realization. Taylor grinned, shouting to the reporters who stood stunned at the doorway. "MY NAME IS TAYLOR DONNER, AND I HAVE AIDS."

Talbott panicked, knowing that every word the boy uttered was a testimony against his government, his overlords. Before he shot Taylor

Donner in the head, spraying his life against the concrete floor that the boy's body sprawled backwards onto, the Captain hesitated. It was just enough time for the young man that was on his knees to whisper his final words. He stared the Captain, the devil, death, squarely in the eyes and muttered in defiant mockery so quietly that only he, Talbott and God could hear it.

"Martyr me you dumb fuck."

The pearl handled revolver fired its solitary bullet, Taylor Donner dead before his spiraling body even hit the stairs. Only after the gun smoke had cleared did the Captain fully comprehend the implications of the boy's words. The red lights blinked behind him, recording the onslaught frame by frame, word by word.

Taylor's blood, his life force, spilled down the steps. His face wore a devilish smile, warm with the crimson fluid that poured from it. His nightmares were ended.

EPILOGUE

The gurney was wheeled down the corridor with precise handling. Its path was speedy, but not hurried. It had been a relentless work day at the crisis center, all the refugees from the inner blockade had been filing in since early that morning. The makeshift tented hospital had changed from being excruciatingly slow to unbearably undermanned in a matter of hours.

A split in the hallway emerged, the gurney turning right as it reached the intersection. From there it entered a room lined with similar stretchers. All of them played host to a wounded citizen or soldier. This particular gurney, though, was looking for a specific patient. Its nurse pushed the stretcher through the room, slowing its speed so the occupant could have time to look at each survivor.

The low beeping of heart monitors rang throughout the tent, alerting the nurses that all, for the time being, was well. It was matched only by the drips of intravenous tubes. The amount of dehydrations had been overwhelming, and needles were running dangerously low. If the Red Cross didn't come through with more supplies soon, the number of casualties would begin to rise drastically.

"Stop," the man in the gurney commanded. "Her."

He pointed to a wounded woman, lying unconscious next to a stable heart monitor. "What's her status?"

"She'll be fine, Lieutenant Gibbs," the nurse answered. "A little girl brought us to her. She'd been abandoned in a field about a half-mile out. She's lost a lot of blood, but we got to her in time."

Leon nodded grimly. He reached behind him, his heavily bandaged head keeping him from being able to turn completely. The nurse grasped his hand, letting him know that she was there.

"Her name is Julie…Julie Patterson," he informed. "When she wakes up let me know immediately."

The nurse patted his hand, understanding. "Yes sir, Lieutenant."

"And don't let her see the television. I want her to hear about it from me."

The heart monitors beeped on, echoing harmlessly throughout the room. The nurse pushed the stretcher onward, down the endless rows of patients. The innumerable victims lined the passing gurney on either side, standing watch over it as it passed out of sight. Out of the tent it traveled, stopping at a line of reporters waiting to jab and stick their microphones at Leon Gibbs.

Printed in the United States
96530LV00001B/368/A